Christmas
Baby
Miracles

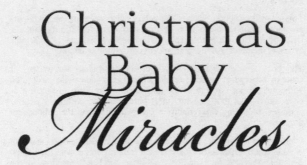

Christmas Baby Miracles

JACQUELINE DIAMOND
LAURA MARIE ALTOM
KATHRYN SPRINGER

MILLS & BOON

Published in Great Britain 2015
by Mills & Boon, an imprint of Harlequin (UK) Limited,
Eton House, 18-24 Paradise Road, Richmond, Surrey, TW9 1SR

CHRISTMAS BABY MIRACLES © 2015 Harlequin Books S.A.

The Holiday Triplets © 2010 Jackie Hyman
The SEAL's Christmas Twins © 2013 Laura Marie Altom
Jingle Bell Babies © 2009 Harlequin Books S.A.

ISBN: 978-0-263-91784-0

025-1015

Harlequin (UK) Limited's policy is to use papers that are natural, renewable and recyclable products and made from wood grown in sustainable forests.The logging and manufacturing processes conform to the legalenvironmental regulations of the country of origin.

Printed and bound in Spain
by CPI, Barcelona

THE HOLIDAY TRIPLETS

JACQUELINE DIAMOND

Growing up as the daughter of a doctor, **Jacqueline Diamond**—author of more than eighty novels—developed an appreciation for the demands and rewards of the medical profession. Most of all, she understands that doctors are just people with a special gift and dedication, who fall in love and wrestle with family issues like everyone else. She's also the daughter of internationally renowned ceramic sculptor Sylvia Hyman. You can learn more about Jackie and see some of her mother's artwork at www.jacquelinediamond.com. If you write to Jackie at jdiamondfriends@yahoo.com, she'll be happy to add you to her e-mail list.

For Arthur Gunzberg
on his 99th birthday

Chapter One

On a Wednesday morning in early December, Dr. Mark Rayburn set out on foot from his house, enjoying the crisp ocean breeze through the palm trees but already eagerly anticipating his arrival at Safe Harbor Medical Center.

This was *his* hospital.

He'd bought a house four blocks away to avoid southern California's infamously long commutes and also because he liked being able to drop in frequently at the center, whether at night or early in the morning or on holidays. Long hours weren't a burden; they were a privilege.

He didn't want or need a family, because he already had one. As administrator, he guided and nudged and cheered for his staff. As an obstetrician, he nurtured mothers and helped babies take their miraculous first breath. And now he had a chance to make a real difference in the world, to help even more women and families. What could be better than that?

At the edge of the medical center, Mark paused to admire the hospital's clean lines and curving, window-lined wings. The six-story structure anchored a complex that included a medical office building, a parking garage and a dental building that the hospital's corporate owner was acquiring to turn into a fertility center.

This was his dream, the reason he'd become an administrator and moved from Florida to California. Soon, he'd be assembling a world-class team of doctors and support staff so that even more families could turn their dreams into reality.

Still, excited as he was about the fertility center plans, he never slighted the less showy part of his domain. Sauntering past a profusion of birds-of-paradise plants and calla lilies, Mark bypassed the staff entrance and walked through the wide central doors into the lobby. Coming in this way helped him stay in touch with what ordinary patients experienced.

Today, the place glittered with holiday spirit. Busy elves from the Hospital Guild Auxiliary had festooned the lobby with twinkling white lights and Santa faces beaming from wreaths. To one side, gingerbread men and miniature porcelain baby dolls dangled from a nonallergenic tree.

Nostalgia and painful memories twisted inside Mark. Brushing aside the ghosts of Christmases past, he quickened the pace of his informal patrol.

At a little past 7:00 a.m., the gift shop hadn't opened yet, but the clatter of breakfast dishes echoed from the nearby cafeteria. As he strode along a corridor, he heard an instructor exhorting an aerobics class to greater exertions in the workout room, and paused to let an orderly pass with a cart full of medications.

"Hey, Dr. Rayburn." The young man gave him an easy grin.

"Good morning, Bob." Mark made a point of remembering his staff's names.

He had a lot of them rattling around in his brain as he mounted the stairs. Names of doctors, nurses, lab techs, secretaries and, of course, patients. Even though he'd been an administrator for the last five of his thirty-seven years, including two here at Safe Harbor, he still found time to provide one-on-one treatment.

On the third floor, he stopped by labor and delivery to greet the hardworking nurses and find out how his maternity patients were doing. He'd delivered five babies yesterday, including triplets born to a young mom.

"Everyone's fine." His nurse, Lori Ross, updated him on the essentials. Two of the three new mothers would be going home today, while the triplets' mom, Candy Alarcon, needed another day or so to recuperate from her cesarean section. "The pediatrician's talking to her now."

"Dr. Sellers?" Neonatologist Jared Sellers had examined the babies in the delivery room. He also happened to be Lori's ex-fiancé, and therefore a touchy subject.

"Uh, no." She gave him a shaky smile. "Dr. Forrest."

"Ah."

You couldn't in all fairness describe Samantha Forrest as a thorn in his side, Mark reflected as he headed toward the patients' rooms. He valued her dedication and her passion for social justice. The problem was that she tended to be a bit of a drama queen.

As did Candy, an unmarried nineteen-year-old whom Samantha had counseled through a volunteer program. That made them an unpredictable combination.

To give them a chance to talk freely, Mark decided to visit his other two patients first.

"NO ONE SAID THIS WAS GOING to be easy," Samantha told the young woman in the bed. "I just don't want you to look back in ten or twenty years and ask, why did I let them go? You've been so eager to keep them until now. It's normal to have second thoughts."

Candy's bow-shaped mouth twisted. Curly hair framed a pretty face that hid the insecurities of a girl who'd grown up alternately indulged and abandoned by troubled parents. "Honestly, Dr. Forrest, I do want to be a good mother. But I feel overwhelmed. And one of them's got that…that thing on her face."

"It's called a port-wine stain." Sam wished she had baby Connie and her sister and brother in the room to remind Candy of how adorable they were, but, as a precaution, they were still being monitored in the intermediate-care nursery. As for the purplish blotch on Connie's cheek, it was superficial rather than an indication of any serious syndrome. "We can treat that with lasers, and if it doesn't completely go away, she can cover it with makeup when she's older."

"It might not go away?" Candy asked anxiously.

"Sometimes a trace remains. But your babies are healthy. That's a blessing, especially with triplets."

Since meeting the young mother months ago at a teen moms' support group that Sam had organized, she'd arranged for prenatal treatment and put Candy in touch with a nonprofit agency that would provide temporary nursing care after the infants went home. In addition, a local charity had pledged to collect baby supplies and used cribs. Sam had spent hours calling and organizing to arrange it all, but it was worth the effort to get this family off to a good start.

"My boyfriend says she's ugly. I thought he'd love them the way I do." Candy drooped against the pillow.

Samantha winced. "Give Jon time. He's falling in love with them already." The previous night at the nursery, she could have sworn the young man's face had lit with pride as he surveyed his children.

"He imagined he could land us a reality TV show." The girl's eyes teared up. "Isn't that ridiculous? I told him we'd need at least eight babies to do that."

"And even then, it wouldn't be in their best interest." Sam tried to cover her dismay. How could people exploit their children? When she had kids of her own, she planned to treasure and protect them with every ounce of her strength.

If I ever have kids. But that was neither here nor there. At the moment, her pediatric patients and the young mothers she nurtured came first with Sam. "Maybe he was kidding."

"I doubt it. He's so immature!" Candy blew out a long breath. "I believed we were in love and he'd marry me once I got pregnant, but he keeps putting it off."

"He'll come around." Samantha searched for a positive angle. "Your mom offered to pitch in, too."

"Yeah, but her idea of pitching in is babysitting once a month. She works awfully hard." The new grandma worked as a waitress, a job that took a heavy physical toll. "And she just hooked up with a new guy. Jerry's not into babies."

"I didn't know that." Sam had only met the grandmother briefly. "The service will be sending aides for the first few months."

"What about after that?" Candy waved her hands helplessly. "My dad was never around. I don't want my kids to grow up that way, too."

Samantha leaned forward. "You have to fight for what matters, Candy. I don't mean to push you into anything you aren't ready for, but if you give up too easily, you might regret it for the rest of your life."

When the stakes were high, you couldn't back down. As a teenager, Sam had nearly given up the most important battle of her life. Thank goodness, with her family's support, she'd rallied. Since then, she'd made it her mission to give others a boost at crucial moments in *their* lives.

Yet, for a moment, she wondered if she'd gone too far. The last thing Sam wanted was to impose her values and dreams on this young woman.

Suddenly a smile brightened Candy's face. "You know what the other girls call you? Fightin' Sam. I'm glad to have you in my corner."

Relieved, Samantha pushed her doubts aside. "That's where you'll find me, all right."

Someone tapped at the open door. Sam didn't have to turn to identify the visitor; she simply inhaled the dangerously thrilling scent of Mark Rayburn's aftershave lotion.

As she listened to Candy's greeting and Mark's deep-voiced answer, Sam kept her face averted so Mark couldn't see her telltale flushed cheeks. Despite her body's traitorous response, she had no intention of letting this man guess how attractive she found him.

In control again, she got to her feet. "Good morning, Mark."

Dark eyes swept her, sending prickles along Samantha's skin. Beneath his white coat, the powerful physique of a former football player loomed in her path. "Good to see you." As if they didn't run into each other practically every day.

Run into each other, and butt heads, and wage polite warfare. Although a fine doctor and an able administrator, Mark Rayburn stood for authority and the bottom line. Which, all too often, made him an obstacle in Samantha's path.

"I'll wait outside till you're done," she said.

His thick eyebrows drew up. "Why wait? Don't you have patients to see?"

"Yes, but there's something I need to run by you."

There was no mistaking the wariness in his expression. "Of course."

With a farewell wave to Candy, Sam went out. She might have a tight schedule, but she never neglected the things that really mattered.

THE INCISION WAS HEALING WELL, and the patient showed no sign of infection. Although Mark lingered for a few minutes after the exam to discuss anything troubling Candy, she insisted she was fine. He left her with a promise to send in the nurse to help her get out of bed. The sooner she started moving, the faster she'd recover.

Triplets. Caring for them would be a huge undertaking for any woman, and especially for this young lady. While he wished her every success, he hoped Samantha hadn't overly influenced Candy's decision to keep them.

In the corridor, he found Sam talking intently with Lori. Just his luck that the two women had become fast friends. So far, they hadn't ganged up on him, though.

As soon as she spotted him, Samantha excused herself. Without prompting, the nurse went in to check on Candy, while Mark pulled off the white coat he'd thrown over his suit.

"Mind climbing the stairs as we talk?" he asked. Although Samantha saw her regular patients in the adjacent office building, she also served as chief of the pediatrics department, which was located on the next floor up. At this early hour, no doubt she planned to make the rounds of her hospitalized patients on that floor.

"Suits me." Her long legs matched his stride easily. Only a few inches shorter than his six-foot height, she had golden hair that, today, swept in waves to her shoulders. He was glad she hadn't stuck it back with a clip or pulled it into a ponytail as she often did.

"What can I do for you?" Mark held the door to the staircase.

"Christmas." She breezed past.

That single word brought back his earlier troubled mood. *His mother and father arguing...Mom drinking some 90-proof concoction she claimed was eggnog...*

stumbling and knocking over the tree, ripping the string of lights out of the socket...

Mark searched for a happier memory when he and his sister, Bryn, were little. Piles of gifts from their physician father, a dinner table laden with treats in their Miami home. He preferred those images to the darker ones from his teen years, when it had fallen to him to dry Bryn's tears and sometimes his mother's, too.

"Yes?" He hoped Sam wasn't about to issue an invitation, because he planned to spend this holiday, like most, either working or playing golf. Probably both.

"I got a great idea last night. I'm going to stage an open-house fundraiser for the counseling clinic on Christmas Day."

As she mounted the stairs ahead of him, Mark admired the feminine sway of her body in tailored trousers and a cherry-colored blouse. Still, that didn't mean he had to endorse her latest scheme.

"Most people have plans for Christmas." Launching the grassroots counseling clinic might be *her* pet project, but she could hardly expect the rest of the world to abandon their traditions. "Why not hold it the weekend before?"

"Everybody throws parties then. Besides, did you know Christmas is one of the slowest news days of the year? We'll get much better media coverage." Her voice drifted back.

Mark stifled a groan. If there was anything Safe Harbor didn't lack, it was media coverage.

A few months earlier, a reporter had stirred up a storm by implying that the hospital had a special connection to California's Safe Haven law, which allowed mothers to surrender newborns safely without legal repercussions. As a result, young moms had showed up in record numbers, babes in their arms and news cameras dogging their every move.

The furor had died down at last, but not before Samantha managed to turn the negative publicity into the realization of a dream. With the claim that she wanted to help prevent future relinquishments, she'd persuaded the hospital's owner, a corporation based in Kentucky, to turn over a large office suite for her to use as a counseling clinic for women and families. As if she didn't already have enough volunteer work to do with the teen support group she counseled—but Sam never seemed to run short of energy.

Since then, donations had enabled the Edward Serra Memorial Clinic to acquire furnishings, a computer system, a handful of volunteer peer counselors and the beginnings of an endowment. Not nearly enough to provide paid staff, however.

Hence this latest proposal, he presumed. While Mark supported the clinic's mission, he considered it peripheral to the hospital's central purpose. Plus, it was always risky to let Samantha speak to the press. She had a gift for stirring up controversy.

"We've discussed this before," he reminded her as they reached the fourth floor landing. "To put the clinic on a solid financial footing, you can't rely on nickel-and-dime contributions. You need major corporate sponsors."

"Mark!" She turned so abruptly he nearly ran into her. "How can I attract sponsors without publicity?"

He'd always appreciated her slim, athletic figure, but rarely had been this close. When she tossed back her blond mane, Mark had to drag his brain back to their conversation.

"Through working quietly behind the scenes. Cultivating contacts. Making presentations." That was how the business world operated.

Sam remained planted one step above him. Unless Mark bodily shifted her aside, he was trapped. And he wasn't eager to put his hands on her body. Actually, he was, but he shouldn't be.

"I am *not* going to spend Christmas assembling a PowerPoint presentation, I'm going to spend it throwing a party! Since I can't celebrate with my parents in Mexico—" both doctors, they ran a charity clinic south of the border "—let's hold a fiesta here. Piñatas, colorful paper flowers and spicy food."

"It does sound like fun," Mark reluctantly agreed.

Samantha dropped her hands to his shoulders, her face inches from his, and teased him with a smile. If he didn't know her better, he might suspect her of flirting. "It will be."

He'd better concede the point before he did something insane, like kiss her in the stairwell. "I'll authorize additional security and cleaning, and I'm sure our public relations staff will be glad to spread the word. But you'll have to come up with the food and entertainment budget."

She bit her lower lip, her brain clearly working hard. "I know a few sources I could tap."

"Glad we see eye to eye on this." Given their relative positions, he couldn't resist adding, "Literally."

Sam cocked her head. "You might be a fun guy if you lightened up, Mark."

"Did I ever tell you I used to be a stand-up comic?"

That startled her into taking a step backward. "You're kidding!"

"Actually, yes." Score one for his side. "See you later." Striding past, he went up the steps, his senses ablaze from the encounter.

For heaven's sake, they'd been discussing business. She'd only been trying to wheedle support out of him, not get him hot and bothered. Yet, intentionally or not, that's what she'd accomplished.

Mark straightened his tie, which probably didn't need

it. Nevertheless, the act reasserted his sense of control as he stepped onto the fifth floor, home to the hospital's main offices. Immediately, he felt his administrator persona settle comfortably over him.

Enough kidding around. He had a job to do, a job he loved.

In the executive suite, his secretary, May Chong, handed Mark a sheaf of phone messages. As he was returning them, the center's public relations director, Jennifer Martin, popped into his office with encouraging statistics about the hospital's toy drive. A few minutes later, staff attorney Tony Franco arrived with a question about a lawsuit. Mark encouraged him to press for arbitration.

He spent most of the morning going over projections for the new fertility center. Although Safe Harbor had remodeled its main building and bragged publicly about its fertility services, it wouldn't achieve world-class status until it recruited a renowned expert to head a showcase program. He or she would bring additional staff and require more lab and office space, so plans were moving rapidly to acquire and renovate the dental building.

Mark felt the adrenaline pulsing through his system. He loved the challenge of pulling together all these different elements and creating something that could enrich people's lives.

Shortly before lunch, May put through a call from Chandra Yashimoto, vice president of Medical Center Management, Inc., in Louisville. As usual, she wasted no time on small talk. "We have a problem."

A quick mental survey of current issues failed to raise any red flags. "What sort of problem?"

"The owner of the dental building has filed for bankruptcy. We're back to square one on the acquisition."

Damn and double-damn. Yet selling the structure would be in the best interest of the man's creditors. "We're so

close to inking a deal. Surely we can come to an understanding."

"You've never dealt with a federal bankruptcy court before, have you? The whole thing could drag on for years."
Chandra released an impatient breath. "We have to look
elsewhere."

No sense debating the point; they needed to move
forward with all due speed. "I'll start researching other
buildings on the market." They ought to be able to find
something within a ten-to-fifteen-minute drive. Safe Harbor was part of bustling Orange County, with a population
of more than three million.

"That will throw us months behind schedule." The veep
went on to say that a delay would cost a fortune in lost
revenue. She was determined to hire a director and get the
new center operational as quickly as possible. "We've decided to use facilities we already own. For starters, we'll
be taking over that office suite on your floor, the one
where you put the memorial—whatchamacallit—counseling clinic."

Sam's center? Well, it didn't *have* to be next to the ad-
ministrative suite. "We could move it next door to the medical building. I believe there are a couple of vacant offices."

"Our new director and his or her colleagues will need
those. That's valuable space, Mark."

He reviewed his rapidly dwindling options. "We have
an empty storage area in the basement that can be fixed
up." Sam would simply have to make the best of the situation.

"I've earmarked that space for an embryology lab,"
Chandra said. "The clinic's going to have to find other
quarters. *Away* from the hospital."

Mark barely stifled a groan. This could mean the end
of Sam's dream. Perhaps not immediately; she might find
space at some other facility in town. But the clinic's asso-

ciation with the hospital gave it prestige and prominence. Without those, she was unlikely to attract more than subsistence-level funding.

"And, Mark?" Chandra's voice roused him from his grim reflections.

"Yes?" he asked warily.

"Put a muzzle on that pediatrician, will you? We can't have her blowing this thing out of proportion."

"I'll do my best." As if you could muzzle Dr. Samantha Forrest.

After he hung up, Mark leaned back and stared at the ceiling. The acoustical tile offered neither inspiration nor reassurance.

Instead, he kept seeing Sam holding her fiesta in the parking lot, proclaiming to the press that Scrooge and the Grinch had merged into the shape of Mark Rayburn, M.D.

No wonder he hated Christmas.

Chapter Two

Before heading for her office next door, Sam paid a visit to the hospital's intermediate-care nursery. Adorable in their tiny caps and booties, the triplets lay in side-by-side bassinets. The low-level lights and quiet environment were designed to reduce stress for the infants, but to grown-ups like her, simply gazing at little Connie, Courtney and Colin was enough to lower her blood pressure.

Sam loved those perfect little fingers and hands. Even the wrinkly, pouchy appearance that distinguished newborns filled her with delight. She found herself humming an old lullaby. "Where are you going, my little one, little one…"

Okay, enough self-indulgence. Time to get moving.

Despite her resolve, she spent much of the morning thinking about kids. That was understandable, considering that her hours were spent peering into small ears, discussing immunization schedules with concerned parents, answering questions about breastfeeding, evaluating rashes, assessing infant development and writing a couple of referrals to specialists.

But she wasn't only thinking about other people's kids. She was thinking about her own—or, rather, the fact that she was thirty-six and hadn't had any yet.

These past few weeks, the combination of holiday cel-

ebrations and her annual physical had reminded her of
how quickly life was racing by. With current technology,
she still had another five years or so to bear children. But
there was the not-so-small matter of deciding whether to
go it alone or put more effort into finding a husband.

She'd had a couple of serious relationships, both with
men she'd met through her activities in championing children's causes. Shared zeal made for hot sex—Samantha
could attest to that. Ultimately, though, either the passion
had cooled along with the cause, or she'd come to realize
the guy was drawn to her energy and purpose because
he lacked sufficient of his own. She needed a man strong
enough to stand beside her as an equal.

On the other hand, not one so bullheaded he was always blocking her path. An image of Mark on the stair-
way this morning kept appearing on her mental screen.
Since the hospital's new owner hired him as administrator, he'd become Public Enemy Number One as far as she
was concerned.

Then, a few weeks ago, she'd stopped into the nursery
to admire Tony Franco's baby, and spotted Mark cradling
the newborn in his arms. His face illuminated with tenderness, he'd cooed to the little girl as if she were his own
daughter. Sam had slipped away, oddly moved.

Why didn't Mark have a wife and children? How unfair that men could ignore the biological clock that ticked
so loudly for women.

Well, no point in woolgathering, Samantha thought as
she washed up following her last patient of the morning.
She had a busy afternoon ahead, dealing with departmen-
tal paperwork and formulating plans for the Christmas
fundraiser. She felt certain she could count on the support
of the PR director, since the clinic was named for the baby
son that Jennifer Serra—Jennifer Martin, since her recent
marriage—had lost during a troubled teen pregnancy.

Sam decided to see if she could catch Jennifer for a quick brainstorming session. As she ducked into the hall, however, her nurse called from behind, "Don't forget!"

"Don't forget what?" Sam swung back toward the ever-efficient Devina Gupta.

"Dr. Kendall wants to see you," said the nurse, a bronze-skinned woman who looked too young to have a son in medical school. "I've told you three times."

Oh, bother. The gynecologist had run tests during Sam's checkup and insisted on discussing the results in person. In Sam's opinion, becoming a doctor ought to excuse you from undergoing medical tests. It should make you immune to all illnesses, too.

But of course it didn't.

"I'll stop by her office," Sam promised, checking her watch. Nora Kendall's office was located one floor below. If she dawdled a few more minutes, she should be safe because Nora would probably leave for lunch.

"I'll call to let her know you're coming," Devina said. "I'm sure she'll wait."

Even the stubbornest person couldn't win every time. "Thank you."

"Not a problem. Better hurry!"

Reluctantly, Samantha obeyed her nurse.

PASTRAMI HEAPED ON RYE. Did a pickle count as a vegetable? And mustard. That had a few nutrients, right?

Mark relished his meal at a corner table in the hospital cafeteria while skimming the latest medical journal. He also kept an eye open for Samantha. Not that he would break the devastating news to her in public, but he hoped to track her movements and catch her on the way back to her office. With luck, he might find an isolated setting where her outraged screams wouldn't attract too much notice.

She often ate with Lori and Jennifer, who were talking

earnestly over their chicken-à-la-something. Judging by Lori's quivering mouth, the subject must be Dr. Sellers.

The cause of their breakup was no secret. As the eldest of six girls, Lori had spent her teen years serving as second mother to five argumentative siblings. She'd sworn off having kids, and her fiancé, who'd recently completed an exhausting residency, had agreed he wanted to spend his free time relaxing with the woman he loved, just the two of them.

Then he'd changed his mind. Mark wasn't sure why, but since the neonatologist spent most of his time around babies, no doubt he'd eventually come to embrace these magnificent little people, so filled with promise and love and...

Am I talking about Jared or about myself?

Mark loved babies and kids of all ages. Delightful images of youngsters he'd delivered filled a folder in his computer. He'd even had a few named after him.

But fathering one? Not a good plan. While he'd escaped his family's weakness for substance abuse, he had no desire to risk passing it on to another generation. Especially since he'd learned the hard way that there were some battles you couldn't win, no matter how much you loved a person.

Besides, he had no time for children of his own. His baby was the new fertility center.

In front of him, the magazine drifted shut. Just as well, since he hadn't read a word.

Mark chewed the last bite of his sandwich. Amazingly, no one had interrupted his meal with an emergency or even so much as a question. That had to be a first.

A glance showed Jennifer and Lori still conferring without their third musketeer. Perhaps Sam was still with patients, or she'd decided to run errands instead of eating. But, he couldn't afford to put this off. News of the dental building's involvement in a bankruptcy had already reached Tony, who'd come in to make sure Mark had received word. Sam needed to be prepared.

Mark cleared his dishes and set out for the building next door.

"I DON'T SUPPOSE IT HELPS to point out that things could be worse," Nora Kendall told Sam ruefully. They were sitting in Nora's office, beneath photos of babies and framed diplomas proclaiming her expertise in obstetrics, gynecology and fertility.

Fertility. The word cut like a scalpel.

"I know I'm lucky to still be cancer-free after twenty years," Sam conceded. "But... Are you certain it's early menopause?"

"Would you like me to go over the results again?"

Sam waved away the offer. Despite her question, she understood the test results all too well. She'd known this was possible; she simply hadn't believed it would happen to her.

Girls who survived cancer treatment as teens were more than a dozen times as likely as other women to suffer menopause before age forty. The greatest risk was for those who, like Sam, had received heavy doses of radiation and chemotherapy to battle Hodgkin's lymphoma. The damage to the ovaries couldn't be repaired.

"What about fertility treatments?" With no husband on the horizon, that would mean using donor sperm. Not Sam's preference, but if it was her only chance to conceive...

Compassion shaded Nora's expression. "At this stage, you'd require donated eggs and heavy-duty hormone treatment. In view of your medical history, I don't recommend it," she added gently.

The instinct to fight swelled in Sam. It was the same instinct that had saved her as a teenager and by which she'd lived ever since. But she had to be reasonable. "You think trying to have a baby might harm my health?"

"That is definitely a concern."

"I don't want to be an idiot about this," she conceded. *And I know the dangers as well as anyone.*

Nora showed no impatience, although she must be hungry. "This is a heavy blow to absorb. If you strongly want to try for a baby, I'll do my best to help you."

Sam tossed back her head. Despite her dejected mood, she relished the bounce of long hair, which she never took for granted. Years ago, she'd put on a brave face about baldness and colorful scarves, but in reality she'd hated them.

"No, thanks. You're right, it could be worse. These past few months, when I started getting irregular periods and night sweats, I was afraid the cancer had returned." Night sweats and swollen glands were the symptoms that had first alerted her to the lymphoma. "I'm darn lucky."

"You pooh-poohed the idea of a recurrence during the exam," Nora pointed out.

"I'd hate to act like a crybaby," Sam explained. "Besides, it's counterproductive to dwell on things we can't control."

"Counterproductive but natural," her doctor responded. "Don't feel you have to hold everything inside and put on a brave face for my sake. Sometimes it's healthy to cry."

"Not for me, it isn't." Because her voice sounded shaky, Sam rose quickly. "I've kept you long enough. Go eat."

"I don't mind skipping lunch," Nora said.

"It's hard to be good-natured with patients when you're hungry." Sam had learned that from experience. "Speaking of eating, you're invited to an open house at the counseling clinic on Christmas Day."

"Christmas? Gee, I'd love to come, but I promised to fix the turkey for my aunt's dinner."

Oh, dear. Perhaps because her family lived far away, Sam had blithely figured most of her friends, at least the unmarried ones, would be available. But she just couldn't focus on that now.

"We'll miss you. Well, thanks for everything." Sam grabbed her purse and bolted for the door. If she lingered one more second, she might break down.

Outside on the walkway, she dragged in a series of deep breaths, trying to ease the sensation of having been punched in the stomach. She would never feel a baby move inside her. Never have any funny-awful pregnancy stories to share with her patients. Never experience the wonder of breastfeeding.

Every day, she cuddled infants and went nose to nose with inquisitive toddlers. For their parents and for teen mothers like Candy, she served as the sage counselor. Sam felt like a sailor lost at sea, dying of thirst while floating on an ocean of undrinkable water.

She wished her parents were here, and her brother, Benton, a cardiologist who lived in her hometown of Seattle with his wife and two kids. They'd rallied behind her before, and they'd do it now. Benton had urged her more than once to relocate to his area, where she had a lot of old friends. The last time she'd visited her parents' clinic in Mexico, she'd also given serious consideration to moving there to work with children in need.

Yet for once she didn't feel like turning to her family. How could they understand? Mom had conceived and given birth easily, and Benton and his wife had produced their kids on a prearranged schedule. *First a boy, then a girl, two and a half years apart.*

Self-pity was not her style, Samantha reminded herself. Neither was resenting other people's good fortune. What she ought to do was square her shoulders, lift her chin and go comfort Lori about *her* problems.

"Oh, there you are." The baritone voice gave her a start.

Mark Rayburn shouldn't sneak up on people. Well, with a delivery truck rumbling across the quadrangle and a medical rescue copter whirring toward the hospital's helipad, perhaps he hadn't actually needed to sneak.

"Samantha?" he prodded, looking much too solid and comforting for her fragile peace of mind. "Are you all right?"

She tried to shrug and look nonchalant. Useless.

"No," she gasped. "No, Mark, I'm not all right."

Then, to her utter humiliation, she burst into tears.

IN THE TWO YEARS MARK HAD worked with the fiery Samantha Forrest, he'd never before glimpsed this lost, little-girl expression. Impulsively, he gathered her into his arms. Felt her collapse against his chest, registered the trace of tears against his neck and tried to soothe the shudders wracking her body. It hurt to see her in such pain.

"What's wrong?" he asked.

The Sam he knew would have volleyed back a sharp answer. Today, she simply went on pouring out grief as if she'd bottled it up for years.

Around them, the medical complex lay calm. During the noon hour, no patients were arriving to notice her distress, and the noise of the helicopter covered her sobs. But any moment that would change, and he suspected Sam would be embarrassed if others witnessed her in this state.

They ought to go somewhere private, as long as that didn't require navigating a hallway or passing a receptionist. Much as Mark loved this place and its people, he deplored the pervasive gossip.

"Let's take a walk," he suggested.

Sam gave a faint nod. She clung to his arm unsteadily as he guided her between the buildings and through a landscaped park strip.

He wondered again what had upset her so badly. It couldn't be related to the counseling clinic, because if she'd learned about that, she'd have railed at him rather than fallen apart. The loss of a patient? That certainly could be upsetting. Still, he'd never seen her react at such a personal level.

They crossed the pedestrian bridge over Coast Highway and reached the edge of the bluffs, where a long wooden staircase led down to the beach. A salty breeze stung Mark's cheeks as they descended and, beside him, Sam sucked in a couple of deep breaths.

"Is your family okay?" he asked as they crossed the beach parking area, largely deserted on a December weekday.

"As far as I know." She sounded puzzled.

"You don't have to talk if you don't want to," Mark said.

Sam peered across the sand toward the soothing lap of the surf. "What're we doing here?"

"Taking a break. Hey, are you lost in a daze?"

"I guess so."

This was unlike her. It worried him.

They found rocky perches on adjacent boulders that bordered the sand. Overhead, a seagull wheeled, mewing plaintively. Aside from a few hardy surfers plying their boards on the low waves, they were alone.

"I figured we could both use a breather," Mark added.

"Thanks."

"You're welcome." The fact that he had a bomb to drop on her bothered him more than a little. But in view of her distress, the clinic's situation could wait.

Samantha managed a weak smile. "You must think I've lost my mind."

He seized on the opening to ask, "What happened?"

She leaned back on the rock, tilting her lightly tanned face toward the winter sun. "You remind me of a doctor on an old TV show. A kind, wise fellow everyone came to for advice."

"Hardly anyone comes to me for advice," Mark said wryly. "And if I give it to them, they don't follow it."

Samantha chuckled. "The heck they don't."

"Well, my patients might be the exception."

"And the staff."

"Not very often."

She fell silent, as if debating how far to trust him. After a moment, she broke the lull. "I got bad news from my doctor."

Clouds drifted over the sun, casting the beach into gray gloom. A chill ran through Mark. Since taking the helm at Safe Harbor, he'd worked his way through the personnel files of his medical staff, acquainting himself with their backgrounds. While they weren't required to disclose their personal medical histories, Samantha had done so freely.

He loosened his tie because he was having a hard time swallowing past the lump in his throat. "The cancer's returned?"

Her startled gaze met his. "No. No, that's not it, thank goodness."

What a relief. "I'm glad to hear it." Very glad.

He waited, in case she had more to say. Out on the water, a surfer rode a puny wave to shore, then stepped off the board with a disdainful grimace. "Pathetic waves," Mark muttered in sympathy.

"I beg your pardon?"

"The surf. It's feeble."

"What're you, a surfing critic?" she demanded.

"I used to surf in high school," he said. "They have surf in Miami, you know."

"I thought you played football."

"The two sports aren't mutually exclusive."

"I never said they were." Samantha kicked at the sand.

The spray hit Mark's freshly shined shoes and sifted into his socks. "Thank you for that."

"My pleasure." She started to laugh. Almost in slow motion, her face crumpled. Finally she rasped out, "It's early menopause."

So that was the bad news. "Because of the radiation and chemo?"

She nodded. "Nora advises against fertility treatments. She says they'd be hazardous."

"I concur," Mark said.

Fresh tears tracked after the ones that had dried in the breeze. "I didn't realize how much I counted on having children. On going through the whole experience of pregnancy."

He checked the impulse to point out that she could adopt. You didn't console a woman who'd lost a child by telling her she could have more, and, in a sense, that's what had happened to Samantha. He'd learned from his patients that the child in a woman's dreams might seem almost as real to her as a baby she'd held in her arms.

How ironic that, despite his medical expertise, he had nothing to offer. Except comfort.

Mark moved to her rock and slid his arm around her. When Sam's head drifted to his shoulder, he brushed a kiss across her hair.

She nestled closer, the scent of springtime enveloping him for a sweet instant before the breeze whipped it away. He couldn't resist tracing the delicate straightness of her nose with his lips, and when she blinked up at him, his mouth closed instinctively over hers.

The warmth drew him in, tantalizing against the cool air. This might be crazy, but Mark yielded to the longing to pull her onto his lap. She shifted readily, clinging to him, answering his kisses with a flick of tongue and a soft moan.

He felt himself stirring, coming alive, wanting Sam in a way he'd never allowed himself before. He lifted his head, breathing fast, and then touched his forehead to hers.

Although he wasn't sure about the wisdom of proceeding with such a combustible relationship, they could hardly deny their attraction. And they were both adults. "We should get together after work. Figure out where to go from here."

"Where to go?" Sam drew back, a pucker forming between her eyebrows.

"I didn't mean literally. I meant…" Grim reality slapped Mark, along with a fresh blast of wind. How could he have forgotten about Chandra's call? "Wait. Before we discuss anything personal, I have a piece of news."

"Hit me with it," Sam replied, sounding more like her usual tart self. "Maybe that'll bring us both to our senses."

Unfortunately, he reflected, it was more likely to bring them to the point of open warfare. "It's about the clinic…"

Chapter Three

Samantha couldn't believe what she was hearing. Yet despite her dismay, she felt conflicted and uncertain. Where was the instantaneous flare of anger that should have powered her into action?

She'd worked hard to bring this counseling service to reality. While she admired her parents' devotion to the poor of another country, there were people hurting in this affluent area, too. Women in abusive relationships who needed someone to talk to, as well as confused teenagers and former foster children who lacked survival skills. They couldn't afford to pay and often shrank from paperwork and bureaucracies.

The Serra Clinic was unusually informal and flexible, using peer counselors who empathized with their clients. Right now, it depended entirely on volunteers, but Sam had hoped to raise funds and find sponsors so they could hire a professional staff, as well. Now, the entire project might be wiped out, or reduced to a catch-as-catch-can enterprise that limped along in second-rate facilities.

She ought to be furious with Mark, who she knew sided with the corporation. Instead, she kept wishing this awful displacement had waited a few more weeks or months so she could go on enjoying the comfort of his arms.

What was wrong with her?

You've received two severe blows in the space of an afternoon. No wonder you're reeling.

Ah, that was the Dr. Forrest side of her brain kicking in. But reeling or not, it didn't explain the way she'd reacted to Mark.

She'd felt a strong urge to skip out on their duties and do much more than kiss him. To pull off his tie, and his jacket, and the rest of his clothes—not in public of course, but...

"Sam? I understand why you're distracted but I'm getting a little worried." The subject of her fantasy stopped pacing along the sand and regarded her with dark-eyed tenderness.

Sam wriggled as the rock dug into her bottom. "Because I'm not erupting like a volcano?"

"That would be a more typical reaction, yes."

"I can't believe they're doing this to people in need. It's cruel."

"It's business," Mark replied. "The hospital has a core mission, and your project isn't part of it."

"That's where we disagree—in spades." There it was, a trace of irritation. Sam did her best to fan it into full-blown righteous anger. "You have to see how important counseling is."

"Yes, of course, but—"

"Keep on compromising your values, and one day you won't have a soul left to call your own."

"Oh, really?" he countered. "You should try compromising more often. You might actually accomplish something instead of spinning your wheels."

"That's what you think I'm doing? Spinning my wheels?"

"Go ahead and pick an argument." He seemed almost pleased. "I prefer that to seeing you defeated. Go on, Sam. Call me names if it makes you happy."

Did he have to look so rumpled and obliging? Mark

Rayburn, guiding spirit of the medical center, everyone's favorite go-to guy. *The enemy.* Yet she still failed to summon any significant fury.

"This is not one of my favorite days," Sam muttered. "I wish I'd checked my horoscope before I got out of bed this morning."

His chuckle reverberated. "I doubt that would have helped. But take the afternoon off. You've got a lot to think about."

"I never take the afternoon off."

"What were you planning to do that's so important?"

She tried to remember. Paperwork. The Christmas fundraiser. Oh, heavens. Was she even going to have a place to hold it? "How soon are they kicking us out?"

"We didn't discuss a deadline," Mark said. "I'm sure I can hold off until after the first of the year, if you like."

"Yes. For one thing, I need to break this to our volunteers." And find somewhere to stow the computers and furniture they'd acquired. Samantha's brain whirred. "I guess I will go home for an hour or so. I can think better uninterrupted."

They recrossed the footbridge in silence. Every now and then, a flicker of indignation crossed her mental horizon—did he have to break the news to her when she was already down and out?—but she had to acknowledge that delaying wouldn't have made things easier.

Sam hated seeing the issue from Mark's perspective. It made her so grumpy, she barely mumbled a farewell when they reached the edge of the hospital complex, and strode off without a backward glance. Nevertheless, she sensed the moment when he stopped watching her and turned onto his own path.

She stemmed an impulse to call out. What would she say, anyway? *Next time I see you, I'll bring poison darts.*

How strange it felt, walking home in the middle of the

day when she ought to be at the hospital. She'd scarcely taken a day off since entering medical school. Even in the summers, she'd worked hard to pay the tuition. Putting two kids through medical school had been expensive for her parents, who'd spent most of their careers doing low-paid work among the poor.

Sam had vowed to continue their tradition, and hadn't entirely written off the idea of someday joining their clinic. But with student loans to pay, she'd had to accept a mainstream medical position and consign charity work to her free hours. Although she'd recently paid off the last of the loans, she still needed to build up at least a modest savings account.

There was, fortunately, an inheritance from her grandparents that she'd invested and saved as an emergency fund. Her parents had refused to let her touch it when she was younger, saying she should only draw on it if she absolutely had to.

She'd always figured the fund was there for the children she planned to have one day. If there'd been any reasonable chance that fertility treatments would work without destroying her health, she'd have spent the money without question now.

It might enable her to adopt. The prospect of a long search and the complex procedures involved seemed overwhelming in her present state of mind, but at least, when she was ready, she had the money set aside.

Silently, she thanked her grandparents. And missed them.

Rounding a corner, Sam had to make way for two women chatting as they pushed strollers side by side along the sidewalk. Their babies, one in a darling miniature ski jacket and the other merry in a green-and-red plaid coat, leaned eagerly forward as if trying to embrace the world.

Feeling a sudden ache, Sam averted her gaze, only to

find herself peering through a house window at a Christmas tree surrounded by gaily wrapped toys. Everywhere she looked, there seemed to be children and families.

A lump rose in her throat. She'd always assumed she would eventually have those things, too. And maybe she could, but not the way she'd expected.

To focus on her loss felt selfish in view of the clinic's crisis and her own fundamental good health. *Be grateful you aren't facing death.*

The problem was, now she had to face life.

ON FRIDAY AFTERNOON, MARK SAT in front of his computer, fingering the mouse as he sifted through applications for the position of fertility center director. Medical Center Management had asked him to narrow the field to three top candidates. Not an easy task. Among several dozen applicants, at least six offered excellent credentials. Not brilliant, perhaps, but close.

Leaning back, he tented his fingers and glanced through the window toward the harbor. Somehow the water managed to sparkle even in the weak winter sunlight.

Was it really only two days since he'd sat on the beach with Samantha? Felt like aeons.

Flexing his hands, he wondered at this nagging concern and the sense that he ought to do something for her. Yesterday, he'd sought a moment to talk to Sam after a staff meeting, but she'd hurried off to admit a patient. He wasn't sure what he'd have said, anyway. He had no magic wand to rescue the counseling clinic nor, despite all his training, could he remedy her medical condition.

Their kiss hadn't softened her attitude toward him. Still the same cautious distance. The same awareness that they stood, irrevocably, on opposite sides of a battlefield.

It had affected *him*, though. He missed her. Those

sparks, that sudden burst of passion—his body heated at the memory.

You must have a death wish, Rayburn.

Mark returned his attention to the résumé on the screen. How ironic that all these fertility experts had no cure for early menopause, either.

Still, the woman whose credentials lay before him had an impressive background at Johns Hopkins and Yale. She specialized in genetic engineering that could enable parents to deliver healthy babies free of their families' devastating hereditary conditions. Her cover letter indicated she was interested in moving to southern California to be closer to her elderly parents.

Much as he admired her, Mark knew she'd be a better fit at a research-oriented university hospital. Safe Harbor needed a clinician concerned with applying proven techniques as well as developing and testing new ones.

The prospect of having the best possible staff and lab facilities thrilled him. He wasn't entirely sorry about taking over existing space at Safe Harbor, because it meant that the new center would be up and running much faster than under the old plan. But he had to find the right director, and so far, respectable as these applicants were, none quite fit what he envisioned.

May Chong buzzed him on the intercom. "There's a woman on line three who says she's your sister. Do you want to pick up?"

A jolt of relief drove everything else from Mark's mind. "Absolutely." Then a wave of apprehension closed over him. It had been five years since he'd seen her. What kind of condition was she in? Would she even be coherent? Was she calling from a jail, seeking bail money?

He punched the button and asked cautiously, "Bryn?"

"You moved," she said without preamble. "I pictured you still in Florida."

"I'd have left a forwarding address if I'd known where to send it."

"I found you on the internet."

Her voice had a huskier quality than he remembered. The last time they'd met he'd seen the toll that drugs and alcohol had taken on his sister, sprinkling her brown hair with premature traces of gray and leaving pouches beneath her eyes.

"You're easy to find," she added. "Unlike me, I guess."

"I hired a detective, but you dropped completely out of sight. Are you okay? Where are you?" He braced for her usual evasions.

"In Phoenix. I've been clean for two years."

"Two years? Congratulations." That sounded like an eternity, considering that she'd begun using as a teenager and hadn't stopped except for the few times he'd persuaded her to enter rehab programs. She must be thirty-three now. Hard to imagine his baby sister being that old. "I wish you'd let me know sooner."

"I wanted to be sure I could do this on my own." In the background, he heard the rumble of a large engine.

"Are you at a truck stop?" That would be typical, sad to say. According to the detective, his sister had put her health and life at risk, picking up men for drug money.

"I work as a receptionist for a trucking company," she told him. "Mark, I don't blame you for doubting me. I put you through hell. But I've found a group that supports me. It's called Celebrate Recovery—kind of like Alcoholics Anonymous, only it's at a church."

"I'm glad to hear it." Beneath her casual tone, he sensed that she'd called for a reason. "I'm happier than I can say to learn that you're all right. You're the only family I have."

"No wife?" Bryn asked. "I was hoping for a few nieces and nephews by now."

"Not yet. I'm still marveling at the idea that a home

can be a refuge instead of a war zone." Now, where had that come from?

"So you choose to be alone?"

"I'm not alone. I run a hospital and see patients. Long hours, but it's what I always dreamed of." Enough talking about himself. He wanted to find out more about his sister. "I was going to ask—"

"Why I'm calling," she finished. "Because I always call with a motive, right?"

"That is the pattern, yes." Blinking buttons on the phone caught Mark's attention. People must be trying to reach him. Thank goodness his secretary had the sense to deflect them.

"One of the steps in our recovery is making amends to people we've harmed. And you're the person I've hurt the most."

"You want to make amends?" He didn't see how a person could atone for so many years of disappointment and pain. Still, he loved her in spite of that.

"Maybe not for your sake, but for mine—if that's okay?" Bryn added quickly. "The last thing I want is to cause you any more problems."

Forgiveness might not come easily, but Mark was willing to try. "I'd be happy to see you."

"I was hoping...how about Christmas?" she blurted. "I could drive out there."

"That's what, seven or eight hours?" A long trek for one person. "I'll send you a plane ticket."

"No, Mark. This is my responsibility." She spoke with a maturity he'd never heard from her before. "I should arrive by late afternoon. But don't let me disrupt your plans if you were going to spend Christmas with someone."

That reminded him of Sam's fundraiser. He'd promised to be there, but that didn't preclude welcoming his sister.

"You should come," Mark told her. "It won't be a proper Christmas without you."

"I don't deserve…" Her words choked off. She cleared her throat. "You're the most wonderful brother in the world."

"Just get here in one piece." He gave her his cell phone number. "You can reach me anytime."

She provided her own number. "I'm not going to disappear again. This is for keeps."

"That's the best Christmas present you could give me."

After they hung up, Mark sat amazed at this development. He'd feared his next contact with Bryn would be a call informing him of her death, or that he might never learn what happened to her. This was beyond anything he'd dared to hope for.

If it was real, and not just another of her deceptions.

A tap at the door broke his reverie. Without waiting for an invitation, a blond whirlwind in a teal blouse and gray tweed skirt breezed in, head high and mouth set in a determined line.

"Sam." Mark got to his feet. "I was wondering where you've been."

"Licking my wounds. Well, I'm done with the self-pity. Now I've got a plan."

"What kind of plan?" he asked warily.

"I've decided to call a press conference."

"Excuse me?"

She beamed. "I'm sure reporters will be very interested to know what's happening to the clinic."

"I decide when the hospital holds a press conference and what information we release to the media."

She held up her hands in a peace gesture. "Sorry. I was just taking a poke at you. I want to announce the Christmas fundraiser. That's all."

"Why not simply send out a press release?" Putting

Samantha together with the media was like cleaning a linoleum floor with gasoline. One spark and the whole house blew up.

"It'll get lost on somebody's desk. There's only a couple of weeks left, after all, and this is the fastest way to reach our supporters. Also, a local caterer agreed to provide food at cost in return for publicity. Jennifer believes we can get the press conference organized by Monday." With an unexpected note of pleading, Sam added, "Please? If the fundraiser fizzles, we're sunk."

It was hard to argue when she spoke so reasonably. "I suppose so. No mention of having to move out of the offices, though," Mark warned. "We'll be presenting the plans for the fertility center in a controlled manner. I can't have you hijacking the subject."

"And flying it into the side of a mountain?" Samantha observed wryly.

"Do I have to remind you about past slipups? Such as the time you announced on the internet that we were giving away beauty makeovers?" Mark would never forget the uproar when a swarm of Samantha's teen moms—including Candy—arrived at the hospital to demand free pampering.

"I just said we ought to make single moms who keep their babies feel like Cinderellas at the ball, even if it meant providing…" She shook her head. "That was over the top, I admit. But it turned out all right." A local salon, glad to reap the TV coverage, had donated makeovers.

"This is much more serious. Bad publicity about the hospital could hurt our recruitment efforts and shake up stockholder confidence." And he'd lose the chance to recruit the kind of director who could put Safe Harbor on the map.

"You don't need to lecture me, Mark."

They faced each other across his desk, a gulf that

seemed wider than ever. He wished he knew how to cross it, not just for the sake of their professional relationship, but because he had a very strong desire to kiss her again. Right now. No matter who might walk in on them.

With a mental wrench, he returned to the topic. "What time Monday?"

"One o'clock."

"We'll go over the presentation beforehand. You, me and Jennifer."

"You plan to be there?"

He shrugged. "I'll put it an appearance."

Sam folded her arms. "If you insist. But honestly, boss, I promise to color inside the lines."

"Spoken like a pediatrician."

When she grinned, sunshine flooded the office. "We really are on the same team, most of the time."

After she left, Mark took a moment to remember how to breathe. Then he got back to work.

Chapter Four

Through the window of the Sea Star Café, the gray sky gave the harbor a flat, subdued air. Once darkness fell tonight, strings of holiday lights on the moored sailboats and yachts would provide a fairyland display, but this morning the scene matched Samantha's gloomy mood.

Lori slid into a seat beside her at the table, the aroma of spices wafting from her steaming cup of chai. Joining them, Jennifer set down a mug of coffee. Their faint reflections in the window showed the contrast between Sam's own blond ponytail, Lori's reddish-brown hair and Jennifer's darker coloring, a tribute to a Hispanic heritage on her father's side.

That reminded Sam: she'd always wondered what *her* children would look like. Well, she wasn't going to have any. Not genetic ones, anyway.

"If you stare out the window any harder, the glass is going to shatter," Lori said.

"Or you'll focus the light and set fire to one of the sailboats," Jennifer added.

"I'm entitled to be moody," Sam grumped. "Deal with it."

She'd broken the news about her medical results to her friends yesterday, and had hoped they could all put the subject behind them before their regular Saturday power

walk and coffee-guzzling. Instead, Sam sat here brood-
ing. Well, they ought to understand.

"We *are* dealing with it, by making jokes," said Lori.

"At your expense." Jennifer softened her words with
a smile. "In the nicest way possible." With an adopted
three-month-old and an adoring husband, the newlywed
beamed at everyone and everything. Constantly. To the
verge of being nauseating.

Honestly, how could she sink so low as to resent her
friend? Sam thought in dismay. Just because she was suffering herself didn't mean she wished the same misery
on anyone else.

She looked up to see Lori frowning. "Sam, I never
thought you were that eager to have kids. You always
seemed preoccupied with saving the world."

True enough. "Frankly, my reaction surprises me, too.
I should be worrying about the counseling clinic, not my
silly personal issues."

"Early menopause is hardly a silly personal issue," Jennifer said.

"Well, it *is* personal. But it's not silly." Lori eyed a cin-
namon-nut muffin passing by on someone's plate. "You
think I worked off enough calories to eat one of those?
I'd hate to lose my girlish figure, especially now that I'm
single again." Perhaps realizing that she hadn't actually
been married, she added, "In the totally unattached sense."

"Do you feel ready to date?" Jennifer asked. "That
would be a good sign."

Lori shrugged. "Wish I did. Then I might stop obsess-
ing about Jared. Only…every guy I meet, when he finds
out I'm an obstetrical nurse, the first thing he says is how
much he wants kids. Can you believe it?"

"Yes." To her embarrassment, Samantha felt the sting
of tears. What was wrong with her?

"I'm sorry. I keep forgetting you can't *have*..." Lori grimaced. "That's even worse, me *dwelling* on it."

"We should find a neutral topic. Unless you two would rather discuss your...issues." Jennifer peered from one to the other. "It's fine with me either way."

"Do you have to be so *nice?*" Sam roared.

Lori held up her hands. "I've got an idea. Let's talk about somebody we all hate."

"I don't hate anyone," Jennifer said.

"Mark," Sam proposed.

Lori shook her head. "It's not his fault he's booting out the counseling clinic. Besides, I can't hate him. He's my doctor."

"Neither can I. After all, he hired me," Jennifer reminded them. "And he's a great boss."

Sam didn't hate him, either. The truth was, she'd done far too much thinking about Mark during the past few days. Did he guess how she melted inside when he drew close? A part of her wished they'd followed up on his suggestion to figure out how to proceed after their kiss. If only the stupid hospital corporation hadn't thrown a wrench into everything.

If only I weren't wildly attracted to the wrong man.

"Why *do* you hate Mark?" Jennifer asked. "Seriously, I realize you two cross swords on a regular basis, but I figured there were sparks."

Was it that obvious?

"He may drive you crazy, but he's supportive when you need him," Lori declared.

That did it. "Let me tell you about men," Sam burst out. "First they're all warm and supportive, but the next thing you know they sucker you into darning their socks."

"Dr. Rayburn would never ask anyone to darn his socks." Lori stirred her tea so vigorously it slopped over. "When they get a hole in them, he throws them away and buys new ones." Amazing what details some nurses noticed about their physicians.

"Who asked you to darn his socks?" Jennifer asked.

"Well, no one, literally," Samantha admitted. "But there was this guy I almost married in college. I nearly dropped my plans for med school so I could put *him* through law school." Brad Worthy. Or rather, Brad *Un*Worthy. She saw his high-boned, angular face as clearly as if she'd dated him last month instead of fifteen years ago at UC Berkeley.

"He must have been an exciting guy, if you cared that much about him," Lori said.

"Smart and passionate." And terribly hurt when his starry-eyed girlfriend came to her senses. "He couldn't figure out why I put my dreams ahead of his."

"Why couldn't you both pursue your dreams?" Jennifer asked.

"Too expensive. Well, from his perspective." Brad had freaked out at the prospect of running up hundreds of thousands of dollars in debt between them. "I didn't care if we ever owned a house or sent our kids to private school. But he did."

"He broke up with you over that?" Lori said. "He sounds like a snob."

"Lucky you discovered that you had such different values," Jennifer added.

In retrospect, their breakup *had* been lucky, Sam reflected as she checked her watch. "I'm afraid I have to go. Candy's being released this morning. I want to make sure she and the triplets are okay."

Lori regarded her dubiously. "It's after ten. She might have left already."

With a guilty pang, Sam realized she'd been dragging her feet. These past few days, seeing those three darling babies had reminded her painfully of her own condition, and she'd found it increasingly hard to sympathize with the serious challenges Candy faced.

First you resent your friends, and now you envy a young mother you've mentored? What's wrong with you?

Sam hauled herself to her feet. "Please forgive my bad mood this morning."

"I will, if you'll forgive *me* for boring you to death about my broken heart," said Lori.

"And if you'll excuse me showing you my honeymoon pictures twice by mistake," Jennifer put in.

"They're great pictures. I didn't mind a bit." Scooping up her oversize purse, Samantha said goodbye and emerged from the cozy café into the chilly seaside air.

She set out at a brisk pace on the uphill march to the hospital. A couple of cyclists swooped by, muscular legs pumping as they bent low over their racing bikes. From a nearby veterinary kennel, a chorus of barks welcomed a visitor or perhaps a meal.

Sam kept an eye out for an empty storefront or sign advertising a small office that might house the counseling clinic. A place right along busy Safe Harbor Boulevard would at least draw walk-in traffic. But how was she going to pay the rent? The hospital facilities had been free.

Somehow, today, she couldn't spare any more energy for other people, even those who were suffering. She just wanted to move past her own deep pain. Thank goodness for exercise.

A few minutes later, her leg muscles burning, she strode into the medical center elevator. On the third floor, the doors opened on three volunteers wheeling a trio of bassinets toward her, trailed by Candy in the obligatory wheelchair. Sam's heart lurched when she spotted sweet little Connie with her strawberry blotch.

I'm going to miss her.

"Hey, Doc!" Toward her ambled the father, Jon, a thin fellow with scraggly facial hair. "Where've you been?"

"I came to the hospital earlier to examine them." She'd cleared each of the babies for release before leaving to meet her friends. "Congratulations. Your children are in great condition. That's not always the case in multiple births."

"I thought you were going to fix her." He indicated Connie.

Like a broken toy? "We'll deal with the birthmark when she's older and stronger." Although the triplets had arrived in remarkably good shape, Samantha preferred to let the infant gain weight before subjecting her to laser treatment.

The wheelchair rolled alongside them, its occupant frowning. "This is kind of scary. I'm not sure how I'm going to care for all these babies when it takes three volunteers just to push the bassinets."

Candy did face a daunting task. Sam had spent a lot of time reviewing the issues with her in advance, and despite the occasional hesitation, the girl had seemed determined. *But was she responding to my enthusiasm? Did I influence her too much?*

This was hardly the moment for a change of heart. Once Candy settled in, with help from her mother and from volunteers, she'd gradually gain confidence. "As I've explained, a nurse will come by your apartment this afternoon to get things organized. Some of our hospital volunteers are going to be relieving you for a few hours a day for the next few weeks. Do you have the schedule I gave you?"

The girl waved a sheaf of papers. "It's in here somewhere with all the hospital forms... I think. Otherwise, I have no idea where I put it."

Irritation surged inside Sam. She'd put a lot of effort into helping Candy. The least the girl could do was hang on to her paperwork.

That wasn't fair. Candy's system must be flooded with hormones and she faced a tremendous amount of adjusting. Regretting her moment of impatience, Sam asked, "Do you want me to come by tonight?"

"No, thanks," Jon said. "A bunch of my friends will be coming over to play with them."

That didn't sound like a good idea. "If you'll check the discharge instructions, you'll see that newborns are very vulnerable to infection. Especially during flu season, we recommend that only family interact with them."

He drew himself up, offended. "My friends aren't infected with anything."

Sam reminded herself that these babies belonged to their parents now. She had to let them go. "Just be careful."

The young man appeared to teeter on the edge of arguing, but Candy's warning glance apparently dissuaded him. "Okay, maybe just a *few* friends. And they'll wash their hands and wear those paper masks the nurse gave us for visitors."

He was showing better judgment already, Samantha reflected. Lots of new parents were young and inexperienced. "You'll do fine. I'll see them for their checkup on Friday, okay?"

Candy nodded and, at her signal, a volunteer pushed the elevator call button. While they waited, Sam gazed down at the little ones. She sympathized with Connie as the underdog, but Courtney's intense expression gave the impression of a little mother hen in the making.

Of the trio, Colin had the strongest grip on Sam's finger and held her gaze for a fraction of a second longer. She'd have sworn he recognized her, but then, why shouldn't he? She'd spent a lot of time around the babies since their birth.

But they weren't hers anymore. Never had been, really.

Then, with the whisper of wheels and the brush of footsteps, they were gone, the double doors closing out her last glimpse of the group.

Samantha stood clenching and unclenching her fists, feeling ridiculously bereft.

MARK FOLDED AWAY HIS CELL phone. There went a perfectly good Saturday afternoon golf game. Tony, the hospital attorney had cancelled to spend the day with his fiancée, planning their wedding. Earlier, Jared Sellers had begged off in order to fill in for an ailing colleague who was signed up to perform newborn hearing and vision screenings at a health fair.

An afternoon on the links would have provided a welcome release after the week's pressures. Mark supposed he could show up at the course and join some random group, but once strangers found out he was a doctor, they tended to interrupt his concentration asking for medical advice.

Rounding a corner in the hospital hallway, he paused at the sight of Samantha, shoulders slumped and strands of hair escaping her ponytail. Although she stood in front of the elevator, neither button was lit.

The events of this week obviously weighed on her. He wished she didn't have to deal with that business about the counseling clinic on top of her medical issues.

When he started forward, his footsteps rang out. At the sound, Sam's spine straightened.

Mark drew alongside. "Up or down?"

Her puzzled glance resolved into a look of understanding as she eyed the buttons. "Down."

He pressed.

"Don't tell me you're done for the day," she said. "So early? Oh, wait! Golf with Tony, right?"

"He cancelled. Sellers, too."

"Poor Mark. Abandoned by your friends."

"You don't play, do you?" That would be almost too

convenient. Mark suspected Sam would golf with the same fierce competitiveness she displayed in her work. Still, he'd be willing to give it a shot.

She shook her head. "Never learned."

"I could teach you."

The elevator opened. "Thanks, but I'll pass."

"Such gratitude," he kidded as they got in.

"I am grateful. To be alive and healthy." She didn't sound very happy, though.

He was well aware of Candy's release a few minutes earlier, since he'd signed off on her medical condition. The departure of those three precious little ones had clearly added to Sam's slump. "You think those kids will rise to the demands of parenting?"

"I have to hope so. Candy's a good person underneath, but she comes from a dysfunctional background. She tends to be impulsive and short-tempered, and so does Jon." Samantha blew out a long breath. "All the more reason to have people around them who will offer support rather than criticism."

Her comment reminded him of his sister. "I grew up with people who wreaked havoc and left it for others to clean up. Support is fine, but there have to be limits."

"I probably set those limits a bit further out than you do." They emerged on the first floor and headed toward the staff exit. "But I'm not an enabler, if that's what you think."

An enabler, in substance-abuse terms, was a person who helped a loved one continue self-destructive behavior by easing or removing the consequences. "There's a fine line between enabling and caring," he told her. "I ought to know. I've crossed it."

"You?" Her eyebrows rose. "You never seem to have trouble enforcing the rules."

Mark preferred to keep his family troubles private. Still, Samantha had wept in his arms and shared her grief. Plus, he could use some objective feedback about his sister. He'd spent a lot of time since yesterday thinking about her call.

"You walking home?" he asked. Although he didn't recall Sam's address, they occasionally arrived on foot at the same time, so her house must be close by.

She nodded.

"Mind some company?"

"Not at all. And I promise I won't harangue you about work unless you deserve it, which depends completely on you."

"I promise to be utterly blameless and saintly," Mark announced as they walked past the parking lot.

"Sounds boring." Her mouth curved in an impish grin.

There was nothing boring *or* saintly about his reaction to that teasing smile. For the sake of his own peace of mind, Mark seized on the first neutral topic that occurred to him. "How are plans coming for the Christmas party?"

"I have volunteers handling the decorations and the music. The theme is 'A Hot and Happy Christmas'—carols set to a salsa beat, Santa draped in a red-and-white serape. You'll be there, right?"

He nodded. "I may bring a guest."

Sam missed a step. He caught her arm as she stumbled, holding her tightly until she regained her balance. The sudden motion sent a few more wisps of hair tickling around her forehead. Irritated, she yanked on the covered elastic as if to pull it off. Instead, it stuck fast.

"Ow!" She added a few pediatrician-appropriate swear words, "Doggone! Blast it," while pulling on the rubbery cord. All she achieved was to get the thing tangled even more tightly in her hair. "I should have just left it alone. Now it's stuck. Got a pair of scissors?"

"You aren't going to cut off your beautiful hair, are you?" he asked in dismay. There went one of his favorite fantasies, the two of them entwined in bed with Sam on top, blond waves curtaining him.

Just as well. He normally made a point of *not* fantasizing about anyone he worked with.

She winced. "No, I didn't mean for my hair. I need to cut off the elastic."

In his pocket, Mark's hand closed around his multifunction pocketknife. Not only could he snip the elastic, he could uncork a wine bottle, file his nails and probably shoe a horse if he really had to. But he'd much rather spend time talking to Sam than leafing through medical journals, so...

He slipped an empty hand out of his pocket. "I have several pairs of surgical scissors at my house. I suspect that's pretty much en route to yours. And I happen to stock excellent coffee."

Sam regarded him speculatively. "Any chocolates? I passed up having a muffin with my friends. Now I'm feeling deprived."

"I have a box in the freezer. Several, in fact." Patients went overboard at holidays with gifts of candy, which he saved for special occasions. "I'd like to use them up before the next round of gift-giving."

"Dark chocolate with nuts?" she queried.

"Plenty. Just don't mess with my caramel centers."

"I wouldn't dream of messing with your caramel centers." She gave her hair one last tweak. "I can't fix this myself, so you're on, Doc."

Taking this desirable woman home with him might not be the wisest move he'd ever made, Mark reflected as they set out again. But for some reason, he felt reckless enough to find out what might happen when he did.

Chapter Five

Samantha had no idea where this other woman had come from. Not the one Mark might be bringing to the Christmas party—she refused to yield to the jealousy-tinged curiosity nipping at her about *that* individual—but the one she herself had become. She'd walked into Mark's large cul-de-sac home, surveyed the spare, clean lines of his living room and immediately pictured it stuffed with her flowery sofa and chairs, along with her collection of colored glassware.

"That's the real problem," she said aloud.

Beside her, Mark pulled off his tie and tossed it over the back of a modern chair so low it nearly didn't *have* a back. He ignored the way the tie slipped onto the seat. "What, exactly?"

"I'm not sure who I am anymore." There, she'd put into words the issue that had been driving her crazy.

"Well, that's a relief." He tossed his jacket after the tie.

As it slid down, too, a trace of his ubermasculine pheromones wafted toward her. Sam could have sworn her brain was floating a few inches above its usual position. "Why?" she managed to ask.

He sent her a lazy grin. "I thought you were about to comment that I decorate like a guy who ran through Ikea throwing items into a shopping cart. Which is basically what happened."

"It's nothing a froufrou addict like me couldn't fix," she said, distracted by the possibility that he might actually enjoy having some of her stuff…no, wait. Back to reality.

"So what's this about not being sure who you are?" He swung a leg over the arm of the couch and sat there, invitingly rumpled.

"I felt impatient with Candy, who's just a kid, after all. I keep thinking about the children I *should* have had, instead of about the counseling clinic. It's like I've turned into a… what are these for?" She stopped pacing to study the sleek, ash-colored cabinets built against one wall. Why had Mark outfitted his living room as if it were a storage facility?

Unable to resist, she opened one. Empty.

Sam couldn't imagine owning cabinets like these and not filling them up. The world was full of so many pretty things.

"They came with the house," he told her. "I only bought it a couple of years ago. Haven't had a chance to put my stamp on the place yet."

"It has your stamp on it," she shot back. "A stamp that reads, Nobody's Home."

His expression turned mischievous. "Is that any way to talk to the man who's going to be holding a pair of scissors close to your hair?"

"I should call Kate."

"Tony's fiancée?"

"She's also my hairdresser, or used to be."

"You don't need a hairdresser—you need a shrink," he observed with a twinkle in his eye.

"Because I'm having a crisis?" She hated feeling disheveled and out of sorts while Mark remained maddeningly cool. "Which you helped cause."

He raised his hands in protest. "You're not the only

person with goals and dreams around here, Sam. Besides, you've always known that the fertility center was the hospital's priority. Your project was a mere afterthought."

He had a point, one she didn't feel up to debating, not in her light-headed condition. "You promised to feed me."

"Are you certain you want to risk eating here? Remember Greek mythology. If you eat or drink anything in Hades, you may be stuck there forever."

"You're crazy."

"But fun to be around."

Someone had to wipe the amusement off his face, so Sam did the only thing she could think of. She walked over and kissed him.

He caught her arms and anchored her there. What started as a gentle exploration deepened, his tongue catching the edge of her teeth, her hands sliding across his shirt and feeling the rise and fall of his chest.

He did some exploring of his own, thumbs tracing the edge of her breasts and smoothing across the swell to reach the hard nubs. When she arched instinctively, he tasted the pulse of her throat, and her blood turned to steaming lava.

Speaking of a hot Christmas, this was quite a preview... or was she having a hot flash? That unpleasant prospect thumped Sam out of her trance. Come to think of it, all of her symptoms might be due to menopause. Wooziness, loss of concentration, cravings...

She retreated beyond the reach of his arms. "Well, that cleared my head."

He studied her questioningly. "My head doesn't feel clear at all."

Her breasts ached for more of his touch, and her lips tingled. "I think we went way off track there."

"Maybe we should try it again and see if it helps us find the right path."

She closed her eyes and registered the sensations rampaging through her nervous system. "I'm tempted, yes," she decided. "Insane, no."

"Samantha, did you have anything to drink this morning?" His joking manner shaded into wariness.

"Nothing stronger than coffee," she said.

"Are you taking medication?"

"I'm not high." She bristled. "Why would you even think that?"

Mark uncoiled from the sofa. "I apologize. The person I mentioned who might accompany me to the Christmas party is my sister, who's a recovering alcoholic. And frankly, I don't trust her claim about being sober. Guess I was projecting."

In fairness, he'd had good reason to ask. "I *have* been acting ditzy," Sam admitted. "And I'm sorry to hear about your sister. I had no idea."

"Lots of people have skeletons in the closet." He led the way to the kitchen. "My closet happens to be a veritable boneyard."

"Your closets were empty."

"My metaphorical closets are stuffed to the gills."

He'd always struck her as the soul of stability. "I thought your father was a doctor, like my folks. I pictured you growing up normal."

"And you consider physicians' children normal?" Although he'd turned away to measure coffee, the tilt of his head indicated he awaited her return volley.

"We may be a bit high-handed." She took a seat at the table. "Also impatient when a man *reputed* to be an excellent surgeon can't manage to extract a simple rubber band that's eating my head."

That remark brought a deep, rich laugh. "One bandectomy coming up." After clicking the coffeemaker into action, Mark examined the contents of a drawer. He selected a small pair of sharp scissors and approached with caution. "I'm not used to doing this without a nurse. Perhaps a whole surgical team."

"I could give Lori a call."

"Too late." Setting the scissors on the table, he lifted the tangle of hair. With scarcely a tug on Sam's scalp, strong, deft fingers cleared away loose strands, freeing as much of the band as possible. The gentle strokes felt like caresses.

In the quiet room, she heard the rush of his breathing. Even facing away, she could detail the muscular length of Mark's body and picture the set of his jaw. She'd watched him perform surgery a few times on complicated cases, and she knew the intensity of his gaze and the way his lips pressed into a firm line.

Snip. One cut must not have been enough, because the scissors snicked again. Then, with the merest of pinches, he plucked out the remnants of the band, and thick waves brushed the nape of her neck.

"Good job," Samantha said.

"You haven't seen it yet."

"I can tell. You have talented hands."

"So I'm told." He came into view, discarding a pathetic clump of elastic and hair into a wastebasket. After washing up, he fetched a box of chocolates from the freezer. "These don't take long to defrost."

"Have you done this before?" she asked, bemused, as he took out mugs and plates. "Eaten junk for lunch?"

"I frequently eat junk for lunch."

"Just curious." Normally, she'd be on her feet, pouring coffee and helping set the table. But today, she felt an unusual lassitude, which translated into an inability to budge. "Just show me the contents, will you? Of your cabinets."

"My cabinets?"

"I'm curious. They aren't bare, are they?"

"Certainly not." Obligingly, he opened one. She cataloged a couple of china plates, neatly stacked, three cups bearing the logos of charitable organizations, four glasses and a lot of open shelving.

"That's disgusting," she said.

"What is?"

"Empty space. Don't you get a burning desire to swing by a yard sale and check out the goods?"

Coffee, chocolates and Mark joined her at the table. "I can safely say that urge hasn't seized me, not once."

"You're urge-free?"

"Of the desire to shop at yard sales? Yes." He studied her across the table. "Where do you find the time?"

"Mostly while I'm supposed to be exercising," she admitted. "Mark, do you want kids?"

His dark eyebrows met in the middle. "Are you offering to have my child?"

"As if I could." She shook her head ruefully. Why *had* she asked him that? Because, she supposed, she wanted to know more about him. Although they worked together and could probably finish many of each other's sentences, she hadn't been aware until today that he had a sister, let alone an alcoholic one.

"I'm doing the world a favor by not having kids."

What on earth motivated him to say such a thing? "You have to be joking."

He shook his head. "My genes are nothing to brag about. Neither is my schedule."

Sam thought this over. Not much to think about, really. "I vote for a world filled with miniature Mark Rayburns, as long as they don't kick poor patients out in the street."

"When have I ever done that?"

"Aside from the clinic?"

"Those aren't patients." He regarded her closely. "I know *you* wanted children, but have you truly considered what's involved? I'm not a hundred percent convinced you'd be willing to make the sacrifices."

She missed her mouth with the edge of her coffee cup, sending a shower of the brew onto her knit top. "Darn." She dabbed her chest with a paper napkin, keenly aware of Mark's interested expression.

"I'd be glad to help," he said with mock earnestness.

She wished her breasts didn't tighten beneath his gaze. "I'm sure you would."

"But that might be construed as harassment."

"I'm the one who kissed you," she reminded him. "Forget it. I'm working up some outrage and I'm not going to waste it by flirting." Deep breath. "How dare you imply I wouldn't be willing to sacrifice for motherhood?"

Whatever it took, she'd do it. When she was ready, Sam amended for the sake of honesty.

"I don't doubt that you'd sacrifice your comfort," Mark told her soberly. "And your finances, and possibly your health. What I meant was that I doubt you'd give up your volunteer work."

She'd never considered motherhood and volunteering incompatible. "Why should I?"

"Because children deserve more than spare minutes between working and saving the world, which is part of why I choose not to have any," he said. "And because *you* deserve the joy of being there for those unpredictable, precious moments when a child says or does or understands something in a unique way."

She didn't have to nurture her annoyance any longer; it sprang up forcefully. "There's no reason I can't manage all that."

"There are only twenty-four hours in a day," Mark cautioned. "And very few years before kids start sharing more with their friends and teachers than with their parents."

"A woman shouldn't have to choose between motherhood and other goals," Sam snapped.

"Everybody has to make choices. Men included."

This conversation wasn't going at all to her liking. Well, two could play at this game, especially since Mark seemed blissfully unaware of his own shortcomings.

"You make choices too easily," Sam countered. "You choose one course of action and push everything else aside without considering whether it's necessary or wise or *right* to compromise."

"That's rather a broad conclusion, don't you think?"

"But accurate." Sam believed in intuitive leaps. "You were quick to doubt your sister's sobriety."

If she'd expected an offended reaction, she'd have been disappointed. "I'd put the odds against her showing up for Christmas at eighty-twenty," Mark said levelly.

Samantha was rooting for his sister, and not only out of compassion. "I'll take those odds."

He tilted his head. "What's the bet?"

She hadn't considered this a real wager, but why not? As long as they kept things light. "A kiss under the mistletoe."

He gave her a heart-stopping smile. "Yes, but which of us gets the kiss?"

"You do, if you win." Sam would enjoy it, too, but she needn't mention that.

"What if *you* win?" he asked suspiciously.

She wanted to suggest he let the counseling clinic keep its quarters, but he'd never agree to that. "You buy me a piece of kitschy glassware at a yard sale." Not that she wanted any more clutter. Rather, Mark needed to loosen up. He might even decide to buy a few odds and ends for those nearly naked cupboards of his.

"It's a deal." He stood and reached across the table, and they shook. Big, warm hand with blunt fingertips, which struck Samantha as very masculine.

"Orange is a nice color, but I like blue, too," she advised him. "Multicolors have a kind of retro glamour."

"You're picky about your cheesy glassware?"

"Just the opposite," she said. "The bigger and more flamboyant, the better."

"You're pretty confident about winning."

"I have faith in your sister. I mean, she's related to you. Take it as a compliment."

"I'm trying," Mark said.

They sat contemplating their bet and stealing glances at each other. Sam couldn't recall the last time she'd relaxed like this with a guy. Male friends occasionally escorted her to charitable functions, and she'd had her share of lovers over the years, but they rarely seemed to find idle moments. Mark, she suspected, was not all that different. Yet here he was, and here she was.

"Why haven't you ever married?" she blurted. "Or did you, and I missed it?"

He pretended to wince. "Is this another of your stump-the-host questions, like whether I want children?"

"Is this another of your evasive answers?"

"I was engaged once," he said. "How's that for not being evasive?"

"You haven't filled in the details yet," Samantha pointed out. While she'd assumed he'd had serious girlfriends, the news of a broken engagement surprised her. Mark seemed like the kind of guy who'd choose with care, and then follow through. "When?"

"A few years ago, in Florida." His shoulders hunched into what she interpreted as a defensive posture.

"Was it that bad?"

"What do you mean?"

"You're bracing as if..." She searched for a football analogy. "As if you're about to be tackled."

He lowered his shoulders, regaining control. "My fiancée was a nurse. Smart and fun to be around. And worth spending my life with, or so I believed."

"What went wrong?"

"She got caught stealing drugs from the hospital. Turned out she'd been addicted to painkillers since a car accident the year before."

His jaw tightened. What an ugly situation. While Sam sympathized with anyone struggling to work through pain and addiction, stealing drugs from the hospital where you worked was a serious breach of trust, as well as a crime.

"How awful. I presume she hadn't confided in you."

He shook his head. "If I'd known anything about it, I could have lost my medical license. I cared about her, but I felt betrayed, too."

"What happened?"

"I helped Chelsea get into a rehab program, but while I understand about addiction, I couldn't forgive the violation of trust. That was the end of our plans together."

"Being addicted and violating trust go hand in hand," Samantha observed sympathetically.

"As I learned growing up."

Her heart went out to him. "Which one of your parents? Not both, surely."

"Dad didn't abuse substances, but he had affairs. That can be an addiction in its own way. My mother drank herself into liver failure." He spoke tightly but without hesitation.

He'd come to terms with his loss, at least at some level, Sam gathered. That didn't mean he'd released all the anger or the pain.

"Do you blame your dad?"

He shrugged. "Did he cheat because she drank, or did she drink because he cheated? Maybe both, or maybe they were drawn to each other's dysfunctions."

That brought them to the subject at hand. "What about your sister? When did she develop problems?"

"She started binge drinking as a teenager. For years, I kept trying to save her, and kept failing." Sorrow shadowed his eyes. "Finally I had to admit defeat and let her go. Now I'm reluctant to buy into the same cycle of hope and regret all over again."

The rough note in his voice touched Sam. "She left scars."

"She did."

"Scars can be stronger than the tissue they replace," she noted.

"Other times, you have to cut out the scar tissue or it limits your ability to function."

"Is that why you're prepared to think the worst of her?" Sam probed.

"We'll see come Christmas, won't we?"

They'd finished their coffee. And, apparently, their conversation.

"We should do this more often," Mark said.

"With healthier food."

"Agreed."

Sam cleared away the chocolate wrappers and washed her hands. It was hard to leave this place, warm despite its starkness, and this man who filled up a room with a subtle sense of power.

And yet, she reflected a few minutes later as she headed toward her house a block away, although Mark seemed contented, he didn't strike her as happy.

She had no idea what anyone could do about that. Oddly, though, she felt an urge to try.

Chapter Six

On Monday morning, between performing several C-sections Mark pondered Samantha's questions. *"Do you want children? Why haven't you ever married?"*

As a rule, he enjoyed his life. Got a jolt of adrenaline from planning the new fertility clinic. Relished bringing babies into the world and helping women lead healthier, fuller lives. And prized going home to a peaceful environment, without the drama, tears and temperaments he'd grown up with.

Today, though, he couldn't escape the image of all that empty space in his cupboards and cabinets. How did it feel to watch a woman arranging her colorful vases and bowls in there? To come home and cook dinner together, and talk over the events of the day? And, watching a new father's face light up as he held his son for the first time, Mark wondered what it was like not simply to appreciate the miracle of birth, but to know you were going to spend the rest of your life caring for that child.

Well, he planned to spend the rest of his life doing what he loved: using the talents and skills he'd been blessed with both as a doctor and as an administrator to make miracles happen.

When he reached his office, Mark listened to his voice

mail. One call had to be returned immediately. It was to
Candy Alarcon.

"I'm sorry to hear you had a rough weekend," he told
the young patient when he reached her. "If you felt it was
an emergency, you should have called my service. They
can reach me 24/7."

She heaved a long sigh. "Everything seems like an
emergency these days, Dr. Rayburn. All these babies. Even
with the volunteers, I feel overwhelmed, and now…" The
sigh gave way to a sob.

Her message had mentioned postpartum depression, a
matter that Mark took very seriously. While many young
moms experienced brief episodes of sadness as they adjusted to their new role, serious cases of depression could
interfere with the vital mother-child bond, or even stir
suicidal thoughts.

If necessary, he'd prescribe medication, therapy or a
combination of both. First, though, he needed to listen
carefully to the patient.

"Can you come to my office in the medical building
this afternoon?" Mark asked. "I'll clear time for you."

"How about right after lunch?"

He checked his schedule. "At one, Dr. Forrest and I
are holding a press conference. Will four o'clock work?"

"I'm not sure. If my boyfriend…" In the background,
a door slammed. "Jon just came home. I told him something I shouldn't have and now he's kind of upset. Can I
call you back?"

"Sure. If you can't reach me, Lori will make an appointment. I'll let her know the situation."

"Thanks, Doc." The phone clicked off.

After a quick call to his nurse, Mark plunged into reading reports, advisories and updates about hospital affairs.
He was immersed in the proposal for installing the basement lab when he got a call from Chandra in Louisville.

"What's this I hear about a press conference?" she demanded.

Mark gave a start. The vice president was nothing if not thorough. She must have scrutinized the hospital's schedule of events, posted on its website and updated daily.

"The counseling clinic is holding a Christmas fundraiser. That's all we're announcing," he assured her. "I have Dr. Forrest's word that she won't mention anything about the fertility center."

"Cancel it," she said.

"The press has already been notified."

"Then un-notify them. That woman can't be trusted not to shoot off her mouth."

Less than two hours remained until the event. While he understood Chandra's concern, Mark found it misplaced. "I doubt we'll be able to reach everyone in the media. In my opinion, it's better to go ahead rather than raise all sorts of questions about why we canceled. I promise I'll keep a lid on things."

"No offense, but you don't exactly have a shining track record for keeping a lid on Dr. Forrest," the veep replied. "I'm sorry I ever agreed to this counseling idea. I should have known it would be trouble."

"Trouble? I wouldn't say that."

Chandra cut him off. "I'm emailing you data about a major fertility conference scheduled for Los Angeles next fall. I want our new staff on board and presenting papers at that event. The prestige will be priceless."

"I agree. However, the organizers may already have scheduled the presenters," Mark warned.

"Then find out who they are and hire them," she snapped. "The fertility center is our number one priority."

"Of course."

"Don't waste your energy on distractions like Dr. Forrest's claptrap."

Samantha would hit the roof if she heard her pet project described as claptrap. But that wasn't the issue. "Even with a cancellation, we're going to have reporters show up. We'll have to tell them something."

"You should never have agreed to this," she said. "Make it go away."

No sense arguing further. "All right."

He put in a call to Jennifer in public relations. She told him what he already knew: it was too late.

"Do it anyway," he said resignedly.

"Okay. I hope you're wearing a hard hat and iron underwear, though. You know Samantha."

Oh, yes. Indeed he did.

It occurred to Mark that when he gave the go-ahead for the press conference, he and Sam had made a deal that effectively muzzled her. Now, thanks to Chandra, he was defaulting on his end of the bargain.

Maybe he'd better add a bulletproof vest to that list of protective gear.

WITH JENNIFER'S WORDS ECHOING in her ear, Samantha clicked off her cell phone. Her thoughts raced furiously. Apparently, she'd made a deal with the devil, and the devil had just reneged.

Sam refused to let her attraction to Mark interfere with her moral outrage. Nor would she yield to the fear of losing her job. Once she started censoring herself, she might as well give up.

This press conference was essential to notify the public about the fundraising event. Her center was losing its home, losing its cachet as part of the hospital and losing much of its momentum in the process. Without a boost at this critical point, it could easily crumble to nothing.

Dedicated as she was, Sam couldn't run a volunteer center on her own. She already counseled the group of teen mothers, and of course her medical practice took the bulk of her time and energy. She had to establish this center on firm financial footing. But how was she going to do that if she couldn't even reach out to the community?

Determination firing on all cylinders, she barreled into the nearest examining room, where two children stopped screaming at each other and stared at her wide-eyed. The little girl ducked behind her mother, who regarded Sam with relief.

"The sight of you puts the fear of divine retribution into them," the woman said admiringly.

"Now let's put the fear of divine retribution into that earache," Sam replied, and helped the boy onto the examining table.

By a little past noon, she'd prescribed antibiotics for earaches and ointments for rashes, completed well-baby exams, stitched a cut in a boy's forehead and persuaded a tearful mom to seek family counseling for her marital problems. Between patients, Samantha's outrage found its focus.

Despite Jennifer's attempts to call off the event, the press would be trickling in soon. The evil powers-that-be at Medical Center Management had seriously misjudged the situation, Sam mused with satisfaction as she took the stairs down. She'd corral the press in the parking lot and fire away.

The center had aroused widespread support in blogs and tweets and social media. While most of the donations that trickled in were modest, sometimes just a few dollars, they came from a significant number of individuals. The public appreciated this nonbureaucratic, caring attempt to reach out. Once reporters learned the whole story of the center's ousting, there'd be a firestorm.

Just what MCM deserved. As for Mark, he'd chosen his

alliances. Despite a pang of concern, Sam refused to back down simply to spare him the embarrassment.

On the ground floor, she met up with Nora Kendall. The gynecologist pinned her with a glance. "How are you doing? I've been worried about you."

"The counseling center..."

"I'm talking about your health."

"Oh, that." Sam glanced around to make sure no patients were nearby. She preferred to keep her medical issues private. "Not sleeping terribly well," she admitted. "I've had a lot on my mind. I'm sure you've heard."

The other woman nodded sympathetically. "The hospital grapevine has been working overtime. I hope you locate new offices quickly."

"I suspect we're about to get a lot of support." Sam explained about the canceled press conference and the opportunity to make a public appeal, free of the restraint she'd promised Mark.

Alarm flashed in Nora's green eyes. "Hold on, Sam."

"Don't you start into me, too!"

"Just listen," the other woman said.

Sam planted hands on hips. "I'm listening. Talk fast."

"I realize that this feels like big business pushing around poor helpless women and kids," Nora began.

"That pretty much sums it up."

"You of all people should understand how it feels to have your chance at motherhood yanked away." She paused as a couple of pregnant women walked past, before continuing in a low voice, "The new fertility center will help people from all over the world."

Because many countries restricted treatments such as in vitro and banned others, including the use of surrogate mothers, couples flocked to California with its open policies. "I sympathize," Samantha said. "But when it comes to these high-tech procedures, we're talking about the wealthy."

Nora shook her head. "Not necessarily. I have patients of very modest means who're willing to spend every penny they can scrape together in order to have a family. And we'll be accepting a percentage of charity patients. Even the wealthy have hearts. Don't declare war on us."

Her use of the pronoun "us" brought Sam up short. She had been associating the fertility project so strongly with the corporate owner that she'd failed to consider the other stakeholders. Her fellow physicians. The patients. The babies that would come into the world loved and wanted.

"I can't just abandon…"

"No one expects you to," Nora said. "But don't take us down as collateral damage. You have a lot of power. The press loves you. You're famous."

"I am not!" Besides, what mattered was her cause, not her personality.

"The media makes instant celebrities, and you fit the bill," Nora countered. "Use your power wisely."

Things no longer seemed as blazingly clear as they had moments ago. While Sam hated shades of gray, the last thing she'd ever do was abuse power. "I'll try to temper my remarks."

"Try hard," Nora said.

A moment later, Sam emerged on the walkway. To her right, in front of the hospital, she spotted a TV van. She should be able to catch the camera crew before Jennifer sent them away. But what was she going to tell them?

THROUGH THE HOSPITAL'S front doors, Mark watched Samantha approaching. "Tell me this isn't going to be the shoot-out at the OK Corral," he muttered to Jennifer. Even though she'd done her best to call off the media, she hadn't—as predicted—been able to reach everyone.

The PR director's only response was an absent nod as she raced to wave down a camera crew. She also rounded up Tom LaGrange, a reporter for a local Orange County newspaper.

"I'm afraid we've had to call off the press conference," she was informing them as Mark came abreast. "The hospital *will* have a major announcement, hopefully in a few weeks, but there've been delays. I'm sorry I didn't get hold of you in time to save you a trip."

Hayden O'Donnell, an on-air television reporter, regarded her and Mark skeptically. "We understood the announcement involved Dr. Forrest."

"And here she is now," added LaGrange. He and the TV crew swung toward the pediatrician.

Mark had to concede that Sam cut a striking figure, her hair just wild enough to give her character, and her face alive with purpose. But apprehension took the edge off his instinctive pleasure at seeing her.

They were in for it now.

"Dr. Forrest." A microphone was thrust toward her. "What's going on? Is someone trying to muzzle you?"

Her gaze met Mark's. Despite everything that separated them, he felt a jolt of connection. And, amazingly, hope.

"I'm not sure what our PR director has told you so far," she began.

Jennifer seized her chance. "That the hospital isn't ready to make any announcement yet."

"That's right, although I would like to tell the public about our upcoming fundraiser." To Mark's amazement, Sam spoke calmly, without a hint of defiance. "There'll be an open house from 2:00 to 4:00 p.m. on Christmas Day at the Edward Serra Memorial Clinic, on the fifth floor of the Safe Harbor Medical Center. Food, piñatas and entertainment. Our theme is 'A Hot and Happy Christmas.' Admission is free, but donations will be appreciated."

He began to relax. Was she really finished?

"And we'll be needing them now more than ever."

Oh, damn. To explain that ominous statement, Mark jumped in to run damage control. "People's generosity always gets stretched thin during the holidays, with so many appeals. Yet during the same period, stresses on families increase. The counseling clinic becomes more important than ever."

"Plus the fact that we have to move," Sam added.

Mark held his breath. If only they were in the auditorium, as planned, he could seize the podium and freeze her out, awkward as that might be. But here on the sidewalk, the reporters were free to ignore him.

Which they did.

"What do you mean?" O'Donnell demanded.

"Is the hospital kicking you out?" That was LaGrange.

"For the past few months, the medical center has generously allowed us to use an office suite free of charge," Sam continued into the microphone. "However, we've always known that was a temporary situation."

She hadn't grabbed the opportunity to bludgeon the hospital's reputation. Or was she building to an attack?

"After the first of the year, the Serra Clinic will need a new home. I appeal to corporations and other generous sponsors in the Safe Harbor area to contact me about any space you may have available free or at low cost."

Unbelievable. The outspoken Samantha Forrest had not only tempered her words, she'd cast the hospital in a somewhat favorable light. And refrained from putting the blame on the planned fertility center.

Jennifer blew out an audible breath of relief. Fortunately, the members of the press didn't appear to pick up on her reaction.

All the same, there was no mistaking the skepticism in the questions that flew at Sam. Both reporters demanded to know if she'd been pressured into downplaying the need to move.

She held fast. "We have the best interests of women and families in mind. No one's forcing us to do anything."

Crisis averted, for now. Mark could have hugged the woman. In fact, he hoped he'd get the chance. Soon.

"Looks like we're in the clear," he observed quietly.

"Uh." Jennifer's voice seemed to stick in her throat. "Sorry?"

Wordlessly, she nodded toward the parking lot, where a van had pulled into the nearest handicapped space. A pudgy young woman with frizzy hair was unloading strollers with the help of a pregnant girl, probably a friend from the teen group.

Candy. He'd specifically requested that she come later, around four.

And, in the process, he'd told her about the press conference. Mark swallowed hard. How could he have forgotten that she was an even bigger drama queen than Sam?

Still, her motives might be innocent. "I'll handle this," he said, and set off to talk to his patient.

"Hey! Over here!" She waved at the press.

"Excuse me." Mark walked in front of her, trying to block their view. "I thought we were going to meet at my office," he said to Candy as quietly as he could.

"My boyfriend dumped me." Her lower lip trembling, the girl stepped around him. Raising her voice again, she declared, "This counseling stuff isn't all it's cracked up to be. Look at these triplets! I should have put them up for adoption, but Dr. Forrest talked me into keeping them. Now I'm stuck with three kids and no future."

"Of course you have a future," he told her, averting his face from the rapidly approaching reporters.

"Not since Jon left! You can't expect me to earn a living and raise three infants."

Sam had gone pale with shock. This had to hurt. Mark knew she'd been trying to meet Candy's needs, not browbeat the girl.

It was also ironic that just when Sam had moderated her pronouncements in the media, her old tactics were being used against her. Even worse, from the hospital's perspective, her attempt to paint Safe Harbor Medical Center as a sympathetic supporter of her project had just backfired.

Because if Candy succeeded in making the clinic look bad, so would everyone connected with it. Including the hospital.

And, Mark reflected ruefully, he'd be top of the list.

Chapter Seven

Had she really talked Candy into making a colossal mistake? Samantha wondered as the young woman and her friend lowered the triplets into strollers. She'd intended to help, not harm.

As she walked toward the new mom, she sorted rapidly through her concerns. For one thing, these newborns shouldn't be out in public, exposed to the gathering crowd of press and passersby. For another, what on earth did Candy hope to accomplish by attacking Sam and the counseling center?

Still, this was hardly the moment for reproaches. Clearly, Candy had suffered a blow.

Sam tried to ignore the riveted members of the press. "Why did Jon leave?" she asked. If this was simply a clash of temperaments, it might blow over.

Candy stuck her chin out. "What do you think? He's, like, twenty-one. You can't expect him to take on this much responsibility."

"Why don't we take this inside where we can talk privately?" Mark said. Sam could have hugged him.

"Why should I?" Candy replied. "I have nothing to hide." She turned one of the strollers to give a photographer a clearer shot of the baby. It was Courtney, her little face scrunched in the sunlight.

"That's too bright. It's hurting her eyes." Sam shifted the stroller. "Please, everyone, stand back. You don't want them to catch an infection, do you?"

The reporters shuffled slightly. Giving a few inches, at most.

"You said you'd told him something that upset him." Mark spoke in a level tone, his gaze fixed on Candy.

"I told him the truth."

"About what?" Sam hadn't suspected there was any hidden truth to reveal. The reporters leaned forward, trying to catch every word.

"That I got pregnant on purpose. I figured he'd marry me." The girl shrugged. "I wasn't counting on triplets."

O'Donnell broke in. "Did you have fertility treatments, Miss, uh—could you tell us your name, please?" He gestured for a crew member to hand the mic to Candy, which was, in Sam's opinion, akin to giving a hand grenade to a three-year-old.

Or to me. For the first time, she understood how Mark must have felt all those times when she had seized the floor.

"Candy Alarcon," the girl said. "No, I didn't need treatments. Twins run in my family. I just got one extra."

More people were gathering, attracted by the TV lights. "Everyone step back," Mark ordered. "As Dr. Forrest pointed out, these newborns are susceptible to airborne illnesses."

At his commanding tone, the onlookers scattered. Even O'Donnell retreated before Mark's stare.

"Let's go inside," Sam murmured.

Candy folded her arms. "No way. Look at that ugly Mark on Connie's face! It's still there."

The TV reporter perked up. "One of them has a birth defect?"

Sam was losing patience. "It's called a port-wine stain

and we're planning to treat it. Connie is a wonderful child with a minor problem. Candy has no idea how lucky she is. Giving birth to three healthy triplets is a blessing."

"Lucky? I'm the victim here." Candy made sure the camera was trained on her before she added, "If people want to help, they can send donations to me. Candy Alarcon. I've set up an account at…"

"Shame on you!" To Sam's amazement, the words burst out of usually low-key Jennifer, who'd been doing her best to shoo away newcomers. "Exploiting these poor little babies when Dr. Forrest arranged for donations of supplies and services! What kind of mother are you?"

For a tense moment, Sam feared Candy would retaliate. The press would love an open battle. Judging by Mark's tense expression, she could tell he was thinking the same thing.

He'd been right, Sam realized. She should have stayed away once he called off the press conference. Matters always seemed to get too volatile around her.

"What are you going to do?" Tom LaGrange asked Candy.

"Are you filing a lawsuit?" added the TV reporter.

Did he have to bring that up?

While the young mother weighed her reply, Sam moved to check on the babies. Courtney was grumbling so low she could barely be heard above the ambient noise. Colin's mouth pursed, likely in search of a nipple. They needed to be fed. Connie waved an arm as if reaching for comfort. For her mom.

Never mind the hullabaloo. Sam yearned to gather them all close. They deserved responsible, caring parents. Why had she foolishly imagined that someone as immature as Candy would rise to the occasion?

Perhaps she'd projected her own feelings onto the young woman, imagining an inner strength that didn't exist. With the best motives in the world, Sam had done these infants a terrible disservice. How was she going to fix that?

The young woman's words broke into her reflections. "I'm going to give them up under the safe harbor law."

"Safe Haven," Jennifer corrected automatically.

"Are you sure?" Mark asked. "Candy, these aren't the best circumstances for making such a decision."

The girl stared at her infants. Courtney let out a cry, and Colin had started fussing. "I feel like I ought to love them, but I don't. Not like a real mom. I thought maybe if I had enough money or something… I was just mad at Jon. I'm sorry, Dr. Forrest. I know you were trying to help."

"But aren't you past the seventy-two-hour limit?" queried O'Donnell, his voice resonating as if he were revealing something of earthshaking importance.

"The what?"

"Under the Safe Haven law, babies can be surrendered with no questions asked if it's within seventy-two hours of birth," Jennifer explained.

Candy frowned. "How many days is that?"

"Three."

She stared at them in dismay. "You mean I'm stuck?"

Colin chose that moment to let out a piercing screech. His mother glared at him.

"Absolutely not." Sam didn't give a rat's tail about the camera swinging toward her or the fascinated observers still lingering around them. "You want to relinquish your babies for adoption? I'll be more than happy to take them. All of them."

"Even her?" Dubiously, Candy indicated Connie.

"Especially her."

"Can she just do that—give them to you?" LaGrange asked.

"It's called a private adoption," Sam told him. "It's more complicated than a Safe Haven relinquishment, but we can take care of all the legal requirements in due time. Right now, she's free to yield physical custody of the babies if she chooses to. What do you say, Candy?"

As she registered the girl's uncertainty and Mark's raised eyebrows, it occurred to Samantha that she might have spoken hastily. Three babies with her full schedule? Cribs and a changing table and all that other stuff wedged into her two-bedroom house with zero preparation?

None of it mattered. She loved these little ones. And she felt suddenly as if the events of the past week, from learning about her early menopause to her sadness at saying farewell to the triplets, had been preparing her for this moment.

If Candy agreed, Sam was about to become a mother. In triplicate.

CRAZY AS THIS WHOLE IDEA might be, Mark stood there silently rooting for Sam. If Candy had any sense, she'd accept the offer.

And if Sam had any sense? Well, that wasn't up to him.

"Okay," the girl said.

The press appeared at a loss for words. That didn't last long. "Tell me, Dr. Forrest," intoned O'Donnell, "exactly what are the differences between surrendering a baby under the Safe Haven law, and signing one over for adoption?"

She glanced past him. "I'll let our staff attorney handle that. Here he comes now."

Mark spotted Tony striding toward them. "That's good timing," he murmured.

Jennifer tapped her cell phone. "I called him."

"Thanks." He appreciated her efficiency.

As the press focused on Tony, Mark felt his concerns ease. He couldn't blame Sam for a colorful tendency to shoot from the hip. In fact, her knack for publicity would no doubt boost the fundraiser, and she'd handily deflected any negative impact on the hospital or the counseling center.

On the other hand, under the glare of the cameras, she'd just made a lifetime commitment with scarcely a moment's thought. Did she understand what she was getting into? While Mark had every respect for Samantha's pediatric knowledge, that didn't necessarily translate to a realistic understanding of parenthood. He might not be experienced in that regard, either, but he at least had the sense to recognize how much he *didn't* know.

Despite his impatience to talk to her, he paused to listen as Tony explained that before the Safe Haven law, a parent who dropped off a baby—even at a safe facility—and fled could have been charged with the crime of abandonment. The tragic result had been that women in desperate circumstances used to dump newborns in trash cans or other unsafe places. Now that they could leave them at a designated hospital or fire station without the risk of charges, far more babies were being saved.

Still, it was better if the mother stayed long enough to provide a medical history and sign legal papers, Tony told them. That way, the infant could be placed for adoption without an investigation to ensure the child hadn't been brought to the drop-off location by an unauthorized person such as a babysitter.

"What about the triplets?" the TV reporter asked. "They're over the time limit."

"Their mother isn't abandoning them, so she hasn't violated any laws," Tony continued. "She's free to relinquish them for adoption by signing the appropriate documents. The adoptive parent or parents must file a legal petition with the court and undergo a home study to make sure they can provide a suitable environment for the child or children. I'll assist Dr. Forrest in making those arrangements."

"Doesn't the father have any rights?" LaGrange queried.

"That depends on the circumstances. We'll try to get his signature, but if he refuses to take responsibility for the children, that may not be necessary."

Reassured that Tony could manage the press under Jennifer's watchful eye, Mark slipped away to join Sam, who was shepherding Candy and the babies into the hospital.

He took her aside. "Everything under control?"

She pushed back a flyaway twist of blond hair. "I checked, and the center's day care has space for them. They'll stay in the isolation room today while I'm at work." That was where employees' children were housed when ill. "In a few days, they should be fine in the regular infant section."

"What about after hours?" Mark asked. "They'll need attention at night, and you have to sleep."

Her gaze bored into his. "Are you lecturing me about my health, Doctor?"

"I'm lecturing you about your common sense, Doctor," he answered in the same half-joking tone.

Wrong tactic, he realized as she drew herself up. "My common sense is fine, Mark. It's my nerve you're doubting, isn't it?"

"Your nerve is the one thing I've never doubted."

She chuckled. "I'll choose a better word. My *resolve*."

"I've never doubted that, either."

"Good." She flashed him a grin that was too contagious for his own good. "Connie, Courtney and Colin were meant to be my children. Don't you see how everything's come together?"

Her early menopause, the delivery of the babies and Candy's very public decision to relinquish them... "What I see is a series of coincidences," he warned.

"One man's coincidence is another man's destiny," she

returned. "Or woman's, in this case. By the way, you've heard of night nurses, right?"

"Yes, but I've also heard that they expect to be paid." While she earned a respectable salary, Mark knew she was far from wealthy.

"My grandparents left me an emergency fund. I've always felt it was there for a reason, and this is it."

That took care of one obstacle, but despite her take-no-prisoners attitude, Sam didn't possess superpowers. "You're well organized, I grant you. But raising three infants can be overwhelming. For anyone."

"Yeah." Without his noticing, Candy had joined them. "I think it's great that Dr. Forrest's going to find out exactly what she wished on me."

"Whoa." Sam regarded the young woman in mock dismay. Or perhaps it was real dismay. "Is this your notion of revenge?"

"You have no idea what my last two nights have been like." Candy held up one hand. "Okay, that's not fair. I *did* think it would be cool to keep the babies, back when they were inside me. My friends encouraged me, too. Plus I had this dumb idea Jon would act like a real father."

Sympathy softened Sam's features. "I'm sorry I didn't prepare you better for the reality. I got carried away with my own fantasies, I'm afraid. But what about your mom?"

"She was helping me last night and all of a sudden she burst into tears. She said she likes the idea of grandchildren, but she's only forty. She wants to have free time with Jerry, not spend every spare minute changing diapers." The girl swept a rueful gaze toward the strollers being piloted toward the day care center by hospital volunteers. "If you'd told me it was a bad idea, I wouldn't have believed you."

Sam gathered her into a hug. "You still have to get back on your feet. You'll come in for counseling, won't you?"

"Oh, yeah. And my friends in the teen group are sticking by me. I kind of wish I could keep one baby, but that wouldn't be fair. They belong together." Candy ducked her head. "Besides, those cribs and stuff are taking up all the room in our place."

"If it's okay, I'll borrow them temporarily," Sam said. "Then I'll pass them on to the other teen moms."

"Cool."

Tony came indoors, moving with an easy stride. Newly engaged to Kate and the happy father of a baby girl, he'd shed his former air of tight control. "Jennifer's finishing up with the reporters. Would you two ladies care to step into my office?"

"You and Candy get started with the paperwork," Sam said. "I'll be right up after I check on the babies." And off she went.

"She's a...what's the word?" Candy asked.

"Force of nature?" the attorney supplied.

Mark had nearly said "maniac." He was glad he'd thought better of it.

Sam had an iron will and an office lined with documents attesting to her pediatric expertise. But three babies at once? Whatever happened next was sure to be interesting, Mark mused.

He'd better go put in a call to let Chandra know that the press conference cancellation hadn't come off as planned.

By a rather wide margin.

Chapter Eight

"Forgive me for being an interfering mom, which I swore I'd never do, but are you certain this is a good idea?" The image of Dr. Lanie Forrest on the computer screen might lag a bit, and her voice sounded fuzzy over the internet connection, but her folded arms and creased forehead spoke volumes to her daughter.

"I never thought I'd hear negativity from you of all people!" Sam fought down the impulse to cross her own arms.

"Just because you agreed to take them, that doesn't make the decision irrevocable on your part," added her father, Dr. David Forrest. His thin face was filled out by a salt-and-pepper beard. "Not that I'm suggesting you renege on your decision, honey. But this is only the first step in a long journey."

"You mean life?"

"I mean the legal system."

That was true. According to Tony, Sam had to wait a month and undergo a home study, then appear in court for a judge's final approval. None of that mattered. From the moment she'd promised to care for the babies, they'd become hers.

Sam didn't kid herself that, even with her emergency fund and her determination, she'd have easy sailing. Raising a baby, let alone three, would be a challenge for any single parent. Oh, heck, she had yet to come to terms with what was involved.

But she'd given her heart. That counted even more than giving a promise.

Determined to dispose of unnecessary tasks, she had thrown her stack of unread holiday cards into a box and instructed Devina to add any other personal notes to the heap. Usually she relished reading messages from former patients and coworkers, but they'd have to wait until she had spare time. Even if that took eighteen years.

She'd checked on the babies several times during the afternoon, and picked them up by 5:00 p.m. Lori had helped her install car seats in the van Sam had hurriedly leased with help from Jennifer, who'd also arranged to have Candy's cribs and other equipment delivered.

Where would a woman be without her friends? Nevertheless, Sam didn't like to depend on them any more than necessary.

Lori had stayed to help feed the infants, leaving a few minutes ago, shortly before 7:00 p.m. Regrettably, they had to rely on formula, but then, Candy had mentioned that she already used it as a supplement. While it was possible for a mother to nurse triplets, it took time and practice.

Breast milk offered many advantages, including the mother's immunities and nature's intended balance of nutrients. But adopted infants generally thrived on formula, and Sam planned to keep a close watch on the babies' development.

The night nurse she'd hired would arrive about ten. So here she sat in front of her computer, cradling a baby as she related the day's events to her parents several hundred miles south in Mexico.

"How are you feeling?" Lanie put in. Her graying hair, once blond like Sam's, had taken on a wiry quality.

"A little tired," Sam admitted. "That's to be expected until we settle into a routine. I'll try to have a nurse on hand until they can sleep through the night."

"That may take longer than with singletons," her mother warned. "They'll tend to wake each other up."

"If that becomes a problem, I'll keep a crib in my room." For now, Sam had turned her home office into the triplets' bedroom, and the furniture crowded around her with narrow passageways in between. Good thing she didn't mind clutter. "I could move another one into the living room at night."

"Great! Then you can run an obstacle course from room to room to room," Lanie grumbled.

"Mom!"

"You're such an overachiever. I hope you won't feel like you have to stick with this if it wears you out."

"Lanie," Sam's dad said in a warning tone.

Time to change the subject. "How're things at the clinic?" she asked.

"We finally got enough flu vaccine for everyone in the area." As hoped, the question distracted her mother, and the rest of the conversation centered on the couple's efforts to improve the health of local residents.

Their village sounded like a warm, caring place. If Sam ever did decide to join them, she'd bet her kids would love it there.

Her kids. What a beautiful term.

Afterward, Sam remained in her desk chair with Courtney dozing against her chest. The little girl smelled sweet and fresh, and from this angle it was amazing how long her lashes looked against her rounded cheeks.

She put Courtney to bed, then studied each of the infants in turn. How precious they were in their footed sleepers, tiny fingers flexing, little bow mouths pursing as they dreamed their baby dreams. In the stillness, she listened to the murmur of their breathing.

For the first time since the press conference, Sam had a moment of actual peace and quiet. It felt like an unbelievable luxury.

The doorbell rang.

She jumped. The babies barely stirred, but she hurried to answer before it rang again.

Not the press, she hoped. O'Donnell had reported the story on the six o'clock news. With the TV playing in the background while she and Lori fed the triplets, Sam had caught glimpses of herself, Candy and the infants. The report had mentioned the fundraiser so briefly that most viewers probably missed it. Thank goodness the newspaper's website, which Jennifer had checked, cited the event prominently.

Reporters who'd missed the impromptu presentation would be trying to make up for lost time. Sam sure hoped some overeager newshound hadn't dredged up her home address.

She supposed she ought to drag a brush through her hair and put on lipstick. But if she stopped to do that, the fool might punch the bell again.

On the doorstep, she found a welcome surprise. Sam's frazzled nerves hummed harmoniously as she took in Mark Rayburn, tie askew and his jaw covered in five o'clock shadow, carrying a sack that smelled like heaven. Garlic, tomato sauce—Italian food. The scent reminded her that she'd missed dinner.

Sam didn't care what a mess she must look. "You were sent by the angels," she said as she ushered him inside.

"That's what I keep telling the corporate honchos. I don't know why they ever doubt it."

At the moment, Sam didn't know, either.

MARK FELT AS IF HE'D STEPPED inside a rainbow. Colored glass vases, candleholders and bowls filled china cabinets and spilled onto the coffee table and end tables. The shimmering effect reminded him of a cut-glass crystal vase his mother used to treasure—until she smashed it against the fireplace one night in an alcohol-fueled rage over one of his father's affairs.

"So this is what's meant by decorating," he said.

"You don't have to tell me it's overkill," Sam replied. "I'll pack the loose pieces away before the babies start crawling."

He hadn't meant to criticize. Best to let it pass. "I hope you're hungry. Papa Giovanni's makes the best ravioli this side of Italy."

"Starved. Right this way." Navigating between pieces of newly arrived baby equipment, she led him into the dining room, where she removed a stack of medical reports from the antique-style table. "I'll grab plates."

While she went into the kitchen, Mark lifted take-out containers from the sack. "I take it the babies are sleeping," he said when she returned.

"Dozing." She set out the plates and glasses of water she'd carried on a tray. "Don't try to be polite. Go ahead and tell me I'm a nutcase. I won't be offended. Much."

He helped place the silverware. "You aren't crazy. I love kids, too. In small doses."

She filled her plate from the containers. "Pardon me for being rude, but I'm starving. Aren't you?"

"The restaurant plied me with breadsticks while I was waiting for my order."

"Lucky you," she mumbled, and dived into her food.

During the meal, Mark took an appreciative look at the watercolor paintings splashed across the walls. A jacaranda tree abloom in lavender blossoms. A seascape carved by a bougainvillea-draped bluff. A waterfall creating its own rainbow. The profusion of colors soothed him.

"These are beautiful," he observed. "It's not what I expected to find in your house. Your offices are so Spartan." The one assigned to her in the hospital as head of pediatrics was practically bare. Her office in the medical building had a corkboard displaying photos sent in by happy patients, plus the expected medical certificates and professional awards. But nothing like this.

She gazed around. "This is my nest. When I was growing up, we lived like we were in the military. Nothing but essentials ready to pack at a moment's notice, although we stayed in the same house practically forever. My parents met in the Peace Corps in South America and they swore they'd be heading south of the border again soon. Twenty-odd years later, they went."

"You're making up for those bare surfaces," he concluded.

"It's more than that," Sam told him. "I guess I've been cramming as much as possible into every day and every inch of space. This past week, it hit me that I've been living as if the cancer might return any day."

"And you finally accept that it won't?" He hoped that was the case.

"I'm trying to accept that I have to live one day at a time like everybody else." She polished off a last bite of garlic bread.

"Let me know if you figure out how to do that," Mark said, "because I haven't a clue. I'm generally thinking at least half a step ahead."

"You never seem rushed."

"I put a lot of pressure on myself." As he spoke, he consciously relaxed his muscles. He'd been tense all day.

First there'd been the press conference business, followed by his strained late-afternoon discussion with Chandra.

Her staccato voice still rang in his ears. She'd been upset that Samantha had spoken to reporters and displeased that the hospital was once again featured on the evening news for a reason other than its medical excellence. Mark had barely hung on to his patience with the woman.

She ought to trust his judgment. He'd made his share of mistakes, but so, he suspected, had Ms. Chandra Yashimoto. Besides, today's situation had turned out well, even if it hadn't been strictly on message.

"Rough day for you, too?" Sam asked.

Rather than dwell on his running skirmishes with the executive, Mark deflected the question. "Occasionally I fantasize about practicing medicine full-time. But then I'd have to work under some idiot administrator who forgets to put patient care first. Instead, I get to *be* the idiot administrator."

"You're not an idiot. Very often."

"Such high praise."

Sam gave him a wry smile through her water glass. "You were pretty darn cool out there in the parking lot."

"I admired the way you handled the press," he admitted. "You were doing great until Candy showed up. When you decided to take the babies, well, that was unexpected."

"To me, too." Her plate empty, she leaned back.

"Were you even considering adoption?"

"Yes, in the theoretical sense." Even after a full meal and a long day, her sharp features exuded restless intelligence. "I didn't imagine it could happen this quickly, with these children, but it seems almost destined."

"And now you're a mommy." Mark found the term endearing when applied to Sam.

Emotions flickered across her face. "Oh, wow, I *am*, aren't I?"

"This comes as a surprise?"

"I mean, of course I know I'm a mother. But I've been so busy putting out fires, I haven't had time to consider the big picture."

He'd suspected as much. "Which part hit you the hardest?"

"That the kids are going to be counting on me to be there for everything." She rested her chin on her palm. "For help with homework and heartaches, for Halloween costumes and Christmas dinners, for proms and college prep. What if I let them down?"

The responsibility *was* a lot to take in. "You don't think you're up to it?"

"I'm embarrassed that I encouraged Candy to take this on, for one thing," Sam answered thoughtfully. "Today it was all I could do to get them fed and diapered, and that was *with* Lori helping. On Saturday, you told me a child deserves attention for those special moments. What if they all fly by and I'm too busy dealing with daily battles to meet the kids' emotional needs?"

He'd harbored those same doubts when she took the triplets. Yet Sam wasn't giving herself enough credit. "There's a bond between you and them. I saw it at the hospital."

Tears glimmered in her eyes. "I love them. When they cry, I feel how much they hurt. When I was working today, there was always a tug, always an awareness, like wishing I could be two places at once."

"I see my patients juggling and balancing the same way," he told her. "It's stressful, but they pull it off."

"But they have husbands. Sometimes grandparents living close by. A support system." Weariness frayed her voice. "I'm out here on the high wire alone."

Her unexpected vulnerability aroused Mark's protective instincts. "I can help. I'll be your backup."

She regarded him skeptically. "What do you mean by that?"

What *did* he mean, anyway? At a whimper from the bedroom, Mark paused, bracing for a cry while he collected his thoughts. The cry never came—the baby must have been fussing in its sleep—but a disturbing thought did.

He felt a powerful urge to cuddle and watch over those little guys. He'd followed their growth from early pregnancy until he'd lifted them from their mother's womb. They almost felt as if they belonged to him, too. But they didn't.

Raising these children was Sam's commitment, not his. He'd come dangerously close to promising more than he should.

Chapter Nine

"You're going to be my backup?" Sam prompted, the corner of her mouth twitching. "This I'd like to see."

Mark chose his words carefully. "I'll pitch in during this neonatal period, until they get stronger. You could obviously use the help." That seemed a reasonable way to see her through this crunch without glossing over the serious issues involved in raising triplets. Sooner or later, she was going to have to make hard choices about her priorities.

"Pitch in how?" Sam pressed. "Details, details."

"Since I live so close, why don't I stop by before work to help in the mornings?" *And play with the babies.* Impulsively, he added, "We could walk them to the hospital together when the weather's nice."

"That would be wonderful. You're great with kids, even if you have sworn off fatherhood." Her brilliant smile made him glad he'd volunteered.

"Before I forget, there's one more important matter to deal with."

Her smile frayed around the edges. "You're not kicking the clinic out before Christmas, are you?"

"Nope." From the Papa Giovanni's sack, Mark retrieved another white container. He flipped the lid to reveal two slices of Italian cake dipped in espresso, layered with a

sweet creamy mixture and topped with cocoa. "I was referring to dessert."

"Tiramisu!"

"My way of leaving a sweet taste in your mouth." His
gaze flew to her lips. Mmm. He'd definitely like to leave
a different kind of sweet taste in her mouth.

"That's fantastic. Thank you."

Better to make an escape while he still had his wits
about him. Mark pushed back his chair. "The cake's for
you, so enjoy it whenever you like. It's been a long day,
and all good things must come to an end."

"Must they?" she broke in teasingly. "You could rub my
shoulders. You did offer to be supportive, right?"

He ought to beg off. Common sense, good judgment...
oh, the hell with them.

"So I did." Without giving himself any more time to reflect, Mark moved to stand behind her and ran his thumbs
across the ridge of her shoulders. "You're knotted up."
Sam was as tense as if she'd been carrying the weight of
the world.

Her hair drifted across his hands. "Hauling babies and
gear does that to you."

He kneaded the lines of tension, probing between her
shoulder blades, exploring her spine. A sigh fluttered from
Sam. Her scent drifted upward, the sharp tang of anti-
septic softened by baby powder and herbal shampoo and
a whisper of femininity. She held so much in check, but
now, in this moment, Mark felt her relax against his hands,
against him. Satisfaction pulsed through him that he could
ease her tension and cares. A healing power flowed from
him into her.

Glancing down, he saw her eyes drift shut. "You going
to sleep?" he teased huskily.

"Dreaming. Fantasizing. Don't stop."

His mind kept veering toward some fantasizing of its

own. Firmly, Mark focused on working out the nubs and knots in Sam's shoulders. The two of them shared a great deal, but he didn't kid himself about their fundamental differences. There was a line he refused to cross, no matter how much he might be tempted.

Yet when she tilted her head back, lifting up her sleepy face, he bent and traced a kiss across her temple. "You *are* going to sleep."

"Think how much easier it would be to help in the morning if you stayed here all night," she murmured.

Mark's body hardened at the suggestion. *And I wouldn't sleep on the couch, either.* With an effort, he dragged himself back to reality. Or, at least, to pragmatism. "Me and that army of nurses you hired?"

"Only one. Did you have to remind me?"

He chuckled and couldn't resist adding, "Besides, you'd regret that offer."

"What offer?"

"The one you just made."

She twisted to look up at him. "What did I say? I was half-asleep."

"You propositioned me."

Her mouth dropped open, but she rallied. "Well, good for me."

"Because sex would relax you?" He quirked an eyebrow.

She brushed her palm across his scratchy cheek. "I give you more credit than that, Doc."

At the inviting touch, he instinctively pressed a kiss into her hand. As if he didn't know better. As if the two of them weren't like gasoline and a lighted match.

With a wrench, Mark pulled away. "Give me credit for leaving while I'm ahead. I'll drop by in the morning around, say, six?"

"Perfect." Sam shifted as if to rise but couldn't seem to muster the energy. "Did you say *all* this tiramisu is for me?"

"Every last bite."

"You're a generous man."

"I'll remind you of that next time we cross swords," he said.

"I'll pretend I don't hear you."

She remained at the table while he wended his bemused way through a living room still reflecting prismatic rainbows from the glassware. He was closing the door behind him when he heard a wail from deep within the house and the instant response as Sam leaped from her chair.

A mother's instincts trumped exhaustion. Whatever he might think of her impulsive decision to adopt, Sam had obviously given her heart to those babies.

ON TUESDAY MORNING, MARK arose half an hour earlier than usual. After a shower and breakfast, he scanned his personal email, as was his custom. A sale at the golf pro shop...updates from former coworkers at his Florida office...and a funny photo from Bryn of a startled-looking puppy and kitten, curled in each other's paws and staring at the camera as if they'd been caught in an indiscretion.

Hope your day is full of unexpected moments read her message.

Failing to think of a clever response, he typed, "Can't wait to see you. I miss your sense of humor. Love, your bro."

Maybe Sam was right and he should have more faith in his sister. People did overcome substance abuse. Due to the drug thefts, his former fiancée had been unable to find another job as a nurse, so she now worked as a receptionist and volunteered at a homeless shelter. Recently, she'd messaged that she and her new husband were planning to start a family.

If Chelsea had shaken off the demon of addiction, Bryn could, too.

Showered, shaved and ready for the day, Mark tossed an old work shirt over his clothes as protection and headed toward Sam's house. He arrived at the bungalow to see the night nurse, a middle-aged woman in a pink uniform, heading for her car. "How'd it go?" Mark asked.

She peered at him dubiously. "Excuse me?"

He hadn't considered the disreputable effect of the torn shirt lumpily covering his suit. "Dr. Mark Rayburn. I promised Sam I'd stop by. How's everyone doing?"

"The triplets are fine, and Dr. Forrest got a few hours' sleep," the nurse summarized. "I tried to let her rest, but someone forgot to tell the babies to take turns getting hungry."

"Thanks for the report." He categorized Sam's first night with the babies as provisionally positive, since no one had fallen ill, but the situation sounded far from ideal. Concerned about the effect of inadequate sleep on Sam's volatile temper, he tapped cautiously at the door.

To a greeting of, "It's open!" he turned the knob.

From a blanket spread on the floor, the baby girl with the port-wine stain—Connie—blinked up at him. Beside her, a red-faced little boy was grunting mightily. The smell confirmed Mark's suspicions.

"Hi." Sam appeared from the hallway with a welcoming grin, Courtney at her shoulder. "I'm nearly done feeding her and then I have to dress." A shower-damp spiral of hair hung over one ear, and without makeup her eyebrows disappeared at the edges. Yet, to Mark, she seemed radiant. And, amazingly, not at all crabby. The woman seemed to thrive on motherhood.

"Where's the diaper changing station?" He indicated Colin on the floor.

"No room for a changing table," she responded. "I use the dryer."

"Seriously?"

"It's in a nook off the kitchen. There's a pad on top and diaper supplies above on the shelf. Hey, that's one of the practical tips I give the teen moms. It really works."

Mark collected the little boy and carried him to the dryer. As he bent to his task, the little one's alert gaze followed him. "Remember me?" he asked Colin. "I'm Dr. Rayburn, but you can call me Mark."

A burbling noise might have been an attempt at communication, although it was too early for the kid to start babbling. The tiny mouth formed an *O*. Or, perhaps, a *D*.

"Daddy? Sorry, no." He felt as if he was letting the baby down. "I'm sort of a father substitute."

Blink. Stare. Yawn.

"Am I boring you?"

Colin studied him as if trying to puzzle out his meaning. Or perhaps marveling at how swiftly and efficiently the doctor changed his diaper, Mark mused.

The job finished, he lifted the clean baby. One wriggle, and the diaper slid down to half-mast.

So much for efficiency.

No wonder Lori always tightened the tabs after he examined a baby, Mark thought with a touch of embarrassment as he pulled the diaper more firmly into place. Thank goodness no one had observed his mishap.

Good thing babies didn't swap stories about their caretakers' dumb mistakes.

After returning the little boy to the living room, he washed his hands. He hadn't paid much attention to the strollers the other day, but a quick glance revealed a double and a single. Mark opened them and was positioning the second baby into place when Sam breezed out, smartly clad in a pantsuit with a receiving blanket safety-pinned to one shoulder.

"Thanks for helping with the strollers," she told Mark, and laid Courtney in the single pram. "Ready?"

"You don't waste time." He'd expected her to take another ten minutes at least.

"The only way I'm going to survive is to put myself on a supertight schedule," she informed him as they maneuvered the strollers outside, with Mark handling the double.

"I thought you were already on one."

"I play hooky once in a while, but I won't be able to do that anymore," she told him. "You were right—I'll have to give up a few things. Hanging with my friends, unless I can bring the kids. Browsing yard sales. Unnecessary stuff like that."

"That's how you recharge. You need to do those things." He paused to tuck in Connie's quilt. The temperature was in the fifties, crisp but not uncomfortably cold.

"I'll recharge by enjoying special moments with my children," she replied.

"Are those on your schedule, too?" He let her move ahead, since the sidewalk wasn't wide enough for both strollers side by side.

"Sure. I'll see them before work, pop in during lunch, and of course there'll be evenings and weekends." Her voice drifted back. "Except when I'm tied up with the counseling clinic."

"You can't do everything."

"Why not? I considered giving up advising the girls at the teen center, but they'll love the triplets. Besides, that's how I met Candy in the first place."

"Sam," he began through gritted teeth.

"You think I'm overcommitted, don't you?"

Since she'd brought it up, he saw no reason to soft-pedal. "You're going to crash and burn. Dial it back for a while."

"Like you?" she challenged. "Dr. Workaholic? You even delivered Tony and Kate's baby on Thanksgiving."

"That's different."

"How?"

"My family doesn't need me, because I don't have a family." The statement gave him an uncomfortable twinge. The words seemed to echo down a long corridor into the future. "Besides, I do relax. I play golf."

"You call that relaxing?" Sam asked as a woman jogger veered around them and continued on her way. "That's exercise, not fun."

"I get fresh air and stay healthy," Mark argued. "Whereas you're sacrificing your sleep and your leisure. You should identify other activities to drop."

Sam swung around so fast he nearly ran the double stroller onto her heels. "Quit harping on how overworked I am."

He *had* sunk to nagging. "Not another word," Mark promised.

She resumed course. Two minutes later, she halted to confront him again. "Quit thinking about my schedule."

"Excuse me?"

"I can feel your criticisms smacking me in the back like BB pellets."

"I was thinking about *my* schedule," he countered.

"No, you weren't," she blazed.

"You can't read my thoughts."

"They're written all over your face."

"You can't see my face—I'm behind you," he pointed out, and then wondered how he'd become entangled in such an absurd argument.

Sunshine highlighted the freckles sprinkled across Sam's nose. "I can read your thoughts from two floors away. Or even in another time zone, and you can do the same with me. You knew precisely how I'd react when you canceled the press conference, didn't you?"

If they kept arguing, they'd never get to work. "Maybe, but I gave you the benefit of the doubt."

"You did?"

"I might have upped my life insurance, but I trusted you to handle the press wisely. And did my best to stay out of it, honestly."

The crease eased from her forehead. "Thanks. Sorry for being so pugnacious."

"No problem." If he mentioned her lack of sleep, it would only make her temper flare again, so he kept silent.

Courtney let out a high, thin cry. Sam hurried to adjust her blanket, and then set out at a faster clip.

When they reached the medical complex, Mark realized how much he'd enjoyed the walk. He'd never known that a squabble could clear the air and bring people closer, yet in a funny way, that's what had happened. In fact, the experience had put him in an upbeat mood for whatever the day might bring.

Then he spotted two news vans parked in front of the hospital and a knot of reporters gathered on the walkway. What on earth was this about? "Any idea why they're here?"

"I guess I should have returned my phone messages last night," Sam said wryly. "Apparently the triplets and I make a great human interest story."

Annoying as he found the press's intrusion, Mark didn't blame her. "I doubt a few phone interviews would have stopped them from showing up."

She adjusted her suit jacket. "Well, brace yourself."

He did his best.

Chapter Ten

As she endured a photo op on the hospital's front steps and answered questions about how the triplets had spent the night, Sam reminded herself that the news coverage was sure to boost support for the Christmas fundraiser. Honestly, though, did the woman from an L.A. paper have to keep asking her to turn Connie to make the birthmark more prominent? And if that radio reporter kept implying that Sam was only taking the triplets as a publicity stunt, she might deck him.

"That's enough," she was relieved to hear Jennifer announce. "Dr. Forrest needs to get the babies settled and she has patients to see."

"They aren't going to keep showing up, are they?" Sam grumbled as Jennifer and Mark provided a protective escort into the lobby.

"Depends on whether it's a slow news day. Pray for a Hollywood scandal." Her friend took over the double stroller from Mark, who departed with a wave.

Watching his jaunty stride as he crossed the lobby, Sam wished she could time travel back to last night's dinner. Having Mark in her house had made everything feel more grounded, more secure. Then this morning a zip of appreciation had run through her when she saw him with Colin. He handled the baby differently than she did, yet with great tenderness. Was it possible babies craved that fatherly touch?

Or that *she* did? When she awoke this morning, her bed had felt wide and lonely. Crazy. She liked having all that room to herself.

Busy wheeling a carriage down the corridor, Jennifer didn't appear to notice Sam was lost in thought. Thank goodness.

At the day care center, Jen planted a kiss on the baby girl she'd recently adopted. Rosalie's birth mother, anguished because she couldn't keep her baby, had seen the public relations director interviewed on the internet and chosen her to be the new mom. Then Jennifer had fallen in love with Ian Martin, the pain-in-the-neck reporter who kept splashing her and Rosalie all over the web, and—not being entirely an idiot—he'd fallen in love with Jennifer, too. Married a little over a month, she and Ian doted on each other and on their new daughter.

A day care worker hurried over to take charge of the triplets. Sam surveyed her to rule out any sign of illness, then yielded the little ones with a tug of mixed emotions.

Colin had already gained two ounces, she'd noticed, when she weighed him this morning. What if being left with a stranger put him off his bottle? As for Courtney, she was peering about with the usual worried furrow between her tiny eyebrows. And Connie seemed so vulnerable.

"Call me if they feel hot," she warned.

The worker fixed her with a knowing smile. "Thank you, Mom. Now it's time to leave."

"That's Dr. Mom. And I'll go in a minute. I'm not sure they're ready."

The woman planted her hands on her hips. "Don't you mean when you're ready? Dr. Forrest, I've been doing this type of work a long time. I know separation anxiety when I see it."

"Me?" Sam asked in astonishment.

The woman gave a knowing nod.

"Right," Samantha said, and tore herself away.

Was that a heartbroken cry from Colin? she wondered as she marched away. No, that screech came from a toddler whose toy had just been snatched by a preschooler.

And I thought my pediatric training gave me an edge on this mom business.

Sam found Jennifer waiting by the door. "Listen, I have an idea about the press," her friend said as they exited.

"Good. I've got more than enough to handle without them." How ironic that in the past, Sam had rather enjoyed talking to the media. Now she disliked having them dog her footsteps, or stroller tracks.

"Once the public's curiosity is satisfied, they'll turn to other things." Jennifer kept pace along the corridor. "Ian still does the occasional interview for Flash News/Global."

He'd covered an international beat for the syndicate until signing a book contract to write about medical advances affecting women. "So?"

"Ian mentioned he'd like to discuss the counseling clinic with you, so why not let him write about the babies, as well? Video, still photos, the whole shebang. His stories go all over the world. That ought to slake people's thirst for triplet news."

Sam paused in a corner to let an employee in a wheelchair scoot past. "What did you inhale for breakfast?"

"Excuse me?" Her friend regarded her in surprise.

"You're usually such an expert, Jen, but *more* publicity? Next you'll be proposing I star in a reality show."

Jennifer tapped her foot angrily. "That's insulting, Sam."

Perhaps she *had* gone too far. "I'm sorry. But I'm also right. Think about it."

"It was a spur-of-the-moment idea. Forget I mentioned

it." Her friend took a deep breath. "Changing subjects here, I have some good news about the clinic. Ian may have found a sponsor. She's dynamic and well connected, and she's looking for a project to pour her energies into."

"To raise funds for—that kind of thing, right?" Not a do-gooder socialite who wanted to play at actually running the place, Sam hoped.

"I'm sure she'd be more involved than that." Jennifer didn't seem to pick up the warning note.

"An amateur who jumps on every health care trend that comes along? Or a control freak who never met a piece of paperwork she didn't love? Email me with the details and I'll check her out."

Jennifer bristled. "Sam, the clinic doesn't belong to you. It's named after *my* son. You decided to take on three babies, which I applaud you for, but you can't keep the clinic under your thumb forever."

"I don't plan to. Once we've found new quarters and a professional director, I'll be happy to let go." Overjoyed, in fact.

"Without help, you may never be able to afford a director," Jennifer answered tightly. "This clinic means as much to me as it does to you. I was thrilled when Ian said he had a patron in mind."

Sam had already done more than enough arguing for one morning. Besides, she valued Jen's friendship. "Let's table this discussion, all right?"

"Fine. But not for too long."

"I'll get back to you. I promise. And I do appreciate how much you and Ian care about the clinic."

All the same, uneasiness dogged Sam as she made her way to the medical building next door. She wasn't trying to hang on to the clinic. She simply refused to see it follow the same misguided path as the medical center itself.

Once a full-service community hospital, Safe Harbor had been converted into a facility primarily serving women and their babies. While that wasn't necessarily a bad thing, it meant taking in fewer charity cases and reaping larger profits. She understood the financial realities involved. For heaven's sake, she'd remained here in part because of her own financial realities—paying off medical school debts.

As for the counseling clinic, she'd established it as a place where women and families could drop in without worrying about who qualified for what or whether they played nice with an intake counselor. What about the cranky, the messy, the offbeat clients who didn't "show" well in front of bureaucrats?

Sam had worked too hard to get this place off the ground. She wasn't about to let it become a plaything for rich dilettantes who acted noble while serving only the right kind of clients, the ones who looked good on posters and appeared suitably grateful.

True, she couldn't hold on to the reins forever. But she didn't intend to let her new status as a mother stampede her into abandoning her vision.

OVER THE COURSE OF THE WEEK, to Mark's relief, press interest was deflected by the birth of twins in Los Angeles to a 60-year-old mother who'd been an Olympic gold medalist. Controversy swirled over the mom's age, but her unusually strong physical condition and determination to have children qualified her for special consideration, according to the world-renowned fertility expert who'd helped her conceive.

The expert, Dr. Owen Tartikoff, flew from his home base in Boston to congratulate his patient and appear on several newscasts. A man of strong opinions—some called him abrasive—he was scheduled as the keynote speaker next fall at the fertility conference that had drawn Chandra's interest.

To his gratification, Mark managed to arrange a private meeting, at which he described the plans for the new fertility center and attempted to recruit Dr. Tartikoff as its director. Intrigued by the idea of building his own program from scratch, the man agreed to further discussions.

That would be an incredible coup. Yet, for now, Mark had to sit on the possibility. Aside from informing Chandra and Tony, he couldn't mention the matter to anyone. If word leaked out prematurely, it would be awkward for Dr. Tartikoff's current employers and might even kill the deal.

As for Sam, she continued her jam-packed schedule, putting in extra hours the following weekend to make sure she had the fundraiser well in hand. In the mornings, when Mark walked to work with her and the babies, she seemed as alert as ever, and insisted she'd slept plenty even though the night nurse advised him privately that Sam caught at most five hours.

He could see for himself that she was pushing too hard. The next time he brought food, Sam thanked him and spent the rest of dinner poring over reports on her laptop, keeping up with her position as head of pediatrics. When he asked why she was so determined not to let up in any area, she brushed aside his concerns.

"That's just who I am," she insisted. "If I'd wanted an easy life, I wouldn't have gone into medicine."

That attitude wasn't unusual among doctors, Mark had to admit. He'd observed surgeons ignoring their bodies' demands while performing complicated operations that lasted more than a dozen hours.

We expect too much of ourselves. Wasn't he almost as bad, seeing patients, performing surgery, running a hospital and getting up early to help Sam bring the babies to work? The busy schedule energized rather than drained him, but then, he was getting sufficient rest.

The next Friday morning, eight days before Christmas, Sam snapped at him for bumping the stroller too hard on their walk. "I hope you're planning to take it easy this weekend," Mark responded. "You're worn out."

From the fiery look she shot him, he expected an argument, but she apparently reconsidered. "I *am* kind of tired. I've arranged for a sitter to come in tomorrow afternoon so I can sleep and catch up on my bills."

"Put the emphasis on the sleep," Mark warned. "I don't want to pull rank, but if you're worn to a frazzle, I'll have to insist you take leave from your hospital duties." Her work with private patients lay beyond his control, however.

"You wouldn't!" She swung around on the sidewalk.

"Your behavior is becoming obsessive." Until he spoke the words, he hadn't fully realized that was the case. "It's almost as if you're addicted to adrenaline."

"I've always been addicted to adrenaline." Her voice had a ragged edge. "So are you."

"You rest tomorrow and Sunday, too. If the sitter lets you down, call me."

"What? No golf?" It was the closest she'd come to teasing him in days.

"Tony, Ian and I are playing tomorrow," Mark conceded as they resumed their pace, Sam leading the way. "But I'll have my cell with me."

She shook back her hair. "Lori's swinging by in the morning. We'll be taking the kids on a stroll and to our coffee klatch. But after the sitter arrives, I promise to hit the hay."

"Glad to hear it."

He didn't remind her that the clinic was running out of time to find new quarters, because the last thing Sam needed was more pressure. Jennifer had mentioned a potential sponsor, which sounded terrific, except that so far Sam hadn't pursued the matter. Mark supposed he could stall the corporation until the end of January. But no longer.

He'd really like to offer more help. When it came to obsessive behavior, though, hadn't his experiences with his sister taught him that more was never enough?

Sooner or later, Sam had to face reality. *That* would be the time to step in and help sort things out.

PLAYING GOLF SLUICED AWAY the pressures and concerns of the week. Although Mark wished Samantha had agreed to let him teach her how to play, he enjoyed being out here with his friends, too.

He loved the pine-scented air of the golf course, the steady, unhurried pace, and the excitement of each hole when the possibility of a perfect shot—a rare hole in one— loomed as a distant but achievable moment of glory. He'd scored a couple of them over the years, mostly through luck, but the joy remained brighter than any trophy.

As Tony collected his ball at the last hole, Mark didn't mind that his score, while respectable, left him behind his two companions. He'd fallen in love with the sport as a teenager, when it was the only thing he and his father shared. If not for golf, he'd have grown up scarcely knowing Dr. Robert Rayburn. And although Mark always played with a competitive spirit, he'd been glad that he occasionally lost to his dad, because the man seemed mellower when he won.

After moving to southern California, Mark had tried skiing. For a while, he'd driven to the nearby mountains at least once a month during the winter and occasionally in summer for a change of pace. He'd even bought a cabin there as an investment. Now he mostly kept it rented out by the week, because after the initial challenge, he'd returned to his first love.

Golf.

At the nineteenth hole, as the on-site restaurant was termed, the men discussed the latest football results over buffalo wings and beer. "I'm hoping to score some press tickets to the Rose Bowl," Ian said. "As a special treat for Jennifer." The game was played on New Year's Day in Pasadena, about an hour's drive from Safe Harbor.

"You're sure you won't be wasting them?" Tony asked. "Most women aren't that crazy about football."

"My sister's a big soccer fan." Ian's twin sister lived in Belgium with her husband and kids. His family had moved all over the world as they were growing up, Mark recalled.

"Well, Jennifer isn't your sister," Tony pointed out. "Did you ask her?"

"If she turns you down, I'll go," Mark volunteered.

"Lucky man. You don't have to check with anyone," Ian said. "Not that I envy you being single."

"Wouldn't have it any other way." And yet, oddly, Mark felt a hollow twinge as he said that. New Year's Day…he *had* no plans. What would Sam and the kids be doing?

Sleeping, he hoped.

"Take Jennifer to the Tournament of Roses Parade instead," advised Tony, the only one of the men who'd grown up in southern California. "You have to practically spend New Year's Eve waiting on the sidewalk to land a good position, but those floats are fantastic up close. And you can attend the game later, if you do manage to get tickets."

"I'll look into it," Ian promised.

"Oh, wait," Tony said. "Forget the sidewalk. There's VIP seating. If you have enough pull to get tickets to the game, I'll bet you could get some to the parade, as well."

"I'll *definitely* look into it." Ian turned to Mark. "By the way, did Jennifer talk to you about Eleanor Wycliff?"

The name rang a bell. "Isn't she the widow of that federal judge who died while under indictment for bribery?"

"Technically, she isn't his widow—they were divorced," Ian said. "But that's right. I interviewed her about the case a few months ago, just before he died."

The man had succumbed to a heart attack, Mark recalled. "What about her?"

"Their seventeen-year-old daughter, Libby, took her father's death hard, as you can imagine," Ian explained. "Eleanor's wealthy, and she's been looking for a project that she and Libby could work on together, not just a charity to throw money at, or a place to serve hot soup on holidays."

"How'd she get interested in the clinic?"

"She heard on the news about it having to move and remembered that it was named after my wife's son," Ian replied. "She's eager to serve on the board, except that we don't have a board yet."

"Sounds promising."

"It would be, except that Sam practically bit Jen's head off when she mentioned I was talking to a sponsor." Ian shrugged. "Jennifer thinks she can't bear to lose control."

"Especially not to some amateur. Isn't that how she put it?" Tony must have discussed this with Jennifer, too.

"How did I miss all this?" Mark wished he'd paid more attention to the PR director's comments.

"You've been busy," said his sympathetic staff attorney.

Mark shook his head. "Not that busy." How frustrating for Ian to find a backer, only to run into Fortress Samantha. In her physical and emotional state, she might be turning down the clinic's salvation. Did she have the right to do that? "I'm not even sure who the clinic belongs to."

"It's not incorporated," Tony said. "It belongs to whoever funds and operates it."

"Up to this point, that's been the hospital," Ian put in.

"Sam would disagree," Mark said. "She believes it's

hers. Besides, the hospital has no interest in holding on to the clinic."

"Well, my wife has strong feelings on the subject," Ian returned tightly.

Squabbling between Jennifer and Sam could only hurt both women as well as the clinic. Besides, once Sam caught up with her sleep, put Christmas behind her and had to stare eviction in the face, surely she'd be more amenable to the offer. Especially if they paved the way diplomatically.

"Here's an idea," Mark told the other men. "Ian, why don't you invite Mrs. Wycliff and her daughter to the fundraiser? Perhaps they could take an hour or so out of their Christmas plans to stop by and meet Sam."

"To discuss the clinic?" the writer asked.

"She might mention her interest, but ask her not to make any specific proposals yet. This is just to break the ice. I have a feeling that seventeen-year-old girl will melt Sam's heart." Mark hoped so. "I'd like this to feel like a partnership rather than a coup."

"Sensible," Tony agreed.

"Mrs. Wycliff is a bit of a powerhouse," Ian warned. "She's used to having her own way. But she's done a lot of organizational work with charities before. I'm sure she knows how to smooth things over."

"Excellent." Mark's cell rang. Not surprising, given the unpredictable nature of childbirth. In fact, he'd enjoyed more uninterrupted time this afternoon than usual. He answered, "Dr. Rayburn," and hoped this wouldn't be an emergency.

Turned out that it was. But not the medical kind.

Chapter Eleven

"She's having a meltdown," Lori gasped into Mark's ear. "I've never seen Sam carry on like this."

"She's supposed to be resting." Surely the sitter should have arrived by now.

"Resting?" his nurse went on. "She didn't even get to finish her coffee this morning. There was supposed to be a Christmas party for those teen girls she counsels, and it got screwed up, so somebody begged her to rescue them."

"She isn't a party planner," he growled. Sam should have better judgment than to take on such an unnecessary task.

"I think it was Candy who called," Lori admitted.

Sam obviously felt an obligation to the triplets' mother. "What happened?"

"Sam insisted on picking up party platters and decorations. She had the triplets with her, so of course I helped."

"Thank you." He hoped Sam appreciated her friend's dedication.

"During the party, Candy started acting possessive about the babies, and she and Sam had some kind of blowup. Candy stomped out, complaining that they were her kids—it was scary. Then we got home late and the sitter had given up waiting and left. Sam's in a foul temper, the babies are crying, and frankly, I'm fed up." Lori's voice broke. "She accused me of being bossy and interfering. *Me!* I'd walk out, but I hate to leave the kids. I'm not sure Sam's up to coping with them right now."

Nearly two weeks of sleeplessness and too much work had finally pushed her over the edge. Somebody had to call a halt to this downward spiral, and like it or not, Mark was elected, both as hospital administrator and as Sam's friend.

Suddenly, he got an idea. Not merely an idea—a potentially dangerous but irresistible plan.

He was going to stage an intervention.

SAM COULDN'T STOP PICTURING the horrible moment at the party when she'd realized Colin was missing. Earlier, she'd seen Candy playing with him, so, trying not to panic, she'd gone in search of the young mother.

After another girl reported seeing Candy take the baby out of the community center, Sam had hurried to the parking lot. There, she'd spotted Candy preening in front of a tattooed, long-haired man astride a motorcycle. Cradling Colin in the crook of his arm, the man stood there revving his bike as if about to shoot into gear.

Sam didn't remember exactly what she'd said, but she'd grabbed the baby away and given both the man and Candy a piece of her mind. Unbelievable, to expose a fragile infant to exhaust fumes, germs and the possibility of being driven unsecured on a Harley.

Candy had pouted and declared that the babies belonged to her. As if they were possessions. As if she hadn't signed them over to Sam.

But she could still take them back. And now, she might, although for today she'd backed off.

Since their argument, Sam's emotions had been roaring around like a lion in search of prey, ready to pounce on anything that moved. She regretted venting at Lori.

Her friend hadn't spoken to her in more than half an hour since then, and who could blame her?

If only Sam didn't feel strung as tight as a wire, she might be able to focus her thoughts.

Pacing through her house, holding Courtney and a bottle that the agitated baby refused to suck, Sam seemed unable to calm down. From a bassinet, Colin's hungry cries scraped on her nerves. At least Connie, settled on Lori's lap, appeared to be taking her formula.

Lori. Today, her friend had done far more than Sam had a right to expect. "I'm sorry I overreacted."

"You freaked out." Lori's hazel eyes regarded her accusingly.

"I apologize. For everything. My rotten mood. My ingratitude." She hoped that wasn't too little, too late. "By the way, who did you call earlier?" She'd heard Lori talking on the phone, but hadn't caught the gist of the conversation.

"Jared. And…" The nurse bit back whatever she'd started to reveal.

"And who?"

"I called my ex-fiancé to come over and help with the babies. Isn't that enough?"

"And who else?" Suspicion threatened to overbalance Sam's delicate restraint. "Lori, you have no business going behind my back."

"You aren't rational today."

"I'm rational at an elevated hormonal level, that's all. Early menopause combined with unplanned motherhood."

"Is this a new medical condition?" her friend grumbled. "It sounds more like an excuse."

"And a pretty poor one, at that." Although Samantha intended the remark to be humorous, it failed to draw a smile. Mercifully, though, Courtney began sucking at the bottle, and Colin's cries had subsided. Perhaps he'd fallen asleep.

At a knock on the door, Lori half jumped from her seat. "I'll get it." She took Connie with her.

Sam drew in a deep breath. If her friends could watch the babies for a while, she might be able to sleep. Or, more important, call Tony for advice about heading off any attempt by Candy to assert her rights. The worst part was the acknowledgment that girl was so irresponsible, she shouldn't be allowed *near* the triplets, let alone have a chance at reclaiming them. If Sam hadn't been so blindly optimistic, she'd have faced that fact months ago and helped Candy arrange...

What? A home for the triplets with a two-parent family? But then Sam would have lost her chance to love and cherish them.

For once in her life, she wasn't sure what the right course would or should have been.

From the front doorway, she detected two male voices: Jared's light tenor, and a deeper tone that had an amazingly soothing effect on her. Rounding a corner, she got a clear view of the entryway. There stood Mark in slacks and a knit golf pullover, his powerful frame overshadowing Jared's slender build.

She could have sworn Jared and Lori wore guilty expressions. Mark looked determined.

She must be a mess, Sam reflected. But she was too tired to care. And glad as she felt to see him...everyone... she couldn't muster the energy to conduct a polite conversation.

"I already hosted one party today, so forgive me if I'm not in the mood to entertain," she said wearily. "Thanks for dropping by, guys. Are you here to babysit?"

"Not exactly." Mark studied her with resolve. Why did

she get the sense that he'd come here for a purpose? "Please hand Courtney to Jared."

His tone struck Sam as odd. Instinctively, she resisted. "She's doing fine. Colin's the one who needs to be fed."

"Let me see her, okay?" With a shy smile that made his mustache twitch, the neonatologist held out his arms. Puzzled, Sam yielded her little charge.

Mark kept his gaze fixed on Sam. "You know how much we care about you, right?"

"What?" Dazedly, she wondered if everyone was behaving strangely or if she was simply imagining it.

"You're one of the toughest, most accomplished people I know," Mark went on. "We're lucky to have you in our lives."

"Wait a minute." His words rang a bell. "This almost sounds like an—"

"But lately, you've driven yourself to exhaustion," he continued.

If she agreed with him, maybe he'd stop talking like a shrink. "I admit, I could use a few hours of sleep. Things went haywire today."

"*You* went haywire today," Lori put in.

"I need a nap," Sam conceded, again.

"You need a break," Mark said levelly. "A nice long one."

"In an institution with padded walls and locks on the doors?" she returned irritably.

"Do you honestly believe you're in any shape right now to be responsible for three infants?" Mark persisted.

"The night nurse will be here in…" How many hours? Seven? Eight? "Well, whenever."

"I'll arrange for her to come to my house," said Jared, who had tipped Courtney's bottle at a jaunty angle that the baby seemed to like.

"Your house?" Sam repeated dully.

"We'll set up a temporary nursery," Lori told her. "That way, you can get some uninterrupted rest."

And Candy wouldn't be able to find them, so there'd be no immediate confrontation. "Not a bad idea," Sam agreed. "I'll bring my sleeping bag."

Mark took her arm and steered her toward the bedroom. What was he doing? she wondered, feeling that she ought to shake him off but too grateful for his strength to react. "You're going to pack an overnight case. You won't need a sleeping bag but be sure to bring warm clothing."

"What's wrong with this?" Sam indicated the clothes she had on. "Okay, I may have spilled some formula on the sweater, but…"

"You aren't going to Jared's house," Mark told her as Lori retrieved Sam's keys from a hook. "They'll transfer the car seats, pack up the babies and drive them to Jared's. You're coming with me."

She blinked. "Mark, there's no reason for me to sleep at your house."

"We aren't going to my house." Holding her elbow, he spoke so close that his voice vibrated through her. "Sam, I don't want you driving and I don't want you staying alone. Accept my help, for once."

"But where—?"

"You'll find out when we get there."

They were running an intervention. Saving Samantha from herself. Any idiot—well, any idiot in the medical profession—could see that.

She didn't need saving. For crying out loud, *she* was the person who saved others. Like Candy, except that today Candy had accused her of being selfish and manipulative. Like the counseling clinic, except that Sam still had no idea how to assure its future. Like the teen moms, except that all they'd done at the party was whine because she hadn't provided a live band.

How had things become so messed up?

Somehow, while these thoughts were rattling around her brain, Sam managed to stagger into the bedroom and stuff fresh clothing into a small suitcase, along with a few reports she'd been meaning to read. Ducking into the bathroom to grab her toiletries, she got a shock when a witch loomed in the mirror. Could this Medusa-like creature really be her?

She burst into tears.

The worst of it was that she had to sob without making any noise. Because if Mark heard her, he might storm in here, grab her pathetically wrecked self and haul her off to…where?

She couldn't bear it if he turned her over to a crew of rehab specialists who talked in the first person plural, as in, "Now, Samantha, *we* shouldn't take responsibility for the entire world on our shoulders, should we?"

Sam felt certain she would commit vicious and unlawful acts if anyone spoke to her like that.

Taking a deep breath, she recalled her mother's advice that when chaos threatened, she should start with the things she *could* control. So she returned to the bedroom, grabbed clean jeans and a clingy pink sweater, and went to take a shower.

While blow-drying her hair, she noted with approval that the sweater did wonders to emphasize her breasts. If she had to spend the weekend feeling like a failure, at least she could make Mark uncomfortable in the process.

In the living room, she found him sitting on the sofa, feeding Colin. Significant amounts of baby gear had vanished, presumably into Lori's and Jared's cars. Outside, she heard them discussing the correct method of installing an infant seat in Lori's subcompact.

Startling, the things a neonatologist and a nurse didn't know, when they'd never actually had children.

"This is an intervention for *them*, right?" Sam joked. "To get them together?"

Mark didn't miss a beat. "You bet. It's like a soap opera in the delivery room these days, with his longing gazes and her red-rimmed eyes. This has to stop."

She set her suitcase on the floor and tossed a windbreaker over it. "Are we going somewhere on a boat? I should warn you, I get seasick."

"No clues." At a coo from Colin, Mark bathed the infant in a warm smile. "Are we done, little man? Ready for Doc Rayburn to burp us?"

Sam grimaced. "Do me a favor. No 'we' and 'us,' okay?"

"Why not?"

"Reminds me of the wrong kind of men in white coats."

Lori banged in through the door. "Jared's heading off with the girls. Is Colin ready for his close-up?"

"You really think this will work?" Sam asked.

Her friend regarded her with uncertainty.

"Exposing Jared to all these babies to turn him off having children," Sam clarified. "You should cancel the special nurse so he has to get up and down with them."

"I already did that while you were in the shower. Although not for nefarious reasons. I just didn't think we needed her." Cautiously, Lori asked, "You're not mad at me for calling in reinforcements?"

"I plan to make Mark suffer appropriately," Sam assured her. "And I forgive you if you'll forgive me for calling you bossy. You never did accept my apology."

"I forgive you—even if you are overbearing and irrational," Lori said cheerfully, and scooped up Colin.

Mark collected Sam's luggage. She locked the house, Mark tucked her into his passenger seat, and off they went into the unknown.

The only explanation for her meekness, Sam decided,

was that she truly had reached the end of her resources.
Either that, or someone had drugged her.

On the plus side, she caught Mark stealing a peek at her
sweater. She'd have teased him about that, but she couldn't
keep her eyelids from drifting shut.

SAM FELL INTO A DEEP SLEEP that lasted the entire two-hour
drive to the mountain community of Big Bear. Although
Mark was relieved, he wished she didn't have to miss the
gorgeous scenery. Late-autumn rains had transformed
California's brown summer landscape into an explosion
of wildflowers and greenery. As they approached the
7,000-foot level, pine trees scented the chilly air, and he
turned on the car heater for the first time that year.

He could swear Sam's condition was improving already.
The farther they got from Orange County, the healthier the
color of her pale skin. As for the form-fitting pink top with
its V-neck, did she have any idea how that affected a man?

He didn't intend to do a damn thing about it. This weekend was an intervention, not a seduction.

Luckily, the cabin hadn't been rented this week. Tour-
ism was slow due to a lack of snowfall, even though many
resorts offered artificial snow on their slopes.

Mark had a spare key, and he kept clothing and toiletries in a locked closet at the cabin. He'd even arranged for
a cleaning crew to tidy up after they left. The only catch
had been the possibility that Sam might go ballistic.

Instead, she'd crashed. Still, he didn't kid himself. Once
she awakened, he might face a battle royal, but surely she
wouldn't insist on interrupting Lori and Jared's chance at
reconciliation. Her comment might have been intended as
a joke, but he wished he'd thought of that angle himself
when he planned this intervention for Sam.

Mark turned off the highway and followed a route

through narrow streets lined with tall pines. Every now and then, he glimpsed a flash of blue from Big Bear Lake below them, before turning onto a bumpy street where cabins lay at odd angles to accommodate the terrain. Unlit strings of Christmas bulbs swathed several of the houses, and on one lawn, a cartoon reindeer and a Santa stood poised for their turn to shine after dark.

While the sky was overcast, no wind disturbed the overhead branches, Mark noticed. Accustomed to southern California's mild climate, he hadn't thought to check a weather forecast, but he doubted they were in for anything severe.

Still, you never could tell.

He swung onto a gravel turnaround and braked to a halt in front of his A-frame. Rough logs gave the exterior a rustic feel, and pine needles crunched beneath his shoes as he stepped out.

Leaving Sam to sleep, he toted her suitcase inside and checked the place. As he'd hoped, the rental agency kept the kitchen stocked and the bathroom and bedroom prepared with towels and sheets.

Outside again, he paused to study Sam through the passenger window. Guiltily, he noticed that she'd huddled in the seat, hugging herself against the cold despite the jacket he'd laid over her.

He tapped the glass, then opened the door. Still sleeping.

"Sam?" Mark crouched beside her.

"Grrr." Was she snarling or shivering?

"Wake up. We're here."

"Beat it." Matted blond hair hid her expression.

"Are you talking in your sleep or giving me a hard time?" he asked.

"Both." She stirred and peered at him. "Where are we?"

"Mountains."

She inhaled. "Mmm. Chilly weather makes me think of hot cocoa."

"If you're willing to lurch a few yards, I promise you all the cocoa you can drink." The rental agency always laid in a supply of that after-ski essential.

Sam stretched and covered a yawn. Her movements dislodged the jacket and provided another tantalizing glimpse of lovely curves revealed by a top so tight-fitting it ought to be outlawed.

"Getting. Up. Now." She swung her long legs out of the car and fixed Mark with a steely blue assessment. "Tell me this isn't an institution for the criminally bewildered."

"It's my vacation cabin," he told her.

She tilted her face toward the sky. A white flake landed on her nose. "Is that snow?"

"Just a flurry." When Mark glanced up, a couple more flakes dampened his cheeks. "At least, I hope it's nothing more."

"We might be stuck here for a long time." Sam sounded merry. "I've never been snowbound."

Before Mark could protest that his schedule simply wouldn't permit him to get stuck in the mountains, she trotted ahead of him into the cabin. For better or worse, he'd whisked her away.

And now he had to make the best of it.

Chapter Twelve

At this elevation, they were literally in the clouds, Sam saw as she turned in the living room and gazed through the A-frame wall of windows. Trees, lake, snatches of fog, drifting bursts of whiteness. This entire cabin might simply float away as in—what was that children's book she'd loved?—ah, yes, *Howl's Moving Castle*.

Impulsively, she headed up the narrow staircase to the loft, where a wide sofa bed faced straight out into the heavens. "I'm sleeping up here!" she called over the railing to Mark, who was prowling through the kitchen cabinets.

"There's no privacy," he said, straightening. "I put your suitcase in the back bedroom."

"You just want the loft for yourself."

"That, too." He considered her assessingly. "Let's play for it."

"Play what?" Sam's competitive instincts surged even before she heard the details.

"Scrabble?"

"I'm not a word person."

"Dominoes?"

"Sissy stuff! Got a couple of swords?" She'd excelled in fencing as an undergrad at UC Berkeley.

"How about wrestling?" he called back.

"Why, Mark, I didn't know you cared."

He had the grace to blush. "You're out of my weight class, anyway."

The altitude was beginning to offset the bracing effect of the cool air. Feeling slightly woozy, Sam descended. "We'll figure out the sleeping arrangements later. Where's my cocoa?"

"Gee, you're pushy." Mark grinned.

"You're the one who brought me here," Sam reminded him. "What exactly happens at this intervention, Doctor?"

"You leave all your cares behind," he said.

"Done."

"That easily?" Standing behind the counter that divided the kitchen from the living room, he produced a couple of mugs and a tin of hot chocolate mix. As he filled the cups, the casual slacks and pullover emphasized a ruggedly masculine build that Sam would definitely enjoy wrestling.

Tearing her thoughts away, she responded to his question. "Sometimes I feel like I absolutely have to fix things, get them right, save the world. To the point of collapse, as you've seen. But up here, I can't do a thing about any of it, so why worry?"

His forehead furrowed as he clinked around fixing their beverages. "You said you're an adrenaline junkie."

"Sometimes I need help breaking loose," she admitted. "Now that it's done, what's next on the agenda?"

"Whatever you want."

"Anything?" she murmured.

He paused with a spoon in his hand. "What would you like?"

A simple response sprang to mind. *You.* "There's one method scientifically proven to relax people faster than anything else."

She could see awareness dawn in the way his pupils dilated and his lips parted. "I don't think that's a good idea."

"You seemed interested enough the last time we were

alone without the triplets," she pointed out. "When you saved me from being strangled by my ponytail elastic."

The microwave timer buzzed. "I seem to be rescuing you a lot these days."

"The way you rescued your sister and your fiancée from *their* addictions?" she prodded.

"I suppose there is some similarity." He set a steaming mug on the counter and located a tin of biscotti in a cabinet. "Except I didn't actually rescue my sister. She rescued herself."

"Yes, but you tried your best." Sam blew on the piping hot cocoa. "Your pattern is to get involved with troubled women, steer them in the right direction and then move on."

He didn't look pleased. "You think that's the way I treat people?"

She nodded, more to provoke him than because she really believed it. "Well, if you plan to dump me as soon as we get home, I hope you'll at least wait until we've had sex."

Mark gave a start. It was a good thing he'd only opened the microwave door and hadn't removed his cup, or she might have had to treat a burn.

Sam wasn't sure why she enjoyed teasing him. Partly, she refused to let Mark stick her in the category of damsels in distress. Also, her body tingled every time he came close, and she was tired of being celibate.

The silence didn't last long. "I may be attracted to women with addiction problems," he conceded, "but I refuse to get caught up in a destructive pattern of enabling them."

"You aren't enabling me," she challenged. "So you have nothing to fear."

"Oh? Who's been saving your bacon every morning, helping you get the triplets off to day care?" He stood across the counter, balancing on both feet as if ready to swat back whatever conversational ball she lobbed in his direction.

They'd bypassed fencing and wrestling in favor of verbal tennis. Perfect—Sam had finally found a sport she could play while snacking.

"That isn't enabling, it's helping," she said. "Being a mother is natural and healthy and wonderful. Besides, you're in love with those babies. Don't bother to deny it."

Crinkles formed beside his eyes. "They're adorable." His expression turned serious. "They're going to need a father. Have you thought about that?"

She'd like to steer this conversation back into more playful areas. "Are you volunteering?"

Alarm flashed across his face. Oops.

Sam reached out and cupped his wrist. "That was a joke, Mark."

"I know." He took a sip of his hot chocolate.

"Twice I've knocked you for a loop," she said. "Does that mean I win the rights to the loft?"

"We'll see."

Or they could share it. In her present mood, Samantha didn't mind the idea at all. Best to get started right now, because given her state of weariness, she was likely to fall asleep early tonight.

Too bad for this inconvenient counter between them. "About that wrestling match," she began.

He pinned her, not with his arms but with a glance. "Behave yourself, Doctor."

"Oh, all right." She stretched her legs along the adjacent stool and turned away to enjoy the sight of snow whirling outside. A naughty impulse prompted her to stretch languidly, giving him an excellent view of her breasts.

"Sam." The low note in his voice sent chills through her.

"Mmm?" She peered at Mark from beneath lowered lashes.

"I'm only human."

"That's what I'm counting on."

He gripped the edge of the counter. "I'm trying to listen to my better judgment."

"What happens in Big Bear stays in Big Bear," she said.

"Is that a promise?" He eased around the counter. Losing the battle? She hoped so.

His hand smoothed along her leg toward her thigh. Instantly, heat sparked through her body, firming the tips of her breasts and warming her right to the core.

"There's not much privacy in this room," Mark observed softly.

"From all those hordes of snow bunnies outside?"

"Why don't we…"

Her phone rang. They both froze.

"Couldn't you have brought me to a cabin without cell reception?" Sam grumbled.

"Don't answer."

"What if it's about the triplets?"

The tone sounded again. Sam wished she'd taken the time to program different ring tones for different people, so she'd know if it was Lori or the answering service or….

The display read: *Candy.* She showed it to Mark.

He nodded resignedly. With a jolt of fear at what the young mother might be about to say, Sam answered.

MARK WASHED OUT THEIR MUGS while Sam listened to her caller. He was grateful in a way for the interruption, because he'd been on the verge of yielding to his impulses. But would that have been so terrible?

It had struck him during their conversation that he'd been in an awful hurry to view Sam's behavior as addictive, to put her in the same box as his sister and his former fiancée. While her behavior could go over the top some-times, did one weakness really erase all the strengths?

She needed a counterbalance, someone to rein her in when she went too far. Wasn't that what couples did for each other? Maybe he ought to take a risk, for once. And today, Sam seemed more than willing to meet him half-way.

This weekend had given them a rare chance to get to know each other...*if* Candy didn't drive Sam right back into a frenzy. And her reaction wasn't the only thing both-ering Mark about this call.

Earlier, he'd been too focused on Sam's meltdown to reflect on Candy's possessive behavior toward the triplets, but if the teenager insisted, she still had the legal right to reclaim them. He'd always doubted the young woman's readiness to parent, and after what he'd heard about her behavior at the party, he felt even more certain it was a bad idea. Eventually, a social worker might determine negli-gence and take them away, but in the interim, there was no telling how much harm she could inflict.

He had a vivid image of Colin this morning, peering trustingly up while taking the bottle. The bond between child and parent had always struck Mark as an instinc-tive thing, predisposed by hormones and nature. But that didn't account for the tightening in his chest whenever he pictured that little boy and his sisters being hauled off by an immature, unstable mother.

Sam was pacing through the cabin, phone pressed to her ear. Mark tuned in to her remarks. "Are you sure you're all right?... Well, I *was* angry... I'm afraid I had to go out of town. Nurse Ross and Dr. Sellers are taking care of them.... No, no, they're not sick... Really? Are you sure he'll agree?... That would be wonderful."

The hope in her words buoyed him. This sounded like good news.

"Yes, I'll set things up with Mr. Franco and call you Monday. Absolutely…. Don't be too hard on yourself, Candy. You've been through a lot. And thank you."

She clicked off and stood there, breathing heavily as if she'd just run a marathon. Perhaps, emotionally, she had.

"Well?" Mark asked.

"I can't stand here and talk. I need to move."

"Closet," he said.

"Sorry?"

"Let's suit up and go for a walk." He strode into the bedroom and unlocked a door half-hidden by the large dresser. From inside, he fetched ski caps, gloves, a windbreaker and boots. Good thing he kept a range of sizes available for friends.

Sam had already zipped her jacket when he rejoined her. They bundled up and set out into a landscape dusted with white. A few flakes still scampered through the air, but, as Mark had guessed, a big snowfall didn't appear likely.

"Candy was in a motorcycle accident," Sam said as they crunched their way across the gravel. "She's scraped and bruised but nothing broken."

She'd ridden on a motorcycle less than two weeks after a cesarean? "She could rupture her incision."

"The ER doctor called in an ob-gyn. She's fine but really sore."

Thank goodness she'd escaped major injury. "How did it happen?"

At the edge of the road, they turned and walked side by side along the shoulder. "She was riding behind her new boyfriend, a fellow with the charming name of Spider. And tattoos to match." Between frosty breaths, Sam explained that the bike had barely started rolling forward when it somehow overturned.

Spider, who'd suffered a sprained arm, had blamed

Candy for throwing him off balance. "She said he was waving to a friend and showing off."

"Sounds like poor judgment all around." Mark was grateful the tumble hadn't been more serious.

"She kept remembering how he'd wanted to take Colin with them, just held in her arms. Something about teaching the little guy not to be afraid. Can you imagine?"

Unfortunately, he could.

"She's really shook up. You know how kids have this sense of invulnerability? Well, hers got stripped away." Sam kicked a pinecone out of her path. "She said that if I hadn't intervened, she might have agreed. All she could think about as she was lying on the pavement was that she might have killed Colin."

Mark's stomach tensed at the mental picture of that trusting little fellow lost forever. "You said something about setting up a meeting with Tony?"

"She got a text from Jon a few days ago, asking if they can be friends again. She promises to drag him in to sign those relinquishment papers." Sam tugged her cap over her ears. "She swears she's given up any idea of taking the triplets. That it scares her just to think about how unprepared she is to protect them."

"How can you be sure she won't reconsider?"

"Well, there's always that possibility. But she sounded, well, like she's growing up, changing. I know this isn't a simple process, but I truly don't believe she's going to want them back."

"Then you can stop worrying about that." He rested his hand lightly on the small of her back. "Congratulations."

Her pace took on a new jauntiness. "They're safe! Isn't that wonderful? Now I can focus on gearing up for Christmas. That party's going to be great fun! You are planning to bring your sister, aren't you?"

Ahead, a squirrel darted up a tall tree. "Someone ought to tell that critter he's supposed to hibernate."

"Tree squirrels don't hibernate."

Mark stared at her in mock dismay. "Next you'll tell me bats don't use radar."

"Technically they don't," Sam informed him. "They use something called echolocation."

"What are you, a nature expert?"

She chuckled. "You'd be surprised at the questions kids ask pediatricians. They expect you to be an expert on everything. *Some* of us don't go around ducking questions."

He tried to figure out what she meant. "Excuse me?"

"I asked if you were bringing your sister to the party. You changed the subject."

"I will if she arrives in time." Wryly, he added, "Or if she arrives at all."

"She has to," Sam told him briskly. "I've got space in my cabinet all picked out for that glassware you're going to buy me."

He'd almost forgotten their bet. "While I'd like to get my kiss under the mistletoe, I hope you're right." Besides, going to a yard sale might be fun. Especially if Sam went with him.

"How exactly do you make a snowball?" she asked sweetly. Too sweetly.

"You're the one who grew up in Seattle. They get more snow than Florida," he answered.

"You're the one who owns a cabin in Big Bear." From a patch where a thin layer had accumulated, she scooped a handful of the white stuff and pressed it like a patty.

"If you throw that at me…"

She tossed it at a tree trunk. "You'll what?"

Spotting another meager drift deeper into the wooded area, Mark beat her there in a couple of strides and snatched up a gloveful of his own. "Return the favor."

"But I didn't!" Sam grabbed his arm.

"Then I guess I'll have to do this." He dropped the snow and gathered her close. On the street, an SUV chugged past, but Mark ignored it as he brushed his lips across Sam's cold cheek until he reached the warmth of her mouth.

Her arms twined around him. Through the thick layers of clothing, he felt her heart thrumming to match his own.

Deliciously isolated in a column of their own heat, he enjoyed the lingering taste of Sam's mouth and the naughty flick of her tongue. As her hands smoothed along the back of his neck, she stood on tiptoe and her hips met his.

Desire arrowed through him. He felt as if the entire woods might burst into snow-defying flame. "Think we can make it home?"

"I don't know," she murmured against his jaw. "Maybe we could just build a snow cave and do it here."

"Impractical."

"Then we should…"

"Go," he finished.

"Fast," she added.

So they did.

Chapter Thirteen

Sam loved the way Mark burst through his usual restraint as he swept her across the cabin and into the bedroom. He tossed his windbreaker onto the floor and, the instant she finished unzipping her jacket, peeled it off, as well.

"Damn boots," he said, flinging aside his ski cap. "Let's leave them on."

Sam shook out her hair. "I don't think that's such a great idea. We might streak mud on the..."

Her protest got lost as he tossed her onto the bed, knelt beside her and smoothed up the pink sweater. The feel of his lips against her breasts sent her reeling.

When he released her, Sam curled around to unbuckle his belt and work open his pants. "You don't play around," Mark said admiringly as he helped her.

"I *do* play around, lucky for you." She basked in the scent of his aftershave lotion and the powerful sight of his chest as he shrugged off his pullover. If she could just get that zipper down... There!

As he rolled her over, her boots clumped to the floor. Muttering impatiently, Mark kicked off his own. "That *is* better."

"And so is this," she said, arching to trace a heated path down Mark's chest with her tongue.

"Incredible." He broke off in a gasp. She had found her way to his erection.

Sam liked feeling this man grow taut beneath her, knowing he was nearing the edge of his control. Then she lifted her head, and Mark seized the initiative. With a few skillful movements, he stripped off her jeans and brought her down, ready for action. Conditioned by years of caution, Sam nearly reminded him that they ought to use protection against pregnancy, until she remembered that she didn't need it anymore.

And she knew she had no need of any other kind of protection with Mark.

Hot longing spread through her as he joined them with long, lustful strokes. Briefly, he paused to brush back her hair and kiss her. Then he filled her again and again, until Sam lost all awareness of anything but him.

At her fevered urging, he drove into her so deeply that she could feel them both melting into a fiery wave. They crested it as one, pleasure leaping and sparking around them like hot lava.

A soft glimmer bathed them in the cool quiet of the room. "Sam," Mark began.

Was he going to say he loved her? She felt a touch afraid, a touch hopeful. Maybe she should say it first. Because she *did* love him.

Sam felt the sting of apprehension. Wonderful things had happened today. To put their feelings into words might tempt fate.

She touched a finger to his lips. "Don't talk."

He nibbled her finger. "Why not?"

Mark wouldn't understand about this silly superstition. "Let's go eat." She wriggled away from him. Shivering in the chill air, she grabbed for her clothes.

"Earlier, you accused *me* of ducking questions. Why can't I talk?" he demanded.

She might as well get this over with. "Because it's bad luck."

"What is?"

Maybe he hadn't meant to say he loved her, or that this was the most special moment of his life, or that they belonged together. Perhaps she'd misread the signs, and he'd been on the verge of suggesting they take up clog dancing.

Sam tossed over his pants. "Get dressed, you stud, and quit quizzing me. I'm hungry."

Aside from a skeptical look, Mark complied without further argument.

Since neither of them felt like cooking, they drove into the town, which early darkness had transformed into a fairyland of Christmas lights. There they discovered a range of cuisines from Italian to Mexican to Chinese, along with mountain-themed names like Lumberjack, Grizzly Manor Café and Himalayan Restaurant. They chose a barbecue place and loaded up on back ribs and fried coconut shrimp.

Being around Mark seemed to involve eating a lot of unhealthy food. Sam couldn't have cared less.

They drove home, lit the gas log in the fireplace, and made love in front of it.

There might be no such thing as perfect happiness, she mused later as she lay in Mark's arms in the loft, with a magnificent A-framed view of pine trees and a brilliantly starry sky. But right now, she couldn't ask for anything more.

ON SUNDAY MORNING, THEY MADE pancakes. Afterward, Mark washed the dishes, while Sam, who'd been reluctant to disturb her friends earlier, put in a call to check on the triplets.

As far as Mark could tell from eavesdropping, everything was all right with the babies. After a lively discussion of their sleep and eating habits, Sam fell silent, listening.

"He did what?" she cried, and grinned. "You're kidding! One night with the triplets and... Which of you changed your mind?"

Hoping he was right, Mark pointed questioningly to his ring finger. Sam nodded.

So the marriage plans were back on. Mark could hardly wait until she clicked off. "Well?"

"They're engaged again," she told him. "Lori swears she isn't going to waste time planning a big ceremony. They don't want to wait."

"But didn't you and Jennifer already buy bridesmaids' dresses? Plus she's got a big family in Colorado." Last fall, Mark had overheard months of chatter about his nurse's elaborate plans for a church wedding followed by a reception.

"She wants a simple ceremony with a few close friends," Sam replied cheerily. "Later, she and Jared will throw a big party."

He finished loading the dishwasher and asked the big question, "Which of them changed their mind about having babies?"

Sam twinkled at him. "You sure you wouldn't rather wait till tomorrow and ask them yourself?"

Mark assumed a bland expression. "You're right. It's no big deal anyway."

"Of course it's a big deal!" she flared. "That's why they broke up."

"Then I guess you ought to tell me."

Sam poured a fresh cup of coffee. "Well..." She took a slow sip, drawing out the tension.

"It must have been Jared," Mark teased, although he suspected the opposite was true. "He's around babies all day. Getting stuck with them at night, too, must have been too much for the man."

"Don't be ridiculous! He didn't feel stuck."

"So it's Lori."

Sam settled onto the couch. "She says Jared's nothing like her father, who refused to get up at night or even change a diaper. And her parents had six kids! That's why her mother dumped so many child-care duties on her."

"And she developed an aversion to motherhood. But Connie, Courtney and Colin fixed her, did they?"

"Those munchkins charmed the socks off her. She asked if she could borrow them now and then. I said yes, of course."

When Mark sat down beside her, Sam nestled against him. He looped an arm around her, careful not to jostle the coffee cup. "After the counseling clinic leaves, we should turn those offices into a wedding chapel. Lori and Jared, Tony and Kate—we've got a full slate of weddings coming up."

Sam's eyes shone. "We could offer a full-service facility. Get married on the premises, conceive in the fertility suite, and deliver right in the same building."

"Dr. Tartikoff's keen on innovation," Mark mused. "He should love it."

"Dr. Tartikoff?" She looked impressed. "I had no idea we were aspiring that high."

"Nothing's firmed up yet," he warned. "In fact, I shouldn't have mentioned it."

Sam sighed. "Don't worry. I've become the soul of discretion."

"How long do you suppose that will last?"

"Two to three hours. Or possibly days. I'm in a beatific frame of mind, what with the Christmas party less than a week away."

At the thought of Christmas, a shadow flitted across

Mark's sunlit horizon. He ought to warn Sam that Mrs. Wycliff and her daughter might attend. But if he brought them up now and Sam went nuclear, that would be unfair to Ian, who'd stuck his neck out to invite them.

Besides, no one had confirmed that they planned to be there. Why risk spoiling today's mellow mood?

Instead, he brought up a happier topic. "I spotted a Christmas tree lot on the way up here. We could surprise the triplets."

Sam set her empty cup on the coffee table. "They're too young to be surprised."

"No one's too young to be surprised," Mark assured her. "Birth comes as a big surprise to newborns, believe me."

"It comes as a shock," she corrected. "You can only be surprised if you're expecting things to be a certain way in the first place. Babies don't have a fixed sense of how things are supposed to be until roughly 18 months."

He regarded her in amusement. "I should know better than to argue about child development with a pediatrician."

"By the way, I'd love to get a Christmas tree." She extended her legs across his, half sitting in his lap. "We don't have to leave yet, do we?"

"No. I have a much better idea of what we could do this morning," he told her.

As it turned out, so did she.

FROM THE TOP OF AN OVERSTUFFED closet in her house, Sam retrieved a box of ornaments she'd collected, by chance and by luck, over the years. Rainbow glass globes and glittery stars, shimmering angels, cherub dolls, along with velvet bows and strings of lights. Some had been gifts, others yard-sale finds or impulse buys at post-holiday clearance sales.

Despite their admitted mutual ignorance of tree trimming, she and Mark managed—with advice from the internet—to wedge the tree into a base, fill it with water and prop it upright. Then they hung and dangled ornaments and lights around the aromatic branches. For good measure, they also tacked a strand of colored lights across the front of the house.

The triplets, who'd been fussy in the car, had calmed once Sam got them home. True, their feedings and diaper changes slowed the tree decorating, but she enjoyed the sense that they'd already begun to feel at home here.

The little innocents hadn't a clue that they'd already worked a Christmas miracle, Sam mused as she stood atop the ladder, capping the tree with a giant star. When she and Mark had arrived at Jared's to pick up the babies, Lori had beamed at her fiancé, who'd scarcely stopped touching her while they regaled their two friends with their plans to get married as soon as next week.

Lori still wanted Sam and Jen to be her bridesmaids, and there'd be a small reception immediately following the ceremony. Her list of a few close friends was expanding to include coworkers, and just before Sam left, Lori had mentioned that she would invite her family, after all.

"I don't want to hurt their feelings," she'd said. "I mean, I only plan to get married once."

Tearing her thoughts back to the present, Sam descended the ladder. Mark gripped her protectively around the waist and lifted her from the last step to slide her down the length of his body.

"I like the way that feels." She draped her arms over his shoulders. "Think anyone would notice if we made the most of it?"

Clearing his throat, Mark dipped his head toward their audience arrayed in carriers around the tree. "Let's keep this G-rated."

"They're too young to tell the difference."

"Science is always discovering unsuspected aspects to

memory," he murmured. "Do you want them to end up on a psychiatrist's couch forty years from now, explaining why they have strange fantasies involving Christmas trees?"

Sam poked him in the ribs. "All right, then. Stand back."

He complied. She turned off the overheads, then switched on the tiny lights.

The tree glowed with a display of treasures transformed into fairy gifts. Outside, twilight had fallen, which only intensified the brilliance inside. One of the babies cooed appreciatively. If it was a burp, Sam didn't want to know it.

"Their first Christmas tree," she said. "Mine, too."

"You mean in this house?"

"Since I've been an adult," she clarified. "How about you?"

Courtney began to cry. Without missing a beat, Mark picked her up. "In Florida, my staff gave me a miniature tree that sat on my coffee table. Does that count?"

"No," she said.

"Then it's the first."

"We're virgins."

"I wouldn't put it that way."

Sam basked in the warmth of his gaze. Who could have imagined two weeks ago that today she'd feel so free and lighthearted?

Must be the spirit of Christmas. And, she conceded as she stole a glance sideways in the dimness, it was because of Mark.

He seemed easy and natural around her and the babies. There was, she supposed, a reserve in him that might always be there, but she'd never wanted the sort of relationship where a couple did everything in lockstep. He could live in his house and keep his schedule, and they could be together when it suited them both.

Things were just fine.

THE WEEK BEFORE CHRISTMAS always passed a bit slowly at the hospital. Patients avoided elective surgeries and the number of births dropped off slightly. As much as possible, doctors scheduled C-sections before or after the holiday period, when many of them went out of town.

As a result, Mark had the treat of performing extra deliveries. Holding each newborn felt even more special than usual, because of the triplets. This little boy showed a trace of Colin's spunk. That girl appeared worried, like Courtney. And when a small defect presented itself, like Connie's discoloration, he could assure the parents from the heart that they would fall in love with the baby just as deeply.

On Wednesday, Dr. Tartikoff called to discuss ideas for adding fertility center staff and to ask about the timetable for renovating the facilities. Although he hadn't officially committed, he promised to make a decision soon after the first of the year.

Informed by phone, Chandra was ecstatic. "Keep him happy, Mark, whatever it takes."

"Within reason." He wasn't sure how much to believe of Owen's reputation for being difficult. So far, Mark had seen no signs of temperament, but then, he hadn't crossed the man, either.

"The board is counting on you to land him," the vice president said. "Don't let us down."

"I'll do my best. Merry Christmas." Mark hoped she didn't detect a note of irony.

"Yes, yes, of course. Merry Christmas."

Chandra had once mentioned having two grandchildren. He hoped that when they jumped onto her lap, they didn't get frostbite on their little rear ends.

On Thursday afternoon, Jennifer stopped into Mark's office to confirm that Mrs. Wycliff and her daughter would be dropping by the party. "She's a real dynamo," the PR director told him. "Honestly, Sam's met her match. Or rather, she *will* be meeting her match."

"Let's hope they hit it off." Mark felt a moment of disquiet. But surely Eleanor's involvement was the best Christmas present the clinic could receive.

"Samantha's been happier this week than I've ever seen her," Jennifer added. "You're good for her."

Obviously, Sam's closest friends knew of the weekend excursion, but Mark felt obliged to sound a note of caution. "I'd rather this didn't become a topic of general discussion."

"It won't."

"Thanks."

"Ready for tomorrow night?" Jennifer asked.

He had nothing scheduled Christmas Eve except on-call duty. "What do you mean?"

"You haven't forgotten our annual caroling?" she chided.

"Actually, I did." Members of the senior staff traditionally sang carols throughout the hospital to cheer up those who had to work as well as patients stuck here when they wanted to be home. "Thanks for reminding me."

"I'll drop the lyric sheets on your desk," Jennifer said. "Seven o'clock. We'll start on the top floor and work our way down."

"Great." He *did* enjoy the tradition. Last year, Samantha had displayed a throaty contralto that struck Mark as incredibly sexy.

After Jennifer left, he checked his email and clicked open an angel-bedecked card from his sister. It included the notation, "See you around three o'clock Saturday."

He emailed back directions to the hospital, details of the party and a reminder of his cell phone number. "I can't wait to see how you're doing."

Bryn was really coming. She'd be keeping her word, at

last. This year, he felt certain—almost—that if he were a fortune-teller, he'd see a yard sale and a glass knickknack in his future.

This was one bet he looked forward to losing.

Chapter Fourteen

On Christmas Eve, after eating a quick dinner at home, Sam took the babies to the hospital nursery. With plenty of cribs available on the holiday, the staff had volunteered to babysit for the carolers.

Jennifer's Rosalie was already here, along with Tara, Tony's month-old daughter. Tiny as they were, each baby already had quite a story, Sam mused. Rosalie and the triplets had been relinquished, while Tara had been born to a surrogate mother. At least, Kate had started out as a surrogate. After Tony's wife, Esther, also an attorney, abandoned him and their unborn baby for a high-powered job in Washington, he'd stepped in as Kate's birthing partner. By Thanksgiving Day, when Tara arrived, the couple had fallen in love. They planned to marry in the spring, as soon as his divorce became final, and Kate now volunteered at the clinic as a peer counselor.

Lingering beside Connie's bassinet, Sam tried to imagine what it would be like to be a bride walking down an aisle. As a teenager, with the threat of cancer hanging over her head, she'd never dared fantasize about her wedding. Later, she'd figured she would rather spend her money on a good cause than a fancy ceremony. Now, she had to admit she'd love to indulge just a little. Beautiful flowers filling a chapel, a couple of friends in elegant dresses, and, most important, a man waiting for her by the altar, his face suffused with love.

Wonder who that could be....

"Dr. Forrest?" A nurse signaled for her attention. "There's a woman in the hall asking for you."

"About the caroling?"

The nurse frowned. "I don't think so."

Sam shifted into take-charge mode. "Thanks. I'll handle it." Who could this be on Christmas Eve?

In the nearly deserted third-floor corridor, a stocky woman with disheveled graying hair stood, arms folded. From her wrinkled housedress to her truculent expression, she inspired immediate wariness. But Sam strove not to judge by appearances.

"I'm Dr. Forrest. What can I do for you?" She dispensed with the usual holiday greetings, since this woman didn't appear to be in the mood.

"I'm Vivien Babcock. I'd like to know why there's nobody at the counseling clinic. You must all be too busy planning your big party tomorrow to waste time on actual clients." The woman's jaw thrust forward.

Sam fought down her instinctive dislike of an exaggerated sense of entitlement. Experience had taught that sometimes the most disagreeable people were the most in need of help. "Is this an emergency?" *It had better be, on Christmas Eve.*

Vivien continued to glare. "I've decided to leave my husband. He's a rotten piece of scum."

Sam scrutinized the woman for signs of abuse. She detected no obvious bruises and no wincing or favoring an arm or leg that might be injured. "You're leaving him tonight?"

"That's right—you know how they always get ugly on holidays" was the vague reply.

Upstairs, the carolers must be wondering what had delayed Sam. Straining for patience, she asked, "Who are 'they'?"

"Men," Vivien snapped. "He's my third husband, so I guess I'm an expert."

An abusive husband *was* likely to use force to prevent his wife from leaving. "I can arrange to admit you to a women's shelter."

"Is that all?" Her lip curled.

"If you feel in danger, you should ask the police to accompany you, or simply leave without telling him," Sam advised. "Walk away from the hospital and don't go home again. Are there children who might be in harm's way?"

"My kids are grown, and a fat lot they care what happens to me. Is that all you have to say?" Vivien's voice rose, with no apparent concern for the open doors to patient rooms along the hall.

"I run a small counseling clinic, not a crisis center," Sam told her. "However, I'd be happy to put in a call to—"

"Never mind." With a toss of her unbrushed hair, the woman marched off. Not limping, Sam noted.

Perhaps she should hurry after her, try to learn the whole story and figure out what resources she needed. Sam hated turning away a person who was clearly in pain and possibly in danger, no matter how obnoxious she might be. But tonight, she lacked both the energy and the will to pursue the matter.

After that wondrously relaxing getaway with Mark, she'd had a busy week. On Monday, the triplets' father had gladly signed papers giving up his rights. Although Candy still had roughly three weeks before signing her final relinquishment, she'd admitted to feeling relief at being free again.

"My aunt in Colorado invited me to move in with her," the young woman had told Sam. "She's a hairdresser and she's going to help me get into cosmetology school. It'll be fun."

"You sure you're okay with this?" Sam had pressed, despite her anguish at the possibility that Candy might renege.

"If I gave them to someone else, I'd probably worry," Candy had said. "But it's you, Sam. In a funny way, I always kind of felt like you were their mother."

"I guess I did, too."

While the situation with the babies seemed on track, the clinic's immediate future still hung in the balance. Several volunteers had suggested possible new locations, but despite Sam's inquiries, none had panned out. Then a salsa band canceled its promise to play for free at the fundraiser. Luckily, she was able to replace it with a mariachi band. She already knew some of the musicians, who were related to a twelve-year-old brain cancer survivor, a onetime patient of Sam's whom she'd referred to Children's Hospital, a few miles away in the city of Orange. According to the last report she'd received, his cancer was in remission.

Another battle won, at least temporarily.

On the top floor, she emerged from the elevator and followed the strains of "We Three Kings" around a corner. There stood a hardy and mostly on-key band: Jared and Lori, on whose finger sparkled a ring; Tony and Kate with her five-year-old son, who kept muffing the words; Jennifer and Ian, nursing director Betsy Raditch, PR assistant Willa Lightner and her teenage son and daughter. And, overshadowing them all, Mark. His gaze lit instantly on Sam as if he'd been watching for her.

Happiness tingled through her. As the carolers launched into "Joy to the World," Sam moved to his side and united her voice with his.

ON CHRISTMAS MORNING, Mark awoke in a bed that wasn't his. Today, however, he felt very much at home in it.

Last night, after caroling, he'd helped Sam strap the babies into the van and then followed them home in his car. They'd lit the tree and let the enchantment ripple through them.

Since they had busy schedules for Christmas Day, they'd exchanged gifts that evening. He'd bought her a quilt handmade by hospital volunteers, with panels that reproduced children's colorful drawings. She'd given him a home golf simulator that allowed him to practice his swing and get it analyzed by computer. Sure to improve his golf game, and possibly his mood.

Then they'd made love and gone to sleep in each other's arms.

During the night, they'd taken turns getting up for feedings, since Sam had refused to ask a nurse to work on a holiday night. Mark didn't mind. Sitting in the quiet hours holding the infants, he'd stumbled into a magical connection with them.

Unbelievable, that such tiny bundles could hold an entire future. As he gazed down at their faces, he saw the future unfolding: toddlers learning to walk, children reading words aloud, teenagers holding hands with a first love or rushing to share the results of a college application. The tears and disappointments, the challenges and triumphs. All this, and they still fit into the crook of his arm.

In the morning, he slept later than usual to compensate for his night duty. Samantha slumbered deeply beside him. Good, she needed it.

As he rose, she shifted to sprawl diagonally across the double bed. Eyes closed, breathing regular, blond hair rioting around her...she might have been the picture of beauty, save for her light snoring. Actually, Mark decided, she was still the picture of beauty, with sound effects.

He'd received only one call from the hospital last night, about a patient in the early stages of labor. Mark had monitored her progress during feedings, and, after dressing and eating breakfast, arrived at the maternity ward in time for the delivery.

A beautiful little boy. The large Italian family that gathered to welcome him showered Mark with thanks, holiday greetings and homemade cookies.

That morning, he ushered three more babies into the world, including one by C-section. As always, Mark was grateful to be part of such miracles.

But, for a change, he was also a little impatient to get back to the miracles that had come into his own life.

SAM HAD A GREAT FEELING about this party. Although she'd wondered whether having it on Christmas Day might discourage volunteers, several came early to finish decorating the suite with paper flowers, a piñata and holiday lights, and more showed up just before the two o'clock start time. The caterer arrived with boxes of hot hors d'oeuvres, while the initial trickle of guests swelled to a torrent, many with checks to contribute. Ian had offered to keep track of those, and drop them off at the bank's night deposit box.

A volunteer Santa distributed small gifts to children, joking with them about his red-trimmed white sombrero. As for the band, its music set people's toes tapping and hips wiggling.

While the actual event hadn't drawn a lot of interest from the press, reporter Tom LaGrange had stopped by with a photographer. Jennifer, who was discreetly steering him around, had presented him with a new brochure about the clinic's plans. Optimistic plans, Sam had to admit, considering what a large amount they'd need now that they could no longer use the hospital's facilities.

They'd taken for granted not only this suite, but free

access to utilities and the internet. She'd also grown accustomed to dropping in here between other duties. That would be difficult when she had to drive to another location.

Sam gave herself a mental shake. This was no occasion for negativity. Her friends and volunteers were laughing and enjoying the alcohol-free punch, and Mark...she kept having to force her gaze away from him as he joked with the appreciative crowd around him.

Were her feelings written as plainly on her face as she feared? It was too soon to let the hospital grapevine get hold of their relationship. Sam wasn't certain yet what kind of relationship they had, except that he'd become so entwined in her thoughts and daydreams that she could scarcely believe only weeks ago they'd been nothing more than verbal sparring partners.

Then, with a jolt, she spotted a boy seated on a folding chair near the band, shaking a castanet in synch with the music. The rest of the room faded, leaving only this youngster. He was small for his twelve years, his face was puffy from steroids, and his tasseled Santa hat had slipped back to reveal a bald head.

No one had told her Artie Ortega's cancer was back.

Mischievous and smart, Artie had recovered from his initial brain tumor. Obviously, it had returned and was being treated aggressively.

Tamping down her concern, Sam pasted a smile on her face and hurried over. "I didn't realize you'd joined the band." She gestured toward his castanet.

"You didn't know I was a rock star?" he shot back.

Sam slid into the chair beside him. "So how's it going?"

"I met a cute girl at a party last night." Doffing the hat, he ducked his head to show the words "Luv, Mellie" scrawled in black marker. "I think she likes me."

"How could she help it?" Sam teased.

Artie's mother, a rotund woman who smelled of cinnamon, perched in the chair on his far side. "He's beating this, Dr. Sam."

"I can see that." She couldn't really, but Sam hoped it was true. If she'd won her battle with cancer, why not Artie?

The pair filled her in on the latest developments in the boy's life. His older sister had had a baby, elevating him to the rank of uncle. His father, laid off from his job, had recently found work again. Good news, all of it.

As the conversation wound down, Mrs. Ortega stared across the room. "Who's that? I think I've seen her on the news." She indicated a tall, patrician woman talking intently with Ian.

"No, who's *that*?" Artie indicated a teenage girl standing with the new arrival. Unlike her mother—Sam presumed they were related, given their similar heights and nutmeg-brown hair—the girl had an open, friendly face. A very pretty face, as the boy had obviously noticed.

"Someone I haven't met yet," Sam informed him. "She looks a tad old for you."

"I'm a man of the world," Artie informed her loftily.

She gave him a hug. "You certainly are."

As soon as she released him, he pulled his hat on, covering the other girl's signature. "Don't want her to think I'm taken."

"Why, you flirt!" Sam joked. "You're going to leave a trail of broken hearts."

Sadness flickered across his young face. "Girls just pretend to flirt with me. I don't look so good right now." His smile returned. "But that'll be over soon."

"Go for it, champ." Reluctantly, Sam excused herself to return to her duties. Mark had joined the group around the tall woman and her daughter, and judging by his serious manner, they weren't merely discussing the punch.

She'd better go find out what that was all about.

FOR THE FIRST HOUR OF THE PARTY, Mark had been swept up by the Hot and Happy Christmas spirit. But while he realized that three o'clock was merely an estimate for his sister's arrival, he'd begun checking his watch instinctively since that hour passed.

When he dialed Bryn's cell phone number, it went through to voice mail. That made sense, since she shouldn't be gabbing on the phone while driving, but he wished he could reach her.

Where was she now on her journey from Phoenix? Surely she'd crossed the state line into California. Possibly she was entering Orange County's northern limits right now, a mere half hour's drive from Safe Harbor.

He wondered how much she'd changed in the past five years. She must be thirty-three, and she'd lived those years hard. Yet to see her healthy and in control of her life would more than compensate for a few added wrinkles and gray hairs, and for the nights he'd spent searching for her in bars and alcohol-drenched flophouses.

But what about the lies, the money he'd wasted on rehab, the sense of angry frustration, and the silence after she disappeared?

Thou shalt not hold grudges. Thou shalt be grateful for the prodigal's return. Except, a tiny voice kept asking, what if she didn't come? What if, once again, she went back on her word?

He pushed those concerns aside when Ian introduced him to Mrs. Wycliff and her daughter. Both were charming, and filled with ideas. Eleanor, as she insisted everyone call her, had already talked to a number of influential friends. "They agree that this sounds like a worthwhile project. True, there are a number of programs asking for money, but how exciting to build something practically from the ground up."

"It's special because it's named after that baby who died," added Libby Wycliff, her eyes bright with tears.

"Don't start crying now!" her mother said. "It's Christmas."

"I won't." The girl bit down on a trembling lip. It was only a few months since her father's death, Mark remembered. Libby must be transferring some of her emotions to this new project.

"I suppose I shouldn't have jumped the gun, but I called the city of Safe Harbor's human services coordinator, and guess what?" Eleanor told him. "She's been trying to figure out how to expand the family and teen offerings at their community center. When she heard this was Dr. Forrest's clinic, she got all excited. We may have a new home already!"

"That's terrific," Ian said.

A new home. It *sounded* great, but Sam already knew the human services coordinator. Why hadn't they discussed this possibility?

"Did I hear my name?" Sam joined them, her cheerful expression a touch strained. A short while ago, he'd seen her talking to a little boy who was obviously a cancer patient.

As Ian made introductions, Mark wished he'd informed her sooner about Eleanor's interest. For one thing, he didn't want to add to Sam's concerns right now. Also, he'd assumed Ian's friend would show up here as an interested newcomer, nothing more. Instead, she'd apparently appointed herself to represent the counseling center to the city.

He checked his watch. Nearly three-thirty. It was just

as well Bryn had been delayed, he supposed; he'd hate for her to walk into the middle of a tense situation.

He glanced at Sam. She didn't seem to take offense. Instead, she listened politely, if guardedly, to Eleanor's explanation of what she'd been doing and how excited she was about the plans. It must be the Christmas spirit. Or was it possible that, as the mother of three, she finally felt ready to hand over the clinic to someone else?

SAM RESTRAINED AN URGE to poke Mark in the side for failing to warn her about this eager-beaver socialite. Still, the clinic had to move within the next few weeks, and it could use a sponsor. Also, when Jennifer mentioned Ian's wealthy contact, Sam had put her off—and never brought up the subject again. No wonder her friends had decided to act independently.

Still, Eleanor Wycliff's imperious manner was likely to intimidate the very people who most needed counseling. Also, from the way she talked about her friends' fundraising balls, Sam doubted they had any real concept of how this low-key, grassroots project operated.

As for coming under the city's sponsorship, Sam had been putting off any discussion of that possibility as a last resort. "Once you get officials involved, there's always red tape," she explained to Eleanor after they'd chatted for a while. "What's special about the Edward Serra Clinic is that teenagers and women can just wander in and talk to a peer counselor, or a doctor, like me. They don't have to fill out a bunch of paperwork first."

Eleanor dismissed the notion with a lift of her elegant shoulders. "I'm sure we can work around that."

"This will be so much fun," added Libby, a sweet girl with an air of fragility. "My best friend's going to collect baby stuff for the clients at her next birthday party, instead of gifts. Isn't that cool?"

"That's very generous." Sam liked the daughter, and she supposed she would like the mother, too, once she got to know Eleanor better.

It *was* a relief to think of sharing responsibility for the clinic. Not that Sam intended to abandon her vision, but recently it had begun to feel more like a burden and less like the realization of a dream.

More playtime with the triplets. More leisurely evenings with Mark, and mornings waking up to his warmth lingering on the sheets. She craved those things, and she deserved them.

"Sam, I think you're needed." Ian nodded toward Jennifer, who was standing across the room with Tom La-Grange and several other people. The photographer's flash went off, and Tom was taking rapid notes as he talked to someone Sam couldn't see.

Jennifer's anxious gaze caught Sam's. Something was wrong. "I'll go see what the problem is." She excused herself and crossed the room. Unexpectedly, Eleanor broke away and walked with her.

At Sam's suggestion that she didn't have to get involved, the socialite replied, "This is a fundraiser for *our* clinic. I'm already involved."

Too late to argue. Besides, at that moment Sam caught sight of the woman who'd been hidden from view. It was Vivien Babcock, her hair even more matted than yesterday, her face flushed and her voice painfully loud.

Whatever she might be saying, the reporter was eating up every word.

Chapter Fifteen

"What a sham this whole thing is!" Vivien proclaimed in slurred tones as Sam and Eleanor approached. "A bunch of fancy people making themselves feel important. You should see the way they treated me!"

"Who *is* that creature?" Eleanor murmured.

"A very troubled woman," Sam answered. "Let's find out exactly what she wants." Despite her irritation, she hadn't forgotten Vivien's declaration that she planned to leave her husband. That was one of those turning points when people's lives could explode, or implode.

"Is she a client?" Eleanor asked.

"She dropped in last night. Christmas Eve, after dinner. Got mad that nobody was staffing the clinic." After this quiet aside, Sam moved to join the group around Jennifer. "Hello, Mrs. Babcock."

Vivien's jaw tightened pugnaciously. "Well! Here's the great doctor who gave me the brush-off last night."

"I tried to refer you to a more appropriate, full-service facility," Sam said calmly. "You chose to leave."

"Well, you didn't try hard enough." With a glittering, almost triumphant look, Vivien peeled back her blouse, exposing a massive black-and-blue patch across her shoulder and chest. With only the bra protecting her from indecency, she turned to display welts across her back. Gasps went up from the observers. The camera was flashing again, and several onlookers raised cell phones to take pictures. "This is what my husband did when I told him I was leaving. You could have prevented this."

No, you could have prevented it. "I advised you to call the police, or simply leave without telling him."

"Easy for you to say!"

Mark was heading in their direction, his face creased with concern. To the reporter, Sam explained, "No one threw anybody out. The Edward Serra Clinic offers informal counseling. We don't have a professional staff yet. I offered to arrange for Mrs. Babcock to enter a women's shelter, and I'll do that now. First, though, we have to report this to the police. Unless you've already filed a report?" She raised an eyebrow at the woman.

Vivien's face crumpled. "My husband *is* a cop."

Sam's stomach tensed. No wonder the woman felt powerless and filled with rage. True, she had unreasonable expectations of the clinic, along with a harsh and not very likable personality, but she was clearly hurting inside and out. "Then I can understand…"

"Oh, you can understand?" Vivien mocked. "Sure you can."

"You're drunk. Drunk and selfish." Eleanor's voice snapped through the air like a whip. "Dr. Forrest offered to help you last night and you threw it in her face. You brought this on yourself."

"How dare you!" Vivien tensed, as if she'd like to land a few blows on this elegant woman, a startling contrast to her own sagging, pouchy self. Both of them were in their late forties, Sam estimated, but what a difference.

"People are giving up their Christmases to help women like you," Eleanor told the interloper. "Of course that man had no right to beat you, but you should get a lawyer and make him pay for it."

"Easy for you to say. Get a lawyer! As if they grew on trees. Maybe for rich people like you."

To short-circuit the argument, Sam caught Vivien's arm. Too late, she realized her mistake. Although it was impossible to see through the sleeve, there must have been a nasty bruise underneath, because the woman let out a yelp.

"I'm sorry." Too late.

"You're both hypocrites!" Vivien cried. "You don't care about the poor or the downtrodden. All you care about is prancing around acting important."

More shutters clicked. Tom held up his recorder, capturing every word.

Barely bothering to yank her blouse into place, Vivien stalked off. "Oh, let her go," Eleanor said. "That woman's beyond saving."

"Nobody's beyond saving!" Sam flared. "If that's the way you think, this is the wrong place for you."

Then she ran to catch up with Vivien Babcock.

MARK, WHO'D BEEN LISTENING from a distance, assessed the situation rapidly. One wealthy donor about to flounce out of the party, deeply offended. A newspaper reporter barely suppressing his glee over stumbling across a controversy. Guests talking and texting on their cell phones, probably sending video around the world.

And then there was Sam disappearing in the wake of an injured woman.

Mark went after Sam.

He found her by the elevators with Vivien Babcock, who had tears streaming down her face. All the anger seemed to have whooshed out of her, leaving her deflated and frightened. "I'm calling someone I know at a shelter," Sam told him. "We have to get her to a safe place and figure out how to handle the situation with the police."

"I'll call the chief at home." Mark occasionally played

golf with the man. "The boys in blue may tend to stick together, but once I explain it, I'm sure the chief will take this situation seriously."

"What if he fires my husband?" Vivien cried. "He'll lose his income and his pension. I'll have nothing."

"You'll have nothing if he kills you," Sam replied. The woman fell silent.

Sam's gaze met Mark's. Clearly, she wasn't any more thrilled than he was about having to deal with this situation on Christmas, but when you were a doctor, emergencies came with the territory.

Fifteen minutes later, Mark had talked to the chief and been assured that the officer in question would be immediately suspended, and a report taken by a female officer. Sam's friend from the women's shelter was on her way, and the last hint of fight had gone out of Vivien.

Leaving the pair in the lobby to wait for Sam's friend, Mark returned to the party, or rather to the office suite, since by now the event had officially ended. The mariachi band had departed, the guests were gone, and the caterer was packing away what remained of the food.

Jennifer and Ian were taking down the decorations. "What happened after I left?" Mark asked.

The PR director regarded him glumly. "Mrs. Wycliff left in a huff. She's furious about the whole scene. Libby was in tears over the woman's bruises."

"Eleanor was right," Ian added. "Vivien had no business barging in here roaring drunk, blaming everyone else for her problems."

Unfortunately, that was exactly what alcoholics did, in Mark's experience. They disappointed, disrupted and discarded others. Take Bryn. She was more than an hour overdue, yet she hadn't called. Maybe she was lying somewhere badly injured in a car crash, or maybe she'd just stopped at a bar for liquid fortification.

He should have insisted on buying her a plane ticket, or gone to Phoenix to meet her. Above all, he should have trusted his gut instinct that she hadn't fundamentally changed.

Nobody's beyond saving. Sam's words rang in his ears. But while he admired her generous spirit, and had done what he could to ensure Mrs. Babcock's safety, today he wasn't sure he shared that optimism. About her client *or* his sister.

"Should I call Mrs. Wycliff and apologize on behalf of the hospital administration?" he asked. "This happened under our roof, and the clinic can't afford to lose her."

"I'll call her," Ian said. "I'm sure an apology from you wouldn't hurt, either. But Sam's the real sticking point."

Jennifer folded her arms. "Sam's heart may be in the right place, but this clinic doesn't belong to her. It's named after *my* son, and it's going to fall apart without someone like Eleanor at the helm."

"Good luck persuading Sam of that. She thinks she can carry the entire world on her shoulders," Mark reflected ruefully.

"Well, she can't," Jennifer said. "She made her choice when she adopted the triplets. Her first duty is to them now. She'll be mad at all of us for a while, but if it's a choice between her and Eleanor, we have to cut Sam out of the picture."

Reluctantly, Mark agreed.

BY THE TIME SHE PULLED INTO her driveway that night, Sam was bone-weary and fed up. Why couldn't other people get their acts together? Eventually, Vivien had quieted down, but she hadn't expressed any appreciation for being taken to a safe place or receiving a promise from Dr. Kendall, whom Sam had also called, to stop by the shelter and examine her injuries. The only positive note was Sam's hope that Vivien had bottomed out and would finally get treatment for her drinking. But what was Eleanor's excuse for *her* behavior?

The socialite had had no business confronting a client or making judgment calls. Her job was to raise funds, not run the clinic. But apparently she felt capable of doing everything.

Sam had been thrilled at the prospect of relinquishing her responsibilities. Now Eleanor Wycliff's arrogance made that impossible.

"Does she have to be such a snob?" she asked Connie as she fumbled with the straps on the baby's car seat.

In the seat behind her sister, Courtney began to whine. Colin was fussing, too. They must be hungry.

Sam tried to focus on one step at a time. She had to take them out of the van and into the house before she could heat their formula and get it into their tiny stomachs. While the day care center and the occasional night nurse were a big help, they weren't enough. She loved the triplets and had been confident that she could handle anything, yet she'd underestimated the sheer physical challenge of dealing with three infants. She needed to hire a nanny, a helper she could rely on day in and day out.

And she needed Mark, his quiet strength supporting her, his tenderness banishing her worries. He'd stood by her tonight, even though, as administrator, he probably should have stayed to placate Mrs. Wycliff. In the past, Sam hadn't minded making trouble for him, because she'd figured he deserved it. Funny how differently things appeared these days.

As she lifted the little girl, headlights prowled along the quiet street, past houses twinkling with Christmas lights. Her spirits lifted. Had he come to spend the evening with her?

At the curb, a van halted, and she spotted the logo of a TV station on the side. *Oh, just go away!*

"Shall we make a run for it?" she asked Connie. But she couldn't, because Courtney and Colin still had to be carried inside. Besides, the press never seemed to take a hint. They'd knock and phone and make pests of themselves.

Steeling her will, Sam turned to face the news crew. With luck, she could fob them off with a few shots of the triplets. Or, if they'd heard about Vivien Babcock, she'd update them on the situation.

One small counseling clinic was hardly a big story, even on the year's slowest news day.

MARK SETTLED ON HIS SOFA—which was much too hard for comfort, he had to admit—and clicked on the TV. Nothing calmed a man's brain like channel surfing, so he flipped through station after station. Every one seemed to be running a movie about Santa Claus, the nativity or angels, with a liberal sprinkling of ads for after-Christmas sales.

He wondered what Sam was doing. Taking care of the babies, no doubt. Given her reluctance to force a nurse to work on a holiday, she'd be handling the situation alone.

The scent of baby powder. The warm softness of infant skin as he changed a diaper. The tiny burp as he patted a triplet on the back. And, later, Sam's legs tangling with his, her hungry mouth seeking him...

He ached to go over there. But, inevitably, the subject of Eleanor would come up, and he'd have to admit that he'd spoken to her at length on the phone. And that, basically, he'd given her full control over the clinic.

Once he soothed hurt feelings and explained that the hospital administration was behind her, Eleanor had agreed to stay involved. But there were conditions he'd been in no position to refuse. After today's blowup, Chandra would no doubt insist the clinic vacate the premises immediately. Hard as Sam worked, she hadn't put together a new home *or* a funding plan.

As he tapped the channel-up button, a painfully familiar, blurred image filled the screen: Vivien Babcock stomping away at the Christmas party, her blouse fluttering out behind her. The image shifted, and there was Eleanor, snapping, "Oh, let her go! That woman's beyond saving."

Then Sam, furious, retorted that no one was beyond saving, and that Eleanor didn't belong there. The sound quality was lousy. Unfortunately, not lousy enough to obscure the words.

"Is this cell-phone video an example of the Christmas spirit, Safe Harbor style?" a newswoman commented gleefully from behind the anchor desk of a TV studio. She briefly recapped the spat as if it were some sort of spectator sport. "Now here's an update."

The screen displayed a photograph of Eleanor. In a staticky recording apparently made over the phone, her patrician voice proclaimed, "I have the assurance of Dr. Mark Rayburn that the hospital is behind me one hundred percent. From now on, Dr. Samantha Forrest no longer has any affiliation with the Serra clinic."

Mark sank back and closed his eyes, wishing he could make this whole business disappear. In his entire career, he'd never had to deal with as much bad publicity as Safe Harbor had suffered in the past four months. First, the misunderstanding about the Safe Haven law had led to multiple baby surrenders, then the press had seized on Sam's silly remarks about beauty makeovers, and now this ridiculous controversy.

Was it him? Was it Sam? Had the medical center inadvertently offended the gods of yellow journalism? He supposed that once the press decided Safe Harbor was newsworthy, any event there got blown out of proportion.

He muted the sound, took out his phone and dialed Sam's number. Mark had no idea if she'd heard the news. If not, he ought to be the one to break it to her. The clinic had been her idea from the start. She'd proposed it, championed it and worked her tail off to make it a reality. She deserved better than to be ousted in a backroom coup, and to learn about it from TV.

Voice mail. Drat!

He sat there fuming. Then, on screen, he saw Sam standing in her driveway, rocking a baby. Looked like Connie, although from this angle he couldn't be sure.

He unmuted the TV. "I've been removed from any role in the clinic's future?" she demanded. "You're sure?"

His heart sank.

The camera shifted to newsman Hayden O'Donnell, his collar raised against the cold. "I'm afraid so. What's your reaction, Dr. Forrest?"

Tensely, she said, "I hope Mrs. Wycliff can put the clinic on solid financial footing." That showed admirable restraint, in Mark's opinion.

"Does the hospital administration have the right to do this?" O'Donnell prodded. "Why do you suppose they kicked the clinic out of its offices in the first place?"

"To make room for their new fertility center, so they can bring in big guns like Dr. Owen Tartikoff." Mark stopped breathing. On the screen, Sam quickly amended, "I mean, someone *like* Dr. Tartikoff."

There was no dissuading the reporter. "Is this true? Dr. Owen Tartikoff is going to head the new fertility center at Safe Harbor?" As Sam remained painfully silent, he addressed the camera. "I think we just got some inside information here, folks. You'll recall that Dr. Tartikoff pioneered a procedure that resulted in the birth of twins to sixty-year-old Olympic gold medalist..."

He went on talking, but Mark didn't hear another word.

He'd carelessly told Sam about Dr. Tartikoff. Pillow talk, that was the term. Now, between them, they'd made a huge mess.

A mess so big he wasn't sure he'd be able to clean it up.

Chapter Sixteen

"I can't imagine that they'll fire you." Lori turned gracefully, her silver wedding gown swishing around her. Open boxes tumbled about her apartment living room, some half-filled in preparation for moving to Jared's house and others displaying gifts. Sam wasn't sure which were Christmas presents and which were for the wedding. Not that it mattered. "Have I lost weight? This feels loose."

"You haven't been eating much the past few months," Sam pointed out, kneeling to check the hem. "Pining away for your lost love. This hangs fine, though. You don't need a tailor unless you're *really* picky."

It felt like forever since September, when they'd shopped together for a gown and dresses. And tasted cakes, and hired a photographer. After the engagement ended, Lori had held on to her dress, which proved fortunate, because she was getting married on short notice.

Sam still fit into her silver-and-blue bridesmaid's dress, and she guessed that Jennifer's probably fit, too. The PR director hadn't been available today, Lori said.

Probably hiding from Sam's temper. Or hanging on to a temper of her own, given that yesterday Sam had likely ruined the hospital's chances of landing the great Dr. Tartikoff.

"I just hope I didn't get Mark into trouble," she said as she straightened. "I feel awful."

"Have you talked to him?" Holding back a hank of reddish-brown hair, Lori leaned over the portable playpen.

"I'm afraid to."

"He hasn't called?"

"Or stopped by, either." Sam shivered. Upset as she'd been, she'd never meant to do anything so destructive. "I emailed him an apology."

"Email? Coward!"

"I texted one, too."

"Just as bad!" Lori eyed the babies. "Hey, I have an idea. Why don't you dress them up as little cupids for the wedding? They're the ones who got Jared and me back together."

"We could hang them from hooks on the church ceiling, and they could flutter overhead during the ceremony," Sam deadpanned.

Lori laughed. "That might be considered child abuse."

"Oh, pooh. They'd probably enjoy it. But wiser heads will prevail."

"Unhook me, will you?" She turned, and Sam performed the honors.

The joy of preparing for a wedding eased the anxiety that had grown since her inexcusable gaffe the previous day. While the disclosure hardly constituted major news, the L.A. press loved celebrity gossip, and Dr. Tartikoff was a celebrity.

In response to the uproar, Jennifer had released a statement saying that the hospital was talking with several distinguished candidates and that nothing had been confirmed. As far as Sam could determine, Dr. T himself remained incommunicado. She hated to think what an uncomfortable situation she'd created for him at his current Boston hospital.

Worst of all, she'd let Mark down. So far, he hadn't said a word to her about it.

Or about anything else.

"Is there a wedding rehearsal?" Sam asked as she helped Lori hang up the beautiful gown on a padded hanger.

"No. Since it's such a small ceremony, the minister offered to tell us what to do right beforehand. I'm just lucky the church was available."

"On a Thursday night? Who'd get married then? I mean, besides you." Sam eased the garment bag over the gown.

"They're booked solid on Friday for New Year's Eve, and on New Year's Day," Lori said. "Some people consider that a lucky time to get married. It was either Thursday or wait until after the first of the year, and we're too impatient."

"Your family must have quite a scramble to come on such short notice." Lori's mother and five sisters lived in Denver.

The bride shook her head. "Only my mom and Louise are coming." That was the next to oldest sister. "The others are tied up with family stuff. They promised to come for the big reception in January."

"I'll look forward to meeting them."

The two women spent the next hour playing with the babies and reviewing plans for decorations and photography, scaled down because of the rush. As Lori noted, she and Jared were saving tons of money, which they'd need for their future children's education.

"You should wait awhile and enjoy each other as a couple," Sam cautioned.

"I agree." Lori knelt on a blanket to change Connie's diaper. "Speaking of couples, what does all this mean for you and Mark? I mean, if he won't even answer your email…"

Sam sighed. "I wish I knew." After the way she'd betrayed his confidence, how could he ever trust her again?

"And what about the clinic? Mrs. Wycliff told you never to darken their doorstep again."

Sam steeled her resolve. "She needs to learn her lesson the hard way."

"What lesson?" Lori returned the baby to the playpen and went into the kitchen to wash her hands.

Since the kitchen opened onto the living room, Sam continued talking. "I'm taking her at her word. Even if it kills me, I'm leaving the clinic to her. Let her find out what it takes to manage the peer counselors, handle emergencies and try to persuade professionals to donate services. Raising money is one thing. Serving as interim director is another. She's unqualified, but she's going to have to discover that for herself."

"You're abandoning the clinic?"

Tears stung at the prospect. Sam blinked them away. "Only temporarily. But I mean it. Hands off."

"You're tough," Lori told her.

"I have to be."

As she cradled Colin on her lap, Sam didn't feel tough. She felt guilty and vulnerable and a bit lost. For once in her life, she didn't have a plan to make things right.

She was almost grateful for Eleanor Wycliff's arrogance. Otherwise, the only person she could be angry with was herself.

BECAUSE CHRISTMAS HAD FALLEN on a Saturday, Monday was considered a holiday, giving most workers a three-day weekend. Mark hadn't scheduled any routine surgeries, which was fortunate, because in between a delivery and an unplanned C-section, he spent most of the morning on the phone.

To members of the press, he issued carefully phrased denials about Dr. Tartikoff. With Eleanor, he listened politely and remained noncommittal as she insisted she was

ready to take on the clinic in any and all capacities. As
for his sister, she hadn't arrived or called. A couple of
times Mark started to dial her number, but each time he
pulled back. Let her make the first move. Let her take responsibility.

His least favorite call was from Chandra, who didn't
believe in taking holidays, either. In fact, he'd reached her
on Sunday and absorbed the brunt of her anger then. It had
cooled, somewhat—or rather, hardened.

"I phoned Owen Tartikoff personally," she announced
when Mark answered. "He's threatening to withdraw from
consideration."

"Only threatening?" That left open a tiny window,
which was more than Mark had expected.

"He'll reconsider if you fire Dr. Forrest as chief of pediatrics and remove her hospital privileges."

A lead weight clamped over his chest. "That's outra-
geous. She's a gifted pediatrician and extremely hardworking. I'm sure she'll be glad to apologize. Privately *and*
publicly if he wishes." Judging by Sam's email and text,
she appreciated how badly she'd screwed up.

"That's not good enough. She has to go."

He couldn't let a personal relationship influence him
on this matter. But Mark considered it his duty to protect
his staff, whether that meant Sam or anyone else. "She
may have a big mouth, but she hasn't harmed patients or
committed any legal or medical errors."

Angry and disappointed as he felt, he saw a vast difference between his former fiancée's drug theft and Sam's
mistake. The first had been calculated and illegal, the second a relatively minor error in judgment.

"She embarrassed us publicly! After the way we
botched this, I doubt anyone of his caliber will look twice
at the fertility center." Her voice bristled.

To keep the peace, Mark refrained from observing

what an exaggeration that was. "Let me talk to Owen myself. I'm sure he'll see things differently once he simmers down." In his experience, people often backed away from ultimatums after a day or so of reflection.

"Simmers down? You're forgetting his reputation."

The man was known for terrorizing nurses and antagonizing coworkers, but Mark had been willing to attribute that to perfectionism. Now, though, doubts bubbled to the surface. Dr. Tartikoff had no business insisting that the hospital fire its head of pediatrics over a verbal blunder. If Owen was that arrogant, he might not be the best choice to head up the new center.

He doubted Chandra would see it that way, however, so he tried a different tack. "Has it occurred to you how it will look if we fire Dr. Forrest under these circumstances? The press will have a field day."

"Then it's your job to persuade her to move on voluntarily," Chandra said. "If she's as outstanding as you say, I'm sure she has plenty of other opportunities."

Sure, but I don't want her to take them. Unthinkable to lose Sam not only as a lover but also as a friend and colleague.

Yet he stopped short of a direct refusal. This position at Safe Harbor had given Mark the chance of a lifetime, to transform a community hospital into a first-rate medical center for women and babies, and the fertility center represented the jewel in the crown. Securing someone of Tartikoff's stature was critical. Two years ago, Mark had made a major life decision to come here, and he wasn't ready to throw away this opportunity without exploring all options.

"I'll discuss it with her," he said into the phone.

"Do this right, Mark."

That, he reflected as he said goodbye, was exactly the point.

DESPITE THE HOLIDAY, SAM SAW patients on Monday morning because kids always managed to get sick on Christmas. She attributed that to a combination of irregular diet, too little sleep and viruses transmitted from person to person at holiday gatherings.

At midafternoon, she wolfed down a sandwich in the hospital cafeteria. About to head for her office on the fourth floor to catch up on paperwork, she saw Mark sitting alone at a table, watching her.

Glad that there was no one around to snoop and stare and gossip, she joined him. Her heart twisted as this man who normally radiated welcome merely lifted a hand in greeting.

It's my own fault. "I'm sorry," Sam replied miserably.

"I know. I got your messages." His voice rang hollowly through the empty cafeteria. "I was just going to call you."

"Did Tartikoff tell you to jump off a cliff?"

"Not exactly."

She saw the conflict in his eyes. He didn't have to say another word. "I'm the sacrificial lamb. Well, I refuse to be forced out. Honestly, Mark! It's not as if I screwed up a diagnosis or was negligent with a patient!"

"I know that," he said quietly.

"I refuse to accept a blot on my record. Getting fired is unreasonable, unfair and a violation of my contract. You know perfectly well I could fight this."

He nodded. "No one's firing you."

"What, then?"

"Chandra asked me to persuade you to leave voluntarily. Sam, it's up to you. I'll fight right alongside you if that's what you want."

On the verge of agreeing, she hesitated. She wanted very much to stay. Not for the counseling clinic, which she seemed unable to save, and not for being chief of pediatrics—heck, she might resign from that position, anyway—but for her patients and friends, and to be around Mark. Mostly, to stay with Mark.

Where could this relationship lead, though? They saw the world from such opposite perspectives that something like this had been bound to happen, sooner or later. If she stayed, it would happen again.

Should she consider her other options? Sam had built a comfortable nest in Safe Harbor, but now that she had children, maybe she ought to consider moving closer to family.

"My brother's been trying for ages to talk me into moving back to Seattle," she said.

"He's a cardiologist, isn't he?"

She nodded. "On the other hand, now that I've finally paid off my student loans, I'd prefer to join my parents in Mexico. It would be great for my kids to live near their grandparents."

"You're sure you're okay with this?" His tone implied that *he* wasn't.

Neither was Sam, yet she ought to be feeling enthusiastic. She'd always planned to make a major contribution to the poor, and here was her chance. So what if she'd miss the life she'd established in Safe Harbor? *I owe a debt to those who're suffering.* Her parents were always talking about the need for more doctors.

"It may take me a few months to work out the legalities with adopting the triplets," she warned. "And I also have to find a pediatrician to take over my practice. But I could make an announcement as soon as I talk to my parents. Maybe right after the first of the year."

He scowled. "I hate this. They have no business forcing you out. I'm the one who leaked sensitive information."

"And I'm the one who shot my mouth off, as usual. Besides, I've always intended to do something like this eventually. And I miss my family." That reminded her. "Speaking of family, did your sister ever get here?"

He shook his head. "I'm a little concerned, but I refuse to climb back on that emotional roller coaster. This time, I'll wait for her to contact me." His brow furrowed as he stared past Sam. "Do you realize it's snowing?"

She glanced out the glass doors to the patio. Sure enough, snowflakes were swirling thickly around deserted tables and chairs. "Wow, that's more than a flurry. It's starting to accumulate. But that never happens in southern California."

"Sure it does. Once or twice a decade."

"Special for us." Sam couldn't believe she was feeling sentimental about snow, but their weekend in the mountains would remain a cherished memory all her life.

Mark's mouth curved into a smile. "Snowballs."

"Oh, come on!"

"Dare you."

She couldn't resist following as he went to open the doors. A blast of chilly air raised goose bumps beneath Sam's sweater, but she didn't care.

Outside, white fluff transformed the nearby hedge and the parking lot beyond it into a scene of pristine beauty. She gazed upward at the unfamiliar sight of snow dusting palm trees.

Crouching by a bush, Mark scraped a thin layer of white into his hands. "Brace yourself."

"Oh, grow up. Just think, we barely missed having a white Christmas. Wouldn't that have been lovely?" Determined not to be outmatched, Sam brushed the snowy accumulation on a tabletop into her own palms and pressed it hard. As soon as she opened her hands, the stuff fell apart. "This won't pack."

"I thought we were supposed to grow up," he reminded her as his own would-be snowball melted in his hand.

"I'll grow up if you will."

Mark tipped his face to the sky. Flakes dappled his dark hair and eyebrows. "I could move to Seattle with you."

"I'm going to Mexico."

"Oh, be a sport. It *never* snows down there."

"Great food, though."

"If you like things spicy."

Sam stopped talking as the snow blotted out the world around them. She loved being isolated with Mark. A week ago, they'd played in the snow and hurried back to the cabin with their arms around each other. If only they could do that again.

Time, stand still. Let me stay here with him.

His cell phone beeped. He glanced at the message. "Delivery."

"I'd better go, too. The paperwork keeps piling up. Whatever made me think I was cut out to be a bureaucrat?" Sam grumbled. "You can replace me as chief of pedes right away. Please."

He slid an arm around her waist. "My pleasure."

"Mark! Anyone can see us."

He kissed the tip of her nose. "Well, they can't accuse me of favoring you, since I'm about to remove you as chief of pediatrics."

His body sheltered hers, warm against the cold, solid against the fragility of snow. "They'll gossip anyway," she said, and touched her lips to his. Immediately, she wanted more.

He lifted his head. "Who cares?" And he proceeded to kiss her thoroughly. They stood there for a while, wrapped up in each other, until his beeper went off.

"Delivery," they both said.

To be discreet, Sam let him go inside ahead of her. When she entered, she saw only a couple of cafeteria workers, whose positions required them to face away from the patio. Lucky break, she supposed.

Sam didn't feel lucky.

She never ran from a challenge, and that was not her intention now. By leaving Safe Harbor she'd be running *to* the kind of commitment she'd always wanted to make. So why was she listening to a selfish inner voice that urged her to stay?

Better tackle those reports awaiting her attention upstairs. She owed a clean desk and an empty in-basket to whoever succeeded her as chief.

On the way, she decided to stop and see if Mark's secretary had his sister's phone number. There was no harm in checking on Bryn, just to be certain she hadn't run into trouble.

Chapter Seventeen

The snowfall amounted to less than an inch, but that was enough to pass for a blizzard in southern California. Although the stuff melted within an hour, the news media provided coverage of freeway jams, farmers struggling to save their citrus and avocado crops, children frolicking and people using hair dryers to deice their front steps. Safe Harbor's latest snafu seemed to be forgotten—except by those who mattered.

True to her word, Sam informed Mark that she'd put in some phone calls about finding a replacement pediatrician and spoken to Tony about fast-tracking the adoption. However, Mark realized that little could be accomplished during this week between Christmas and New Year's, when half the world had gone out of town.

The situation had almost driven the counseling clinic from his mind, until Eleanor stopped by his office late on Thursday afternoon. "I never thought I'd say this, but would you please tell Dr. Forrest I didn't mean to drive her away entirely?"

"You could speak to her yourself." Mark hated to rush this conversation, but he still had to pick up his tuxedo from the cleaners for Jared and Lori's wedding tonight.

"She scares me."

He regarded the aristocratic woman in her designer suit. "You're kidding."

Her chest heaved. "I suppose I'm having trouble acknowledging how high-handed I was. It never occurred to me that, without her, there truly isn't anyone in charge. Clients show up without appointments, peer counselors go on vacation and don't tell anybody, and there's no one to keep a lid on things. I've had to drive down here two days in a row. This is crazy."

"I'll ask her to pitch in." He felt certain Sam would do her best.

Eleanor drummed her fingers on his desk. "I suppose I was unreasonably optimistic about budgeting and staffing. I doubt we'll be able to afford a real director for at least a year. We need Dr. Forrest."

He took a deep breath. "I'm afraid that, at best, she'll only be around for a few more months." He explained about Sam's decision to relocate.

"Is this because of me?" Eleanor asked in dismay.

"It's a lot of things," he said. "She's always intended to work full-time at a low-cost clinic eventually."

"But she's got three children! Has she any idea what an education costs these days?"

"If I could change her mind, I would." Listening to his own words, Mark realized he meant it. And that he'd accepted her decision to leave much too readily.

He loved Safe Harbor Medical Center and everything he'd accomplished in the past couple of years. Even more, he treasured the prospect of what he planned to accomplish in the years to come.

Yet without Sam, all the flavor went out of the place. He couldn't imagine coming to work every day without looking forward to seeing her. Or going home to his sterile house, knowing he'd never hold her in his arms again.

If he wanted to change Sam's mind, he had to do something drastic. And he'd better do it soon.

The problem was, he had no idea how to accomplish that.

AS CO-MAIDS OF HONOR, Sam and Jennifer had been instructed to walk down the aisle side by side. They stood waiting their turn in the church foyer, wearing identical silver-and-blue dresses, Jennifer's dark hair and Sam's blond curls pinned back with matching silvery ornaments. Sam hoped the three-inch difference in their heights didn't look awkward.

Oh, well, who would notice? Lori's auburn splendor and the joy on her face were bound to steal the show.

"Have I apologized enough?" Jennifer asked in a low voice. She and Lori were among the few Sam had told about her decision to leave. "I feel like I helped push you into this."

Sam tried to reassure her friend. "I'm famous for shooting my mouth off. I just did it one time too many." She didn't bother to repeat her contention that she'd always intended either to join her parents in Mexico or work at a similar facility elsewhere. Her closest friends knew that she wouldn't have chosen this particular timing.

Her mom, too, had cautioned her not to make a snap decision. "Not that I wouldn't be thrilled to have you here. Either way, I'm coming to visit my three new grandchildren next month, the first chance I get," she'd added.

The thought of the triplets soothed Sam. They seemed to get stronger and smarter every day. Since they still weren't big enough to sleep through the night, she'd used a referral service to find a nanny who specialized in caring for twins and triplets. Nanny Nancy had started two days ago and was holding down the fort this evening.

Already, she'd organized the house so Sam no lon-

ger banged into furniture and tripped over supplies. The
woman was capable, cheerful and experienced.

Wonder how she'd feel about moving to Mexico.

The music shifted into their cue. "Don't trip," Jennifer advised.

"I wasn't planning to."

"I'm talking to myself, not you."

"Let's hope neither of us trips," Sam suggested.

"Go!" Lori urged from behind.

Silver bells and green-and-silver wreaths gave the small
chapel a wintry charm. In the pews, friendly, familiar
faces greeted them. Tony Franco and his fiancée, Kate.
Ian Martin and nursing director Betsy Raditch. Doctors
and nurses, childbirth educator Tina Torres, secretary May
Chong…people who'd become like family over the past
five years. How could she leave them?

But she had to. Controversy aside, this was what she'd
always meant to do.

Finally, Sam allowed herself to focus on the man standing beside Jared at the altar, studying Sam with a gaze that
could melt chocolate. In that crisp tuxedo, Mark Rayburn
might have been a Mediterranean prince or an old-time
movie star. Or simply the man she loved.

I didn't really admit that, did I?

Her chest tightened as she struggled to come to terms
with her sudden romanticism. It must be the effect of walking down an aisle clutching a bouquet, she told herself
desperately.

What she should have done was paid more attention
to her footing. As she reached the front, she took a misstep, stumbled and might have fallen if Jennifer hadn't
grabbed her arm.

"You promised!" her friend hissed.

"Sorry." Regaining her balance, Sam took her place
beside her fellow maid of honor. When she glanced over

at Mark, she caught the edge of a grin and a small head-shake. *Hopeless*, it said.

She didn't have time to dwell on her clumsiness. The wedding march swelled and, along with the guests, Sam turned her attention to Lori. The bride glowed with happiness as she strolled down the aisle on her mother's arm.

Sam's eyes misted as Lori reached Jared and the couple joined hands in front of the minister. Thank goodness these two people hadn't lost each other, because they obviously belonged together.

Sometimes things worked out the way you hoped. And sometimes, she conceded with a pang, they didn't.

SINCE THE COUPLE HADN'T BEEN able to find an affordable facility at the last minute, the cake-and-champagne reception took place in the hospital's workout room, which was also used for childbirth classes. Lori had assured Mark that she didn't mind, since her "real" reception would be held at a restaurant the following month.

Nevertheless, it was hard to ignore the posters detailing the stages of labor, and another graphically depicting exercises for pregnant women. "I think every couple should have posters like these at their reception," joked Tina, the childbirth instructor.

"I didn't realize they were still going to be up," Lori said tartly. "I may deal with pregnancies every day, but on a personal level, I'd rather not think about it for a few years yet."

Jared gave his new wife a hug. "We can start practicing, though, right?"

"For which part?" she challenged.

"You don't expect me to spell it out here, do you, sweetheart?"

As Lori's cheeks flushed, Mark raised his glass. "I propose a toast. To the couple best qualified of anyone I know to practice for childbirth."

Amid the laughter, he saw a wistful expression fleet across Sam's face. Did she still regret losing the chance to experience pregnancy? But what a blessing to have Colin and Connie and Courtney.

She still had the chance to enjoy every step of parenthood. As for Mark, he'd felt thousands of babies move inside their mothers, seen them on ultrasounds, and listened to their heartbeats. He'd never minded that he didn't get to keep any of them.

He minded now. How could he let the triplets grow up without him?

Jennifer appeared at his side. "I just got an alert about a website you ought to see."

"We're both off duty," he protested.

"I still get alerts on my cell phone. This one concerns Dr. Tartikoff."

The name no longer inspired enthusiasm. More like antipathy. "Oh?"

"He's been selected scientist of the year." A prestigious journal had just announced the honor, she explained as she brought up the magazine's website on her phone. Reluctantly, Mark accepted the device and scanned the story, which could only make matters worse as far as the corporate owners were concerned. Now they'd want him more than ever.

A flattering photo made Tartikoff look like a TV star. Mark was less impressed with the interview, in which the doctor went on at great length about the latest developments in manipulating DNA to eliminate genetic diseases. While he hadn't pioneered the techniques, a reader might get that impression from the way the guy boasted about his stellar record with patients.

Sour grapes on my part. But Mark had to admit he'd

still love to have Owen's name attached to the fertility center.

Chandra had told the doctor of Sam's willingness to leave, but so far he'd made no decision. After this coup, Mark supposed offers would flood in from all over the globe. How ironic if they lost Dr. Tartikoff, anyway.

He returned the phone to Jennifer. "That's quite an honor. Thanks for showing it to me."

That night, Mark slept badly. He tossed and kicked off the sheets and felt angry at everyone. *Okay, so Owen's a genius. But who's the administrator of this damn hospital, anyway?*

Mark didn't intend to spend the next few years catering to the fellow's ego or his touchy temperament. Professional respect had to cut both ways. Three ways—to Samantha, as well.

Regardless of her claim that she wanted to join her parents in Mexico, she was being forced out. Taking Mark's joy and sense of purpose with her.

Maybe eventually he'd regain his dedication to the hospital. Maybe he'd find satisfaction in landing an incredibly gifted and innovative surgeon for his staff, whether Dr. Tartikoff or someone else. But it wasn't enough.

By the time he dozed off at last, he'd come to a difficult decision.

Mark spent much of Friday morning making notes on what he wanted to say to Chandra, then deleted all of them. On impulse, he pulled up the website from last night and reread the article. Spotting an option for reader comments, he clicked over to scan them.

Amid a profusion of posts, many lauded Dr. T's accomplishments. Others took a less pleasant tone, including several that accused him of playing God. A nurse who claimed to be a former coworker called him arrogant to the point of cruelty. A former patient contended he'd unsuccessfully pushed her into high-tech procedures, and that, later, another doctor had helped her get pregnant with simpler and less costly techniques.

Suddenly Mark knew what he wanted to say. Not to the corporation vice president, but to Owen himself.

He put in a call, and got the man's voice mail. Too impatient to delay, Mark left a message that might very well end his career at Safe Harbor.

SAM WASN'T SURE WHEN PEOPLE had fallen into the habit of calling the entire day of December 31 "New Year's Eve." As far as she was concerned, the evening didn't begin until after five. To her, Friday was just another workday.

She spent the morning seeing patients, then took her nurse to lunch and broke the news that she might be leaving but would make sure her staff still had jobs.

"I hate—who is it I'm supposed to hate?" Devina demanded. "Who did this?"

"I always planned…"

"Yes, yes, the suffering poor." Her nurse waved a perfectly manicured hand. How she managed to keep those nails beautifully shaped and polished despite the demands of her profession was the subject of speculation among her coworkers. "This is a terrible idea."

"I appreciate your support." Sam waited while a waiter wearing Papa Giovanni's white-and-red-trimmed green uniform refilled her glass.

Devina sniffed a piece of garlic bread and set it aside. An obsessive calorie watcher, she claimed to satisfy her cravings that way. "Dr. Tartikoff should think about which doctor is going to take care of the babies *after* they're born. What does he imagine, that he brings them into the world and they disappear into a cloud of happiness? He's only a small part of their lives."

"I doubt that idea ever pierced his ego." Sam was going

to miss her nurse. Just being around Devina lightened her spirits.

"He'd better not cross my path." Her nurse stabbed a single tortellini with her fork. "I hear he reduces his nurses to tears. Huh."

"Good thing you're a pedes nurse so you won't have to work with him."

Devina chewed and swallowed carefully. "Don't leave, Samantha. You belong here."

Sam felt that way, too, even though her higher self told her otherwise.

After lunch, she gave her staff the rest of the day off. In her medical building office, Sam clicked through emails, glad to get this chore out of the way. Once she collected the babies for the holiday, she wanted to devote her full attention to them.

A message from Mark's sister apologized for being short when Sam called earlier in the week. "I'm sorry I was defensive. Like I said, I'll drive out there one of these days and surprise my brother. I spent Christmas with my mentor, dealing with old guilt feelings. I know I let Mark down. I'm really good at that, aren't I? I haven't even worked up the nerve to apologize yet."

"Don't let guilt rule your life," Sam wrote back. "We're all guilty of something. Put it behind you. Happy New Year."

She returned to scrolling. Near the end of the email queue, a message line caught her eye. "From Artie Ortega's family."

Before she could read it, the phone rang. It was the nursery.

"Your daughters don't seem well," the worker said. "Could you come over and check on them?"

Sam's heart leaped into her throat. "Right away," she said, and instantly forgot everything else.

Chapter Eighteen

Having put his job in jeopardy, Mark did something else uncharacteristic: he left work early on New Year's Eve to go shopping.

There were, he saw as he cruised the residential streets of Safe Harbor, no yard sales on holidays. He did, however, find a thrift store that hadn't closed yet.

Fortified with a couple of purchases, he drove to Sam's house. Before leaving the hospital, he'd learned that she'd taken the triplets home, so he knew she must be there. The day care worker had also mentioned that Connie and Courtney suffered from colds. Good thing they had a pediatrician for a mother.

He parked in front of her bungalow. A strand of colored lights blinked at him flirtatiously, slightly off synch with the neighbor's flashier display.

Mark had no idea when he'd fallen in love with Samantha. But after he left the message for Owen and sat there hoping with all his heart that somehow he'd find a way to keep her on staff, he'd realized the "somehow" wasn't enough.

Well, here he was. Nervous, but too impatient to delay.

He got out of his car. Since he could hear the babies crying, he didn't have to worry about waking them, so he gave the bell a jab.

"It's open!" called a thick voice that sounded like Samantha's.

Mark cracked open the door to a blast of moist air and the scent of pine. "Hello? It's me."

"Over here." She sat on the couch, her face puffy and red as if from crying. Blond hair straggled every which way, some of it stuck behind her ears, some sweeping over the baby cradled in her arms. Her jogging suit bore splashes of formula.

From an inside room, he heard the other two triplets fussing. While he considered it unlikely that a trio of babies with head colds could have reduced Sam to such a state, Mark didn't stop to quiz her. First things first. "Do the kids have temperatures?"

"Low grade," she told him. "Just the girls."

He set the thrift-store bag on an end table. "Coughing and sneezing?"

"Yes."

"Leave this to me."

Half an hour later, Colin—the easiest of the three to deal with today—was fed, diapered and asleep. Courtney, who'd been in Sam's arms, had also been settled in bed, her congestion eased by saline nose drops and a cool-mist vaporizer.

His specialty might not be pediatrics, but Mark kept up with the latest research and agreed with Sam's decision to avoid over-the-counter medications. These didn't work well and in newborns could have dangerous side effects, such as thinning mucus into fluids that might literally drown a baby.

Sam was feeding the last of the trio a bottle as Mark settled in a chair. On the Christmas tree, the cherub dolls watched with painted smiles and sad eyes.

"Now tell me what's wrong," he said.

She indicated a wrinkled sheet of paper beside her.

When he picked it up, he saw that she'd printed out an email. The subject line mentioned Artie Ortega, the young cancer patient from the Christmas party.

His parents wrote that he had died three days after Christmas.

"Thanks to friends like you, our son had the happiest childhood a little boy could ask for. He was an angel and an inspiration in our lives, and he will be with us always."

Like most doctors, Mark tried to distance himself from the fact that, no matter how much you wanted to heal the world, sometimes you failed. But Artie was twelve years old. It shouldn't happen.

"I'm sorry." He wiped away a tear of his own.

Sam blew into a tissue. "Well, that's my news for the day."

"I have some, too."

She regarded him questioningly.

"I just told Owen Tartikoff...well, I more or less told him where to get off." He swallowed. "I said I'm not running a tyranny that penalizes caring and dedicated physicians like you. I said you may be leaving over this, and that in my opinion, it's as much a blow to this hospital as losing him would be."

She adjusted the baby's bottle. "How'd he react?"

"I have no idea. I had to leave a message." Mark described the comments he'd read on the website and explained, "I reminded him that innovative fertility treatments are bound to generate controversy. Does he really want to work with an administrator who cuts and runs in a storm? Because if he does, he's a fool."

Sam had stopped crying. "Did you clear this with Chandra?"

"Nope." What was the point? No matter what she'd said, he'd have done this anyway.

Her forehead puckered. "That was risky. I don't suppose she'd fire you but…"

"I don't care if she does."

"Liar!"

He refused to worry about that. Besides, he had other, more pressing business to deal with. "Do you realize nobody holds yard sales on New Year's Eve? How inconvenient."

She set down the bottle. "Why do you care? You won the bet about your sister."

"But I never collected my kiss. So I figured *one* of us ought to come out ahead." Before she could question his logic, he fished his purchase from the bag and handed it to her. "How's this?"

With an air of wonder, she held up the glass candy dish shaped like a swan and studied the light filtering through the shades of blue. "It's lovely. Thank you."

"It's only a reproduction, according to the clerk," Mark said. "She mentioned something called Depression glass. I was too embarrassed to admit I had no idea what that is." Since Sam was having trouble manipulating both baby and bowl, he transferred the blanket to his shoulder and lifted Connie gently.

"During the Great Depression, companies used to give away cheap glassware to lure buyers," Sam explained. "Manufacturers put pieces in boxes of cereal, and movie theaters handed them out to ticket buyers. They've become popular with collectors." From the center of the bowl, she removed a small item wrapped in newspaper. "What's this?"

"Open it." His hands prickled.

From the paper, she plucked a rainbow-hued glass ring. "This is beautiful. What's it for?"

Now, Mark. "Will you marry me?"

Sam regarded him questioningly. "Are you serious?"

"I love you. Whatever we're doing and wherever we're going, let's do it together. Our future shouldn't depend on other people's decisions." He couldn't put it any more plainly than that.

She gave him a wry, tender smile. "I never pictured myself getting a proposal wearing old sweats covered with baby spit-up."

"I hope that's a yes," Mark said.

When she shook her head, his heart squeezed. "I can't do this to you. Mark, you'd never be happy working at a small clinic."

He refused to give in, because he knew, more certainly than he'd ever known anything, that getting married was the right course for them both. "Just say yes and we'll figure out the details later."

Sam sank back against the cushions. "I'm in no condition to give you an answer right now. Can you be patient with me?"

"Of course." After a beat, he added, "For how long?"

"That's your idea of being patient?"

"You love me. Admit it."

Sam's gaze fell on the email. She stroked the paper lightly. "Tell me something I don't understand. Why did he die and I lived?"

She must be thinking of her own battle with cancer, Mark realized. "You mean, when you were a kid?"

She nodded. "I made friends in the cancer ward. A girl a few years older than me, and a boy about Artie's age. We'd buck each other up. Joke about our bald heads. Plan reunions for when we got better."

She didn't have to spell it out. "Both of them died?"

"The same week." Fresh tears dampened her cheeks. "I nearly gave up. I *did* give up. I went to bed and cried for days. I got mad at God, and felt sorry for myself, and missed my friends. It was all so wrong. Ironically, my own treatment was going well, but why did I deserve that?"

"Survivor's guilt." Mark had run across the syndrome in his practice. Patients who'd lost loved ones, even in circumstances where they were blameless, sometimes questioned why they deserved to live.

"My mom pulled me out of it," Sam continued. "She sat on the edge of the bed and told me I'd been spared for a reason. That I had the gift of healing. While I was always patching up animals and giving first-aid to my friends, I hadn't been sure I could handle medical school. After that day, I had no doubt. I was spared so I could save other lives."

"And you'll go right on doing that," Mark said. "Wherever you decide to practice."

Sam clutched the paper. "I've been far luckier than I deserve. Yes, it was a blow learning about early menopause, but then I was handed these wonderful babies. I can't go on being selfish, indulging in a cozy job, a comfortable income, a nice house. I have to remember why I was kept alive."

"Marrying me does not amount to thumbing your nose at fate," Mark countered.

She gazed at him tearily. "You're the most wonderful man I've ever met, but living my way would make you miserable."

He disagreed with every cell in his body. On the other hand, she'd been right about being in no condition to make a life-changing commitment.

"Give the idea a chance to sink in. We'll talk about this later." Since Connie had started squirming in his arms, Mark went and put the baby in her cradle. He paused to watch the three little ones sleeping, their breathing steady against the hum of the vaporizer. *I'm not letting you go. Or your mom, either.*

Standing there, he asked himself a hard question: Was he prepared to move to Mexico to keep them? Could he give up the joy of running a hospital, of building new programs for the future, of harnessing the latest technology? Could he spend his days treating ailments in a struggling clinic, and his nights living in near-poverty?

Maybe for a while. But after that?

Marriage required finding a way to keep them both happy. Sam was right about that.

Well, this was New Year's Eve. In a new year, all things were possible.

He went and broke a twig off the Christmas tree. "What's that for?" Sam asked sleepily.

"My prize. It's not exactly mistletoe, but it's close enough." Holding it above her head, he sat on the couch and claimed his kiss.

THE MONDAY AFTER NEW YEAR'S was a holiday, and, of course, Mark went to the hospital anyway. Delivered babies, cheered the staff members who had to work and stewed about his inability to nail down Sam's agreement to marry him.

They'd spent the weekend together and walked to work today, taking turns pushing the babies in a double-decker triplet pram that her brother had sent for Christmas. To his amusement, they'd spotted some yard sale signs but there hadn't been time to do more than glance at the objects displayed on tables and blankets. In any case, he'd glimpsed nothing much in the way of glassware.

"I do plan to buy a real ring, you know," he'd commented to Sam as they approached the medical center.

"That isn't the issue, Mark. As you well know, you big gorgeous lug." She'd kissed him, and never mind who might see. He rather regretted the discovery afterward that there hadn't been any witnesses.

Today, he wouldn't at all mind stirring up a bit of scandal. Mark the peacemaker, Mark the master of the artful compromise, really wanted to take a poke at somebody. He just had to figure out who.

Certainly not the woman who walked into his office early that afternoon. A tuft of pure white had replaced the sprinkling of gray in his sister's dark hair, but her skin had a healthy glow and her tremulous smile revealed teeth a lot whiter than when he'd last seen her.

"Sorry I'm late," Bryn said.

THAT MORNING, THERE WAS ONLY a trickle of patients. Sam used the extra time to clear out old papers that had accumulated in her desk drawers. Then, eating a sandwich at her desk, she started riffling through the box of holiday cards. Once she finished with each, she set it aside for children's craft projects at the day care center.

As always, the notes and photos warmed her. A gawky boy she'd treated for severe acne stood proudly in his high school graduation robes, his skin clear. His mother thanked Sam for referring him to a dermatologist. "I didn't know it then, but he was so depressed he'd considered suicide," she wrote. "Until you told us, I had no idea that medication might cure him. Thank you from the bottom of my heart."

A bad complexion might not pose as dramatic a threat as cancer, Sam mused, but it could have a profound effect on the patient. Tucking the note into a personal file of keepers, she read on.

"SAM CALLED YOU?" MARK ASKED as he absorbed his sister's explanation that she'd spent Christmas with her mentor, fighting feelings of despair and self-loathing.

"Dr. Forrest told me to stop letting guilt run my life. Which is basically what my mentor said, but somehow it

felt different, coming from a friend of yours." Bryn faced
him across a cafeteria table after a late lunch.

"That's interesting, considering that Sam lets guilt run
her life," Mark observed drily. But since he didn't feel right
discussing Sam's issues with Bryn, he said, "I still don't
understand why you didn't email or call."

"Oh, Mark." When she shook her head, crystal ear-
rings flashed. She'd loaded on the costume jewelry, an
effect their mother would have dismissed as gaudy. Now
that he'd developed an appreciation for Depression glass,
however, he enjoyed the glitter. "You have no idea how
intimidating you are."

"Me?" That didn't fit his image of himself. "I never
yelled at you, did I?"

"You didn't have to," his sister said ruefully. "I hated
hearing that cranky edge to your voice. I felt like, if I ever
pushed you hard enough, you might explode."

"Maybe I should have exploded more often," Mark
mused. "Would that have helped?"

"Nothing would have helped." Bryn's mouth twisted
ironically. "I had to do this on my own, one step at a time."

"Apparently you've succeeded," he said with approval.

"I'm an alcoholic. I'll always have to be careful." She
paused as a couple of nurses, sauntering past with their
trays, paused to greet Mark.

He made introductions and was grateful that they didn't
linger. Once he and Bryn were alone, he picked up the
thread of the conversation. "You're right. There's no cure
for addiction, but it can be controlled."

"Coming here is a big step," she admitted. "I want you
to understand how sorry I am for what I put you through.
You're the best friend I ever had. You cared more about
me than anyone, maybe even our parents. And I repaid
you by acting like a jerk."

"I forgive you." Now that she sat in front him, this

woman he remembered through so many stages of her childhood and adolescence, he felt only gratitude for her recovery.

"Do you really?"

"To prove it, I'm going to take the rest of the day off. You said you don't have to leave till tomorrow morning, right?" He had an idea how they might celebrate their reunion.

She nodded. "I worked New Year's Eve, so I get an extra day off."

"You used to enjoy playing laser tag," he recalled.

"Still do."

"Well?" he said. "What're we waiting for?" Then he added, "There is one stop I'd like to make on the way."

"I hope it's to meet Samantha."

"You're way ahead of me."

SAM WAS BARELY HALFWAY through the accumulation of cards when Mark stopped by to make introductions. She immediately liked his sister's straightforward manner. In Sam's experience, people who'd come to terms with their own failings didn't waste energy on pretenses. They simply accepted others as they had learned to accept themselves.

"I hope I'm not interrupting any plans you guys had for this evening," Bryn told her. "We could all get together if you like."

"With three screaming infants?" This was Nanny Nancy's night off. "I'll let you enjoy your evening together." Mark had explained that Bryn planned to drive back to Phoenix first thing tomorrow.

"Thanks." He gave Sam a look full of tenderness. "For encouraging Bryn to contact me and for that excellent advice you gave her."

She wasn't sure what he meant. "Advice?"

"About guilt." He left it at that and guided his sister toward the door.

"I hope I get a chance to know you better," Bryn added. "Next visit, okay?"

"Absolutely." *But it had better come in the next month or so, because after that I'll be gone.*

Sam's chest tightened at the thought. Despite her attempts to whip up some enthusiasm, she hated the idea of leaving Safe Harbor.

If she married Mark, Bryn would be her sister-in-law. Sam pictured them all gathered around his living room or at the cabin, laughing as the triplets toddled and plopped on the floor.

No. Erase that image.

She'd be somewhere else, doing what she was meant to do. After all, how many people were lucky enough to have a mission in life as significant as hers?

Wistfully, she went back to reading, but didn't get far before her phone rang. "Dr. Forrest."

In the split second before the caller replied, she heard a girl's voice in the background say, "Mom! Quit eating all the fudge."

"I'm only testing it" came a crisp voice. "Sorry. This is Eleanor Wycliff."

"Happy New Year." That seemed a civil greeting, which was the best Sam could do. She and Eleanor hadn't crossed paths since their fencing match in the media a week earlier.

"Mark told me that you're leaving and I think it's ridiculous. Please stay. I hope you'll continue as the clinic's adviser, too. We need you."

"I'm sorry—I can't," Sam said.

A long sigh. "I was afraid you'd say that, but I hoped…" Eleanor broke off, and in the background Sam heard her daughter say, "Tell her about Vivien."

"What about Vivien?" Sam asked.

Eleanor gave a dry chuckle. "I stopped by the shelter to see Mrs. Babcock and apologize for being rude to her. I won't say that I like her, but she's much more tolerable when she's sober. Thanks for showing me that even people who lack social skills deserve sympathy."

"You're welcome." If Eleanor was mature enough to apologize for her mistakes, the clinic wasn't in such bad hands after all.

"Now, I have another request. If you insist on leaving, at least keep guiding us long-distance. Answer our questions and keep us focused on why the clinic was established in the first place."

Sam's mood lifted at the notion that she didn't have to give up all contact with the project. "I'd be happy to consult by phone or email."

"That's wonderful."

"Remember the slogan" came Libby's voice over the clang of a pot.

"Watch where you put that, dear!" her mother said. Back to Sam, she explained, "We've decided we need a slogan. Something to keep the staff, volunteers and clients in a positive frame of mind. Any ideas?"

A slogan? "That's more Jennifer's area than mine."

"She suggested Optimism in the face of adversity, then shortened it to, Think positive, but I'd prefer something with more snap."

"I'll let it simmer in my brain." Perhaps one of the cards would provide inspiration.

After the call, pleased to have made peace with Eleanor, Sam resumed reading. A young mother thanked her for a referral to counseling to treat her depression. She also heard from a girl with curvature of the spine, who now stood straight and was training to become a dancer. A mother wrote that her autistic son, referred for early intervention, had improved enough by age five to enroll in a regular kindergarten.

By the time she finished, Sam ached with longing to stay here in this place where she'd done so much good. But her higher and better self responded with a resounding "no."

Although it was only midafternoon, she felt too restless to linger. Pushing the stroller home through the crisp air ought to clear her mind and perhaps help her come up with a slogan for Eleanor.

If not, at least she could stop at yard sales and indulge in a little shopping.

Chapter Nineteen

Mark's urge to give someone a sharp poke, which had gone into hibernation during his sister's visit, came roaring back early Tuesday morning when he realized Owen Tartikoff still hadn't returned his call. Annoyed, he dialed the man's number in Boston.

"Tartikoff," came the curt response.

"This is Mark Rayburn. In case you didn't get my message..."

"I got it," the man said. "Let me be sure I understand correctly. You consider Dr. Forrest as much an asset to Safe Harbor as I would be."

"That's about the size of it."

"I'll take the job."

Having braced for an argument, Mark tried to make sense of Owen's words. "You're accepting the position as director of the fertility center?"

"Unless you've changed your mind about offering it to me."

"Welcome aboard." Mark struggled to bring his reaction in line with this unexpected development. "When can you start?"

"I have a contract to fulfill here, so I won't be able to come full-time until next summer. But we can get started implementing policy." As they agreed on a timetable, Mark wondered whether to ask what had influenced Owen's decision. The new director saved him the trouble. "I admire a man or woman who can stand up to me. In the long run, it leads to better outcomes. I look forward to working with you and to meeting this fire-breathing pediatrician."

"We're excited to have you join us." Mark decided against mentioning that Sam seemed resolved to leave. Or that he, too, might depart.

"Shall I give Ms. Yashimoto a call with my decision?" the fertility specialist asked.

"I'll handle that." Mark had a piece of business to settle with Chandra, as well. After a bit more discussion with Owen, he put through a call to the vice president and, when she answered, broke the news about Tartikoff.

"That's fantastic!" Her voice registered relief. "How on earth did you pull this off?"

"I stood up to him," Mark said. "And that's the second reason I'm calling you. It's about the chain of command."

"Excuse me?"

"You shouldn't have called him in the first place. The corporation hired me as hospital administrator, and that means I'm the person Owen reports to. I don't want him going over my head every time there's a disagreement."

A long silence greeted his remarks. Finally, she said, "I didn't mean to undercut your authority, but this project is of the utmost importance."

"I thought the hospital as a whole was of the utmost importance," he answered coolly. "*Including* the fertility center."

"Well, of course."

Might as well go for broke. "I should warn you that I'm considering leaving when Dr. Forrest does. She and I may be taking on a new challenge together." That was a stretch, since Sam hadn't agreed to any such thing, but Mark was in no mood to pull his punches.

Chandra gasped. "Mark, we can't afford to lose you."

"I suspect that's an exaggeration." He'd expended far too much energy these past months mediating between Chandra and his staff— Sam in particular—to fall for idle compliments.

"You have no idea what a brilliant job you're doing. Safe Harbor is our flagship hospital. One of our other hospitals is in bad shape due to poor leadership, and a couple of others are struggling. You're even more important to us than Dr. Tartikoff." Chandra spoke in a rush, with no sign of her usual calculation. "I hope you'll reconsider, Mark. And Dr. Forrest, as well. We'd like for her to stay in any capacity you deem fit."

Hmm. Interesting. "I'll take that into consideration."

"Naturally we'll be raising both your salaries by ten percent," Chandra added.

Even more interesting. "Much appreciated. I'll get back to you soon."

After hanging up, Mark sat staring out the window toward the harbor. He loved this view and he'd really hate to abandon it.

Now for the tough part: persuading Sam to stay.

A tap at the door ushered in Eleanor Wycliff. "Good morning," she said, far too cheerily for someone who'd presumably driven all the way from Beverly Hills in what he'd heard on the radio was heavy postholiday traffic. "How do you like the clinic's new slogan?" She indicated a bright yellow lapel button bearing a prominent single word: Yes!

"Excellent." Mark tried to show more interest than he felt. Right now the clinic was the least of his concerns.

"Dr. Forrest found a box of them at a yard sale yesterday," Eleanor continued. "Well, I won't keep you. Ciao!"

After she'd gone, he reflected on the fact that he and Sam had been offered substantial raises. What a shame to give those up. Still, she'd never let money influence her decision.

He was marshalling his arguments when Lori popped in. "Just a reminder that you have patients scheduled this morning."

Mark checked his watch. "In half an hour. I'm aware of that, thanks."

She tapped her own Yes! button. "I like the clinic's new slogan so much, I thought I'd wear one, too."

"I hope you sanitized it. I understand they came from a yard sale."

"Grouch." Quickly, she added, "Yes, I did."

Something occurred to Mark. "Wait a minute. Shouldn't you be on your honeymoon?"

"Jared couldn't reschedule his duties on such short notice, so we took a long weekend in Palm Springs," the nurse answered. "Anyway, I wouldn't miss this."

"Miss what?"

She gave him a broad smile and ducked out. He imagined her grin still hanging in midair, as if she were the Cheshire cat.

What was going on?

Then Sam came in. "Hi." She pointed to her yellow Yes! button.

"Good morning." Mark took a deep breath. "I have good news."

"Oh?" She quirked one of her amazing eyebrows. The gesture seemed to convey a world of meaning, but at the moment, he had no idea what it was.

"Dr. Tartikoff's going to be joining our staff. Also, Chandra wants you to stay at Safe Harbor and she's offered us both ten percent raises."

"What's the punch line?" Sam asked. She looked particularly lovely today, he observed, with her hair curling seductively around the shoulders of her tweed suit. He'd missed walking to work with her this morning, but he'd wanted to have breakfast with Bryn.

"No punch line. I'm serious."

"Good thing." She indicated her button again.

"I like the new slogan," Mark said politely.

"It's also the answer to your question."

Which question? "Refresh my memory."

She held up her left hand. The rainbow ring, adapted to fit with a thick Band-Aid, clung to her third finger. "That question."

When Mark started to rise, his knees defied him, and he sank down again. "You'll marry me?"

"I love you. Whatever we're doing and wherever we're going, let's do it together."

"That's the most brilliant thing I ever heard." This time, he propelled himself upright and strode around the desk.

"Actually, you said it." Sam reached for him. "I was quoting you."

"I did? I must be a genius." He gathered her in his arms, exactly where she belonged.

"I finally figured out," she murmured, "that I shouldn't let defying death take over my life."

"You're a genius, too."

"And since you'd be monstrously unhappy in a small clinic, I've decided to stay here." She nuzzled the curve of his throat. "As long as I'm getting a ten percent raise."

Mark breathed in the scent of baby powder and peppermint. A practical woman, his future wife. "I'm glad you dressed for the occasion, by the way. You're smashing."

"I had to erase that image of myself receiving a proposal in sweats and baby spit-up."

He wanted to be sure she wouldn't regret this. "What about that dream of yours? The idea that you were saved for a reason?"

"I still believe that," Sam replied. "The thing is, I kept

saying no to my own instincts. After I bought these buttons, I felt them nagging at me all night. Finally I got the
message about saying yes. That I can save the world one
child at a time just as well right here in Safe Harbor."

Mark kissed her for a very long while. Not as long as
he'd have liked, though, because he heard giggling and
whispering in the outer office. Reluctantly, he lifted his
head. "What now?"

Catching his hand in hers, Sam stepped back and called
out, "Okay, guys."

Lori entered first, with Eleanor and Jennifer right behind. "Can we pop the champagne now?" his nurse asked.
"It's really sparkling apple juice."

"Please do." As Eleanor twisted off the lid, Mark didn't
even mind that Sam had told her friends about her decision before she'd told him. Otherwise, how could she have
arranged this celebration?

"I had my fingers crossed for you both," Jennifer added.

"Was there any doubt about how I'd react?" Mark had
already proposed, after all.

Lori poured juice carefully into plastic champagne
flutes. "With the two of you, we never can tell."

Come to think of it, neither could he.

ON A BALMY MORNING IN February, Dr. Mark Rayburn
and Dr. Samantha Forrest set out on foot from their large
home on a cul-de-sac. While he lowered the oversize
stroller to the walkway, she locked the door on the once-
austere house, which seemed much friendlier now that it
was stuffed with a flowery sofa and chairs, baby furniture
and a collection of colored glassware.

Dr. Rayburn and Dr. Forrest, who had discussed merg-
ing their names when they said their vows but decided
Rayburn-Forrest would be too much of a mouthful, enjoyed the salty breeze that blew from the ocean and the

early spring flowering of pansies, snapdragons and primroses in the yards they passed.

A couple of times, they stopped to tug a blanket into place over one of the triplets, who were getting feistier every day, much like their parents. And occasionally the two doctors' voices rang out in cheerful disagreement about some policy or other. But when they neared the complex, their steps quickened as they eagerly anticipated their arrival at Safe Harbor Medical Center.

This was—and for a very long time into the future would surely remain—*their* hospital.

* * * * *

THE SEAL'S
CHRISTMAS TWINS

LAURA MARIE ALTOM

After college (Go, Hogs!), bestselling, award-winning author **Laura Marie Altom** did a brief stint as an interior designer before becoming a stay-at-home mum to boy/girl twins and a bonus son. Always an avid romance reader, she knew it was time to try her hand at writing when she found herself re-plotting the afternoon soaps.

When not immersed in her next story, Laura teaches art at a local middle school. In her free time she beats her kids at video games, tackles Mount Laundry and, of course, reads romance!

Laura loves hearing from readers at either PO Box 2074, Tulsa, OK 74101, USA, or by e-mail, BaliPalm@aol.com.

Love winning fun stuff?
Check out www.lauramariealtom.com.

This story is dedicated to my fellow 'professional dieters.' May someday soon scientists develop fat-free cheesecake that actually tastes of creamy, gooey goodness as opposed to cardboard!

Chapter One

"Wait—she's *dead?*" Navy SEAL Mason Brown covered his right ear so he could hear the caller. His team was at Virginia Beach's joint base, Fort Story, immersed in close quarters combat training. If his CO caught him on his cell, there'd be hell to pay. Just in case, he locked himself in a bathroom and crossed his fingers to not lose his already-shoddy signal. "Come again. I'm sure I didn't fully hear you."

"M-Mason, I'm sorry, but you heard me right. Melissa and Alec died. Their plane went down, and…" Hattie's voice was drowned out by the sort of electric, adrenaline-charged hum he usually only experienced at the height of combat. No way was this real. There had to be a mistake, because even though his ex-wife had betrayed him in the worst possible way, even though there'd been thousands of miles between them, he couldn't imagine life without her at least sharing the planet. "I'm sorry to break this to you over the phone, but with you so far away…"

"I get it." What he didn't get was his reaction. Melissa had cheated on him with his old pal Alec six years ago. So why had his limbs gone numb to the point he leaned against the closed bathroom door, sliding down, down until his carefully constructed emotional walls shattered, leaving him feeling raw and exposed and maybe even a little afraid.

"Mason, I know this is probably the last thing you want to hear at a time like this, but Melissa and Alec's lawyer needs to see you. He says you're in the will, and—"

"Why would I be in the will?" He clamped his hand to his forehead.

"I don't know. He wanted to call you, but I asked him to let me. I didn't want this kind of news coming from a stranger."

Isn't that essentially what we are? Though he and Hattie used to be tight, once he and Melissa split, Melissa had taken custody of the rest of her family, as well. In Divorce Land, wasn't that the natural order?

"Mason? Will you come?"

He groaned.

Just beyond the bathroom's far wall, gunfire popped like firecrackers. That was his world. Had been for a nice, long while and he felt comfortable here in Virginia. Back in his hometown of Conifer, Alaska, he was a pariah— which still burned his hide, considering he'd been the wounded party.

"Mason? I don't know why, but Melissa's lawyer's adamant you be present at the reading of her will."

Pop, pop, pop. Considering the fire knotting in his stomach, those shots might as well have been to his gut. "Yeah," he finally muttered. "I'll be there."

THURSDAY NIGHT, Hattie Beaumont volunteered for pickup duty. Her mother was too grief-stricken to leave her bed after having just lost her eldest daughter to a plane crash. Her dad wasn't faring much better. Glad to be inside and out of the blustery October wind, Hattie lugged her sister's five-month-old twins to the nearest row of chairs in Conifer's airport terminal—newly constructed after the old one collapsed following a heavy snowfall.

River-stone columns now supported the vaulted ceiling of the otherwise modest space that housed three regional airlines, two charter air companies, one rental-car agency, a coffee bar, sundries shop and diner.

At nine, everything was closed. Only three other parties waited for the night's last incoming flight from Anchorage.

The infants, finally sleeping in their carriers, had been heavy, but not near as heavy as the pain squeezing Hattie's heart.

Her sister Melissa's husband's twin-engine Cessna had gone down in bad weather on Tuesday. Alec died upon impact, but Melissa lived long enough for a search-and-rescue team to get her to an Anchorage hospital, where she'd passed Wednesday morning.

The realization that her sister was well and truly gone hadn't quite sunk in. It felt more like a nightmare from which she couldn't wake.

Alec's parents, Taylor and Cindy, understandably hadn't taken the news well. They'd retired in Miami, and it was their flight she was meeting. They planned to be in town until Saturday's double funeral. After that, Hattie wasn't sure of their plans—or anyone's plans for that matter. Would her parents and Alec's share custody of the twins?

Covering her face with her hands, Hattie fought a fresh wave of the nausea that she hadn't been able to shake since she'd first heard the news of Melissa's accident. Granted, people of all ages died all the time. Funerals were a sad fact of life, but having a close family member die didn't seem possible.

Then there was Mason…

Yeah. She'd table thoughts of him for another time. Too much history. *Way* too much pain on top of an already-crushing amount of grief.

Steeling herself for her eventual reunion with him at her sister's funeral, then again at Sunday's reading of the will, Hattie was thankful that she wouldn't have to see him until then. Despite the fact that she'd had years apart from him to think of what she might say should she ever see him again, she still couldn't quite string together the words.

How was she supposed to act around the one guy she'd secretly adored? The guy who hadn't just gotten away, but had married and divorced her sister?

Minutes elongated into what felt like hours.

She tried playing a game on her phone but, after losing a dozen times, gave up.

Finally, the drone of the twin-engine Piper Chieftain taxiing to the passenger offloading area signaled the near-end of her grueling night. She doubted she'd even be able to sleep, but if she did, the break from reality would be most welcome.

She rose to wait for Alec's parents. Since the twins were still sleeping, she left them in the seating area that was only thirty feet from the incoming passengers' door.

"Hattie?"

She glanced to her left only to get a shock. Mason's dad, Jerry Brown, stood alongside her, holding out his arms for a hug. "Girl, it's been ages since I last saw you—though I hear you and Fern visit all the time."

"True. I can't get enough of her shortbread cookies." Fern was Jerry's neighbor. She was getting on in years, and Hattie enjoyed chatting with her. What she didn't enjoy was passing Mason's old house. The mere sight reminded her of happier times, which was why she hustled by, carefully avoiding a possible meeting with Jerry. The last thing she wanted was to hear about his son. For hearing about Mason would only serve as a reminder of how much he was missed.

He laughed. "That makes two of us." His smile faded.

"Addressing the elephant in the room, how're you and your folks coping? Both your sister and Alec gone..." He shook his head. "One helluva blow."

"Yeah." She swallowed back tears. "I'm here to pick up Alec's parents."

"I'm grabbing Mason. It'll be damn good to see him, though I wish our visit was under happier circumstances."

Mason will be here? Now? As in the next thirty seconds?

Considering her sister had just died, fashion hadn't topped her priorities. Hattie wore jeans, a faded Green Bay Packers sweatshirt a patron had left at her bar, and she'd crammed her hair into a messy bun—as for makeup, it hadn't even occurred to her. *Jeez, what is wrong with you? Why are you worried about how you look?*

She shook her head, suddenly feeling jittery.

Sure, she'd known Mason would be coming for the funeral, but she'd assumed they wouldn't run into each other until Saturday. This was too soon. What would she say or do?

Whereas moments earlier grief had slowed her pulse, panic now caused it to race. She couldn't see him. Not yet.

And then an airline representative stole all options for possible escape by opening the doors. In strode Mason. Out went her last shred of confidence.

She took a few steps back into a shadow. With luck, Mason wouldn't even see her.

The plan proved simple, yet effective, as Mason and his dad were soon caught up in their reunion.

Two strangers entered the terminal, and then Alec's parents. What were their thoughts about Mason having been on their flight? Or were they so absorbed in their grief, they hadn't noticed?

"Cindy? Taylor?" Hattie waved them over. "Hi. How was your flight?"

Cindy's eyes appeared red and sunken, her expression hollow. Taylor didn't look much better.

"It was fine," Taylor said, "but we're ready to call it a day."

"I understand. Should I get a cart for your luggage?"

He shook his head. "We don't have much."

"Okay, well…I'll grab the twins, and we'll be on our way." *Awkward* didn't begin to describe the moment, especially when she accidentally glanced in Mason's direction, but he turned away. Purposely? She hoped not.

SUNDAY AFTERNOON MASON shoveled for all he was worth, but still couldn't keep up with the mid-October snow. Located on the eastern shore of Prince William Sound, Conifer was known for impressive snowfalls. As an oblivious kid, he'd spent hours happily building forts and snowmen and, if he'd been really ambitious, even tunnels. Now he needed to dig out his dad's old truck, carefully avoiding the passenger-side door, which was barely attached to the vehicle after it had been rammed by an angry plow driver some ten years earlier.

His dad's trailer was dwarfed by towering Sitka spruce. Mason used to like playing hide-and-seek in them. Now, having grown used to the open sea, the dark forest made him feel trapped.

It had been six long years since he'd been home.

Best as he could remember, he'd once enjoyed the whisper of wind through the boughs. Today, the world had fallen silent beneath the deepening blanket of snow. If pressed, he'd have to admit the evergreen and ice-laced air smelled damned good. Fresh and clean—the way his life used to be.

"This is the last place I expected to see you."

"Same could be said of you." Mason glanced toward the

familiar voice to find little Hattie Beaumont all grown up. He'd seen her in the airport when he'd come in, but with Alec's parents having been there, the timing was all wrong for any kind of meaningful conversation. That morning, at the funeral, hadn't been much better. "Not a great day for an afternoon stroll."

"I like it." At the funeral, he'd been so preoccupied, he hadn't fully absorbed the fact that the former tomboy had matured into a full-on looker. She was part Inuit, and the snow falling on her long dark hair struck him as beautiful. Her brown eyes lacked her usual mischievous sparkle, but then, given the circumstances, he supposed that was to be expected. "Feels good getting out of the house."

"Agreed." He rested his gloved hands on the shovel's handle. "Snow expected to stop anytime soon?"

"Mom says we could see ten inches by morning."

"Swell." Around here, pilots flew through just about anything Mother Nature blew their way, but a major storm could put a kink in his plans to fly out first thing in the morning.

"We still on for this afternoon?"

He nodded. "Two, right?"

"Yes. Benton's opening his office just for us, so don't be late."

He couldn't help but grin. "Little Hattie Beaumont, who never once made it to school on time, is lecturing me on punctuality? And how many nights did your mother send me out to find you for dinner?"

Eyes shining, she looked away from him, then smiled. "Good times, huh?"

"The best." Back then, he'd had it all figured out. Perfect woman, job—even had his eye on a fixer-upper at the lonely end of Juniper Lane. Considering how tragic his parents' marriage had ultimately been, he should've known better than to believe his life would turn out any different.

Joining the navy had been the best thing he'd ever done.

"Well…" She gestured to the house next door. "I wanted to thank Fern for the pies and ham she brought to the wake. Might as well check her firewood while I'm there."

"Want me to tag along?" He'd forgotten the spirit of community up here. The way everyone watched out for everyone else. He'd lived in his Virginia Beach apartment for just over five years, but still didn't have a clue about any of his neighbors.

"Thanks, but I can handle it." Her forced smile brought on a protective streak in him for the girl who'd grown into a woman.

"I'm not saying you can't. Just offering to lend a hand. Besides…" Half smiling, he shook his head. "I haven't seen Fern since she ratted me out for driving my snow-mobile across her deck."

"She still hasn't built railings. I'm surprised nobody's tried it since."

"What can I say? I'm an original."

"More like a delinquent." She waved goodbye and walked down the street, then shouted, "Don't be late!"

"I won't."

"Oh—and, Mason?" He'd resumed shoveling, but looked up to find her biting her lower lip.

"Yeah?"

She looked down. "Thanks for coming. I really appreciate it."

"Sure. No problem," he lied. Actually, returning to Conifer had brought on an unfathomable amount of pain. Remembering Hattie's big sister, Melissa—the love of his life—was never easy. Not only had she broken his heart, but spirit. She'd taught him *trust* should've been a four-letter word. He hated her on a scale he'd thought himself incapable of reaching.

Now that she was dead?

All that hate mixed with guilt culminated in killer heartburn and an insatiable need to escape.

Chapter Two

Hattie had believed her childhood crush on Mason long over. Then he'd gone and flashed his crooked smile, opening the gate for her flood of feelings for him to come rushing back.

Along with her parents—the twins were being watched by their neighbor Sophie—Hattie now sat outside the office of family friend, and the only lawyer in town, Benton Seagrave, waiting for Mason to arrive. The metal folding chair serving as his trailer's bare-bones reception area made her squirmy. The scent of burnt coffee churned her stomach.

As with many folks in Alaska, Benton had a personal drive outside of his profession. He practiced law from October through May—and then, begrudgingly. His summers were spent on his gold claim in the Tolovana-Livengood region. The only reason he'd agreed to see the family today was because Mason and Alec's folks flew out in the morning.

Holding her hands clasped on her knees, Hattie closed her eyes, contrasting her remembered images of Mason with ones recently gained.

He'd always been taller than her, but now she felt positively petite standing beside him—not an easy feat for a woman a few local teens still called Fattie Hattie. Not only had he grown in height, but stature. He'd shoveled in his Sorel boots, jeans and a brown long-johns top that had clung to broadened shoulders and pecs. When he'd shoveled, his biceps could've earned their own zip code. Sure, in the bar she owned plenty of fit men came and went, but none caused her stomach to somersault with just a flash of a crooked smile. Mason's blue eyes had darkened and lines now creased the corners. His perpetually mussed dark hair shone with golden highlights. She was two years younger than him, and while the few other kids they'd gone to school with mercilessly teased her about her weight, he'd actually talked to her, sharing her love of astronomy and fishing and most of all…her sister.

On Mason and Melissa's wedding day, Hattie had tried being happy, but in actuality, she'd suffered through, forcing her smile and well-wishes, secretly resenting her sister for not only her too-tight maid-of-honor dress selection, but for marrying the only man Hattie had ever loved.

Of course in retrospect, Hattie knew she hadn't loved Mason, but crushed on him. Daydreamed of him holding her, kissing her, declaring it had never been Melissa he'd wanted, but her. Now that Melissa was dead, the mere thought of those traitorous longings made her feel dirty and disrespectful.

Melissa was—had been—the bronzed beauty every guy wanted. For as long as she could remember, Hattie battled jealousy and resentment she'd never wanted, but seemed to have always carried. When Melissa destroyed Mason by cheating on him, well, Hattie had secretly sided with him in believing her own sister heartless and cruel. Years later, when Melissa struggled to conceive, Hattie's guilt doubled for believing her sister's infertility was karma paying a call.

Now that Melissa was dead, self-loathing consumed Hattie for not only all of that, but not being able to cry.

Since the accident, she'd been the strong one, shielding her parents from the painful process of burying their perfect child, their pretty child, the one their Inuit mother had called *piujuq*—beautiful.

From outside came the clang of someone mounting the trailer's metal steps. Seconds later, the door was tugged open. Mason ducked as he entered, brushing snow from his dark hair. He still wore his jeans and boots, but had added an ivory cable-knit sweater that made his blue eyes all the more striking. For a moment, Hattie fell speechless. Then she remembered she wasn't seeing Mason for a happy reunion, but the reading of her sister's will.

Her parents, still holding tight to their resentment over the divorce—and especially his attendance at an intimate family moment such as the reading of Melissa's will—barely acknowledged his presence.

"Am I late?" He checked his black Luminox watch, the kind she'd seen on divers around town. Certain times of year, Conifer was a bustling port.

"W-we're early." She struggled knowing what to do with her hands. "Alec's parents should be here soon, so Benton said to let him know when we're all ready."

"Sure." Mason shoved his hands in his pockets.

And then they waited.

No one said a word. Aside from wind gusts and papery whispers of *Reader's Digest* pages being turned, all in the cramped space had fallen silent. Thank goodness Hattie's racing thoughts and pulse had no volume or everyone would know the extent of her panic. For years, she'd dreamed of a reunion with Mason, but never under these circumstances.

Twenty minutes passed with still no sign of Alec's parents.

A muffled landline rang in Benton's office, then came a brief, equally muffled conversation.

"Look," Mason said, "if you all don't mind, I'd just as soon get started. I can't imagine what Melissa would've left me. The whole thing's bizarre."

"Agreed," Hattie's father said, also rising, offering his hand to his wife. Akna and Lyle led the way down the short hall leading to Benton's office.

Before Lyle had reached the door, Benton opened it. "Good, you're all here." He waved Akna and Lyle into the room. "That was Taylor and Cindy on the phone. They're not going to make it."

"Everything all right?" Lyle asked.

"As well as can be expected."

While her parents and Benton made polite conversation, Hattie hung back with Mason. He made the formerly smallish space feel cramped. She needed to get away from him. And take time to process what losing her sister really meant.

"Ladies first." He gestured for her to lead the way, which was the last thing she wanted. She felt most comfortable in jeans and a roomy sweatshirt. Her black slacks and plum sweater clung in all the wrong places and she'd never wished more for a ponytail holder to hold her long hair from her face.

The graying lawyer greeted them at the door, shaking their hands. "Damn sorry about all this. Melissa and Alec were good people."

Really? The weight of what her sister and Mason's former best friend had done hung heavy in the room.

Her parents had already been seated.

Mason cleared his throat. "I don't mean to be rude, but can we get on with this?"

Hattie sympathized with what he must be going through. Just as she had guilt, he must harbor anger. Granted, Mason had left Conifer years ago and his absence no doubt tempered the initial sting of finding his wife in bed with his best friend, but there wasn't a statute of limitations on that sort of thing. Hattie couldn't imagine how Mason now felt regarding the lovebirds' sudden deaths.

Benton's office could've been featured on a special episode of *Hoarders*. Stacks upon stacks of files leaned precariously on every available surface.

Behind his desk, Benton shuffled through three more leaning piles. He tugged one out, only to have the whole pile follow in a paper-work avalanche. "Oops." He flashed them all a reassuring smile. "Happens all the time. Give me a sec, and we'll be back on course. Hattie, Mason, please, have a seat."

Mason knelt to assist with the cleanup.

Normally, Hattie would've helped, too, but at the moment, she lacked the strength.

"There we go," Benton finally said, reassembling the file he'd previously held. "Thanks, Mason."

"No problem."

"All right, then, let's skip formalities and get right to the meat of the matter."

"Perfect." Lyle took Akna's hand.

Hattie wished for someone to comfort her.

Two additional padded folding chairs faced Benton's desk. Mason sat in the one nearest the window.

Hattie took the other.

To Hattie, Benton said, "Having Vivian and Vanessa changed your sister—softened her to a degree I'm not sure she allowed most people to see."

Resting his elbows on his knees, Mason grunted.

Hattie commenced with squirming, carefully avoiding brushing against Mason in the too-close space.

"She was highly superstitious about Alec's flying. After their marriage, he had me write up a will, stating her his sole beneficiary."

Sighing, Mason asked, "What does any of that have to do with me?"

Hattie pressed her lips tight to keep from saying something she might regret. Mason had a right to be angry with Melissa, but he didn't have to be rude. Even though Hattie had her own issues with her sister, when it came down to it, she'd loved her as much as everyone else had in their small town. Melissa's beauty and spirit had been irresistible. Their parents hadn't been upset with their eldest for having an affair. Instead, they'd believed Mason—formerly a commercial fisherman—in the wrong for being gone so many days at sea, especially at a time when she'd needed him more than ever.

The lawyer closed the file and sighed. "I'm afraid this has everything to do with you, Mason—quite literally. Alec left the entirety of his estate to Melissa…."

Akna held a tissue to her nose. "Please, hurry."

"Of course." Benton consulted the file. "Bottom line, Melissa bequeathed everything to Hattie and Mason in the event both she and Alec passed at the same time."

"What?" Lyle released Akna to stand. "That's ridiculous."

"Surely, not everything—not…the girls?" Tears streamed down Akna's weathered cheeks.

Benton nodded. "Afraid so."

"Why?" Hattie asked.

"This might explain." He handed a letter to Mason, but Mason held up his hands. "You read it. I don't want anything to do with any of this."

Akna shot him a dark look.

"Very well…" Benton took the sealed letter, opened it, then began to read.

"Mason—
If you're reading this, my dreams were indeed the premonition I'd feared. I know you never held much

faith in my Inuit heritage, but we place great significance on dreams, and as I have had the same dream of Alec and me passing on three different occasions, I feel compelled to make arrangements should the worst indeed happen.

First, I owe you an apology. Our losing the baby was a horrible accident, nothing either of us could've prevented. I'm sorry I not only blamed the miscarriage on you, but was too cowardly to admit I'd outgrown our relationship."

Mason stood, hand over his mouth, eyes shining with unshed tears.

Benton asked, "Would you like to read the rest in private?"

"Get it over with." Hands clenching into fists, Mason stared out the window on the far side of the room.

"You're a monster," Akna said. "How dare you disrespect my daughter's last words."

"Honey…" Lyle slipped his arms about her shoulders.

Hattie wished for an escape hatch to open beneath her chair.

Benton cleared his throat, then continued to read from the letter.

"I'm ashamed to admit, my whole life was spent in the pursuit of pleasure. Now that I'm a parent, I understand how much more to life there is. Honor and self-sacrifice. The kinds of traits I now recognize not only in my sister and parents, but you.

I doubt you're aware of this, but Hattie has harbored quite the crush on you for as long as she could walk well enough to follow you around. If my dreams are true, and I am soon to die, I want to do something well and truly good.

The best thing I can think of is to play match-maker. If you and Hattie end up together, not only will my gorgeous twins end up with a great set of parents, but my beautiful, kindhearted sister will live happily ever after with the good guy she's always deserved.

"That's it." Benton folded the note, returning it to the envelope. "Lyle, Akna, I hope that answers your questions as to why your daughter chose to leave her twins to Hattie and Mason."

"We'll contest it." Akna held a white-knuckled grip on her purse. "My grandbabies need to be with me. Family."

"Wh-what am I?" Hattie managed past the wall of tears blocking her throat.

"Your mother didn't mean it like that," Lyle assured her.

"Lord almighty…" While the wind howled outside the trailer's paper-thin walls and windows, Mason shook his head. "I feel like we've been here ten days. This is nuts. No one gives away kids based on a few stupid dreams."

Akna fired off a round of Inuit curses at Mason.

Hattie's chest had tightened. As much as she adored her baby nieces, in no way, shape or form was she ready to become a mom. Melissa had tossed around formally naming Hattie as the twins' godmother a few times, but that'd been just talk. Hattie had always dreamed of being a mom, but considering her lackluster social life, she'd resigned herself to the fact that unless Prince Charming breezed in on a white snowmobile, her only destiny was to become an old maid. She couldn't even process the fact that her sister had just outed her feelings for Mason.

"No." Mason paced the cramped, sterile office. "I want no part of this. Clearly, Melissa wasn't in her right mind, and I sure as hell don't believe Inuit dream voodoo."

"You hush!" Akna demanded.

Hattie shot him a look. "Leave my culture out of this." Of Benton, she asked, "Are you sure Melissa didn't want the girls to be with their grandparents? My mom and dad have already taken them in."

"As you heard in not just the letter, but on all legal documentation, Melissa was quite clear in her wishes. She wanted the girls raised in their own home by her sister and her ex-husband."

Mason snorted. "Look, I can tell you right now this isn't happening. I'm due back on base first thing Tuesday morning, and want no part of Melissa's twisted matchmaking scheme—no offense, Hattie. You're a great gal, but..."

"I get it," she said, mortified her own sister would stoop so low as to embarrass her from beyond the grave.

Benton said, "It's understandable you'd need a few days to adjust to something of this nature."

"There's no adjusting. Deal me out."

Hattie glanced over her shoulder to find Mason's complexion lightened by a couple shades. He'd narrowed his eyes and held the heels of his hands to his forehead.

"Hattie?" Benton asked. "How do you feel regarding the matter?"

She straightened, drawing strength from not only herself, but her ancestors. "If this is what Melissa wanted for her children, who am I to deny her? Not sure how," she said with a faint laugh, "but I will raise my nieces."

"This is wrong," Akna said.

"I agree." Lyle shifted on his seat. "Weren't there other letters from our daughter? Why'd she leave just the one?"

Benton rifled through the file. "That appears to be the only one. She gave me the packet herself. Before now, I never checked the contents. But, Hattie, if you feel capable of raising your nieces, there's no reason Mason should feel compelled to stay."

"Good." Mason now rested his hands on his hips. "Perfect solution. The kids are in capable hands, and I'm back on my base. Problem solved."

"Not so fast." The lawyer wagged a pen. "Mason, while I understand your reluctance to take on such a challenge, as of now, you and Hattie share legal custody of Vivian and Vanessa. A family-court judge can release you from this responsibility, but it will take time."

A muscle ticked in Mason's clenched jaw. "How much time are we talking?"

"Well, let's see…" Benton took a few endless minutes to consult his computer. "Ironically, the nearest family-court judge for five hundred miles is on maternity leave. A judge in Valdez is temporarily hearing her cases. First thing Monday morning, Mason, I'll get you on Judge Dvorck's docket, but considering the fact that, like it or not, Melissa's twins are your legal responsibility, I'd strongly advise you to assume their care until the judge releases you from all financial and custodial ties to the estate." Withdrawing a legal-sized envelope from his top desk drawer, he opened it, then passed along two sets of keys. "These belong to Melissa and Alec's home and cars. Counting real estate, life insurance and investments, the twins— and you—should live quite comfortably." He gave Mason and Hattie each copies of the files. "These contain detailed listings of all assets."

Hattie felt near drowning. Was this real?

Her mother quietly sobbed.

Lyle helped his wife to her feet. "Let's go. It's clear we're not needed."

Damn Melissa for doing this to their parents.

"So wait—" Mason said once Lyle and Akna had gone. "Me and Hattie are supposed to drag Melissa's kids from their grandparents, then camp out at Alec and Melissa's house until we see the judge?"

"That's about the size of it. Any further questions?" Benton raised his considerable eyebrows.

Oh—Hattie had plenty more she needed to know, but for the moment, the most pressing issue was how was she supposed to keep her sanity while playing *house* with stupid-handsome Mason?

Chapter Three

In the time they'd spent with Benton, the weather had turned from pretty lightly falling snow to downright blowing ugly. The trailer's grated-steel stairs were snow-covered and treacherous. This time of year, on a clear, bright day they only had maybe ten hours of sun. During the two hours they'd been inside, darkness had settled in.

Mason held out his hand to Hattie, who stood behind him. "Let me help."

"I'm fine!" she said above the wind.

Ignoring her, he took firm hold of her arm. "You won't make it five feet in those heels. Forget you live in Alaska?"

When she struggled to escape him, common sense took over and he scooped her into his arms.

"Put me down!"

He did—once he'd reached her SUV. "There you go. I'll follow you to your folks'. I'm assuming that's where the twins currently reside?"

"Not necessary. I'll take it from here."

"Why are you being so stubborn?"

She ignored him to fish through her purse for her keys, which she promptly dropped in the snow.

They both knelt at the same time and ended up conking heads.

"Ouch," they said in unison, rubbing their noggins.

Mason had to laugh. "This reminds me of that time I took you salmon fishing and you damn near knocked yourself out just leaving the boat's cabin."

"I tripped and you know it."

"Yeah, yeah…" He found her keys, then pressed the remote. "Climb in. I'll see you in a few."

"Mason…"

Her dark, wary tone told him she'd prefer he stay away, but he'd never been one to shirk duty and didn't plan on starting now. For whatever time he was legally charged with caring for Melissa's kids, he would. Out of the memory of what they'd once shared, he owed her that much.

The storm made it tough to see the road, but Mason was familiar enough with the route to his former in-laws' he could've driven it blindfolded. He'd shared a lot of good times with Melissa and Hattie's parents. This afternoon, like the day of Melissa's funeral, wouldn't be one.

The back-and-forth drone of the wipers transported him to another snowy day. Weeks after his divorce had been finalized, he'd been fresh off the boat from a grueling two-month Yakutat king-crab season to find himself with his dad at the Juniper Inn's Sunday brunch seated two tables down from newlyweds Melissa and Alec. As if that weren't bad enough, Akna and Lyle were also in attendance. As long as he lived, he'd never forget their disapproving stare. Melissa's betrayal—and Alec's—had been hard enough to bear.

His dad counseled to play it cool. Not to let them get beneath his skin. They weren't worth it. But all through middle and high school, throughout his and Melissa's two-year marriage, he'd loved Akna and Lyle. They were good people. It killed him to think for one second they blamed him for his marriage falling apart. Yes, he'd spent a lot of time away from home, but he was working for Melissa— them. Their future.

Losing their baby hadn't been anyone's fault.

He remembered a fire crackling in the inn's too-fussy dining room. His chair had been too straight-backed and uptight. Even though the weather outside was bitterly cold, inside struck him as annoyingly hot. As long as he lived, he'd never forget the way the snow pelting the windows melted on contact, running in tearlike rivulets that reminded him of Melissa's tears when she'd asked for a divorce.

She'd claimed his distance had driven her to Alec—not physical distance, but emotional. She'd said the miscarriage changed him. Mason believed that a crock. She was the one who'd changed. His love had never once faltered.

On autopilot, back in the present, he parked his dad's old pickup in front of Akna and Lyle's house.

Though the temperature had dropped to the teens, his palms were sweating. Countless dangerous SEAL missions had left him less keyed up.

Hattie pulled into her parents' driveway ahead of him. She now teetered on their front-porch steps. What'd gotten into her? The Hattie he remembered struck him as a practical, no-frills girl who knew better than to wear high-heel boots in a snowstorm. But then, that girl had also been a tomboy, doe-eyed dreamer who'd preferred the company of her dogs over most people. It saddened him to realize he no longer knew the striking woman she'd grown into. They might as well be strangers.

She damn near tripped, so he hastened his pace to a jog.

"Slow it down." He took her arm. "You act like this is somewhere you want to be."

Wrenching her arm free, she grasped the railing instead of him. "Where else would I be? This is my family. Used to be yours."

He snorted.

At seventeen, he and Hattie had helped Lyle build this

porch over a warm summer weekend. Melissa had sat in a lawn chair, *supervising.* Over ten years later, the wood groaned beneath their footfalls. Bitter wind whistled through the towering conifers that had given the town its name.

The front door popped open. Lyle ushered his daughter inside. "Hurry, it's cold. Your mom and I were just wondering what took so—" He eyed Mason. "What're you doing here?"

"Nice to see you, too." Mason trailed after Hattie, easing past her father. In the tiled entry, he brushed snow from his hair.

Hattie bustled with the busy work of removing her coat, then taking his.

Took about two seconds for Mason to assess his surroundings well enough to realize he'd stumbled deep into enemy territory.

Akna sat on one end of the sofa holding an infant wrapped in a pink blanket. Sophie Reynolds—a buxom busybody he remembered as being a neighbor and clerk down at Shamrock's Emporium—held another pink bundle in a recliner. Despite a cheery fire, the room struck Mason as devoid of warmth. As if the loss of their child had sucked the life from Hattie's parents.

Unsure what to say or even what to do with his hands, Mason crossed his arms. "Brutal out there."

Akna flashed a hollow-eyed stare briefly in his direction, before asking her daughter, "I suppose you're here for the girls?"

"Mom…" Hattie leaned against the wall while unzipping one boot, then the other. "Honestly? You probably need some rest. And it's not like you can't see the twins as often as you like."

Sophie noted, "A body can never see too much of their grandbabies."

Mason didn't miss Hattie's narrow-eyed stare in Sophie's direction.

While Mason stood rooted in the entryway, Hattie joined her mother on the sofa, taking the baby into her arms. Her tender reverence reminded him that Alec had been the one who'd ultimately given Melissa her most cherished desire. Part of him felt seized by childish, irrational jealousy over his once best friend filling his wife's need for babies. But then the grown-up in him took over, reminding Mason the point was moot, considering both parties were dead.

"It's not the same, and you know it." Akna angled on the sofa, facing her daughter and granddaughter. "Right, Sophie?"

Sophie nodded. "Amen."

Akna said, "Your sister betrayed me." By rote, she made the sign of the cross on her chest. The official family religion had always been an odd pairing of old Inuit ways blended with Lyle's Catholicism. A gold-framed photo of the Pope hung alongside Melissa's and Hattie's high school graduation pictures.

"Oh, stop. Melissa loved you very much." Hattie's voice cracked, causing Mason to shift uncomfortably. As much as he'd told himself he hated Melissa, wanted her to hurt as badly as she'd hurt him, he'd never wanted this. Hattie regained her composure. She'd always been the stronger of the two sisters.

"Obviously, not enough. And how could she have ignored Alec's parents? When your father called to tell them the news, poor Cindy had a breakdown. Taylor's got them on the first flight out in the morning so she can see her doctor."

"Such a shame," Sophie murmured.

"Akna, I'm sorry about all this." Mason left the entry to join them. "Which is why—soon as possible—I'll sign over my rights to Hattie. What you all do from there is your business."

"Hattie," Akna asked, "with the time you spend at the bar, do you even feel capable of raising twins?"

Hattie shrugged before tracing the back of her finger along her sleeping niece's cheek. "If this is what Melissa wanted, I feel honor bound to at least try."

Lyle ran his hands through his hair and sighed. "A few weeks ago, Melissa and the girls rode along with me while I covered for one of my delivery guys." A former bush pilot, Lyle now owned a grocery distribution center that served many nearby small communities. "Looking back, she acted jumpy. She mentioned not having been sleeping. Didn't think much of it at the time—chalked it up to her being a new mom. She talked a lot about wanting Hattie to be the girls' godmother, and that if something ever happened to her, she wanted them raised young."

"What does that even mean?" Akna asked through the tissue she'd held to her nose.

"Ask me, this is all unnatural," Sophie said. "The girls should be with their grandparents who love them."

Hattie ignored the neighbor and forced a deep breath. "Mom, no offense to you and Dad, but Melissa brought up the godmother thing with me, too. At the time, I told her she was talking crazy, but she said she wanted the girls raised by someone young. I guess her friend Bess was taken in by her grandmother, then lost her, which is how she ended up in foster care until she turned eighteen. Melissa didn't want that for her girls."

"We'd never let that happen," Lyle said.

Hattie took her niece from Akna's arms. "Look, I know this is a shock for everyone—me, too—but if this is what Melissa wanted—"

Her mother interjected, "What about *our* wishes?"

Lyle sat beside his wife, taking her hand. "Honey, what

we want doesn't matter. All we can do is support Hattie as best we can."

"I would be calling a lawyer," Sophie said.

"Sophie," Hattie said, "please, stay out of this family matter. And, Mom, I don't mean to be harsh, but you're acting petty." Standing, Hattie cupped her hand to the infant's head. Hattie's brown eyes narrowed the way they always had when she dug in her heels to fight for what she wanted. "Why can't we raise the twins together? As of now, Mason and I might have legal custody, but what does that really even mean? I'll move into Melissa and Alec's, which is—what?—three miles from you? You used to watch the girls all the time for Melissa and Alec. Won't you do the same now for me? Vivian and Vanessa will be raised in the only home they've known, by people they love. I fail to see how this isn't the best all-around solution—especially since Mason already agreed to take himself out of the equation."

"It isn't the best," Sophie said, "because grandparents are best. You've never been around little ones. How will you even know what to do?"

While Sophie, in her infinite wisdom, rattled on, Mason was unprepared for the personal sting he felt at Hattie's speech. Did she have to make him sound so heartless and uncaring? But what else could he do? He had no stake in these little lives. Prior to their parents' funeral, he'd never even seen the girls. If he had his way, he'd be on a return flight to Virginia first thing in the morning.

Akna had been silently crying, but her pain now turned to uncontrollable sobbing. "Wh-why did this h-happen?"

Lyle slipped his arm around her.

Sophie closed her eyes in prayer.

Mason felt emotionally detached from the scene, as if he were watching a movie. What was he doing here? This was no longer his life.

Sophie abruptly stood. The once-sleeping infant she'd cradled was startled by the sudden movement and whimpered.

"Here, Mr. Mom." She thrust the baby into his arms. "You think yourself an expert, take over."

Mason didn't even know which baby he held, let alone what to do when her fitful protest turned into a full-blown wail.

THIRTY MINUTES LATER, Hattie held Vanessa with her right arm, struggling to unlock her sister and brother-in-law's former home. Mason stood behind her with Vivian, who hadn't stopped crying since leaving her grandparents.

"She always like this?" Mason set the bulging diaper bag on the porch.

"Usually, they're both easygoing, but it's been a rough couple days—for everyone."

"Yeah."

She finally got the key turned and opened the door on a house cold and dark and lonely enough to have been a tomb. When Melissa and Alec had been alive, the A-frame log cabin glowed with warmth and laughter. Her sister had been a wonderful cook and she'd always had something delicious baking or bubbling in one of her cast-iron pots.

The storm had passed and the two-story living room featured a glass wall looking out on all of Treehorn Valley and Mount Kneely beyond. Moonlight reflecting off the snow cast a frosty bluish pallor over what Hattie knew to be warm-toned pine furniture upholstered in a vibrant red-orange and yellow *inukshuk* pattern.

"Cold in here." Mason closed the door with his foot. "Think the furnace is out?"

"Probably. It's a wood-burning system with propane backup. The temperature's been so mild, Alec probably didn't have it going for the season yet."

"Is it downstairs?"

She nodded, wandering through the open space, turning on lamps and overhead lights.

"I'll check it out, but in the meantime, what do you want me to do with this one?" He nodded at still-sniffling and red-eyed Vivian.

"I'll take her." Melissa kept a playpen in the warmest kitchen corner. Hattie set Vanessa in it, then took Vivian. Since the air was cold enough to see her breath, she kept the girls' outerwear on while she made a fire in the living room's river-stone hearth.

Being in her sister's home without Melissa unnerved her. Hattie normally occupied the one-bedroom efficiency apartment above her waterfront bar. It was small, cramped and cozy. Just the way she liked it. This space was too large for her taste. Though beautifully decorated in what she supposed was the classic Alaskan hunting lodge look, featuring an antler chandelier and an oil painting of snow-capped Mount Kneely over the mantel, this was her sister's dream house—not hers. Hattie thrived among clutter.

The house shuddered when the sleeping furnace lumbered awake.

A few minutes later when warm air flowed through the vents, gratitude swelled in Hattie for Mason handling at least that issue. She would've eventually gotten the unit started, but having one less worry was welcome.

Vivian fussed, reaching for her hat.

"I know, sweetie, it's annoying, but until it warms up in here, let's keep it on, okay?" Hattie knelt before the playpen, patting the infant's back.

Mason's boots clomped on the hardwood stairs. "Alec has enough wood to last the week, so as long as one of us remembers to feed the beast, we'll at least be warm for the time being. Before winter sets in, though, I'll have to stockpile a legit supply. I'll make a fire up here, too."

"Already did, but it probably needs stoking."

Both babies were back to fussing. Were they hungry?

Hands to her throbbing forehead, Hattie wished she'd taken more than a casual interest in her nieces. Playing with them had been a much higher priority than an activity as mundane as meals. Hattie knew Melissa had breastfed, supplemented by formula, but the exact powder-to-water ratio escaped her.

"Since I'm over here, handling man work," Mason said from the hearth, "how about you do something about the kids' racket?"

"Love to, but it's gonna take a sec to get the formula mixed."

By the time Hattie finished, dancing firelight banished the living room's dark corners, but did little to ease the pain in her heart.

Both babies still fussed, which only made her fumble more. At the bar, she thrived under the chaotic pressure of a busy Friday or Saturday night. This was different.

"Need help?" Behind her, Mason hovered. His radiated heat further unnerved her. The situation was already beyond horrible. Tossing her old high school crush into the mix only made matters worse. And here she'd thought Melissa and Mason's wedding had been hard? This was a thousand times tougher.

"Sure." She managed to swallow past the emotional brick lodged in her throat. "You take Vanessa and a bottle and I'll grab Vivian."

In front of the playpen, he scratched his head. "Love to do just that, only I don't have a clue which one is Vanessa."

"You'll learn. Although there are still times I'm not sure, Vanessa typically has a more laid-back disposition. Vivian has no trouble letting you know she's displeased."

As if she knew her aunt was talking smack about her, Vivian upped the volume on her wail.

He snorted. "Sounds like you and your sister."

For the first time since the funeral, Hattie genuinely smiled. "Never thought of it like that, but you nailed your assessment—which makes me an awful person, right?"

"Not even close," he said over the infant's cry. "Melissa was a handful and were she here with us, she'd be first to admit it—with a proud smile."

"True."

When they each cradled an infant, they settled on the sofa in front of the fire.

Hattie plucked off the twins' hats and mittens, then gave Vivian her bottle. The sudden silence save for the fire's crackle and the twins' occasional grunts and sighs made for much-welcomed peace.

"Sorry about what happened at my parents'. That was an ugly scene."

"No worries." He shifted Vanessa to hold her in the crook of his other arm. "I don't blame them for being upset—Alec's folks, too. They've got to be feeling out of the loop."

"I suppose. But it doesn't have to be that way. They're welcome to see these two whenever they'd like. They chose to run back to Florida."

"I know, but think of this from their perspective. Alec used to be my best friend, then I caught him sleeping with my wife and never spoke to him again. Cindy and Taylor were like second parents to me. Growing up, I ate more dinners at their house than mine. Everything's so mixed up, you know? Part of me was glad to see them at the funeral—at least until I remembered they were part of the enemy team. I imagine they feel the same?"

"Probably." Vivian had thankfully drifted off to sleep. Hattie gently leaned forward, setting the empty bottle on the coffee table. "Wonder if my sister even talked about her will with Alec? Or her prophetic dreams?"

"Guess we'll never know."

On the surface, Mason's words were simple enough, but the finality of that word—*never*—hit Hattie hard. Up until now, she'd been too wrapped up in the ceremony of her sister's death to consider the impact of losing someone she'd dearly loved.

At the hospital, during Melissa's last hours, Hattie had stayed strong for her parents—especially her mom. Then there'd been planning the funeral and reception. Steeling herself for the reading of Melissa's will. Now there was nothing left to do except begin her new life by essentially stepping into her sister's.

How many times when Melissa had been married to Mason had Hattie prayed for just such a thing?

In light of her current situation, this fact shamed her. So much so that the tears she'd so carefully held inside now spilled in ugly sobs.

After handing Vivian to Mason, Hattie dashed upstairs, not even sure where she was going, just knowing she needed to be alone.

Chapter Four

Swell.

Mason glanced over his shoulder at Hattie's departing back, then down at the two sleeping infants. What was he supposed to do now? How had he even landed in this impossible situation?

From somewhere upstairs, a door slammed. But the house wasn't solid enough to mask Hattie's cries.

His heart went out to her. Losing Melissa had to be tough.

He'd have no doubt been upset himself if he hadn't already mourned their relationship's death. Then there was the stunt she'd pulled with her letter—the matchmaking bit. What the hell? Poor Hattie had plenty to be upset about, and he hoped she didn't think he'd taken any of her sister's ramblings seriously.

"Ladies," he mumbled to what amounted to maybe twenty pounds of snoozing babies, "I should probably check on your aunt, but that leaves me in a bind as to what to do with you."

They didn't stir.

Since he already cradled one, he made an awkward position change on the couch in order to scoop up the other. Holding both, he slowly rose, then headed for the kitchen, assuming the kiddy corral would be safe enough until he got back.

Their little arms and legs jolted upon landing.

The house was still on the chilly side, so he left them on their backs, wearing their coats.

At the top of the stairs was a loft library he ventured through to gain access to a hall. He forged down it, intent on not just finding Hattie, but stopping her tears. The sound ripped through him. Took him back to when she'd been thirteen and broke her ankle after using scrap sheet metal for a sled. He'd carried her home and made sure she was okay back then and he'd sure as hell do the same now.

He passed a bedroom, the nursery and a bath before reaching the one closed door Hattie had hidden behind. He opened it to step into what could only be the master. A miniversion of the living room's A-frame window wall overlooked a spectacular snowy night scene.

Hattie sat hunched over and crying on the foot of a king-size bed positioned to take maximum advantage of the view.

Mason's first thought should've been comforting her, but all he seemed able to focus on were Alec and Melissa. What they'd done in that cozy bed. How his wife and best friend had betrayed him to an unimaginable degree.

Snapping himself out of his own issues with the deceased, he sat next to Hattie, easing his arm around her as naturally as he always had. "I'm sorry."

She cried all the harder, struggled to escape him, but he drew her closer, onto his lap, where he held her for all she was worth, all the while gently stroking her hair. "Shh… everything's going to be okay."

"No," she said with a sniffle and shake of her head. "Part of me feels like I did this. I hid so much resentment that she had not one amazing man, b-but two. Then she got the perfect babies I'd always wanted. H-her life was everything mine wasn't. I used to wish I could be her—

just for a day. But I never wanted her gone, Mason. I—I loved her so much...."

Sobs racked Hattie's frame, and for the first time since losing Melissa to divorce, Mason felt helpless. As a SEAL, he'd been trained to handle any contingency. Make flash life-or-death decisions, but this one had him stumped. How did he begin comforting Hattie when he harbored such ill will toward her sister and brother-in-law? Now that he was both legally and honor bound to care for their children?

It was too much.

"What if she's somehow looking down on me? And knows I coveted what she had? But I never in a million years wanted it like this. She meant the world to me. More than anything when we were all kids, I wanted to be just like her. As an adult, I realized that wasn't going to happen, but that didn't stop the yearning. Still, I did love her. She has to know. Has to."

"I loved her, too, Hat Trick." He used to call Hattie that when she'd challenged him to pond hockey. "For her to leave you her children, you have to know she loved you every bit as much?"

She nodded.

Drawing back, he lightly touched her chin, urging her to meet his gaze. Though the room was dark, moonlight reflecting off the snow reinforced the fact that she was far from being the little girl and teen Mason remembered. Hattie was all grown up. Even tear-stained, her face was one of the loveliest he'd ever seen. In many ways, she resembled her sister—big brown eyes and long dark hair. Yet she had higher cheekbones, fuller lips. Where she lacked Melissa's petite stature, her full curves made her more womanly.

Pushing back, she turned away, fussing with her hair. "I'm sorry. I didn't mean to flip out on you like that. Some parent I'll make, huh?"

"Give yourself a break. This is a full-on nightmare—even if neither of us had any issues simmering on the old back burner. Honestly, I didn't even want to come to the funeral and figured the will could be handled via email or over the phone. Dad convinced me I'd regret it if I didn't come."

"Speaking of him, have you let him know?"

Mason shook his head. "I'll give him a call."

A few feet away, she shivered. She crossed her arms and ran her hands up and down them.

He should've gotten off the bed to hold her—at least find a blanket to wrap her in, but his feet were frozen in place.

"Guess I should check on the babies."

"They're fine. As open as this place is, if they were in trouble, we'd hear them crying."

"Still…"

He sighed. "They're *fine*."

Ignoring him, she left the room, heading toward the stairs. A few minutes later, just as he'd suggested, the sound of her cooing over them carried all the way to where he still sat.

Honestly, he felt more than a little shell-shocked by the whole turn of events. Now he was not only mad at Melissa for hooking up with Alec, but for apparently thinking so highly of herself as to presume he'd want her matchmaking services. As if that weren't despicable enough, she'd thought it a good idea to use her own babies as manipulative tools? The whole thing was psycho. He might've long ago loved her, but at the moment, he didn't even kind of like her.

Hattie's big brown eyes flashed before him, reminding him why he hadn't told Benton to take a flying leap. His being here, in this house, in the very room where Alec and Melissa had made love, wasn't about allegiance to his ex, but her sister.

Hattie had always been there for him and he now owed her the same.

He made a quick call to his dad, bringing him up to speed on the will and how he'd be staying at Melissa and Alec's until his day in court. His dad wasn't the chatty type, so once the facts were delivered, Mason hung up.

Downstairs, he found Hattie removing the girls' coats and soft boots. "Want me to help you get them in their cribs?"

"Sure. But they both need fresh diapers."

He blanched. "Not my idea of a good time, but show me what to do."

Together they took the babies upstairs, and Hattie walked him through a diaper change. "Diaper removal is pretty self-explanatory. From there, use a few wipes, assess if you think she needs rash cream or powder, then—"

"Okay, whoa—I'm great at assessing, but I usually have a list of parameters to work with."

Hattie wrinkled her nose, and damned if she didn't strike him as cute. "You lost me."

"What am I supposed to look for in order to know if either of those contingencies apply?"

She cocked her head. "In English?"

"What am I looking for? Like, if I'm supposed to use the powder or cream, how will I know?"

"Oh. Well, the cream you'll use if anything looks red or irritated. As for the powder…" She shrugged. "Honestly, let's table it for now. I'll look it up online or ask Mom. Pretty sure it's a moisture thing."

"Want me to research it? I'm much better with that than diapering."

"Sure. Thanks." She returned her attention to the baby.

"No sign of rash, so we'll grab a fresh diaper, open it, then slide the back part under her—like this."

Stepping alongside her for a better view, he nodded. "Got it. Next?"

"Pull up the front, fasten it with the sticky tabs, put her clothes back on and you're good to go."

"Wait—you didn't say anything about the clothes. All of them come off?"

She sighed. "Now you're being deliberately obtuse."

"No, really. For whatever time I'm here, I want to be as much help as possible. I'm viewing this as a mission."

"Wow. Please tell me you didn't just equate my sister's babies with battle." Keeping one hand on the now-squirmy baby, she grabbed a pair of footie pj's from a nearby drawer.

"What? You don't want my help?"

"Mason, Vanessa and Viv are real-live babies—not burp-and-feed dolls you'd read about in a manual."

"Duh. Why do you think I'm concentrating on what you tell me? I want to get this right. We're in a zero-tolerance mistake zone, right?"

"Wow. Just wow." She finished her task without so much as looking his way.

Whatever. He took her ignoring him as an opportunity to study the nursery layout. Two cribs, built-in shelves loaded with toys and books. Two upholstered swivel rockers. Changing table. Adequate stockpile of supplies on shelf beneath said table. Easy-access traffic flow—although down the line, the potted Norfolk pine in front of the window could pose a spooky shadow problem.

Overall impression? *Way* too much pink.

Once Hattie placed her baby in the crib, Mason took his turn at diapering. Forcing a deep breath, he rolled down minitights. It was still chilly, so he left the baby's long-sleeved dress, undershirt, sweater and socks on her.

Watching Hattie, the diaper process had seemed straightforward enough. He easily undid the sticky tape but, upon lifting the front flap, was accosted by a smell so vile he damn near retched.

"Oh, my God…" He stepped back. Fanning the putrid air, he asked, "What the hell? Is she sick?"

Hattie glared. "Welcome to the wonderful world of babies. Lesson 101—poop stinks. Standard operating procedure."

"If that last part was a dig at me, stow it. I'm doing the best I can here, okay?"

Her indifferent shrug told him she wasn't impressed.

Had he really only a few minutes earlier felt sorry for her? Regardless, he forged ahead. "You didn't mention Number Two in your lesson. Any special spray needed? Protective gloves or eyewear?"

"Want me to do it?"

"No." And he was offended she'd asked. "I've got this."

Dear Lord. Mason struggled to maintain his composure while cleaning the baby's behind. Was this poop or tar?

He made the mistake of looking at the kid's face and their gazes connected. Was she smiling? This one had to be Vivian—the baby whose personality matched Melissa's. She'd get a kick out of seeing him tortured.

Finally finished wiping, with Hattie supervising, Mason found a fresh diaper and tried grabbing the kid's ankles to raise her behind, but she kicked so hard it was tough to grab hold. Settling for one ankle, he tried lifting her sideways, then sneaking the diaper under.

"Not like that," Hattie complained. "You'll put her in traction before her first birthday." Nudging him aside, she dived right in, catching the baby's ankles one-handed on her first try.

"As much as it pains me to admit this," Mason said with a round of applause, "you're good."

"I've had at least a little practice. You'll get the hang of it." She took the diaper from him and, once she had it properly positioned, stepped aside for him to finish. "She's all yours."

When Mason stepped back into place, their arms brushed. The resulting hum of awareness caught him as off guard as practically flunking his first diapering lesson. He and Hattie had never been more than friends, so what was that about? Had she felt it, too? If so, she showed no signs, which told him to chalk it up to his imagination, then get his job done. Another part of him couldn't get Melissa's words from his head. *Hattie has harbored quite the crush on you for as long as she could walk well enough to follow you around.* Could it be true?

Perhaps an even bigger question was, what did he feel for her?

Nothing romantic, that was for sure. For as long as he could remember, she'd been his friend. For sanity's sake, he planned to ignore that rush of attraction in favor of putting Hattie safely back in the friend zone.

Subject closed.

It proved no big deal to get the diaper perfectly positioned, and while a few of his new-father SEAL friends whined about the whole sticky-tab thing being tough to tackle, Mason thought that part a piece of cake. He liked lining them up perfectly straight. Precision in all things—especially diapers—was good.

"There." He couldn't help but smile upon completing his goal. "Now what?"

"Take her dress off and put these on." Hattie offered a pair of pj's that matched Vivian's sister's.

"Just a thought—" Mason struggled to unfasten the row of tiny buttons up the back of the dress "—but what if we started color-coding the twins? That way, we'd know who's who."

"You mean dress Vivian in one color and Vanessa in another?"

"Exactly. That way, they won't be sixteen and realize their whole lives they've been called by the wrong names."

"While I applaud your suggestion, I don't think we're in danger of that. Besides, they already have so many pretty matching clothes, I'd hate to toss everything Melissa bought and was given as shower gifts."

"Hadn't thought of that. When I'm researching powder, I'll see if I can find tips on telling twins apart."

"You do that." Though she didn't smile, he'd have sworn he saw laughter spark her still-teary eyes.

Once both girls had been tucked beneath matching fuzzy pink blankets, Mason asked, "Now what?"

"Know how to do laundry?"

"Sure."

She pointed toward an overflowing hamper. "Mind tackling that while I'm out?"

"Where are you going?"

"I have to at least make an appearance at the bar. I haven't been in since first hearing the news."

"But it's Sunday. Thought no alcohol was sold or served?"

She patted his back. "You *have* been gone awhile. Two years ago, the new mayor, who's a huge Cowboys fan, exempted every Sunday during football season."

As a general rule, Mason never pouted, but he was damn near close. "But I'd rather go with you than be stuck here doing laundry."

"Sorry." She flashed a forced, unapologetic smile. "One of us has to bring home the bacon."

"Hattie Beaumont, you turned mean."

"Nah." She ducked across the hall and into the bathroom. "Just practical."

WITH HER PRACTICAL boots crunching on the city side-walk's hard-packed snow, Hattie realized she had never been happier to be away from someone in her whole life. Was she really supposed to live with Mason for however long it took him to get unattached from her sister's will? Couldn't he just fly up when it was his turn in court?

Aerosmith's "Walk This Way" spilled out the bar's door at the same time as Harvey Mitchell.

"Got a ride?" Hattie asked.

Breath fogging in the cold night air, he hitched his thumb toward the road. "Wife sent the daughter to pick-me-up." His last three words slurred into one. Looked as though someone should've gone home a few drinks earlier.

Hattie waited outside for the few minutes it took for Harvey's sixteen-year-old, Janine, to show. The bar stood at the end of a pier. She took a deep breath, appreciating the water's briny tang.

With Harvey safely gone, she headed inside, glad for the warmth and cheerful riot of Halloween decorations she'd put up weeks ago before knowing how tragically the month would end.

"Hey, sweetie." Her best friend, Clementine Archer, stepped out from behind the bar, enfolding her in a hug. They'd gone to school together since kindergarten. When Clementine's husband had lost his job at the fish-canning factory, Hattie had suggested her friend take an online bartending class, then come work for her. Five years later, Clementine's husband had run off to Texas, leaving her on her own with their two sons, but she still worked be-hind the bar four days a week. Her mom watched the boys. "How's it going? You've gotta be a mess."

"Oh—I passed mess a long time ago. I'm currently a disaster." Hattie deposited her purse in a lower cabinet beside the fridge. Before leaving, she needed to run upstairs to switch it out for her usual cargo-style bag. Might as well grab extra clothes, too.

"You leave Mason with the twins?"

Hattie nodded. "He wasn't happy about it. Pouted like a second grader."

"How is it?"

"What?" Hattie poured herself an orange juice on the rocks.

Hands on her hips, Clementine shook her head. "Don't even try playing it cool with me, lady. I'm the one person aside from Melissa who ever knew exactly how much Mason meant to you. No way is his being here not impacting your life."

Hattie looked at her drink. "Yeah, so maybe I'd like a splash of vodka for this, but you know…" She stared at the crowd of regulars: some played pool, others poker, others still watched one of the four flat screens or just talked. Everything about the night was normal, yet not a single thing in Hattie's life felt the same. Her eyes welled with tears again. She blotted them with one of the bar's trademark red plaid napkins she'd had monogrammed with *Hattie's*. "It's all good."

"Oh, sweetie…" Clementine ambushed her with another hug. "You don't still have a thing for him, do you?"

"No. Of course not." Which was why when he'd swooped her into his arms outside of the lawyer's her heart had skipped beats. When he'd stood beside her in her sister's kitchen or they'd shared feeding time on the couch or he'd tugged her onto his lap for a comforting hug, everything she thought she knew turned upside down.

And that was bad.

It didn't matter that Melissa was no longer with them. Mason would always belong to her. Their bond had been unbreakable. So much so that not only had her sister reached from beyond her grave to ask Mason to raise her girls, but she'd had the audacity to suggest he also be Hattie's man.

Chapter Five

"Thanks for bringing all of this by, Dad—and thank you, Fern, for driving." His ditty bag and iPad couldn't be more welcome sights in this unfamiliar home.

While his dad grunted, prune-faced Fern waved off Mason's appreciation in favor of snooping about the kitchen. She'd tossed her red down coat on the granite counter, but still wore her orange cap and a hot-pink sweat suit with striped blue socks. She'd abandoned her sturdy Sorel boots at the front door. "Where'd Melissa keep her coffee?"

"Couldn't tell you."

"Times like these folks need coffee. Hattie didn't make any? And Danish. Doughnuts. At the very least, she could've set out a bag of Oreos."

Mason tried like hell not to smile. "In Hattie's defense, she hardly expected anyone to be here. I'm sure her mother's got plenty of food left from the wake if you two want to head over there?"

"Lord..." Hands on her hips, Fern surveyed Melissa's top-of-the-line Keurig K-Cup–style coffeemaker. "Prissy and downright pretentious is what this is. If I were you, I'd run this straight out to the dump and get you a nice stove-top percolator."

"Sure. I'll see what I can do." What he failed telling Fern was that he thought the whole single-cup thing pretty damned cool. He'd never known coffee technology existed until his friend Heath's new bride, Patricia, had it listed on her bridal-shower registry. The damn thing had been pricey, so Mason and his pal Cooper had gone halvsies on it. Which reminded him, he needed to call his CO and SEAL team roomie about not being home as scheduled.

"Ready?" His dad, Jerry, joined them. "I've got shows."

Fern furrowed the caterpillars she called brows. "For cryin' out loud, Jer', step into this century. Haven't you heard of a DVR?"

"Haven't you heard the government uses those things to bug your house—they put pinhole spy cams in there, too."

After a grand eye roll, Fern sighed. "S'pose next you'll be telling me sittin' too close to my TV'll make me blind?"

Jerry shrugged. "Judging by your outfit, you may want to push your recliner a ways back."

"Oh, for God's sake…" Mason grabbed Fern's coat and held it out to her. "Get a room and leave me in peace."

"I wouldn't sleep with your father if he laid gold nuggets."

"Thanks for that visual." Wincing, Mason held out the garment, wagging it in hopes of enticing Fern to slip it on and then slip right out the door. "I appreciate you two bringing my gear, but if you don't mind, I've got baby-care research to do. Oh—and, Dad, here are your keys." Mason fished them from his pocket. "Thank you for letting me use your ride."

"No problem, but what're you gonna drive now?"

"I suppose Alec's Hummer."

"Talk about pretentious." Fern snorted. "I don't mean to speak ill of the dead, but I never did approve of that car—if you could even call it that. More like a tank."

Jerry snapped, "You didn't seem to mind much last winter when you stuck your Shirley Temple curls out the sunroof for the Christmas parade."

"Shut your pie hole, old man. You're just jealous no one asked you."

Fingers to throbbing temples, Mason counted to ten to keep from blowing. Fern and his dad had always been combustible neighbors, but he'd forgotten to what degree. At least they could now retreat to separate vehicles.

After ten more minutes' bickering, Fern and Jerry finally left Mason in peace. Only, even then he didn't truly feel calm because of the emotions warring in his head. Guilt for not feeling more sadness in regard to Melissa's and Alec's deaths, confusion over the sheer logistics of caring for their infant twins, hurt over being treated like a pariah by two families he'd once very much loved and felt a part of.

Thank God for Hattie.

Even though she'd temporarily left him in charge, he appreciated knowing he wasn't ultimately alone. Knowing that by the time the babies woke she'd be back comforted him when otherwise he'd have been in a panic.

Mason tossed a couple logs on the fire, then grabbed his iPad, only to find the battery near dead. He rummaged through his bag for the charger but, when he returned to the sofa to do baby research, found his cord wasn't near long enough.

In need of an extension cord, he headed downstairs to the utility room. His first trek to the home's lowest level, he hadn't ventured farther than the heater. Now he noted the kind of party room he and Alec had only dreamed of when they'd been teens. A fully stocked wet bar complete with two kegs on tap and a loaded wine fridge. A few half-empty beer mugs sat on a counter covered in longneck twist caps sealed in clear acrylic. Mason had never seen anything like it. Had the creation been his idea or Melissa's or their architect or designer's?

A pool table sat lifeless with all the balls scattered as if fresh from a break.

Bright lights from three vintage slots and an assortment of pinball machines and video games stood out in the gloom.

A dozen or so weary red balloons hung at various elevations. Some waist-high. Others an inch from the floor. What had the happy couple been celebrating? Was their current group of friends comprised of the same old crew he'd once also considered his?

He caught a movement in his peripheral vision and discovered Hattie reflected in the mirrored wall behind the bar.

"Impressive, huh?" She trailed her fingertips along a felt-covered poker table still littered with cards and chips. "Almost as nice as my bar on the wharf, but I have more than one TV." Gesturing to a wall-mount model that was damn near half the size of his truck, she swiped at glistening tears. Her faint smile twisted his heart. He couldn't imagine what she must be going through.

"If you don't mind my asking…" He swatted a balloon. "What were they celebrating?"

"Remember Craig Lovett from your senior class?"

He nodded.

"It was his birthday." Behind the bar, she took the three mugs and washed them in the sink. "I'm surprised Melissa left even this little of a mess. Practically her only hobby was cleaning."

"Fun." He snagged the nearest balloon. "Want me to grab all of these?"

"Sure. Thanks." Though it'd been years since their last meaningful conversation, Hattie's current cool demeanor unnerved him. A childish part of him wanted things back the way they used to be between them. Hattie had been his go-to girl for when he'd just wanted to chill. They'd always been able to talk about anything from sports to politics to, hell, even stupid issues like annoying road construction.

Now he wasn't sure what to say.

Her new, more polished, infinitely more curvy look threw him for a loop. Not only didn't she look the same, but she carried herself with more confidence. Shoulders back, long hair loose, wind-tossed to the point of being a little wild. Her scent even threw him. Gone was the tomboy blend of sweat and bubble gum, replaced by a complex crispness that on this snowy night embodied the town's conifer trees and ice.

"Here's a trash bag." She held the top open for him while he shoved in the balloons. She was quiet for a moment and then said, "What's wrong?"

"Not sure what you mean?" He focused on his task rather than her uncomfortable proximity.

"You're tensed up—kind of like when we were in grade school and all of you guys used to freeze when the girls threatened to give you cooties."

"Whatever..." He shook his head. "I'm just tired." Of the whole situation. If Melissa and Alec hadn't died, he'd be safe and sound back in Virginia—even better, off on a mission where his thoughts were occupied 24/7 by things that mattered. The issues currently fogging his brain were the kinds of details he found best avoided. Women and kids were so far off his radar they might as well be alien life forms.

"Me, too. Hopefully, after a good night's rest all of this will feel less overwhelming." Her eyes shone.

Mason knew he should say something kind and reassuring, but how could he when panic consumed him? Even worse, once they met with the judge, his ties to the whole mess would be cut, but poor Hattie was stuck with two kids for a lifetime. Inconceivable. "Yeah. I bet everything will seem better in the morning."

HATTIE WOKE TO the not-so-melodic sound of her nieces screaming. She bolted from her guest-room bed, nearly colliding with Mason as he charged up the stairs from where he'd slept on the sofa.

She winced. "Thought you said everything would be better in the morning?"

"Yeah, well, guess I was wrong. You take the one on the left. I'll take the right."

Hattie scooped squalling Vivian from her crib.

Mason picked up Vanessa.

Neither baby showed any sign of calming soon. Above her nieces' now-frantic tears, Hattie shouted, "I'm guessing both need fresh diapers and feeding, so should we divide and conquer?"

"What do you mean?" He lightly jiggled Vanessa, which only agitated her further.

"I'll make bottles while you handle morning cleanup." Honestly, could her sister have left her in any worse position? The instant upgrade from aunt to mom was rough enough; tossing in an incompetent baby daddy like Mason compounded her already-considerable woes.

His eyebrows shot up. "You mean you're leaving me alone with them?"

After placing Vivian temporarily back in her crib, she patted Mason's back. "I have total faith in you to do a great job."

Five minutes later, bottles in hand, she'd just mounted the steps to check on Mason's progress when she spied him carrying both babies and heading her way. Vivian and Vanessa were still red-eyed and huffing, but at least the near-deafening wails had calmed. While moments earlier, she'd have seen this as a good thing, the lull in the storm afforded her the relative luxury of getting her first good look at Mason that morning. He wore no shirt and a pair of low-riding sweats with *Navy* written down one leg. He'd always had a great body, but now? Wow.

Mouth dry, she hastily looked away from six-pack abs partially blocked by her squirmy nieces.

She met him halfway up the stairs, taking Vanessa. "Did you have any trouble?"

"Nah. Compared to bomb demo, diapering's no biggie. This one's a pistol, though. Fights me every step of the way." Taking the bottle she offered, he nodded to Vivian. "She's only four arms and legs shy of being a human octopus. I feel bad for you when she learns to walk."

Hattie laughed, though inside, his innocent statement brought on cause to worry. The twins still had months before they started walking, but the day would come. She'd soon need to worry about baby-proofing and figuring out solid foods and brushing tiny teeth. She didn't even want to think about the girls walking yet.

She settled onto the sofa with her charge.

Mason, cradling Vivian, sat on the opposite end. He initially fumbled getting the bottle into the baby's crying mouth, but once he did, the house fell blessedly quiet. "That's better. When they tag team like that, I feel desperate."

"Me, too...."

After a few minutes' companionable silence, he asked, "What's the plan for today?"

"I suppose we need to nail down a firm date for you to appear in court. Then, if you don't mind, I could use help moving a few things from my place over here."

"Sure." He repositioned Vivian. "Think your mom would feel up to watching these two?"

"I don't see why not."

"Good." His smile did funny things to her stomach. "I don't know about you, but I could use a breather."

"We've only been awake ten minutes."

He shrugged. "There's no politically correct way for me to say this, so I'll just go for it. Have you thought about taking the same route I am? You know, signing over your parental rights?"

"You mean passing the buck?"

His smile morphed into a scowl. "I mean, getting your life back on track. Your mom seemed genuinely upset that she won't be raising these two. Why not give her what she wants? Hell, give a girl to Alec's mom, too. That way, they can each have a kid, all problems solved."

"Hear that rushing sound? That was my respect for you, flying out the window."

"How LONG ARE you going to stay mad at me?" Mason asked Hattie as they snatched boxes from her dad's warehouse's recycling bin.

"Forever." She wouldn't even look his way.

They'd each spelled each other for showers, then loaded the eight tons of gear needed to drop the babies with Akna. During all that time, she'd barely said three words.

When Benton had called, dropping the bomb that it would be three weeks before Mason's meeting with the Valdez judge, the mood hadn't grown much brighter.

"Look," Mason said, "I was only stating the obvious. What you're doing for Melissa is a noble, lovely gesture, but it's also going way above and beyond when if you get right down to it, what did your sister ever do for you? Melissa was a taker. She took from me and you."

"Stop." Tears shone on Hattie's cheeks, making Mason instantly ashamed, even though in his heart he believed he'd spoken the truth. "What happened to you? I never remember you being this cruel."

"Cruel?" He couldn't contain a sarcastic laugh. "Is there

a statute of limitations on me being allowed to harbor ill will toward a woman who essentially ruined my life?"

"Stop being a drama queen. That all happened years ago."

"Right—" he grabbed an undamaged box and tossed it on their pile "—just like the time Melissa totaled her car and instead of making her earn a new one, your parents gave her yours? Or how about when you won the role of Juliet in the school play, but then Melissa told the drama teacher she should get it since I was playing Romeo and we were dating, and that would sell more tickets?"

Hattie sharply looked away. "I refuse to do this. Melissa's dead. Whatever she did back then is ancient history. Right now, her babies need a mom—they already have grandmothers. My mother and Alec's mean well, but you, of all people, should realize what it's like growing up without a mom."

"Leave my past out of this." Jaw clenched, he pitched a box hard enough at their growing pile to crush one of the corners.

"But it's all right for you to air my dirty laundry?"

"I gave you Melissa-specific examples."

"I'm done with this discussion." She raised her chin. The air outside the loading dock was cold enough to see her sharp exhalations manifest in angry clouds. Her cheeks reddened, probably more from fury than cold. Regardless, her determined stare reminded him of better days. Times when that determination landed them on epic climbs to mountaintops and fishing in places he'd sworn they'd never find their way home from. She'd been one of his best pals, but for whatever reason, that dynamic had changed, which made him sad. He'd already lost her sister; he didn't want to lose Hattie's friendship, as well.

"I'm sorry," he said. "I can see where my suggestion could come across as crass, but, Hat Trick, you're no more ready to be a parent than I am. I was only trying to give you an *out*."

"That's just it…" She brushed away more tears. "I don't want an out. These are my nieces we're talking about—not a pair of Yorkies. If Melissa had enough faith in me to handle the job, then I can. Period."

"Okay. I get it." Had she always been this beautiful? Her anger intensified the color in her high cheekbones, making her appear warrior-fierce. In that moment, he believed she could single-handedly raise the twins. He just wished she didn't have to. But did he wish it enough to quit the navy? Stay in Conifer to help?

Not just *no. Hell no.*

Chapter Six

"Clem, come on—focus." Hattie waved her hand in front of her friend's blatant stare. "Can you cover for me tonight?"

"I remember Mason being decent looking, but *damn*..."

"Hush." Hattie gave her friend a well-placed elbow to her side as Mason effortlessly hefted another box down the narrow staircase that led from her apartment to the bar's main floor. "He's nothing special."

"Says the girl who lusted after him for the vast majority of her life—at least until her sister married him."

"Can you please save this for another time?" Hattie closed her eyes on the not-too-shabby view of Mason's jean-clad behind.

"Look, I understand what you're going through must be rough, but Melissa dumped him a long time ago. In my mind, that makes him fair game."

"Please stop."

"He's single. You're single. Those babies go to bed early, leaving a whole lot of time for fooling—"

"Hush!" Hattie hadn't meant to shout, but when the five patrons at the bar looked her way, she reddened. Her voice at a more appropriate level, she said, "You're being ridiculous. Now back to the topic at hand—can you cover for me tonight, or not?"

"Sorry, but Dougie's got a nasty cold. Once I'm done here, I wanna run him over to the urgent-care clinic to get him checked out."

"How's Joey?" Clementine's son Doug was three and Joey was five.

"So far, he's fine. But Mom had sniffles when I dropped Dougie off this morning. If she goes down, I'm screwed."

"Hopefully, they'll both feel better soon." Hattie had five other bartenders she could call, but she thought working the shift herself, and having a night away from Mason, would probably do her good.

He appeared. "That was the last of it. Ready to head out?"

"Sure." Hattie took her purse from behind the bar. "But I'll need to come back later."

He frowned. "Clem, how've you been?"

"Good, thanks." Oh, for heaven's sake. Clementine visibly flushed. Mason wasn't *that* great to look at.

The lie created heat in her own cheeks. Okay, so Mason wasn't exactly unfortunate when it came to his appearance, but that didn't mean Clementine's matchmaking had been warranted. The whole issue was wildly inappropriate.

"Hear you've done real good for yourself." Hattie's friend actually fluffed her hair. "Even so, we've missed you around here."

"Thanks." He shrugged. "It's nice being back. Just wish the circumstances were better."

"I understand." Could Clementine be more obvious? She'd struck a pose against the bar that showed a royal gorge of cleavage. "We're all pretty upset."

Really, Clem? The only thing she looked upset about was Mason standing too far away.

"Okay, well…" Hattie grabbed Mason by his arm, tugging him toward the door. "Glad you two could catch up, but I'd like to unpack all my stuff at Melissa's before it's time to pick up the girls."

Outside, though the day was sunny, a blustery north wind seized Hattie's hair, tangling it in her face.

"Hold up." Mason stopped her midway down the pier, way too deep into her personal space for her liking while helping her tidy the mess. "You look like Cousin Itt from— What was that show?"

"The Addams Family?" For years, they'd watched the show every day after school. Hattie could probably still recite every episode.

"Yeah. That's it." Resuming their walk, he said, "I used to love that show."

"Me, too." Only not for the stellar acting, but because Melissa had hated it, which meant Hattie and Mason were usually left alone with the TV and Oreos.

At her SUV, he asked, "Want me to drive?"

"Why?"

"You look tired. And a couple times when you were packing, I caught you crying."

She yanked open the driver's-side door with extra force, then climbed behind the wheel. "I'm fine. In fact, having just lost my sister, I figure I'm doing pretty damned good to even be upright."

"Excellent point," he said from beside her. "You are putting on a good show of strength, Hat Trick, but I know you. It's a show. Honestly, you look ready to break."

"Thanks for the appraisal, but you *used* to know me." She started the car and pulled away from the curb. "Now? I'm not sure what we are. Maybe strangers who used to be friends?"

HATTIE'S ASSESSMENT OF their relationship sobered Mason.

While she unpacked her belongings in the guest bedroom, he lounged on the living room sofa, surfing the web for baby-care sites. He was determined to treat this bump in his road as he would any other mission. Professionally, with a cool detachment from any issue close to getting personal.

They were due at Hattie's mom's in a couple hours, so he made good use of the uninterrupted time.

He'd just found an excellent page outlining the reasons for not using baby powder when a crash sounded from upstairs, followed by a feminine yelp.

"Hattie? You okay?"

When she didn't answer, he abandoned his iPad to charge up the stairs.

He found her beneath a pile of clothes tall enough to have damn near buried her. Looked as if the closet's hanging rod had given up the ghost. "Damn, girl, good thing you use plastic hangers or you'd have poked out your eyes."

She popped her head out from between the legs of faded jeans. "Less commentary and more help would be appreciated."

"Oh, I don't know..." He couldn't resist tugging his phone from his back pocket to snap a quick pic. The closet was a walk-in, but Hattie and her sweaters, jeans and blouses occupied a huge portion of the floor. "I think we should sit back for a minute to savor the moment."

"You're a beast." She gave a mighty shove to the clothes in front of her, struggling to get back on her feet.

"A good-looking one, though," he teased, offering her his hands to tug her free from the mess.

Her only answer was a glare.

"How'd you manage this? I always thought Melissa was the fashionista?"

"Have you seen the size of her closet? Trust me, this isn't much. I guess she and Alec just used cheap rod brackets when this place was built."

"In their defense—" Mason grabbed as much clothing

as he could, piling it on the bed "—probably most guests don't have as much stuff as you."

For a brief moment, the old Hattie stuck out her tongue. It happened so fast, Mason couldn't even be sure he hadn't imagined her return to that old playful habit, but he hoped he hadn't. Holding her hands even for the brief seconds it'd taken to free her from the fabric avalanche hadn't felt ordinary, but somehow special. As if he'd stumbled across a long-forgotten part of himself that up until now, he hadn't even known was missing.

He looked at Hattie.

Really looked, and found himself riveted by the view. Even with her long hair more disheveled than usual and her cheeks prettily flushed, there was something about her that kept drawing him in. The fact that she wore the hell out of faded jeans and a plaid shirt didn't hurt, either. The woman had curves in all the right places.

Hands on her hips, she asked, "What?"

"Huh?"

"You're staring." She fussed with her hair. "Do I have a bra hanging from my head?"

He laughed. "Can't a guy appreciate a nice view?"

EVEN AT TEN that night while working her shift at the bar, Hattie struggled to get Mason's cryptic words from her head. When he'd mentioned that "nice view," she'd been standing in front of French doors that led to a balcony overlooking the valley. At that moment, she'd brushed off his unexpected comment, but now her stomach knotted. Had he been talking about her?

No. She scrubbed harder at the greasy hot-wing residue someone had smeared on the bar. For as long as they'd known each other, Melissa had been the only girl for him. Their divorce, and even her death, couldn't erase that kind of history.

Mason had 100 percent admired scenic Treehorn Valley. Which was a good thing. According to unwritten, yet explicitly understood Sister Code, Mason would always belong to Melissa. As he should. Even if he did by some miracle find her attractive, Hattie had more pride than to even want a man who no doubt viewed her as second best.

"Didn't expect to find you here." A familiar voice jolted Hattie from her thoughts.

"I could say the same to you." She jogged around to the bar's front to hug her dad. With dark circles under his tear-reddened eyes, he was a walking example of how shattered their whole family felt. "Why aren't you with Mom?"

Shifting on his stool, resting his elbows on the bar, he sighed. "She hasn't had a decent night's rest since…" In that small hesitation, Hattie all-too-easily filled in the blank. "I called Doc Amesbury to prescribe her a sedative. She's finally asleep."

"What about you? Not that I'm knocking the healing benefits of the occasional shot of whiskey, but, Dad, maybe you should've also gotten medicine for yourself?"

He waved off her concern. "I might look like hell, but I'm all right. Need to stay strong for your mom. She's already torn up enough about your sister, but to then have the twins taken from her, too…" He shook his head. "I get what your sister was trying to accomplish, but in the process she broke your mother's heart."

Hattie struggled to compose her thoughts. "Are you suggesting I follow Mason's lead and sign away my rights?"

"No. Absolutely not—unless you want to. Your mom likes to believe she can do anything and everything, but as exhausted as she was from watching the rug rats this afternoon, no way is she ready to start parenting all over again from scratch."

On autopilot, Hattie poured her dad two fingers of his favorite bourbon.

"I think what she doesn't realize, but your sister in some crazy way did, is that if your mom were to assume primary custody of those babies, she'd for all practical purposes lose out on the joy she finds in being their grandmother." He took a long sip of his drink. "You and I were blessed to have both in our lives, and there's a difference."

Hattie nodded. Though all of her grandparents had passed—her maternal grandmother just two years earlier—Hattie would never forget the unconditional love and downright spoiling she'd found in their loving arms.

"That said, if you feel like you can't handle raising those girls on your own, move home. Between the three of us, we'll figure it out."

"Dad, I'm fine." And one of these days, possibly years down the road, she'd believe it. For now, all she could do was honor her sister's last wish as best she could. "I'm sorry Mom's upset. She's not mad at me, is she?"

He shook his head. "More like mad at the world." After another drink, he said, "Give it some time. I'm sure she'll come around."

HATTIE DIDN'T CLOSE until 2:00 a.m., meaning by the time she'd poured her last customer into the town's only cab, it was two-thirty when she reached Melissa and Alec's.

Would the supersize house ever feel like home?

The night had turned bitterly cold and her footfalls crunched in the icy snow.

By the time true winter cold set in, she'd have to sell her ancient SUV in favor of driving Melissa's much-newer Land Rover that was parked all warm and toasty in the garage.

She'd just mounted the freshly shoveled porch when the door opened and Mason stepped out.

"Hey." He held the door open for her.

"Hey, yourself. Why are you still up?" Brushing past

him, Hattie found herself wrapped in his all-masculine scent of sweet woodsmoke and the leathery aftershave he'd started using in tenth grade. She wanted to act as if it was no big deal, but at this time of night her defenses were down and the comfort of their shared pasts stirred a warmth she'd thought gone forever.

He shrugged. "Couldn't sleep till I knew you'd made it home safe."

"Thanks."

With her inside, he closed and locked the door—not that there was much need for it with Conifer's almost-nonexistent crime rate.

"Hungry?" He took her coat and hung it in the entry-hall closet. "I made a couple boxes of mac and cheese."

"Yum," she teased. "Didn't know you'd become a gourmet."

"If that was a dig at me flunking home ec, I shouldn't have even been in there and you know it." Only in Alaska could the woodshop teacher be on extended leave because of a bear attack. "If I'd had a little longer, that cake would've been delicious."

"Yeah, yeah…" She couldn't help but grin at his dear face that had changed so much over the years, but in her mind's eye not at all. "Keep telling yourself that. One of these days it might come true."

"Just for that, next time you're at work, I'm making you a cake so you'll be forced to eat your words." While she removed her boots, he took a covered bowl from the fridge.

"From scratch?"

He put the bowl in the microwave. "Is there any other kind?"

"Sure. Duncan Hines, Pillsbury and the really fancy ones from Ann's Bakery."

Leaning against the counter, waiting for the food to

warm, he grinned. "How is it that after all these years, you're still a pain in my ass?"

"Language," she said primly. "You forget, children are present."

"Whatever." The microwave dinged.

Hattie sat at the counter bar while Mason delivered her a fork and the bowl of leftovers. What the meal lacked in flavor, it made up for in companionship. She'd forgotten how much fun she and Mason could have with simple banter.

He took a beer from the fridge and twisted off the cap. After hefting himself up to sit on the kitchen's island counter, he asked, "In all seriousness, how are you?"

"I'm good. Don't get me wrong, this isn't going to be an easy adjustment, but I'll deal. What about you? You're the one who pulled the short end of the straw tonight. How were my adorable nieces?"

His handsome half smile did funny things to Hattie's insides. "Vanessa was a doll, but I swear Vivian's got it in for me. During bath time, she pitched soap in my eyes and I'm pretty sure she deliberately tried to drown my cell."

"Uh-huh…" Now Hattie was the one grinning. "All this from an infant who can barely roll herself over?"

"Don't let that innocent act fool you." He raised his bottle. "She's a tough cookie. Before too long, you'll be catching her smoking out behind the woodshed."

"Right. If my memory serves me correct, that was you and Melissa who got caught in that particular act."

"There was never any proof we smoked those butts. Could've been anyone." He winked before hopping down to finish off his beer and toss the bottle in the recycling bin. "Ready for bed?"

"I should be—" she speared a few noodles "—but I'm too wired. Wanna watch a movie—or at least part of one?"

He yawned. "Sounds better than another night on the sofa."

"There is another bed."

A scowl marred his otherwise-gorgeous face. "Yeah, and it's got more ghosts than the town graveyard."

MASON WOKE GOD-ONLY-KNEW how many hours later in the basement's home theater to the sound of the opening loop for *Alien* playing over and over. Laced in with that were frantic cries from upstairs.

A glance to his left showed Hattie out cold, lightly snoring.

Bolting to action, Mason raced from the room to find bright sun streaming through the living room's glass wall. The baby monitor he'd meant to carry downstairs with them sat on the kitchen counter, echoing the twins' wails.

Feeling lower than low—like the worst babysitter in the history of the world, Mason bounded up the stairs and into the nursery. "I'm so sorry, ladies."

He scooped first Vanessa, then Vivian into his arms. Vanessa calmed soon enough, letting out offended huffs, but there was no consoling Vivian.

After making a precision-swift diaper change, Mason marched downstairs with his troops, setting them in the playpen while mixing formula. A few minutes after that, he sat on the sofa with both pretty girls nestled into the crooks of his arms.

"I'm so sorry," he said over their greedy suckling. "Rookie mistake that will *never* happen again."

Vivian's blue-eyed stare warned him it'd better not.

The fact that he'd forgotten such a basic necessity as the baby monitor reinforced Mason's belief he had no business being any child's parent—let alone, Melissa and Alec's kids.

Though Hattie claimed she was ready, he had serious doubts as to whether or not she was any more capable than him. Not three minutes into the movie, clearly exhausted, she'd fallen asleep.

He'd watched her for a spell, worrying about how she'd manage both her bar and new family.

She'd always been one of the strongest people he knew, but in that moment's peace, she'd appeared vulnerable. Almost fragile. Her complexion had paled and her cheeks bore telltale signs of tears.

Guilt consumed him for even thinking of leaving her on her own with the girls. But honestly, what else could he do? Even if the twins weren't the product of a marriage he'd viewed as a betrayal, that whole mess had forever changed him. It'd stolen whatever softness his heart might have once contained and exchanged it for unyielding steel.

He was now a soldier.

That was all.

Chapter Seven

"I'm a horrible person," Hattie said as she pushed their cart at Conifer's only grocery store. While Princess Vivian rode in her carrier in the cart, Mason held Vanessa. "You should've shaken me awake."

"Knock it off, will you?" He took five cans of the organic formula Melissa had preferred from the shelf. "We both screwed up. I'm as much to blame as you. Luckily, other than Vivian giving me the stink eye, no real harm was done."

She tossed three bags of diapers atop their growing pile. "Yeah, but what if there'd been a fire or burglar?"

"Armed robbery a big worry in Conifer nowadays?"

It took Hattie a sec to see the smile lighting his eyes. Then she restrained herself from pummeling him. "You know what I mean."

"Yeah, I do. But we got lucky and both girls are fine. Lesson learned." They rounded the corner to the cereal aisle, where he asked, "You still a fan of Cap'n Crunch?"

"Love it," she said with a wistful glance toward a box, "but my hips don't."

"What's wrong with your hips?"

Seriously? He was going to make her explain the obvious? She'd always been big-boned, but lately her weight had become more and more of an issue. One she had no intention of discussing with Mason.

"Did you have an operation Dad forgot to tell me about?"

Hattie clenched her teeth to keep from saying something she may later regret. After adding bran flakes to the cart, she asked, "Anything in particular you want?"

"Whoa." She'd moved a good ten feet from him, when he grabbed her arm, lightly tugging her back, flooding her with an old, achy longing for him she'd thought had been tucked safely away and forgotten. "Talk to me, Hat Trick. What's with the sudden deep freeze?"

Tears stung her eyes. Her friends constantly told her how strong she was and funny and hardworking, but never had anyone said she was pretty or looked darling in a dress the way they had her sister. She would give away half her credit score to have Mason look at her just once the way he had Melissa. With heat. Longing. Appreciation.

"What'd I do? Does this have something to do with missing your sister?"

Wrenching free from him, she continued to the next aisle, desperate to get away.

Unfortunately, he was not only a head taller than her, but faster. In a heartbeat, he'd rounded the cart, bracing his hands on either side. "You're not going anywhere until I'm out of the doghouse. If we're stuck living together for the next three weeks, let's at least be civil."

Stuck? Oh—that made her feel much better.

"For the last time, what do your hips have to do with our old pal The Captain?"

"I'm fat, okay? There. I said it. Happy?"

He actually had the good graces to appear dumbfounded, with his mouth partially open. "Are you kidding me?"

"Can we please finish up?" Unshed tears blurred her vision.

"We will, but first things first. For the record, what the hell? Fat? You're not fat, for God's sake. You're voluptuous and a one-hundred-percent beautiful woman. Melissa used to spout this dieting crap all the time and it pissed me off. If I were sticking around, I'd tell Vanessa and Viv every day that they're pretty just the way they are."

But you're not sticking around. The words caught in Hattie's throat. For an awkward moment, she wasn't sure what to do with herself and then Mason caught and held her gaze.

Finally, he looked away before stalking to the delicious, sugary cereal they'd both eaten by the bushels as kids. He tossed two boxes in the cart, then shot her a dirty look. "You're not fat."

"WOULD YOU QUIT lookin' at that thing and get back to chopping?" Mason's dad rammed his ax extra hard on the log he'd been splitting, coming dangerously close in the process to knocking off the baby monitor Mason had set on the porch rail. The temperature was falling fast, and a stiff breeze howled through the pines. With another winter storm heading their way, and Alec not even having a fraction of the wood supply needed to carry a home as large as his and Melissa's through the winter, Mason was grateful to his dad for pitching in. "Fern knows more about babies than anyone in this town."

"How?" Hattie had gone to work at the bar and her father reported Akna was in no shape to watch the girls, so Fern, a former long-haul trucker, had volunteered to watch Vivian and Vanessa.

"Remember a few years back when Fern had that puppy? Well, Rascal grew into a fine dog."

"Dad, even I know there's a helluva difference between raising a dog and kids."

His father used his shirt sleeve to wipe sweat from his brow. "Fern's a good woman. Those kids could do worse."

"Since when are you two getting on so well?"

"What do you mean?" Had his longtime bachelor dad's cheeks actually reddened from something other than exertion?

"You know…" Mason winked. "I think Fern has a crush on you."

"Me and Fern?" Jerry laughed. "We have a complicated relationship. Although, folks at the coffee shop have been speculating on the prospect of you and Hattie ending up together. Said it'd be shameful—Hattie taking up with her dead sister's husband."

"They can talk all they want—" Mason took a fresh log from the truck bed "—but not only did the gossips leave out the bit about Melissa's having been my ex, but I'm expected back on base in three weeks. Besides which, one Beaumont woman was more than enough for me."

His dad grunted. "Guess you've got a point there."

"You're actually agreeing with me?"

"Not so much agreeing as remembering. Not to speak ill of the dead, but Melissa put you through the ringer. Alec, too. Wasn't right. Still…" He stopped chopping to lean back against their growing, neatly stacked pile. "I suppose if I'm ever going to get grandkids, sooner or later you're gonna have to climb back on that horse."

Mason winced. "If only it were that simple. And since when did you start wanting to be a grandpa?"

"I'm getting up in years. For that matter, so are you." He resumed chopping. "Speaking from past experience, growing old alone isn't all it's cracked up to be."

"Then why don't you find a good woman? And when you do, then you can leave me alone."

"Jerry, hon?" Fern poked her head out the front door. "You two want chili or tacos for dinner?"

"Hon?" Mason aimed a smile in his dad's direction. "If I were you, I'd take that as a sign." As for his own love life? Those days were long gone.

"WHAT'S WRONG WITH HER?" Hattie asked her dad, who was sorting his DVD collection. When he'd reported earlier that her mom was too sick to watch the twins, Hattie worried the rest of the day.

"Not sure."

She removed her coat and boots to curl onto an end of the sofa. Strange how the room looked the same as it always had. Soothing blue walls covered in dozens of family pictures. Hand-crocheted doilies covering tabletops decorated with lamps and her mom's many ballerina figurines. A stranger looking in would never suspect the tragedy their family was going through. "What are Mom's symptoms?"

Rather than look at her, he studied the back cover of a DVD case. "Pretty sure she's just tired."

"But she loves caring for the girls." Standing, she said, "I'll talk to her."

"Wish you wouldn't." Her dad abandoned his movie to block the hall.

"Okay, now you're scaring me. What's going on?"

"She's having a hard time with this—we both are."

"By 'this,' do you mean what happened to Melissa? Or are you talking about the will?"

After a sharp exhalation, he shook his head. "Leave it alone."

"Okay. Sure." Hattie had tired of crying, but the knot that had become all too familiar at the back of her throat made it difficult to breathe.

Though the last thing she wanted was to be distanced

from her parents when she needed them most, Hattie abided by her father's wishes and left the two of them alone.

"IT WAS AWFULLY nice of Fern and your dad to step in to help." Hattie passed Mason the last of the plates to dry.

Vivian and Vanessa shared the playpen, alternating between gumming teething rings and each other. It was good for a change, seeing them not upset.

"With Fern watching the girls, Dad and I got a lot of wood cut."

"Thanks." The pain of her father's rejection still stung, and though Hattie had held her emotions in check while sharing their meal with Jerry and Fern, she now felt dangerously near her breaking point. Not a good thing considering the meltdown she'd already had that morning at the grocery store. "I really appreciate your help. While you're still in town, I need to get a new schedule established at the bar."

"Sure. I'm happy to do whatever you need."

Though his words were kind, as were his actions, Hattie couldn't help feeling tension simmering between them. Despite the years between them, she still felt as if she knew him better than just about anyone—at least anyone other than Melissa. His shoulders were too squared for him to be relaxed. The set of his jaw too tight.

They finished washing and drying the dishes. While Hattie wiped down the counters, Mason brushed crumbs from the place mats Fern had set on the table.

"Look," Hattie finally said, unable to bear a moment's more tension, "about this morning at the store... I was—"

"Stop. I should've stayed out of your business." He left the table, approaching her until he stood perilously close. "But I meant it, you know? Hat Trick, you're a beautiful woman. One day, you're going to make some lucky guy seriously happy."

But not you?

After what she'd just been through with her dad, the last thing Hattie needed was Mason's vacuous compliment. What he didn't know—what he must never know—was that no matter how many guys she'd dated, none of them had ever meant more to her than him. Melissa had known it. Hattie was still furious with her for matchmaking via her will. That letter should've been a treasured keepsake, but instead, Hattie found her sister's last words mortifying. Before losing her sister, Hattie's life's tragedy had been loving a man she could never have. It struck her as ironic that even with Melissa no longer in the picture, Mason was just as off-limits—not only because of her own conscience, but his clichéd "some lucky guy" declaration.

Covering her face with her hands, she wasn't sure how much more she could take.

"Hattie?" With his elbow, he delivered what she assumed he meant to be a playful nudge. The kind of gesture he'd made a hundred times when they'd been friends and later, when by law he'd technically been her brother. "I know this pouty look. What's going on? With Fern and my dad here, I didn't have the chance to ask if everything's okay with your mom."

She pitched the dishrag in the sink. "No. Things are far from okay with both of my folks. Though Dad wouldn't give me specifics, I'm guessing Mom's still freaking out about the will."

"I'm sorry." He drew her into a hug. The kind of friendly gesture they'd exchanged countless times.

His strength, his warmth, his mere presence meant more to her than he would ever know. She had to pull herself together. Grief was making her an emotional basket case when she'd always prided herself on being strong.

"A few months from now, when you're settled into your new routine, I'll bet things will be better."

"Hope you're right." Hattie pressed her cheek against his impossibly toned chest. Her mother's words had been so cruel, yet in the same respect, given the opportunity, would she not only kiss Mason, but more?

For the longest time, they stood together, bodies so close they'd become one. She allowed herself the weakness of letting him be the strong one, because she was tired of holding it all together when all she wanted was to fall apart.

She glanced up at him, at his dear lips. How long had she dreamed of holding him like this? Having him hold her? Hattie had been mortified by Melissa spilling Hattie's most closely guarded secret about her crush on Mason. How embarrassing, but at the same time, liberating. For if all of her cards were already on the table, what did she have to lose by standing on her tiptoes, touching her lips to his for so brief a tantalizing second? She wasn't sure she had actually kissed him at all. But then he groaned, easing his hand under the curtain of her hair, and suddenly what she'd meant to be a simple gesture turned very complicated, and he was kissing her, sweeping her tongue, chilling her yet warming her, until everything in the room vanished, save for him and the raw emotions their connection evoked.

"Oh, my God..." Just as shockingly as the kiss had begun, it ended. "I'm sorry. That shouldn't have happened."

"No, *I'm* sorry...." Her hands pressed to her swollen, still-tingling lips. *Mortification* didn't come close to describing how deeply she regretted what had just transpired. "It'll never happen again."

"Of course. Shouldn't have happened the first time."

"Agreed."

For an endless minute, they stood frozen. Just as well, considering Hattie didn't have a clue where to go from here. She'd kissed her dead sister's ex-husband. On the morality meter, she couldn't get much lower.

"On a lighter note…" Mason rocketed to the other side of the kitchen. "Did you know that at six months, a baby's brain will have already grown to half the size of an adult's?"

In no mood for baby trivia, Hattie simply stared.

"YOU LOOK LIKE death warmed over."

"Love you, too," Hattie said to Clementine early the next evening upon arriving to tend bar for the rest of the night.

"Sorry, but are you getting enough sleep?"

Hattie's only reply was a sad laugh.

"Wait—let me guess. Mason's not helping out with the babies?"

"Guess again. Turns out he's SEAL Nanny. When the twins are sleeping, he researches infant care online, then somehow assimilates it, only to brag about all he knows, which leads to making me feel guilty for all I don't know."

"Chin up." Clementine took her purse from under the counter. "In a few weeks, Mason will be gone, and with any luck, you won't have to deal with him again."

"Guess you're right." What Hattie couldn't share with her friend was that she feared Mason's leaving was a big part of her problem. He'd already adopted the role of the twins' primary caregiver. He could practically change a diaper one-handed and somehow managed feeding both girls their bottles at the same time. The guy was like a highly trained human octopus!

Clementine took her gloves from her purse. "I'm having a Halloween party next Saturday night. You and Mason wanna come?"

"Thanks, but I'm sure Mason would feel awkward around the old crowd and my mom's acting weird, so I don't know if she'd watch the twins. Plus, I really should be here. On any holiday, you know how it's usually nuts."

"Which is why Trevor and Rose have volunteered to cover for you. Come on—" she gave Hattie an elbow nudge "—say yes. It'll be fun."

"I'll think about it."

"You have to at least take the babies to Wharf-o-Ween." Hattie had forgotten about the town's annual Halloween festival that was held on the wharf—hence the kooky name.

Hattie sighed. "I don't know. We'd have to get costumes, and what if people talked? You know—like it's too soon after losing Melissa to have her kids out partying?"

"So what if they do? Melissa might be gone, but the whole reason she left her girls with you is for them to live. Meaning the question you have to ask yourself is, what would she want you to do?"

A WEEK PASSED.

Mason wished he could shake the melancholy that had settled over Hattie, but they seemed to have fallen into a rhythm of orchestrated avoidance—at least on Hattie's part.

Whenever he tried talking with her about anything more in depth than weather, she dashed off to her room—which made him crazy because he really needed to debrief. Compared to his usual workdays, caring for the twins was no big deal physically. What got to him was the mental game of sitting by himself all day every day. Sure, his dad and Fern dropped in occasionally, but other than them, he'd been pretty much left on his own.

Which was making him nuts.

Toss in that off-the-charts hot kiss he and Hattie had shared and he was really a goner. Being anywhere near her without touching her was proving incredibly hard.

Which was why when Hattie finally came home at 1:00 a.m. on a Tuesday night, he all but pounced on her when she walked through the door—at least, verbally. Physically, he kept his hands to himself. "It's about time you got here. Don't you have employees without kids who could take over your late night shifts?"

She froze midway through the process of removing her bulky coat. "Maybe you're not familiar with how businesses work, but if I pay out more in salaries than I take in, that's not a good thing."

"You know what I mean." He returned to the living room to pick up where he'd left off reading an online article about infants' strong sense of smell. "If you're hungry, I figured out a fairly decent pork-chop recipe. Left a plate for you in the fridge."

"Thanks."

He was trying. Why couldn't she?

Might be childish, but he refused to even look her way while she banged and clattered through the kitchen. She acted as if she was furious with him, but why? What the hell had he done other than bend over backward trying to make her life easier?

He hadn't even helped her with taking her coat off— not out of a lack of courtesy, but because he feared what the seemingly simple act of touching her may unleash.

Once the microwave dinged, she removed her plate to park at the kitchen bar with her back to him.

Really? She was going to sit there, eating his food without saying a single word? Okay, no more Mr. Nice Guy.

He got up from the sofa, rounded the counter to face her and braced his palms on the granite countertop. "Am I so repulsive that you can't even look at me while eating the meal I prepared?"

For the longest time, she stared at him, then had the gall to laugh—but it wasn't her ordinary laugh; it was more in the range of a guffaw with snorting and side-tears. "I'm sorry, but you sound like a housewife."

"Glad you think it's funny. I'd like to see you sit here, caring for two babies day after day. I'm going out of my mind."

"I can tell." Sobering, she toyed with her green beans. "Me, too. Sorry, I haven't been sharing the workload around here."

"I could give two shits about laundry or burping, but I could really just use a friend. So many guys on my team have kids and they ramble on about how great it is. Maybe I'm approaching this whole thing in too clinical a manner, but as cute as Viv and Van are, when I look at them, I see what their parents did to me. I loved Melissa. Alec was like a brother." Hands fisted, he slammed them to the counter. "Being back has stirred up all this crap I thought was behind me, you know?"

Boy, did she know. Hattie knew all too well what Mason meant, only in her case, it wasn't anger rising from the deep, but so much more. More than anything, she longed to take his hands, unclench his fingers, then kiss them one by one until his anger faded.

"The more I'm around the girls, caring for them, showing them *genuine* love every day, the more I realize this is no joke. But how can I love them when thinking about how they came into this world brings me nothing but pain? Nothing—save for losing my mom—has ever hurt as bad as Melissa and Alec's betrayal."

"Well…" Sighing, she pushed her half-eaten dinner aside. "Lucky for you, you're a short-timer in this whole thing. Even though I have no right, part of me is seriously ticked off at you for even thinking of leaving. Don't get me wrong—I understand you can't just up and quit the navy, but in the same respect, my mind's reeling. I know my folks will eventually come around, but in the meantime, I've got a sharp learning curve in raising these two on my own."

"For the next couple weeks, you don't have to. So how about I help you figure out the hourly logistics of infant care and you help me deal with the touchy-feely side of once and for all getting over your sister."

Hattie extended her hand for him to shake. "Deal."

When he pressed his palm to hers, shivery awareness danced through her, striking a humming chord of attraction low in her belly. How long had she wanted more from him than to be only friends? How long would the memory of the next precious two weeks last, knowing once Mason was gone, it might very well be forever?

"You okay?" he asked, still holding her hand.

"Yeah. I'm good." Her voice cracked with emotion and confusion and wistful longing for what she knew could never be.

"You don't look good— I mean…" With his free hand, he brushed away tears that lately never seemed to stop. Sure, grief played a role in Hattie's current emotional roller coaster, but so did unearthing her long-hidden feelings for this man. "You're pretty as ever, but what do I have to do to help you not look so sad?"

What did he have to do? *Everything.*

Hold her, kiss her, never leave. But honestly? Not only were the odds of all that occurring about as likely as a palm tree sprouting in the front yard, but she owed it to herself to once and for all forget her lame childhood fantasies of them being together and finally get on with her life.

As for their kiss? She *really* needed to forget that!

Chapter Eight

"Good morning, sleepyhead." The next morning, for once, Mason was awake before the girls wailed for room service. In the short time he'd been with them, he'd already seen developmental changes. At nineteen weeks, they were all about exploration, and when he entered their room, Vivian was studying a stuffed frog that shared her crib.

Vanessa was still snoozing.

Sunlight streamed through windows overlooking majestic mountain views.

Vivian caught sight of him and whimpered.

He scooped her into his arms. "Don't start, munchkin. It was a long night and I don't need you making this an even longer day."

Her smile took his breath away.

"Think that's funny?" Cradling her, he tickled her belly.

As much as he kept telling himself he was immune to the girls' charms, he feared many more encounters like this may lead to him having his heart broken all over again by this fresh crop of Beaumont girls.

"Hey…" Hattie stood at the room's threshold, yawning and rubbing her eyes. "I promised myself to be out of bed early enough for you to sleep in."

He grinned at his drooling charge. "I'm used to early mornings with no sleep." Talking in a goofy voice to coax

Vivian into another smile, he said, "Caring for babies is a cakewalk compared to defusing nukes."

Hattie sighed. "Wish I had your confidence."

"You'll get the hang of it."

"Wasn't I just saying that to you?" Cocking her head, she'd unwittingly sent her long hair into a sexy cascade. Her short flannel nightgown hugged her in all the right places, and exposed even more spots he wouldn't mind exploring. Since when had she stopped being just plain old Hat Trick, and started being sexy?

Laughing, he nodded. "What can I say? The navy taught me to be a fast learner."

After a halfhearted smile, she eased onto one of the room's upholstered rockers, drawing her feet up to hug her miles of bare legs. "No need to get cocky, sailor. I know the basics. Diapering, feeding, baths. What scares me is handling those basics, plus my regular full-time job."

"I thought your mom would be helping?"

"Me, too, but all of the sudden it's like she's checked out. I feel like she's blaming me for Melissa's will. It's crazy."

Mason changed Vivian's diaper. "What about Alec's folks?"

"Since they left for Miami, they're a nonissue." She took Vanessa from her crib. After kissing the infant's chubby cheek, she said, "For all the fuss your grandparents made when they heard I'd be caring for you, where are they now?"

"Wanna see your folks this afternoon? Might make it easier if we go together?"

She made a face. "Do we have to?"

"No. Just thought I'd throw it out there." He approached her with Vivian. "Trade with me and I'll get Van cleaned up." The exchange should've been no big deal, but for whatever reason, for however briefly, Mason appreciated the brush of Hattie's warm, smooth forearms against his. Unfortunately, it also left him craving another kiss. "Anything you want to do?"

She'd returned to her chair, only this time holding Vivian upright on her lap. "Let me run something by you."

"Sure. Shoot."

"At the bar last week, Clementine invited us to a Halloween party."

"Cool. I love Halloween."

There she went again with another frown. "Ordinarily I'd agree with you, but we'd need a sitter and—"

"I'm sure Fern and my dad would help out."

"Okay, well, Clem also brought up Wharf-o-Ween. I always have a huge, kid-friendly booth to represent the bar, and—"

"Wait—" he snorted "—are we talking, like, tequila for toddlers?"

She stuck out her tongue. "I know, it sounds weird, but all of the other wharf businesses participate, so why shouldn't Hattie's? And for the record, obviously, no alcohol's served."

"I get it, but what's your question?" He shifted his weight from his left leg to right, but apparently the movement was too sudden for Vanessa's taste. The baby burst into startled tears. "Hey…" he soothed.

"Never mind. We should probably get these two fed."

"Can't we walk and talk?"

In Hattie's defense, she tried, but once Vivian heard her sister's wail, she started in. Neither quieted until their mouths were too busy with breakfast to scream.

Once they all shared the sofa, Mason exhaled. "Damn, that was intense. If these two are this demanding as babies, I can't imagine them as teens."

294 The SEAL's Christmas Twins

He cursed silently as yet again, Hattie's eyes filled with tears.

"Good times." She smiled faintly. "Anyway, what I started to ask was if you think it'd be inappropriate for us to take the girls to the festival?"

He took a moment to chew on that one. "You know, if the twins were older, you could let them dictate what they want to do. With them being so little, the decision's yours."

"Which lands me right back to the heart of my question. Wharf-o-Ween or quiet night at home?"

"Might just be me," he said, "but I'd enjoy the crap out of getting away from this house."

HATTIE'S SIDES HURT from laughing.

Conifer's generic equivalent of Walmart—Shamrock's Emporium—carried a meager, yet fun stock of Halloween masks, costumes and makeup. Mason plopped a giant, green Hulk head on Vivian and surprisingly, far from her being upset about it, she giggled while playing peekaboo, peeping out the mask's eyeholes.

The girls sat in their stroller and Mason held up Vivian's little arms, waving them while saying in his best Hulk voice, "Don't make me angry! You won't like me when I'm angry!"

"Stop!" Hattie pleaded in a loud whisper when people started to stare. "We're going to get kicked out of the store." With a permanent population of just under two thousand, but a seasonal flux that jumped as high as four thousand, Hattie knew a lot of people, but thankfully not everyone.

Vanessa took one look at the back of her sister's green head and burst into tears.

Hattie's heart melted when Mason lifted the sniffling

baby girl and cradled her close. "I'm sorry. I didn't mean to make you angry."

Vivian kept right on giggling.

Hattie crouched alongside her, making sure to keep the mask from covering her nose or mouth.

"How about a halo for you?" Mason perched a heavenly headband on the still-spooked girl.

"Aw…" Hattie fished through her purse for her phone. "Keep that on her. I've got to get a picture."

Just as her camera app flashed, Sophie Reynolds rounded the corner with a pricing gun in hand. She took one look at the cheery foursome and turned right back around, all but running to escape them.

"Sophie, wait!" Hattie removed Vivian's mask before chasing after one of the town's biggest gossips.

"How could you?" Nearly to the checkout, Sophie spun around to face her. "Poor Alec and *your sister* are barely in their graves, yet this is how you choose to pay your respects?"

From behind her, Mason approached. "Sophie—not that it's any of your business, but I've done a lot of research on infant grief and the best thing we can do for these two is provide constant love and support—and yes, maybe even a little fun."

Sophie snapped, "What do you know about grief, Mason Brown? It's no secret why Melissa left you. The poor woman had just lost your child and you—"

"Stop," he said in a dangerously low tone Hattie had never before heard. He shifted Vanessa, holding her protectively against his chest, cupping his hand to her ear, shielding her from the brunt of their confrontation. "Don't you dare make excuses for the inexcusable. If *my* wife needed comfort, she should've come to me—not Alec. And thanks

for remembering that I know all too well what it's like—having also lost my mother when I was a kid."

Sophie stashed her pricing gun under the checkout counter, then dashed to the stock room.

The pimple-faced kid behind the register stared after her.

A muscle ticked in Mason's clenched jaw.

"I'm so sorry she said those things to you." Acting on pure instinct and adrenaline, Hattie hugged him from behind. In the moment, he was no longer a tough-guy SEAL, but the little boy she'd once known. He'd been in the fourth grade when his mom died of cancer. Hattie didn't remember the funeral specifically, but she had sad memories of what happened after. She'd asked him if he wanted to play Matchbox cars. He'd said he couldn't. All of his best cars were gone.

"Where'd they go?"

"To heaven with my mom."

Later, when Hattie had asked her mom what that meant, she'd explained that Mason had placed his favorite cars in his mother's coffin.

Patting him, trying to soothe him as she would her nieces, Hattie swallowed the latest knot in her throat. "I've never liked that woman. At Melissa and Alec's wedding, she pulled me aside to ask if I wanted to borrow her shawl to cover my *inappropriate* strapless dress."

"You're kidding."

Hattie shook her head, but then smiled. "Right after downing two shots of Johnnie Walker Black, I told her I *like* being inappropriate."

Chuckling, he turned and set Vanessa into the stroller before drawing Hattie into a hug. He kissed the top of her head. Held her and held her until she felt they'd connected on another level—an indefinable place that was deeper, and infinitely more meaningful, than just friends.

"Thank you for that," he said into her hair.

"I didn't do anything."

"Sure you did. When it felt like this whole damn town sided against me, you were always there. Still are. And now..." He exhaled sharply. "I wish I could be there for you."

"WHAT DO YOU think he meant?" Clementine asked when Hattie relayed the incident at Shamrock's later that night at the bar. "Could that have been his stab at declaring his undying love?"

"Don't be ridiculous." Hattie filled two draft-beer orders, delivering them to the regulars at the end of the bar.

"Stranger things have happened," Clementine pointed out upon Hattie's return.

"And Bigfoot could kidnap me on my way home, but I'm not going to dwell on it. Sorry I said anything."

Rufus Pendleton, a regular, sat at the far end of the bar and signaled for another beer. "I ever tell you 'bout the time Bigfoot paid a visit to my mine?"

Clementine delivered his order. "Only around ten times, darlin'." She leaned over the counter to kiss his leathered skin.

He blanched, wiping the spot she'd touched.

Hattie had been so stunned by Sophie's cruelty—the pall it'd placed over what had previously been a nice day— that she'd needed to talk it over with her friend. But now? She realized she should've kept her big mouth shut. What Hattie had viewed as a sweet moment, Molly Matchmaker saw as the launchpad for a smoking-hot affair.

What about that lone, spectacular kiss?

Had that been significant? Hattie kept that informational nugget to herself.

After an exaggerated eye roll, Clementine popped a green olive from the garnish tray into her mouth. A lot of bars rarely—if ever—cleaned their trays, but Hattie found that practice disgusting and washed theirs once per shift. "What'd you decide about my party and Wharf-o-Ween?"

When Clementine helped herself to three cherries, Hattie said, "Didn't we have an employee meeting about that?"

Her friend feigned wide-eyed innocence. One downside to sanitary trays was the fact that everyone enjoyed snacking from them. "A meeting about what? Our Halloween booth?"

Hattie gave Clementine's hand a light smack the next time she tried to grab a snack. "Knock it off. And yes, we will be hosting our usual booth, only we're adding a pic of my sister and her husband. I think it'd be nice to remind people to live in the moment because you never know what could happen."

SINCE TREVOR VOLUNTEERED to cover the late shift, Hattie used the free time to stop by her parents' home. She'd brought a foil-wrapped plate of hot wings for her dad and mozzarella sticks for her mom.

Inside, she set the snacks on the entry-hall table, then removed her coat and boots. The place was dark as a tomb.

"Hello?" she called out.

When no one answered, she found the kitchen empty. She opened the door leading to the garage to find her dad's truck gone. Hattie's old room, which her mom now used as a craft room, was also empty. Melissa's room remained much as it had when she'd left to marry Mason. Even back then, Hattie had known she was second best in her parents' eyes and hearts.

The last place Hattie checked for her mom was the master bedroom. She found Akna curled onto her side, eyes wide-open, staring into the darkness. "Mom? Are you all right?"

"What do you think?"

Hattie sat gingerly on the side of the bed. "It was sunny today. Still not quite dark. Wanna watch the sunset? It might make you feel better."

"Don't even try pretending you're innocent."

"Wh-what?" The anger behind her mother's statement stung.

"Sophie told me about your plans to carry on as usual for Halloween. The whole town's talking about your abhorrent, downright scandalous behavior. Don't think Sophie didn't tell me everything you and Mason did down at the store."

"Good grief, all we did was pick up a few Halloween items for the girls."

"Didn't sound so simple to me. I remember your sister's letter—the way she made it seem like she was playing matchmaker. I know there's more to it, and now you're cozying up to Mason like he's your boyfriend, but he'll always belong to your sister. I'll bet you're loving that big, old house of hers, too, huh? And her new car? Melissa had everything you ever wanted, and now that she's dead, pretty as you please, tied up with a neat bow, you've had her whole life handed to you on a platter."

The horror of her mother's words caused Hattie to raise her hands to her mouth.

"You should be ashamed." Akna sat up in the bed. "You're an abomination—stepping into your sister's shoes like that."

"I—I don't even know you...." Trembling head to toe, Hattie backed out of the room. She had to get away before she said something she regretted.

"Run!" her mother shouted. "You should run straight to church! Pray for the sin of wishing your sister dead!"

Hattie ran, all right, but in the direction of sanity.

Straight toward Mason, who, at the moment, felt as though he was one of her only friends.

THE NEXT MORNING, Hattie had just finished washing the breakfast dishes when her cell rang.

The babies had long since been fed and were lounging in their playpen. It hadn't escaped Hattie's attention that the girls cried and slept more than they ever had in their mother's care, so times like these, when they seemed content, she especially cherished.

Mason sat at the bar, drinking coffee and reading the paper. "Who's that?"

Hattie frowned. "Mom. I'm sure she's doing better."

On a line filled with static, Akna said, "Did you go to church like I asked?"

"Stop this. You've already lost one daughter. Do you really want to lose another?"

Sobs filled the line.

Part panicked, part incensed, part unsure how to be the adult when the woman she'd looked up to her whole life was obviously falling apart, Hattie said, "Mom, I think you should have Dad take you to the clinic. You're not acting rational."

"You're the one who—"

Unable to bear a moment more of her mother's ranting, Hattie pressed the disconnect button on her phone. "Think it's too early for a beer?"

"That doesn't sound good." He put down the paper.

"Aside from my mother having gone so far off the deep end, she's on the verge of discovering a new continent, there's the issue of how much I despise living in this fishbowl of a small town."

"What happened?"

"Apparently, Clem opened her big mouth about the bar sponsoring our usual festival booth. Sophie had already given Mom an earful about our *shocking* behavior at Shamrock's and now it seems everyone's gossiping about what a disrespectful sister I am. A-and now my mother seems to think that I'm a little too happy about stepping right into Melissa's life. Apparently, the only possible chance I have for changing my evil ways is through plenty of prayer." Using a paper towel, Hattie blotted tears that lately never seemed to stop. "H-how could she say that to me? H-how could she be so cruel?"

"Come here...." Mason stood and held out his arms for her to step into. She did, and honestly, his strong embrace felt akin to that first delicious sensation of sinking into a hot bubble bath. Though her emotions were still all over the map, physically, she was content. "I'm sure she didn't mean it. That was her grief talking," he murmured.

"St-still..." she sobbed against his chest, grateful for his strength when she had none.

"Shh..." He stroked her hair, flooding her with warmth and well-being. "Everything's going to be okay."

Will it? Because judging by how good Hattie felt standing there in her sister's ex-husband's arms, she couldn't help but fear at least part of her mother's accusations may be true.

"WHAT'S THE MATTER with them?" An hour later, fresh from the shower, still embarrassed at having yet again emotionally bared herself to Mason, Hattie entered the nursery to find baby bedlam.

From where he sat on the floor, holding the two girls, he shrugged. "I found this lullaby CD I thought they might like, but within the first couple minutes of it playing, they both flipped out. Think Melissa played it a lot? And they're wondering why she's not here?"

"Wouldn't surprise me." Hattie turned off the haunting music she'd heard her sister sing to the girls, then joined the trio on the floor. She took Vivian from Mason, holding her close, rocking her back and forth. "I'm sorry, little one. I know you miss your mom and dad."

She looked up to find Mason hugging and patting Vanessa.

Having recently been the recipient of his strong, reassuring hold, Hattie knew his brand of comfort to be effective.

In a few minutes, both girls had calmed. The silence was a relief. "That was intense."

"No kidding. Makes me wonder—how many other memory bombs are around here, just waiting to go off?"

Fingers to her throbbing forehead, she rubbed.

"Anything I can do for you? It's been kind of a crappy morning."

"You think?" Her half laugh didn't begin to cover how much she still hurt from her mother's call. Witnessing her nieces' grief only compounded Hattie's troubles.

"Come on. What can I do to make all three of my girls smile?"

His girls? She met his perilously handsome gaze, warning herself not to read anything other than friendly concern into his statement. It didn't matter that lately, the man had become her lifeline. Not only was he leaving in a week, but just like the perfect house and beautiful babies, he didn't belong to her. Would *never* belong to her.

"Hit me," he teased. "There's gotta be something selfish you've been craving."

She tilted her head back and smiled. "All right, if we were in an idyllic, happy universe, I think I would very much enjoy a pedicure and brownies."

"Done and done."

"Really?" She arched her right eyebrow. "And just how do you propose to make that happen?"

"First…" He set Vanessa on the carpet before standing, then scooping her back up. "We're going to traipse down to that ridiculous home theater and pop in a sappy chick flick."

"I'd rather watch an action-adventure."

"Or that…" He kissed the crown of Vanessa's downy head. What did it mean that Hattie craved another of his kisses so badly for herself that she could practically feel the one her niece received? "Then I'm going to make that brownie mix I stashed in the grocery cart when you weren't looking…"

Hattie frowned, but not too hard.

"And while the brownies are baking, I'm going to paint your gorgeous toes."

"What in the world would you know about nail polish?"

He sobered. "I may be a bit rusty, but when my mom was sick, she always asked me to paint her nails Candy Apple Red. It made me proud to be able to make her smile." Outside, the day was cloudy, but even in the nursery's dim light, Mason's eyes shone. "Will you let me do the same for you?"

Swallowing hard, she nodded.

Then she wished for the power to not only forget their lone kiss, but to stop craving another.

Chapter Nine

To say Mason felt horrible for what poor Hattie was going through would be the understatement of the century. They'd lived together for nearly two weeks, and in that time, he felt as if he'd had a front-row seat to watching her world crumble.

For as long as he could remember, she'd been his little buddy. His pal. But lately? He'd felt the stirrings of something more. Not only the desire to see where another kiss might lead, but a fierce protective streak was emerging regarding her and the girls. Yet as much as one part of him couldn't wait to return to base, another part dreaded leaving Hattie and the twins on their own.

The morning of Wharf-o-Ween, while his dad and Fern watched the girls, Mason hauled the heavy plywood pieces to Hattie's carnival-style booth from the bar's dusty attic. Thankfully, their latest snow had melted and the sunny day already boasted temperatures in the balmy forties.

While Hattie wiped dust from everything with a damp cloth, Mason used his shirt sleeve to wipe sweat from his brow. Only he wasn't sweating from exertion, but the excellent view of her derriere and thong teaser visible every time she knelt to scrub a board. "You owe me big-time. I would hardly call this the quick job you described."

"If I'd told the truth, would you have still offered to

help?" The grin she cast over her shoulder tugged at his heartstrings. Lord, she'd grown into a fine-looking woman.

He couldn't help but smile back. "You've got me there. What's next?"

"Help me get these pieces clean, and then we get to start assembling."

"Swell…" After three hours of torturing himself by keeping his hands off Hattie and busy with power tools, they'd constructed an Old West–styled ringtoss game, with plenty of fun toys and candy they'd purchased at Shamrock's for kids to win as prizes.

Hands on her sexy-full hips, she stood back to survey their work. "Looks pretty good."

"And who do you have to thank?"

"You." She ambushed him with a hug, then stepped back as if checking herself. Part of him wished she hadn't. She smelled good. Like fabric softener and the strawberries she'd sliced for their breakfast. Being with her not only felt comfortable, but exciting—like jumping out of a perfectly good airplane for a stealth night mission. Hattie still held all of the qualities he'd enjoyed about her while growing up, but this new, adult version of her was even better. She had an edge to her. That kiss ignited a curiosity that left him wondering what might happen—not that anything needed to happen. "I appreciate everything you've done."

"Aw, shucks, ma'am…" He tipped an imaginary cowboy hat. "It were my pleasure."

"Layin' it on a little thick, cowboy?"

"Probably so, but considering the looks the good Lord failed to give me, I have to rely on purdy words to impress the ladies."

That earned him a playful swat. "Fish for compliments much?"

He just smiled, realizing he liked the rise in his pulse that their playful banter had created. Only, considering he practically had one foot on the plane that would fly him from town, was that really a good thing?

THAT NIGHT, as Hattie manned the game booth with Mason, Princess Vivian took one look at a kid dressed like a werewolf and that was all it took for her to break into a wail.

Vanessa, on the other hand, stared up from her perch in the crook of Mason's right arm with wide-eyed wonder.

"Want to take this one," he asked, offering Hattie Vanessa, "while I get Viv calmed down?"

"Thanks." She watched with awe as all it took to calm her niece was Mason's magic touch. He sang, but with a local rock band playing and children laughing, she couldn't make out his words, only that the sentiment was apparently sweet enough for Vivian to find comfort nestling into the crook of his neck.

By feeding time, when the girls had grown cranky again, Mason handled that situation, too, by carting both girls off to the peace and quiet to be found in her old apartment.

After a thirty-minute crush of ghosts and vampires and even a pint-size Britney Spears, Hattie finally got a breather, only to have her dad wander up to the booth.

"Looks good," he said with a faint smile.

"Thanks. The bar was too busy for any of the guys or Clementine to help out, so Mason did most of the work."

"Where's he now?"

"He's got the twins upstairs for a quick bottle and diaper change."

Her dad's expression read confused. "Why aren't you handling that?"

"Honestly? He's better at it. The girls adore him."

Scowling, he shoved his hands in his pockets, nodding toward the plastic pumpkin she'd set out with Melissa and Alec's wedding picture attached, along with a sign asking for donations to Conifer Search and Rescue, who'd so valiantly tried to save her sister. "That's nice."

"I figure every little bit helps."

He nodded.

"How's Mom?"

"Still in bed. Hope the doctor won't give her any more sedatives. She's not in her right mind."

Hattie wasn't sure how to respond. The pain of her mother's accusation was still too fresh.

"I heard about what she said to you. Didn't like it." He took a few seconds to stare at her sister's photo. "You have to know it's her grief that has her talking crazy. She'll come around."

Wiping tears from her cheeks, Hattie nodded.

"Everyone's smiling again." Mason stepped around the booth's corner, holding both bundled-up infants in his arms. "Oh—hey, Lyle."

"Mason."

The two men seemed wary of each other. Hattie remembered a time when her father had considered Mason his son.

"How's Akna?"

Not one to easily share his emotions, her father said, "She'll pull through."

"Gotta be tough." Mason settled the twins into their stroller.

For Hattie, the tension between the only two men who'd ever meant anything to her was becoming unbearable. Hoping to smooth things over, she suggested, "How about you and Mom come for dinner on Sunday?"

Mason hovered behind her, and as Hattie awaited her father's answer to her impromptu invitation, she appreciated her friend's silent support.

"It's awfully nice of you to ask," Lyle said, "but I don't

think your mom's up to it. Soon, though. We'll get to-gether real soon."

"Sorry," Mason said after her dad left as quietly as he'd arrived.

"It's okay," she said, even though nothing could be further from the truth. More than anything, she longed to turn around and lose herself in the strength of one of Mason's hugs, but what would that do except prove Hattie was the despicable person her mom and Sophie and apparently the whole rest of the town believed her to be.

"TURN RIGHT BACK AROUND," Clementine said to Hattie when she arrived for her usual Saturday night shift. "I told you I've got you covered for tonight so you can come to my party."

Hattie made a face. "I'm not really in the mood to play quarters or beer pong."

Clementine waved off her concerns. "This is a grown-up party. I'm planning for Pictionary and dancing in the living and dining room and *Halloween I, II* and *III* on TV."

"What?" Hattie feigned shock. "No *Friday the 13th?*"

"Think that would be better?" She reached for an olive.

"What have I told you about eating the bar garnishes? And for the record, I'm messing with you. Sounds like a good time."

"Then you and Mason are coming?"

Hattie set her purse behind the bar. "Not sure if you're up on current events, but my sister just died. I shouldn't even be talking about going to a party."

"What was Wharf-o-Ween?"

"That was different." She poured herself a Coke. "I wanted the girls to hear laughter again. Plus, my donation pumpkin raised over four hundred dollars for search and rescue."

"Oh—so it's all right for the girls to laugh, but not you?"

"They don't know any better. But it's been suggested I do."

"By who?" Clementine crossed her arms.

"Lately, I feel like everyone. You know Mason and I had that run-in with Sophie, and now my mom has totally lost it—not that I blame her. I'm upset about my sister, too, but—"

"Wait. What else happened with your mom?"

Hattie relayed her mother's most recent call.

"Ouch." Clementine winced. "I'm sorry she went off on you, but you can't internalize her grief. Everyone has to deal with this in their own way. Melissa didn't give you the luxury of crawling into bed for a month. Yes, mourn your sister, but her girls also need you to celebrate her."

THE WHOLE RIDE HOME, Clementine's words refused to leave Hattie's head. Was she taking her mother's grief too personally? To be fair, having no children of her own, Hattie couldn't begin to fathom the depth of her mother's pain. Yes, Hattie was sad, but no comparison to what her mother—or Alec's—must be going through.

Upon entering her sister's home, thundering racket alerted her that she'd find Mason and the girls in the movie room.

Sure enough, while Mason reclined in one of the sumptuous leather chairs, the girls lounged on their play pads. Vivian stared in wonder at the colorful screen on which *Finding Nemo* played out. Vanessa focused her attention on gumming a cloth-polar-bear rattle.

"Hey," Mason called upon seeing Hattie. "Not that I'm complaining, but what're you doing home?"

After depositing her purse on one chair, Hattie sat in the one nearest Mason. "Clementine informed me we are going to her party. If your dad and Fern don't mind sitting, do you feel up to it?"

He groaned. "How many of the old crowd will be there?"

"Actually, I doubt many. Clementine and I are more the blue-collar type."

"Doesn't matter. If that's what you want to do—" he paused the movie "—I'll call Dad."

Just like that, Hattie had a date for Halloween—not just any date, but the man of her dreams. So why didn't she feel happier about the situation? Why was she allowing her mother's hateful accusations to ruin a fun night out—a night Hattie deserved?

Why? Because if Hattie so much as touched Mason, then Akna's horrible claims about Hattie's lack of morals, and lack of loyalty to her sister, would be true.

"REALLY?" HANDS ON her hips, scowl firmly in place, Clementine appraised Hattie's and Mason's impromptu costumes. "I shouldn't even let you in the door. What are you supposed to be?"

"Duh. TV antennas." Hattie brushed past her and, in the process, adjusted the tinfoil cap Mason helped make.

He passed their hostess the tray of pumpkin-shaped cookies they'd picked up at the grocery store on the way over. "Clever, right?"

Clementine just shook her head.

The party was already in full swing with classic Kid Rock booming from the stereo speakers. The house was decorated with orange and black streamers along with dozens of orange light strands. Hattie knew most of the twenty or so guests, but had to introduce Mason to a few of the men and women who were new to town.

Joey and Dougie were spending the night at Clementine's mom's place.

Hattie and Mason played Pictionary for a while, but when they lost every round, and Hattie found herself forcing good cheer, she was glad when Mason offered her a beer, then asked if she wanted to get some air.

"Good idea," she said, standing alongside him on the two-bedroom home's back deck. Just being near him produced a fierce longing for a forbidden, elusive *more*.

"No offense, but you looked a little out of it in there."

She laughed. "You've got a good eye."

"Anything in particular got you down?" He rested his forearms against the railing, glancing back at her, moonlight kissing his handsome features. The mere sight of him took her breath away, transported her to a magical place where there were no worries, only the two of them. "Or just our situation in general?"

"Remember how when we first got to Melissa and Alec's place, the game room still had the remnants of Craig Lovett's birthday?"

"Sure."

"Obviously, this is the first party I've been to since then, and it just occurred to me how different that night would've been had any of us known what was to come." When her eyes teared up and the familiar knot in her throat formed, Hattie forced herself to stay strong. The worst had already happened. Her job now was to steel herself for whatever the future held.

Mason groaned before tugging her in for a hug. "Hat Trick, if there's anything the navy has taught me, it's that tomorrow's never guaranteed. You have to take what today gifts you and be good with it."

"I know...." Clinging to him, knowing he'd soon be leaving, too, she fought not to lose herself in fears of her uncertain future and of being a single parent to her sister's girls. "But it's easier said than done."

He tenderly placed his hand beneath her chin, forcing her gaze to meet his. "Come Friday, when I sign away my rights to your nieces, I need you to know that has nothing to do with you. I might be back on base, but I'll only be a phone call away."

"Th-that's supposed to make me feel better?" She wrenched herself free, yanking off her stupid tinfoil hat, wadding it in a ball and tossing it out into the yard.

"I hoped it would. Last thing I want you thinking is that I'm abandoning you." She turned her back on him, but he stepped up behind her, curving his hands over her shoulders. "What your sister did—leaving her kids to me..." He sighed. "What the hell was she thinking?"

A question Hattie asked herself every day.

TRUTH BE TOLD, by the time Friday morning rolled around and Mason stood in line at Era Alaska with Hattie to board their short flight to Valdez, he was more than a little relieved. The sooner this custody thing was behind him, the better off he'd be.

Ever since the party, Hattie had been a sullen mess. The twins weren't much better. As for *his* mood? It ranged between sympathy for what Hattie was going through to annoyance over her shutting him out. On the surface, she was polite, but he knew her well enough to recognize the camaraderie they'd shared before the party was long gone.

Thank God for Fern and his dad watching the twins, because after the week he'd had, he could use the time away.

His dour companion mumbled, "Just when I think life can't get worse."

"What's wrong?"

She held up her cell to show him a weather-radar image. "What're the odds of this storm affecting our flight home?"

"Nil." Had circumstances been different, he'd have pulled her close for a reassuring kiss. "Stop making up worries, and let's try to enjoy our day."

"Impossible. The closer I get to officially being a single parent, the more my stomach hurts."

"What do you expect me to do? Even if I wanted to, I can't just up and quit. I can ask for more leave, but at some point, I will want to finish at the very least my current enlistment."

"I know. And I'm sorry to be dwelling on this. Consider the subject dropped."

"Oh, no, you're not going to launch a—"

"Sir." The attendant leading them to their plane gestured for him to follow. Just as well, considering their circular argument had been getting them nowhere.

He waved at Hattie to lead the way, and then noticed her gray complexion. He felt like kicking himself. She'd just lost her sister to a plane crash. Why hadn't he suggested they take a ferry?

"Hey—" He clamped his hand around her upper arm. "I didn't even think of the implications of you getting on a plane. We don't have to do this—at least, you don't. Let me sign the papers on my own."

"Benton advised us to present a united front."

"What if I advise you to spend your afternoon soaking in a nice hot bath?"

"Do you ever shut up?" Her legs wobbled visibly and she planted both hands on the rails to mount the prop plane's short set of stairs.

About a dozen snappy comebacks came to mind, but it wasn't the right place or time for sniping at each other. If she refused to get off the flight, the least he could do was ensure she knew he was there to lean on—assuming that at this point she even wanted his support.

She chose to sit in the back. He followed, ducking in the cramped space.

Only three other passengers were on the flight, and they occupied seats near the front.

As the pilot cleared them for takeoff, Hattie's complexion grew more waxen.

Mason reached across the narrow aisle and took her hand. She tried valiantly to rip it from his, but he said in a low tone, "Knock it off. I might be leaving Sunday afternoon, but for now, I'm here, and I *will* help you through this."

From that point through the duration of the flight, Mason held her hand, and she let him, and when the sun broke through the clouds just before landing, dowsing them in brilliant warmth and light, he couldn't help but wonder if Hattie's sister was sending her own form of comfort.

But when the aircraft's wheels touched ground and Hattie dropped his hand as if he'd burned her, his own nerves set in. Was he doing the right thing? Even if a small part of his conscience said he wasn't, what could he do about it? At the very minimum, he owed the navy a solid two years. And regardless of what she'd put in her will, he owed Melissa nothing.

What about Hattie?

What about that kiss you can't forget?

He ignored the voice in his head. Three weeks earlier, he'd rarely even thought of her. So why did thoughts of Hattie—and her adorable nieces—rarely leave his head now?

Chapter Ten

"Relieved?" Hattie asked Mason on the cab ride from the courthouse to the airport. The storm she'd shown him earlier had yet to materialize, which was a relief as the sooner he got away from her the better.

"No." He stared out the window at the hodgepodge of hangars and less-than-tourist-worthy homes. The judge had been ahead of schedule, and signing away his parental rights and monetary claims to any of Melissa's and Alec's possessions had taken all of ten minutes. "Look, we're about three hours early for our flight. Let me at least buy you a decent meal. Steak? Sound good?"

She shrugged. "If you want."

It beat the hell out of sitting with her at the airport for three hours. "Ah, sir," he said to the cabbie, "would you mind running us back to that two-story steak place with all the antlers?"

At the restaurant, Mason paid the driver and got his business card so they'd have his number for their return trip.

A hostess seated them at a table near a crackling fire. The antler theme went a little overboard with antler candle holders, chair backs and even an antler railing on the stairs leading up to the inn's few guest rooms. What space on the walls that wasn't graced with antlers, there were framed head shots of celebrity guests.

A country singer crooned over a radio in a thankfully low volume about his cheatin' ex.

Once the waitress left with their drink orders, Mason said, "I don't know about you, but I'm thinking this place could use a few more antlers."

For the first time that day, Hattie cracked a smile. "You think?"

Their Jack and Cokes arrived, and after ordering two steaks, Mason was fresh out of conversational fodder.

First downing a good third of her drink, Hattie said, "Mom dragged me and Melissa up here for a quilt festival a couple years ago. We ate here one night." Down went another third. "It was pretty good."

"Glad to hear it."

"Quilting's never really been my thing. Had more fun the next year when Dad and I stayed over at the Robe Lake Lodge. We took a charter—caught a salmon shark. Took nearly ninety minutes to reel him in." Her drink was gone. "He'd never admit it, but I'm pretty sure Dad's still jealous."

"Don't blame him."

"You see our waitress?" Considering at two in the afternoon, the dining room only had three other guests, it wasn't too hard to find the young woman seated in a corner booth, texting on her cell.

"What do you need?"

She waved to the girl and held up her empty glass, jiggling the ice.

"You didn't eat breakfast or lunch. Think you might wanna pace yourself?"

"This time Sunday, you'll be long gone. Why do you care?"

He took the empty glass from her. "Because I care about you."

"Bull."

The waitress delivered Hattie's second drink.

"This time next week, you won't even remember my name." Down went her latest third, as did the zipper on her red sweater. "It's *waaay* too hot in here. Oops," she said when going low enough to expose a seriously sexy black lace bra.

An instant, damn-near-painful erection had him shifting positions. He didn't need reminding about his recent dry spell. He sure as hell didn't want to even ponder the notion of ending it with an innocent like Hattie.

Pointing to her bountiful breasts, he made a zipping motion. "You, ah, might want to assess that situation."

She glanced down only to wave off his concern.

He leaned across the table, doing the job himself by raising her zipper to a respectable position.

"You know," she said in a perfectly sober tone, "this situation sums up my life. I've always been seen as the good girl. Everyone's always zipping me up." Her second drink emptied. "Well, guess what? I'm tired of being good. And now, here I am mom to two kids and I didn't even get great sex before getting knocked up."

Mason choked on his drink, then did a quick check of the room to make sure no one had overheard Hattie's complaint. "The guys you've been with haven't been doing it right?"

"Not even a little bit...." She took a moment to ponder her revelation. "Pretty sure this is a sign I need more liquid courage."

"Courage for what?"

"The whole single-mom thing, but mostly, I'm drinking however much it takes to remind me to keep my hands off of you."

She tried signaling the waitress, but he managed to snag her arm before she got the woman's attention.

"Would it be so bad?"

"What?"

"Putting your hands on me?"

She snorted. "It'd be the worst thing in the history of the world. Don't get me wrong, you're tastier than hot apple cobbler, but I'm not going to take a single bite—not even a lick."

The thought of her licking him sent a fresh jolt to regions better left ignored. What Mason had intended to be a simple celebratory meal had suddenly become a sexually frustrating adventure. By the time the waitress brought salads, then their steaks, snow fell so hard that the parking lot vanished from the windows' view.

He pulled up radar on his phone to find the snow had not only arrived ahead of schedule, but stronger in intensity than forecast.

When a tipsy Hattie damn near stabbed herself with her steak knife, he cleared his throat and asked, "Um, Hat Trick, how about letting me cut your meat for you?" Her all-too obliging come-hither smile did little to erase the image of her *assets* that had been burned into his retinas. Up close and personal, her floral shampoo reminded him of their many summer outings.

He may have married Melissa, but he'd had fun with Hattie.

Guilt from the realization had him retreating to his own personal space.

The waitress stopped by with the dessert menu.

Mason ordered cheesecake.

"Do you have beefcake?" Hattie asked with a snort.

After clearing his throat, Mason tugged his phone from his pocket. "I'll check on our flight."

"Why?" Her seat faced the river-rock hearth and its mounted moose head.

"Look behind you."

She did and closed her eyes. "You do know Alec and Melissa's accident was because of bad weather?"

"Yeah." His dad told him the visibility had been fine when the couple had left Conifer, but roughly fifty miles south of Anchorage, they'd run into a snowstorm. One more glance out the restaurant's window had Mason doubting they'd be going anywhere soon. "Let me give Era a call."

"Well?" Hattie asked when he disconnected.

"Nothing's going in or out for a while." Snow already had day quickly fading to night.

With a groan, she dropped her head to the table. "Just when I thought I wouldn't have to resist you much longer…"

"Hang tight." Lord, what he wouldn't give to break her resistance, but his dad had raised him better than to take advantage of a girl who'd had a few too many. Mason finished off his cheesecake, then pushed back his chair. "I'll grab a couple rooms. We'll get a good night's rest, then re-group in the morning. I'm sure Dad and Fern won't mind staying with the twins. Sound good?"

She may have nodded, but judging by her crestfallen expression, he'd had dogs more excited by the prospect of spending more time with him.

Five minutes later, Mason returned, but not with the news he'd expected. He dangled a key from a canoe key chain. "Hope you're not a blanket hog, because they only had one room."

HATTIE WOKE FROM a three-hour nap to find Mason on the king-size bed beside her, pillow propped behind him. A woman on *Wheel of Fortune* had just snagged a Hawaiian vacation, but he didn't seem all that excited. If anything, his handsome profile struck Hattie as stoic—resigned to riding out the storm with her when he'd probably rather be with a flashy blonde.

Save for the TV's glow, the room was dark. Wind howled just beyond closed drapes. The old building shuddered from occasional gusts.

Most ordinary folks would be battened down for the duration, but typically, the word *ordinary* and Alaskans didn't match up. Judging by the muted bass and laughter coming from downstairs, a blizzard party was in full swing.

Hattie envied the happy game-show contestant. "What would you give to be lounging on a Maui beach right about now?"

His unexpected smile raced her pulse. "Sleeping Beauty awakes." He tugged a chunk of her hair. "You were a handful at lunch."

"Yeah?" She yawned. "I don't remember much past my third drink."

"Likely story," he teased. "Come here."

He snagged her around her waist, tugging her close, landing her head atop his chest—exactly where she'd wanted to be, but knew she shouldn't.

"I like tipsy you." He kissed the top of her head. "Your honesty was quite the turn-on."

She groaned, squirming to get away, but he tugged her back.

"My head's fuzzy on your exact phrasing, but at one point, I'm pretty sure you admitted you'd like to lick me."

Groaning even louder, she covered her flaming face with her hands. "Stop."

"I would, but you pretty much seared that image into my brain. Then there were your asparagus tricks…"

"Stop…"

"Nah…" Lifting her up to him, he kissed her real slow, doing plenty of searing with his lips. When she groaned, he pulled her closer, easing his big, rough hand under her sweater. Being with him like this felt so natural, so right, so— What was she thinking?

"Mason, no—" She pushed him away, then tidied her hair. "We can't do this. It's wrong."

"Why?"

Images of her mother and beady-eyed Sophie Reynolds flashed before her, as well as her radiant sister on the long-ago day she and Mason married. "It just is. I can't—won't—be the kind of woman who—"

"Actually lives her own life?"

That very question was what had led her to drink. After Mason signed the forms releasing him from his parental duties, he'd essentially stepped one foot out the door of their shared life. The thought of no longer playing house with him, exchanging brief touches with him or even lingering looks had sent her running straight for liquid courage.

Oh—she'd be leading her own life, all right—her very-much-alone life!

"Ha-ha." She slid off the bed, straightening her sweater in the process. "You're so *not* funny."

"Just keepin' it real, Hat Trick." After a yawn and stretch, he asked, "Hungry?"

"Not really." *Yes.* When wasn't she? But thinking of her latest abandoned diet would hardly stop her downward emotional spiral.

"Mind at least sitting with me while I grab a burger?"

"Sure. Help me find my shoes and we'll head downstairs."

What a difference a few hours made. The place was packed.

The only seats to be had were a couple stools at the bar.

While Mason called his dad to check on the twins, Hattie called her own establishment. Clementine had long

since gone home, but Craig and Trevor reassured her all
was well and that they'd also been slammed with folks
seeking an excuse to party through the inclement weather.

"Wanna beer?" Mason asked.

"Yes, please."

After agreeing to share onion rings, Hattie raised her
longneck brew. "How about a toast?"

"To what?"

"There are good ships and wood ships. Ships that sail
the sea. But the best ships are friendships. May they always be."

Mason said, "I'll drink to that."

They clinked bottles.

Desperate to avoid the elephant in the room—his immi-
nent departure—Hattie said, "Since you've been in town,
we've talked about babies and wills and more death than
I care to remember, but you've said nothing about what's
really going on with you. Have a good group of guys you
hang out with? A girlfriend?"

He reddened. "My guys consist mostly of my SEAL
team. My best bud, Calder, just got married and had his
second kid." After a long swig of beer, he turned intro-
spective, swirling his bottle against the smooth wood bar.
"For the longest time, I was pissed at him for turning
to the Dark Side. Your sister really did a number on my
head." He drew a deep breath. "As for the second part of
your question—the longest relationship I've had recently
was a gallon of milk I forgot to toss before leaving for
Afghanistan. Can you believe she stayed with me for six
whole months?"

"Not sure whether the similarity of our love lives should
make me laugh or cry—although I did have a guy stick
around for that long. Constantine…" She finished her beer.
"Great in bed. Hopeless at keeping a job." Mortified by
what she'd just admitted, she pressed her hands to her

flaming cheeks. "Could I sound like any more of a money-grubbing hussy?"

"Don't sweat it." He finished his drink and signaled the bartender for two more. "I happen to very much like hussies."

Before she could even wonder if she should take his statement at face value, he winked. "I get it. You're over thirty and entitled to a satisfactory roll in the sack—hell, we all are. As for the cash? Seems to me a man's work ethic speaks volumes about his character."

"True..." Mason's had always been top-notch. "Melissa used to bitch a blue streak about you working too much. I lost count of the number of times I reminded her you were working for her—your future kids."

"See? I love that you get that—you've always gotten that. You're good people, Hat Trick. Wise beyond your years."

"I try." Fresh drinks arrived.

The dining room furniture had been compressed, allowing for a makeshift dance floor. The roaring fire, combined with gyrating bodies, upped the room's heat—both figuratively and literally. Lights had been dimmed to almost nonexistent and she found herself embracing the dark.

It made her bold.

Made her forget herself and her worries and everything but this moment with the only man she'd ever wanted.

Hattie lowered the zipper on her sweater, then fanned herself with a napkin. "You'd never know it's probably ten degrees outside."

He laughed, then held out his hand. "I love this song. Let's dance."

Rod Stewart's "Da Ya Think I'm Sexy" morphed into a slow and sexy Def Leppard number that had Hattie pressed against Mason in an anything-but-friendly manner. Swaying to the music, they abandoned themselves to the fire's hedonistic glow, and he settled his hands low on her hips. Was it the fire's heat or his touch that had her skin flush and thoughts dizzy?

Everyone knew blizzard parties were like Vegas. What happened at the party stayed at the party.

Mason eased his hands under her sweater and up her bare back as she pressed her hands to his chest, fisting his shirt when their gazes met in a way they never had before. How many times had she stared into Mason's eyes? She liked to think she knew him inside and out—that she'd always known him, but never like this.

The song ended and another came on. Still slow, but with Justin Timberlake's painfully sexy vibe. She'd always associated his music with the pretty people—the glamorous party set who'd hung with her sister—but tonight, with a blizzard raging outside and her hair swinging loose and wild, with Mason's wicked hands sliding up her sides, beneath her bra, skimming her breasts' side-swell, she felt pretty. Wanton and wicked. All grown up and, for once in her life, refusing to back away from what she wanted.

He angled his head as if planning to kiss her.

Panic seized her, stopping her heart, then racing it to a frightening degree. What was happening? This was Mason. Her sister's boyfriend—her husband. Her *ex*-husband.

Not asking permission, Mason's hands were out from beneath her sweater to cup her cheeks, pulling her close for a kiss she'd waited a lifetime for. His lips were firm, yet supple, drawing her in, only to tease her by backing away.

She had never been more out of breath—out of control. She couldn't have stopped kissing him if the room caught on fire.

He played his teasing game until the end of the song, but then things got serious when he grasped her hand and led her away from the crowd to the stairs.

There, he took things to a whole new level, lowering her to sit on the nearest step, then arching her back, kissing her, haunting her with the sweep of his tongue—for he had to know regardless of where the night led, she'd never forget his kiss. His faint taste of beer and raw masculinity.

He hovered over her, pressing his swollen need against her. "You okay with taking this upstairs?"

She somehow found the strength—the courage—to nod.

Chapter Eleven

Safely hidden behind their closed door, their urges broke free. Hattie didn't even try pretending being with Mason in every way a woman could wasn't exactly what she wanted.

She ripped at his shirt just as he did away with her sweater. Like a blind woman seeing the sun for the first time, she reveled in gazing at his every muscular nuance and groove. Where her body was soft, his was hard. Honed from she couldn't even imagine how many hours of working out.

Cloaked by darkness, she forgot to care about what he thought of her body in favor of savoring his every touch.

He backed her against the nearest wall, but it turned out to be the door leading into the bathroom. It didn't matter, as he slowed things down while impossibly racing her pulse all the more.

"You're beautiful…." His words were a ragged whisper.

"No…"

"Shh…" He was back to exploring, kissing her abdomen and still lower until he was between her legs and she buried her fingers in his hair, abandoning herself to a swift climax that built into another. His touch transported her to a place where anything was possible, where dreams really did come true.

By the time he'd left her to grab a condom from his

wallet, she thought she'd been ready for him, but nothing could've been further from the truth.

Eyes closed, the sheer beauty of his motion, of the two of them finally uniting as one, knotted her throat to the point she was no longer able to hold tears at bay.

"Hey…want me to stop?" He paused, which prompted her to press her fingers into his back, urging him to continue—to never stop.

"No. Please…" Her mind was too addled for speech.

"What's wrong?"

"Please, Mason…don't stop."

He braced his hands against the wall, giving her an opportunity to dance her fingertips along his impressive biceps.

"What else can I do? You're crying."

"Lately, I'm always crying. It's not a big deal."

"Hattie…"

She kissed him, hoping to convey the depth of her riotous emotions through her actions. "Th-this is a big deal for me—huge. Trust me. I want this—us—more than you'll ever know."

"Well, all right, then…" Mason struggled for thought, let alone words. He had never seen a more beautiful sight than Hattie standing before him, naked, shyly smiling, unflinchingly meeting his gaze. "Wanna take this to the shower?"

"Sounds a little wild," she said with a giggle. "I like wild. D-do you?"

"Hell, yeah…. As long as you're sure."

She turned on the water. "You think too much. You've also apparently been away from Conifer too long. How could you forget the rule about blizzard parties?"

"I didn't. Trust me, I'm all for getting buck-ass wild tonight, then forgetting come morning. But, Hattie, I'm not willing to do it at your expense. You were crying."

He wanted to hold her gaze, but lacked the strength when she'd presented herself like a womanly buffet. He drew her to him, so damned relieved he hadn't botched things up.

"In case it escaped your notice, lately I'm always crying. But this time—" she drew back to gift him with the sweetest kiss "—my tears were happy. More than anything I want to be with you. I've always wanted to be with you. If my parents knew, they'd permanently disown me, but for now—tonight—no one ever has to know besides me and you."

"And you're okay with that?" He searched her dear face, those chocolate eyes.

She nodded.

"Sweet. Let's get busy." To once and for all dispel any concerns about her weight, he backed her against the wall, lifting her, urging her arms around his neck and her legs around his waist. "Wanna go for a ride?"

WHEN HATTIE WOKE to use the bathroom, then settled into an armchair, though it was still dark, she could tell the storm had passed and enough moonlight reflected off the snow to afford her a mesmerizing view. Sleeping Mason was a sight to behold. The wall heater worked a little too well, meaning that after making love a third time, he'd fallen asleep on his back. The sheet only covered his midsection and left leg, leaving the rest of his godlike physique on display.

If she weren't sore in places, she wouldn't believe their shared intimacies had even happened.

But they had.

As a realist, she knew being with Mason changed nothing. He'd still leave bright and early Sunday morning and she'd still raise her nieces on her own. She'd never been a fairy-tale girl; rather, she lived more in the realm of Cinderella before the ball. But now that she'd had her one, sparkling night, no matter what other tragedies fell her way, she'd finally had her chance to be a princess. And it'd truly been a magical affair.

Mason stirred.

On her feet, she rummaged through her purse for the bottle of water she'd stashed earlier that day. She took three long sips.

Upon her return to the bed, Mason mumbled, then kicked the sheet from his right leg. Whatever he dreamed of seemed fitful.

Should she wake him? She recalled once reading never to wake a sleepwalker, but she'd never heard any rules on standard dreamers.

When his moaning resembled pain, she touched his shoulder. "Mason? You all right?"

He thrashed his head. "No. No."

"Mason? Wake up." She nudged him again, only this time slightly harder.

With a start, his eyes opened, his gaze unfocused, and for a moment he seemed lost. "Melissa?"

Hattie froze. No way had he said what she thought she'd heard. Moments earlier her happiness had been hard to contain, but now she shrank inside herself, only just realizing the depth of her mistake. She knew he wasn't still hung up on her sister, but that didn't change the fact that they'd shared a significant past. So significant that Melissa still popped up in his dreams—or nightmares…

Hattie had no business being with him. Nothing good could come from anything they shared.

Eyes again closed, he fitfully kicked his legs. "Baby? Is that you?"

Though Mason drifted back into peaceful slumber, for Hattie, sleep never came.

At 5:00 a.m., she tired of trying. Instead, she dressed in the previous day's clothes, ran her brush through her tangled hair, then wrote a hasty note for Mason, telling him that when he woke, she'd be in the lobby.

For now, she needed coffee, pastry and the space to process her thoughts—however dark they may be.

MASON WAS SORRY Hattie hadn't been in bed when he woke. After the wild night they'd shared, he wouldn't have minded kissing her good-morning.

How crazy was it that after all these years of being friends, they'd discovered something more. On the flip side, how depressing was it that he was soon leaving. Somehow, he had to make her understand that despite that fact, their night hadn't been purely about sex. She'd always meant the world to him and still did. He wasn't quite sure how she fit into that world, but he'd worry about that another day.

For now, he took a quick shower, toweled off, then tugged on clothes still in a rumpled heap from where they'd been tossed the night before.

Damn, Hattie had been a closet hottie. No more calling her *Hat Trick*—more like *hellion*.

Downstairs, he found the sun-flooded dining room restored to its former sedate pace. Two business-types sat at tables, reading newspapers and drinking coffee. Then there was Hattie, seated cross-legged on the sofa in front of the fire, reading something on her Kindle. She'd crammed her long hair into a messy ponytail, and even from a distance, he could tell she wasn't her usual self.

"Hey…" He kissed the crown of her head before sitting next to her. "Quite a night, huh?"

Her smile didn't reach her bloodshot eyes.

After placing his hand possessively on her thigh, he asked, "Everything all right?"

She nodded. "I'm glad you're here. We should head for the airport. Our flight leaves in just over an hour."

"Wish you'd told me sooner. Might've been nice to share breakfast."

She shrugged.

He glanced over his shoulder. "Mind telling me what I'm missing? In light of, you know…last night. Your cold shoulder's kind of freaking me out."

"Good. Then we're even." Before he had the chance to ask what that meant, she was on the phone with the cab-driver. Upon hanging up, she stood. "We're in luck. He's only a few minutes away."

"Swell. That'll hopefully give you just enough time to explain what the hell's wrong with you? Is this about me leaving?"

She shook her head. "Can we please just get back to Conifer? Last night was a mistake. We both know it."

"Are you kidding me?" After a quick check to make sure the other guests were ignoring him, he took Hattie's hand, easing her fingers between his. "Last night was not only hot, but opened my eyes to a whole new part of you. You're like Hattie, but better. I have to get back to the base, but I was thinking, for the holidays, how about you and the girls fly out for a visit? Wouldn't that be fun?"

There she went again with her waterworks, but not be-fore jerking her hand free. "You have no idea, do you?"

From outside came a honk.

"No idea about what?" Mason asked. He'd grown seri-ously tired of this game.

"Come on. That's our ride."

"What about the bill?"

"Already paid."

She was midway to the door when he caught her by her upper arm, spinning her to face him. Under his breath, he said, "Damn it, Hattie, tell me what's wrong or we'll stand here all day."

"You called out for Melissa, okay?" She took a tissue from her purse, blotting her eyes. "After spending the whole night making love with me, turns out your subconscious prefers my sister."

While he stood dumbfounded, taking in the gravity of what Hattie had just said, she was already at the inn's door, tugging it open.

Mason chased after her, and when she slipped on snow-covered stairs, he almost caught her, but hadn't been quite fast enough to break her fall. The way she landed on her right arm didn't look good. In his line of business, he'd seen a lot of men get hurt, and to him, this looked potentially serious. "Are you okay?"

"Fine," she insisted, brushing off his attempts to help. "Please, leave me alone."

He at least opened the sedan's back door for her. When she'd climbed in, he closed the door and walked around to the other side.

With no desire to air their dirty laundry in front of a captive audience, he waited until after they'd checked in for their flight to pick up where they'd last left off.

"So, about last night..." he said in a quiet corner of the airport terminal. "Are you honestly blaming me for something I said in a dream? Hell—" he raked his fingers through his hair "—I don't even remember what it was about."

"Must've been good. After a lot of groaning, you said her name, then called her 'baby.'"

"You're being crazy," he had no problem telling her. "I can see you being upset we didn't use a condom or that I hogged the blanket, but this?" He laughed. "You, of all people, should know how much pain your sister brought me. You, on the other hand, have always been the one who made me smile."

Whether she liked it or not, he leaned in to kiss her, and damn if her whole body didn't seem to exhale in relief.

"Hattie, I'm sorry if I accidentally hurt you. But the God's honest truth is that—for me, anyway—last night was amazing, but that's where it has to end. You and I both know sheer logistics make it impossible for anything life-altering to happen."

She nodded. No matter how much his speech hurt, his words made sense. "Thank you for the apology. And I totally get what you're saying. Our already-gossipy town would have a field day should they ever have an official report of us being together." She forced a breath, then swallowed the knot in her throat. "Not gonna lie, hearing you call out my sister's name shattered my heart in about a zillion tiny pieces, but what I was too punch-drunk on fun sex to realize was that, like you said, last night can never be more than that—fun. Pleasure shared between two consenting adults at a blizzard party."

Leaning forward, he rested his elbows on his knees. "Want a coffee?"

She shook her head.

Due to so many flights having been canceled the previous afternoon, the airport was buzzing that morning. After Mason stood in an endless line for standard black coffee, it was time to board their flight.

Once again, Hattie's complexion paled as she reached her seat, but this time she had no interest in holding his hand. Which just so happened was fine by him.

The sooner he got away from her and back to Virginia Beach, the better off he'd be.

THE FLIGHT LASTED thirty-five minutes, and it took another fifteen of his father's agonizingly slow driving for Mason and Hattie to reach Melissa and Alec's house, where Fern sat with the girls. An added hour of polite small talk just about did him in.

On a trek outside for more firewood, his father asked, "What's with the chill between you and Hattie?"

"Long story."

"Good or bad?"

Mason laughed. "Little of both."

His dad grunted. "What time you want me to fetch you for the airport in the morning?"

"Six, please."

"You got it." His dad's rare hug couldn't have come at a better time. Mason didn't feel right about going, but he sure as hell knew it would be a huge mistake staying.

By the time Mason and Hattie had the house to themselves, he couldn't tell if she was still upset with him or something else was wrong. Her color was seriously *off,* and she'd winced when picking up or even holding either baby.

"You all right?" he finally asked when they both happened to be in the kitchen.

"I'm fine. But as soon as I wash these bottles, can we talk?"

"Here, let me help." Alongside her at the sink, he took one look at her swollen right hand and turned off the faucet. "Are you kidding me?" She tried turning from him, but he'd already reached for her left arm. "You're seriously hurt, aren't you?"

"It'll be fine. I want to apologize for this morning. Last night was so… And I just…"

"I get it. Apology accepted. Right now, since your arm looks too swollen for me to even roll up your sleeve, I'm taking your sweater off, okay?"

She nodded.

Last night he'd unzipped her sweater for purely selfish reasons, but he now found himself in a wholly altruistic position, tensing when Hattie winced with pain. Her arm had turned a dozen shades of purple and that told him it had to be broken. "Jeez, woman, were you ever planning to do something about this?"

"I figured after a couple days it'll feel better."

"Uh-huh." He tossed her sweater on the counter, wishing he had her top off under more fun circumstances. He ushered her to the sofa. "Wait here while I grab you a T-shirt. Then we're running to the clinic."

"That's not necessary. Besides, after being crazy this morning, I want to do something nice for you. Maybe wash your clothes?"

From the stairs, he said, "How about once we get home you take a nice nap? Then we'll call it even."

"COULD YOU HAVE misread the X-ray?" An hour later, Hattie sat on an exam table at Conifer Clinic. Mason had stayed in the waiting room with the twins, and from the muted cries, she guessed he wasn't having fun, either.

Dr. Murdock laughed. Five years earlier, the town had paid her med-school loans in exchange for her services. Turned out she was a great fit. "Sorry, hon, but I'm afraid you're looking at a minimum of six weeks in a cast. The good news is that we just got in a really great pink."

Hattie groaned. "Not only am I not really a girlie girl, but I don't have time for being even temporarily down one arm."

"Well, I can't help you find more time, but I do have lots of colors. Red? Orange? Black? Christmas is just around the corner. How about green?"

"Guess that'll work."

Thirty minutes later, sporting her two-ton green arm and a prescription for pain meds, Hattie found Mason in the crowded waiting room, jiggling a baby on each of his knees.

He looked up only to catch sight of her and frowned. "Told you so."

She stuck out her tongue.

He winked. "Don't threaten me with a good time."

"Hush. I'm in pain and just realized no meds for me."

After settling the girls in their carriers, he joined her at the checkout desk.

In the sunny parking lot, amid mounds of melting snow, he asked, "Why can't you have medicine?"

"Do you think it'd be a good idea to be loopy while single-handedly caring for two infants?"

"Hadn't thought of that."

He set the carriers alongside the SUV while opening Hattie's door. "Hop in. I'll load everyone else."

"Thanks." Because he wouldn't be around much longer to help care for the girls, Hattie closed her eyes, soaking in the warm sun while he tackled the chore of fastening them into their safety seats.

Everything would be all right. As long as she stayed positive and worked hard, she was fully capable of raising the twins, healing her family and running the bar. The cast wouldn't even slow her down. Piece of cake.

They were midway back to the house when Mason asked, "What would you think about me extending my leave?"

"What? Why?" Her heart skipped a beat at the mere prospect of him sticking around. Trouble was, the more she was with him, the more she realized he needed to go— not just for his job, but her peace of mind. The doctor had reminded her the holidays had nearly arrived. Hattie had to somehow get her family back to normal and she sure couldn't accomplish that when Mason's mere presence made her feel anything but!

"You obviously need help. Since there's no way my mind will even be on my work if I'm worried about you, I figure why not see about extending my leave? Great idea, right?" He aimed his killer, white-toothed grin in her direction.

With the memory of what he could do with that mouth all too fresh in her mind, she tried covering her face with her hands, but instead, conked her nose with her cast. Could this day get any worse? Whether Mason left in the morning or after New Year's made no difference. Sooner or later he would go. And even though she had no business wanting him to stay forever, she did. Feared she always would.

An even bigger worry was the one Mason's own subconscious had proved real. The fact that in his sleep he'd cried out for Melissa told Hattie that no matter how hot their night had been, in his mind, she'd always finish a distant second to the way he'd once felt about her sister.

And she deserved better than being a guy's second choice. If she couldn't be Mason's top pick, then she'd prefer not having him at all.

She pasted a smile on her face and said, "You're sweet to think of me, but the girls and I will be fine. It's probably for the best that you go."

Chapter Twelve

Mason wasn't sure what to think of Hattie's negative reaction to his suggestion that he stay. She obviously needed the help, so what was her problem? "If this is about last night…"

"No, not at all," she assured him. "I just think it's best to get on with the inevitable. Last night was…well…"

Freaking incredible. "I get it. Yeah, you're probably right." If she'd been hoping for a different reaction, her expression gave nothing away. Had she truly been that unaffected by what they'd shared? "I'll leave as planned."

"Good."

Her attitude was really pissing him off. How could she be so cavalier? Or was it an act? If so, why did she feel compelled to lie to him, of all people? They'd known each other forever. If there was anyone she could be her true self with, he hoped it'd be him.

But then, why should she feel allegiance to him? The genuine friendship they'd shared might as well have happened a hundred years ago. Had her sister's death created what was essentially an artificial reality, thereby forcing a reunion? A reunion that was actually an illusion?

Was Hattie the only one of them smart enough to call last night for what it had been? A blizzard-party hookup between old friends who were better off *just* friends?

Ignoring Hattie's protests, he swung by the pharmacy, filling her prescription so at the very least she'd have relief for tonight.

Back at the house, she tried helping get the twins inside, but he fended her off. "Go on in and take your medicine."

"I'm perfectly capable of handling the girls, you know?"

"Yep."

"Then let me—"

"Hat Trick, please...you're only stuck with me for one more night. Do me the favor of letting me take care of you till I'm gone?" He held her gaze, silently signaling her to chill. Leaving her and the twins was already hard enough. Leaving under these circumstances made him feel like the world's biggest jerk.

"Sure. Whatever. Toss me the keys, though, so I can at least unlock the door."

Finally in the house, Mason corralled the twins in their playpen, then got Hattie settled on the sofa, bringing her a Coke, her medicine bottle and her cell so she could ask one of her employees to cover her shift. "Need me to bring you a few crackers? You probably shouldn't take it on an empty stomach."

"Thanks, but I'll be fine."

He started to make a fire, but instead took a seat on the cold stone hearth. The chill seeped through his jeans, but had nothing on the deep freeze that had settled over Hattie. "You ever talking normal to me again?"

"Thought I was?"

He snorted. "Right."

"Sorry. I'm not trying to be difficult. I'm just hurting and mad at myself for being in such a rush this morning that I fell."

Mason wanted her to keep talking—admit she was also upset by his leaving. Instead, she made an awkward grab for a movie magazine Fern had left on the coffee table.

"Where do you think you'll be this time tomorrow?"

Her question caught him off guard. Truthfully, he was surprised she even cared. "Jeez, I guess I'll still be in the air. I leave Anchorage at 9:25 in the morning, but don't land in Norfolk till 10:15 at night. Gonna be a long day."

"But a good one." Her faint smile tightened his stomach. Damn, he wanted to kiss her. "When I was a kid, I always dreamed about traveling. It's gotta be exciting, going all over the world like you do."

"It is—was—but it's not often the navy takes us anywhere sane people would want to be."

"I suppose…."

There was so much he wanted to say to her, but where did he begin?

Never did Mason think he'd be happy to hear either of the twins cry, but in this case, he was glad for the distraction. "Guess it's dinnertime, huh?"

"Want me to help?"

Hopefully, his glare conveyed how serious he was about her resting.

"Come here, you little bugger." With Vivian in his arms, Mason set about making bottles, finding comfort in the routine. When she turned her tear-filled baby blues on him, he melted. "You're going to grow into one helluva heartbreaker."

From the playpen, Vanessa wasn't happy about her sister hogging the attention.

"Just a sec, sweetie. I'm almost finished, then heading your way."

In his peripheral vision, Mason caught a flash of movement from the sofa to the stairs. He turned back in time to see Hattie vanish in the hall. "What the…"

HATTIE REACHED THE bathroom just before retching into the commode. Why hadn't she listened when Mason told her to eat something with her medicine? What else had he been right about? Wanting to stay?

She'd wanted so badly to agree with his plan, but what was the point?

Seated on the tub's tile edge, she rested her elbows on her knees. More than anything, she wanted to call out to Mason, ask him for a cool rag, but in the morning he'd be gone and she had to once again learn to not only live on her own, but be happy about it.

Twin cries rose faintly upstairs.

Seconds later, Mason stood in the bathroom's doorway. "You okay?"

Nodding, she drew strength from just knowing he was near. "Hate to admit it, but you were right about those crackers."

"Sorry." As if reading her mind, he took one of Melissa's designer washcloths from the towel rack, dampening it before holding it to her forehead.

"Thanks. I should've listened, huh?"

From downstairs, the wailing grew louder.

He knelt, kissing the top of her head. "You gonna be all right if I leave you for a sec? I'll grab those two and bring them up here to feed them."

"I'm fine. No need to hurry." *Or even come back to me at all.* Because his presence only worsened her pain.

The babies soon enough quieted, but then she heard what sounded like Mason talking on the phone. Creeping from the bathroom to the stairs, she eavesdropped on his conversation.

"Yes, sir....Thank you....Same to you, sir."

Who was he talking to? His dad?

"I'll be sure and let you know....Yes, sir. Thanks, again."

She'd never heard him call Jerry "sir."

One of the twins whimpered, so she headed that way to

help. And maybe get a better feel for who Mason was chatting with. His whole demeanor had changed. He'd deepened his voice and squared his already-broad shoulders.

For a split second, her mind's eye returned to their shared shower, and the way those shoulders had looked all soapy and wet. Mouth dry, she willed her pulse to slow and her mind to get out of the gutter.

"Who was that?" she asked, striving for a casual tone.

"My CO." He scooped a sniffling Vivian from the playpen, teasing, "What's the problem, princess? Your appetizer wasn't adequate?"

The infant's giggle only further degraded Hattie's foul mood. The twins had already lost their parents. Having bonded with Mason, would they mourn his loss, too?

He knelt for Vanessa, and then, once he held both girls, he took their bottles from the counter before heading for the sofa.

"Want me to take care of them so you can pack?"

His slow grin destroyed her. "Didn't I tell you to rest?"

"Since when do I ever do what you tell me?"

Laughing, he said, "Good point."

Seated alongside him, she used her good arm to take Vanessa. "Wanna hand me her bottle?"

He passed over a bottle, and they finished feeding the girls. Darkness had fallen and she shivered from a sudden chill. Her medicine made her eyelids heavy.

After tugging an afghan from the back of the sofa to drape over her lap, Mason said, "I'm going to give these two monkeys a quick bath, then put them to bed. If you're still awake, want to watch a movie or just make out in front of a fire?"

"Excuse me?" If she'd thought for one second he was serious, her choice would be all too obvious.

"Just kidding. See you in a few."

"Mason, if you need to pack, I can handle tub time. It's not a big deal."

"Relax..." There he went again with his grin. "We have all the time in the world."

"Yeah, if you don't sleep a wink. Didn't you ask your dad to be here at six?"

"Guess I should give him a call, huh? Tell him his taxi services are no longer needed."

Eyes narrowed, she asked, "What're you talking about?"

"Wouldn't you like to know?"

In no mood for teasing, she snapped, "Actually, yes, I would."

"Jeez, Hat Trick, chill. I won't need Dad for one simple reason—I'm not leaving."

Had she heard him right? "Wh-why?"

"Isn't it obvious? You've got a broken arm, these angels need pretty much around-the-clock care and selfishly," he murmured, and dropped his gaze only to then pierce her with his direct stare, "I wouldn't mind further exploration of that sexy genie we let out of the bottle."

While he exited up the stairs, Hattie leaned her head back and sighed. *He's staying.*

Which meant her sanity would soon be going...

ALMOST TWO WEEKS later on a snowy, extra-busy Friday afternoon, Hattie struggled using her free hand to stock the bar. With Mason available to take the baby monitor at night, she was able to take her pain meds for sleep. During the day, however, her pain was light enough for her to soldier through.

"Why are you even here?" Clementine asked. "You know we banded together to cover your shifts indefinitely."

"Thank you. I love you guys for that, but I'm all right. Just a little slow. Besides, I seriously needed out of the house." Or, more specifically, away from Mason. Aside from his occasional X-rated double entendres, he'd been a perfect gentleman, not even delivering a peck to her cheek. Which should've come as a relief. Ha!

The more space he gave her, the more she craved jumping into his arms.

"Sure was good of Mason to stay. Your dad told me he's not leaving till you get your cast off, which is, like, what? Just after New Year's?"

"Somewhere around there." Hattie stretched her back, taking a break from the chore of stocking the glass-front fridge.

"You've gotta be relieved."

"I guess." Thank God for the fridge's cool air dowsing her flaming cheeks. If Clementine learned Hattie's dirty secret, she'd never hear the end of it.

"Could you be any more apathetic? The guy has no legal reason to be here, but turned his whole life upside down to put himself at your beck and call."

"It's not like that. For the most part, we share watching the twins."

"Then there must be some other reason he's staying."

"Ask me," grizzly old Rufus Pendleton said from down the bar, "the man's got it bad for you. Not a good thing, considering past history and such."

"Keep out of it," Clementine snapped to their regular.

"Just sayin'…" He finished off his shot and signaled for another. "No good can come from a union between those two. For him, it'd be like shackin' up with a ghost. For her, steppin' right into her big sister's fancy shoes."

"For the record, Rufus," Hattie said, "there's nothing going on between Mason and me." She tried ducking back into the fridge, but too late. Her friend had already spied her using a collapsed six-pack case as a makeshift fan.

"Oh. My. Gosh." The size of Clementine's grin rivaled

the half-mile wonder of Conifer Gulch. "You two totally did the deed?"

"Shh!" Hattie held her finger to her lips, eyeing Rufus. "Don't be so crude!"

"Excuse me, did you make *sweet love?*"

Hattie refused to answer. Damn her stupid, flaming cheeks!

"You've liked him forever. But you've got to be freaking out. Your mom's already having a tough time with Melissa—no way is she going to be okay with you sleeping with her ex."

Hattie released a relieved sigh when Rufus and his latest shot headed to the nearest pool table.

"Thanks for reminding me." Hattie started unloading the next case. "And for the record, we were only together one night. It's not happening again."

"Is that what you really want?"

Hattie sat on the stool they kept behind the bar for when it was slow. "I don't know what I want, other than for things to go back to normal."

"Sweetie," Clementine said, with a hand on Hattie's forearm, "I'm no expert, but after suffering a loss like you have, I think you have to fight your way to a new normal. Thanksgiving's coming, then Christmas. For those babies, you have to get your family back on track. If that means officially welcoming Mason back into the fold, then your mom's just going to have to deal."

"Yeah..." Was now the time to admit her deepest fear had nothing to do with her mom's disapproval and everything to do with the fact Mason still dreamed of Melissa?

"I'D BE LYING if I said I wasn't disappointed you're not gonna be here for Christmas." Since Hattie was at her bar, Mason navigated Shamrock's, using the twins' stroller as a shopping cart for detergent and trash bags, while listening to his SEAL friend "Cowboy" Cooper whine for the past five minutes about losing his drinking buddy, even if only temporarily. "I swear to God, if you get hitched like Calder and Heath, I'll lose what little respect I have left for you."

"No worries," Mason said with a laugh, maneuvering down the chip and soda aisle. "Just as soon as Hattie's cast comes off, I'll be back on base."

"She's your ex's sister, right?"

"Yeah. We're just friends, though. No big deal." Unless Mason counted the number of times a day his mind replayed their wild night.

"Glad to hear it. Thanks for the reassurance, man."

With another laugh, Mason said, "No problem."

They swapped stories for a few more minutes, Mason retelling Vivian's Halloween scare and Cooper relaying his latest wild night with a blonde. How times had changed. Used to be they talked about weapons, video games and women—not necessarily in that order. Never had babies made it into the conversational mix—unless they were bitching about how nauseating it was for their married friends to blather on about their kids.

After finishing his call, Mason found lightbulbs and a new movie magazine for Hattie—who claimed she didn't read them, but had devoured Fern's cover to cover. Oh—and while he was thinking about it, he also grabbed more brownie mix.

Facing the girls, he asked, "Can you two think of anything else we might need?"

Though he'd have a long wait before they officially said their first words, both girls had grown more adept at babbles and coos.

"Ahhh..." Vivian hummed while gumming her rattle.

Vanessa gurgled while staring up at the store's fluorescent lights.

"She needs all of that, huh?"

Vivian performed a few excited wiggles.

Thanksgiving bouquet displays graced both sides of the checkout. Mason took one for Hattie, but then also for Akna and Fern. Hattie never talked about how much the rift between her and her mother bothered her, but she'd visited twice the past week and both times returned home crying. He could only imagine what Hattie might have to say concerning his olive-branch attempts. She'd tell him to stay out of it. Mind his own business. Everything would be fine.

All of that was well and good, but it'd been a long time since he'd had a traditional Thanksgiving—the last decent one had been with his friends Calder and Pandora. He couldn't even remember the last time he'd celebrated with his dad. If pressed, it'd probably been the year Melissa left him.

By God, if making Hattie smile meant hand delivering folks to her Turkey Day feast, he'd do it.

He cringed to find Sophie manning the sole checkout line. "Flowers?" she asked with eyebrows raised.

"For Hattie and her mom—and Fern."

The old bat had the audacity to snort. "You do know folks are talkin'? Doesn't seem natural for you to be with your dead ex-wife's sister."

"Thank you for your opinion, Sophie. Next time I'm looking to ruin my day, I'll be sure to make this my first stop."

Mason ignored the pit in his gut that Sophie's condemning glare had left and loaded up the girls and his purchases, then drove toward Hattie's childhood home. "You gals ready to see Grandma Akna?"

Vivian did her happy bounce, but Vanessa rubbed her sleepy eyes.

"Ladies, let's make this an in-and-out mission. We'll

hand Grandma her flowers, then remind her Melissa might be gone but you're still here."

And please, God, let Akna be more welcoming than Sophie, because his patience with busybodies was wearing mighty thin.

Chapter Thirteen

"Mom, please," Hattie pleaded, "at least tell me what I can do to help. I know you miss her, but you can't spend the rest of your life in bed." She eyed the row of prescriptions on her mother's nightstand. After her confession to Clementine, the last place Hattie had felt like staying was the bar, but her snap decision to check in on her parents wasn't turning out much better.

"I'll be fine," her mother assured her.

"Then prove it by coming over on Thanksgiving. You do know it's next week?"

"Honey, it's too soon. It's not appropriate to celebrate holidays with your sister gone."

Hattie counted to five in her head. She lacked the patience to get all the way to ten. "Thanksgiving isn't known for loud music and balloons. It's about family, and sharing what we're thankful for."

"I have nothing." She rolled over to face the wall.

Hattie wanted to go off, reminding her mother she still had a husband, daughter and two granddaughters who needed and loved her, but she sensed nothing she said would break the drug-induced fog.

After drawing the quilt her grandmother had made higher on her mother's slim shoulders, Hattie left the room.

She found her father stoking the fire.

"Heard you two talking," he said. "Have a good visit?"

"No. In fact, it was awful. You have to get her off of the sedatives."

"I know." Seated on the hearth with his shoulders hunched, her father looked defeated.

"Just take away the bottles. She hasn't been on them long enough for her to be addicted, but if she doesn't stop soon, she could be. Please, Dad, don't let it get to that point."

He nodded.

To make sure he'd heard her, she went to him, clutching his hands. "I want to have a big Thanksgiving with all the trimmings, okay? We'll use Melissa's fancy dining room and china. She'd like that. You know how she used to love to entertain. And instead of being morose about missing her, let's celebrate her life, okay?"

Sighing, he said, "You make it sound so simple, but for your mom and me, it's different."

What else could she say? Since losing Melissa, life had been *different* for her, too, but she didn't have the luxury of hiding. If her sister hadn't asked Hattie to raise the twins, would her mother still be in this funk? Or had the will's directive stolen her purpose?

Dragging in a fortifying breath, Hattie said, "Okay, well, I'm going to go. I'm sure I'll see you before Thanksgiving, but in case I don't, please bring Mom over around noon. I'll fix some appetizers—plenty of the stuffed mushrooms and hot wings you love from the bar—and we'll have dinner around two. Sound good?"

"Sure. We'll be there."

Hattie wished with all her heart she believed him.

She'd just made it to her car when Mason pulled in behind her. Even seeing him through the windshield made everything feel better.

"What are you doing here?" she asked when he rolled down the driver's-side window.

He took a cellophane-wrapped fall bouquet from the passenger seat. "I grabbed these at Shamrock's. Thought your mom might like one to help get her in the holiday spirit."

His thoughtfulness blasted a hole through the defensive wall she'd built around her heart. "You're kind to think of her, but she's dead to the world. I'll take them in and leave them with Dad."

"You sure? Seeing the girls might make her feel better."

"Yep. I'm sure." Recalling her mother's spaced-out stare, Hattie didn't think fireworks accompanied by turkeys dancing beneath a candy-corn rainbow would restore her usual cheery demeanor. Deep down, she was scared for her mom—and for herself. Hattie had already lost Melissa; she couldn't bear losing her mom, too. Knowing she was on borrowed time with Mason already hurt bad enough.

"All right, how about we meet back at the house, then you climb in with us so we can all take flowers to Fern?"

Eyes tearing, she asked, "Does the navy know their big, tough SEAL is actually a teddy bear?"

"Hat Trick, you can't go around staying stuff like that. You'll ruin my manly reputation."

On her tiptoes, she recklessly kissed his whisker-stubbled cheek. "Sorry. I promise not to let it happen again."

What she'd have a tougher time with was honoring the promise she'd made to herself to keep her distance from this amazing man.

As if fate agreed with Hattie's decision to back off from Mason, Sophie pulled her Impala into the driveway she shared with Hattie's parents. Judging by her sour expression, not only had she seen the kiss, but she'd disapproved.

"ARE YOU SURE you didn't give me a cup of salt instead of sugar?" The night before Thanksgiving, with Mason's help,

Hattie was attempting to make her grandmother's pumpkin pie, but something about the texture didn't seem right.

"Pretty sure," Mason said. "Taste it."

"It's got raw eggs."

He rolled his eyes, then dredged his index finger through the mixture. He swallowed and said, "I've eaten worse."

"What does that mean?"

"Just bake it. I'm sure it'll be fine."

The babies had been in bed for an hour and the house felt eerily quiet. "Want me to put on some music?"

"Sure." He washed the measuring spoons. "What's next on the menu?"

"Pumpkin bread. Mind getting the walnuts from the pantry?"

She turned on Alec's pricey Bose stereo. He'd subscribed to satellite radio and she hadn't yet called to cancel, so she used the remote to find a soft-rock station.

Mason emerged from the pantry, wearing a grin. "Wanna dance?"

"No, thank you. Clearly, the last night we danced, I'd had way too many beers."

"Uh-huh…"

He'd wedged behind her and settled his hands on her hips, swaying them in time to the music. His actions, his body heat, the sexy smell of his breath when he nuzzled her neck made Hattie shiver. "Stop. We need to bake." *And I can't go down this road with you again. It's too dangerous to my heart.*

"Really? You'd rather bake?"

No. "Yes."

"What if I did this?" He spun her around real slow, kissing her neck, her collarbone, the indentation at the base of her throat.

Her breathing hitched. Desire pooled low and achy in her belly. *Never stop.* "You *have* to stop."

"Okay, but what if I accidentally did this…" He slid his tongue in a tantalizing trail down her chest and into her T-shirt's deep V. As if that weren't torture enough, he skimmed his warm, rough hand under her thin cotton T, following her waist's inward curve.

"Mason…" She wanted him so bad. Knew being with him again was the worst thing she could do. No good could come of them being together. *"Please…"*

"You don't have to beg," he teased. "I'd be happy to kiss you." He tugged out her ponytail holder, freeing her hair. After easing his fingers beneath her black waves, he pressed his lips to hers, stealing every shred of her good judgment in the process.

Somehow, he was then dragging her T-shirt over her head and then she tugged at his shirt. Last time they'd been together it'd been dark or she'd been covered with suds and then a quick towel. He hadn't seen the real her. Would he stop once he noticed she wasn't a size two? "Should we go to my room? Dim the lights?"

"Why?" He paused, then made her die a thousand times under his slow appraisal. Her bra was simple and flesh-toned. Nothing fancy or lacy or anything she was certain his usual type might wear.

"Well…" She licked her lips. "Dim—even dark—is better."

"I like seeing all of you. Do you have any idea how gorgeous you are?"

"No…"

"Yes. Oh, hell yes." He reached behind her, deftly unfastening her bra, then easing the straps from her shoulders. Under his appraisal, her nipples hardened. She instinctively tried crossing her arms, but he stopped her, drawing her arms back to her sides. "I could stare at you all night."

Was this a dream? She couldn't be sure, because he was back to kissing her, kneading her aching breasts. Unable to believe any of this was really happening, she closed her eyes, abandoning herself to pure pleasure.

When he fumbled for the button to her jeans, she helped him. Together, they tugged them down. Her plain white panties went along with them and for a moment she stood before him completely naked and stunned. No one but her mirror had ever seen her fully unclothed. Would he think her hideous? The way her hips and thighs were way fuller than any woman's in magazines or on TV?

"I—I can't do this," she said. *Mortified* didn't begin to describe how she'd feel if he rejected her.

He groaned. "Baby, don't do this to me." He'd taken off his own jeans and boxers, leaving no question to the matter of whether or not he was aroused.

A giggle escaped her, but she covered her mouth.

"Think this is funny?" he teased, sweeping her into another heady kiss. "I'm in agony. You're so damned sexy it literally hurts."

"No..." She shook her head.

"Woman, have you ever really looked at yourself?" She'd only just noticed their reflections in the living room's plate-glass windows. With no one around for miles, Mason took her hand, guiding her closer to their mirror images. He knelt in front of her, kissing the belly she thought too round. The hips she believed untouchable. "You're curvy and sexy and soft." Rising, he effortlessly lifted her onto a solid oak sofa table. "I want to bury myself in you, leave you begging for more..."

The shock of his entry was soon tempered by pleasure so intense she lost all sense of space and time. In and out he thrust and her body willingly swallowed him whole. Pressure built and blossomed until erupting into all-encompassing joy.

Breathing heavy, she clung to him, needing a few moments to come crashing down.

He kissed her again, this time deep and slow, sweeping her tongue with his. "How could I have missed knowing you were right here all along?"

She couldn't answer because for her, it'd always been him.

"RELAX." MASON STOOD behind Hattie at the kitchen counter while she added more crackers to her cheese platter. With her sexy bottom pressed against his fly, it was all he could do not to drag her into the pantry and have his way with her all over again. Unfortunately, since his dad and Fern sat only a couple dozen feet away, bickering about whether to watch football or John Wayne, Mason behaved, chastely kneading Hattie's knotted shoulders. "They'll come."

Leaning against him, she asked, "What if they don't? How can they stand being away from the girls? Should I run over there? Check if they're all right?"

"They're adults. They know they're invited." He spun her to face him, wanting more than anything to kiss her worries away. Instead, he settled for a quick hug, hoping his dad and Fern didn't see.

"I guess. But it hurts, you know? I don't understand how they lose one daughter, then make a conscious decision to throw their other one away. Not to mention, their grandchildren."

"Babe, I don't think it's like that at all. Surely, by Christmas, your mom will come around."

"Hope you're right." Had it been his imagination, or had she held him extra close? Almost as if she'd craved his touch as much as he had hers? "Whatever happens, thanks for your help. Everything looks great—although it's a miracle anything got done."

"Complaining?"

He loved the way she reddened. "No, but—"

Mason silenced her with a kiss.

Stunned, she put her hands to her lips. "You can't do that. Not when we have company. In fact, we shouldn't be doing it at all."

She was right, but that didn't stop him from landing a light smack to her behind when she left him to deliver the tray to their guests.

By the time the turkey was browned to perfection and Hattie had whipped mashed potatoes and candied sweet potatoes, his heart broke for her because Akna and Lyle failed to show. She'd even invited Alec's parents, who were all the way down in Miami. Her hands' slight tremble alerted him to her distress.

Fury didn't begin to describe the malice he felt for the two couples. Ever since learning the contents of Melissa's will, they'd taken out their pain on the one person who'd been just as surprised as them—Hattie. That fact royally pissed him off. Granted, as of late, he might be biased, but she was a good woman. She deserved to have only caring, devoted people in her life.

Which category are you?

His conscience's question hit Mason square in the gut. When it came down to it, when he did finally return to Virginia, at the rate their connection was progressing he stood to hurt her more than anyone. He was married to the navy, and even if he weren't, he'd tried marriage and look where it had landed him. He wasn't sure what kind of relationship Hattie was ultimately in the market for, but he felt fairly certain that once she finally did settle down, she'd expect—she deserved—for it to be for the long haul.

Ignoring what would inevitably be his own role in Hattie's pain, Mason sneaked off to the bathroom to make a call to Lyle.

The son of a bitch couldn't even be bothered to answer.

"Dinner's ready!" Hattie called from the kitchen.

Mason tucked his cell in his pocket, then joined everyone in the dining alcove.

"Your table's pretty as a picture." Fern smoothed the tablecloth. She held Vanessa, who kept making valiant attempts to nab Fern's sparkly barrette. "I've never seen so much bling."

"My sister loved putting on a good show. She bought all the crystal and china on one of Alec's business trips to L.A."

Mason thought all of it a bit much. Give him a paper plate and plastic fork and he'd be good. Toss in a campfire and he'd be even better.

On his way from carrying one of the high chairs in from the kitchen, he noticed a series of silver frames. The dining alcove was a spot in the house he'd never much paid attention to, and now he was glad he hadn't. Picture after picture of Alec and Melissa lined a buffet. Smiling. Hugging. Kissing. Turning his stomach. Why, after all these years, did he still let them get to him?

Maybe because they were the reason he now felt incapable of sustaining any relationship. Because they'd taught him not to trust.

His dad carried in the other high chair and eased Vivian into it.

Though Hattie had set the table for six, only four presided around her delicious-looking spread.

She said a brief prayer, and then they dug in. Save for the clinking of silverware against plates and the girls' occasional grunts and giggles as Fern and Hattie took turns feeding them pureed pears, all was quiet. The girls had grown a lot in the short time Mason had been with them. Seemed hard to believe they were already eating solid foods.

A couple times, Mason figured when she'd thought no one was looking, he caught Hattie glancing at the empty place settings.

Finally, having had enough of her torturing herself over other people's poor manners, he pushed his chair back and cleared the empty plates. "I don't know about the rest of you, but I could use more elbow room."

"Me, too," his dad said, rising to help.

"Hattie, this turkey is as moist as any I've ever had," Fern noted.

"Thank you."

His dad nodded. "I could take a bath in these potatoes."

"You should probably take a bath in something." Fern pinched her nose.

"Ha-ha." Jerry helped himself to thirds of everything.

The meal wound on, and though Hattie didn't say anything, Mason sensed her mood growing ever more somber. By the time they helped each other serve dessert, she was hardly saying a word.

"You okay?" he asked while unearthing the whipped cream from the overstocked fridge.

She nodded.

Back at the table, Mason took charge of serving. "Who wants pumpkin pie?"

"Heck," his dad said, "I'll have a little of everything."

"You'd better get me some, too." Fern held out her plate. "At the rate he's going, there won't be any left."

Jerry dived for his plate, too, only to spit out his most recent bite. "No offense, Hattie, but this pie tastes like a salt lick."

Chapter Fourteen

Paling, Hattie said, "Mason, you tasted it and told me it was fine."

Yeah, he'd also been distracted. "Honestly, not only have my taste buds been ruined by dousing hot sauce on MREs, but I'm more of a pecan pie kind of guy. I'm not even sure what pumpkin's supposed to taste like." And to prove it, he dived his fork right into the pie's center. He chewed and chewed, and when he couldn't hold his fake smile a second longer, he deposited the bite into his fancy cloth napkin. "Okay, so it might be a little salty, but otherwise, it's pretty good."

"Oh, stop." Hattie tossed her napkin on the table, then dashed off up the stairs.

Fern scowled at both men. "Good Lord, were you two raised in a barn? Poor girl. It's her first time hosting a big holiday. Couldn't you lie? I ate my whole piece."

Snorting, Jerry said, "That's because you're crazy."

"No," she argued, "I have manners. Mason, you'd better go after her. It's not every day your own parents stand you up, then your pumpkin pie sucks." She hacked off a chunk of pumpkin bread, slathering it with butter. "Everything else is real good, though."

Mason followed Fern's advice, charging upstairs. The closed guest room door may have muffled Hattie's sobs, but that didn't help him feel better about the situation. Quiet tears were still tears and he hated knowing she was hurt.

He knocked. "Hat Trick? Can I come in?"

"No! And stop calling me that!"

For a split second he considered respecting her apparent wish for privacy, but then barged in, closing the door behind him. "What's with the waterworks? It was only a pie. And Dad and Fern have eaten damn near every crumb of the other stuff you cooked."

"You're such a man. The pie was just the cherry on top of what has been a seriously awful day. Everything was supposed to be perfect, but nothing went right."

Perched on the bed beside her, he skimmed hair from her eyes. "Funny, because up until a few minutes ago, I thought it's been a pretty great day. I've got you and the girls with me. My dad and Fern. I'm sorry your parents and Alec's chose not to come, but that's their loss."

"You're just saying that to be nice. And don't think for a second I didn't see the way you were looking at all of Melissa's pictures in the dining room."

"Yeah? What about it?" He didn't have a clue what she was talking about. "You sound as nutty as Fern."

"Don't even try pretending you don't know what I mean. You slept with me last night, then today, stared like a love-sick puppy at her and Alec's parade of exotic vacation pics."

"Those? Are you kidding me?" He crossed his arms. "Yeah, I looked at them, all right—in disgust. If I looked sick, that's because I was. I'm sorry those two died, and if this makes me sound like the most heartless ass on earth, then so be it, but the God's honest truth is that to me, those two died the day Melissa left me to marry my so-called best friend."

He stood and moved in front of the window. "Look,

you have to forget the past. I don't mean erasing your sister's memory, but the role I once played in her life. Anything I felt for her has been over for a long time. As for me and you…"

"Oh, my God, do you ever shut up? As soon as my cast comes off, you're headed back to Virginia. Last night and what happened in Valdez was fun, but you and I both know it'll never go further than that."

Jaw clenched, Mason tapped his closed fist to his mouth.

"My sister was the dreamer. I've always been a realist." She combed the guest room's designer pillowcase's fringe. "I'll be first to admit our hookup has been a nice surprise, but—"

"Aw, Hattie, you mean a helluva lot more than just a hookup to me. Don't you know that? But circumstances being what they are, I don't have anything else to offer."

"Trust me, I know."

AFTER A FEW semifriendly days, followed by smoking-hot nights, Mason had never been more confused. The second Hattie left for the bar on Tuesday, he called his pal Calder.

"Hey, man, we were just talking about you." One of Calder's kids cried in the background. He and his wife, Pandora, shared an almost-three-year-old boy and a one-year-old girl, as well as her daughter Julia from a previous marriage. Mason figured if anyone could help him figure out how to handle the mess he found himself in, it'd be Calder. "There's a betting pool going on whether or not you're coming back."

"Of course I'll be back. I still owe the navy two years."

"You know enough people in high places to bail if need be."

Mason sorted through the day's mail. "That's not my style."

"Didn't say it was, but I know what suddenly having a kid is like—and here, you have two."

"Not anymore. I mean, yeah, I'm still taking care of them until Hattie's arm heals, but I signed away my custody rights."

"Cooper told us." Yipping competed with kid-cries for loudest background noise.

"Sounds like you've got a zoo."

"Pandora and the kids gave me a puppy for my birthday. It's a Yorkie barely big enough to fit in the palm of my hand. Damn thing pees and craps chocolate-chip-sized turds everywhere, but it's so cute you can't stay mad at it long."

"Sounds like you've got your hands full. Should I call back?"

"Not at all. What's up?"

"Not sure where to even start." His doodling on the back of the water bill took on a frenetic pace. "After what Melissa put me through, never in a million years would I believe I'd be thinking about another commitment, but things have developed between Hattie and me that I—"

"Whoa, stop right there." The connection sounded muffled while Calder yelled at either a kid or dog. "Sorry. Crowd control. Listen, before I knew I wanted to marry Pandora, my stepdad gave me some great advice."

"Lay it on me."

"You know when you know."

That's it? "Care to elaborate?"

"Nothing more to say." Something howled. Mason couldn't be sure whether it was a dog or kid. "Sorry, man, but Pandora's out shopping with a friend and I've got a situation. Seriously, think about what I told you. Best thing I ever did was trust myself enough to believe in what I was doing."

Mason disconnected and contemplated throwing his phone.

Clearly, his usually logical friend had been brainwashed by love. Nothing he'd just said made sense. Mason had entered his marriage planning to be with the same woman for the rest of his life, but now that the illusion of a *forever* relationship had been shattered, he recognized love for the sham it was.

Sure, he loved his dad, but that was different. No one else could ever have that kind of permanent connection. Melissa proved it wasn't possible.

As for what he felt for Hattie? Mason didn't have a clue.

WITH CHRISTMAS ONLY three weeks away, a sense of urgency had settled over Hattie, driving her to make every minute of each day count. Thanksgiving might've been a bust—at least where her parents were concerned, but no matter what, she was determined to make Santa's big day extra special.

The holiday was always a big deal in Conifer. With a limited amount of decorative items shipped in, homeowners had to be quick in buying items the second they hit Shamrock's or the grocery store.

Tuesday morning, she and Mason loaded the girls into Melissa's SUV to go to a Christmas-tree farm. Hattie had her heart set on the biggest tree she could find.

"You sure we're on the right road?" Mason drove, while both babies gurgled and babbled along to *Elmo's Sing-a-Long*. "And could you please find a different CD?"

"The map said Owl Creek Road. That's what we're on, right?"

Braking, he lowered his mirrored sunglasses to give her a dark stare. "We're on Deer Creek Road because that's what you told me we needed."

"Oops." She hoped her smile encouraged Mr. Grinch

to better appreciate the importance of their mission. This would be the girls' first Christmas, and as such, Hattie thought it important to do everything perfect—just the way her sister would've. Hattie had always wanted to visit the farm, but her parents put up an artificial tree. "You have to admit that with all the snow piled on the shoulders, it looks the same?"

"Sure. Except for the sign that says Owl Creek Road."

"Sorry. Once we get there, you'll be superhappy we drove all this way. Clementine got her tree here last year and it was gorgeous."

He shook his head.

Thirty minutes later, they finally reached Olde St. Nick's Tree Farm. On a weekday, the train wasn't running, but there were plenty of trees and a black pony named Coal for the girls to ride. The building that housed Santa, as well as hot chocolate and cookies, had been decorated to resemble a Dickensian village. Thousands of lights twinkled from most every surface, lighting the suddenly cloudy day. With carols playing over loudspeakers and scents of cinnamon and pine lacing the air, Hattie couldn't imagine a better place for Mason to finally find his holiday spirit.

The place was so popular, families from neighboring towns rode the ferry to catch the farm's specially outfitted retired school bus that hauled trees on top. Since it was open only two weeks out of the year, customers had to be on their game to make sure they were there in time to make the best selection.

"Isn't this adorable?" Hattie asked Mason as they left the car, each carrying a girl. "Should we take pictures of the twins riding the pony first, or visiting Santa?"

"I thought we were here to get a tree? Should be an in-and-out mission. Precision all the way."

"What is it with you and missions? This will be Van's and Viv's first time to see the big guy. I want to soak it in."

He locked the car. "Thought you were asking your mom to come with you?"

"I did, but as usual, she turned me down."

"Sorry."

"It is what it is," Hattie said in a forced cheery tone. She was tired of feeling hurt by her mom. In the same respect, she refused to give up on making their relationship as special as it had once been.

"What happened to the sun?" He tucked his sunglasses into his coat pocket. "I thought it wasn't supposed to snow till tonight?"

"I say bring it on. It'll create an even more festive mood."

"You do know you sound like a lunatic elf, right? From all I've read, I doubt the girls will even remember this Christmas."

"But they'll have pictures. Do you want them being the only kids at school who didn't meet with Santa?"

"News flash—" he opened the gate to the pony corral "—they've got a while till kindergarten."

"Just hush."

Since the lot was nearly empty, Coal's wrangler gave the twins an extralong ride. While Mason walked alongside the pony, holding both girls in the same saddle, Hattie took pictures with her phone, trying not to think how lucky Vanessa and Vivian were to be held by such a handsome guy.

A few minutes in, the pony snorted. Vivian got spooked and launched into an instant wail.

"That's it." Mason plucked both girls from the saddle. "Ride's over. Let's grab the tree before snow sets in."

"Nope," she said. "Santa's next."

While the quintessential Kris Kringle jiggled the now-smiley twins, Hattie snapped more shots. "Aren't they the cutest things you've ever seen?"

"Ho, ho, ho," Santa said. "I'll bet you two want some pretty new rattles for Christmas." His boisterous laugh terrified Vanessa.

Mason was first to snatch Vanessa and Vivian back into his arms. "Now that both babies have been thoroughly traumatized, can we get on with this?"

"What's up with you?" she asked out of earshot of Mrs. Claus, who'd handed them all candy canes.

"This just isn't my thing, okay?"

"What do you mean?" She took Vanessa from him.

"The over-the-top holiday scene."

"I never knew you didn't like Christmas." She glanced his way to find his profile darker than the approaching storm clouds.

"I don't have anything personal against it." He stepped over an extension cord, then extended his hand to steady her. "But Mom died the week before, so ever since, that memory overrides anything else."

"Please don't think I'm being flippant, but have you ever thought about making new memories? You spent lots of holidays with us and seemed happy enough."

He snorted. "That's because Melissa was always nagging me to smile."

"I'm sorry." And she really was. All too clearly she recalled the sad little boy he'd long ago been. It hurt her that he still missed his mom. It also made her all the more determined to help heal her own mother's emotional pain.

After interlocking her fingers with his, she squeezed.

"See any of these you like?" They'd reached the portion of the lot where precut trees stood in neat rows.

"Nice stab at changing the subject." Standing on her tiptoes, she kissed him. "What if this Christmas you remember the happy times with your mom? Even better, what if I make this holiday so perfect you can't wait to have dozens more just like it?"

Groaning, he drew her into a hug. "You're too good to be true. I don't deserve you."

"No, you don't," she teased, "but for now, anyway, I'm here and you're here and the most adorable baby angels are here. What if we make believe we're a real family?"

"That what you want to do?"

She swallowed hard. Hattie didn't know what she wanted beyond being with this man, which went against everything she knew to be true. If he played along with her silly game, it'd be just that—a game. After New Year's, he'd be gone, just like the season. But it wouldn't even be like a legitimate breakup because how could she claim a man who'd never really been hers, but her sister's?

Making matters worse, as was usually the case in their small town, their hug had been witnessed. Her opinionated regular from the bar, Rufus, had apparently secured seasonal work at the farm and stood a few yards away, trimming a tree bottom—and wagging his finger in her direction.

Chapter Fifteen

Back from the tree farm, Mason unearthed Melissa's tree stand from the downstairs storage area, hauled it upstairs, then crammed the odd little tree they'd purchased into it. "Want me to pile a few books under it so it looks taller?"

Hattie held Vanessa on her hip while appraising the partially bald tree. "It seemed bigger outside."

She'd gotten her dates mixed up and missed the farm's famed opening weekend. It was then, the salesman had explained, that the best trees were sold. All of the majestic ones Hattie had set her heart upon regally standing in the cathedral-like living room had already been sold. The tree they'd bought was cute—if a little lopsided—but barely stood five feet tall.

Vivian honked the horn on her new walker toy.

Mason chuckled. "Viv seems to like it, so it can't be all that bad."

"Yeah, but I wanted a perfect tree. You know how Melissa always wanted even her old bedroom to look like it was out of a magazine. How could I have gotten the tree farm's opening dates so wrong?"

"Gee, could it be you lost your sister, your mom and dad dived off the deep end, you broke your arm and suddenly are the primary caregiver to not one baby, but two?"

She sat on the sofa arm. "When you put it that way, guess I have had a lot on my mind."

"You think?" He went to her, enfolding her in his arms. "Tell you what, tomorrow morning, if you still find this tree lacking, let's go out and cut our own."

"Really?"

"Have you looked outside? This land is covered in Christmas trees. How hard can it be to chop one down?"

HATTIE WOKE SPOONED alongside Mason the next morning. Though the clock read 6:00 a.m., it was still dark and would be for a while. He'd molded his fingers to the curve of her stomach. She placed her hand over his, toying with the fine hair on his knuckles.

"You're up too early," he said with a sexy growl, burrowing beneath her hair to kiss her neck. "If we're lucky, the munchkins will snooze for at least another thirty minutes."

"I'm up because I'm excited."

"Yeah? Me, too...." His claim was confirmed by the size of his erection. "What are we going to do about all this excitement?"

"I thought we were headed into the woods to find a giant Christmas tree?"

He rolled her over for a long, leisurely kiss that tugged an invisible string of arousal. "Wouldn't you rather stay in bed?"

She giggled when he nibbled her ear. "I suppose we could, but then what are we going to do about getting a bigger tree?"

"Oh—something's getting bigger as we speak."

"You're awful!"

"You're delicious," he said after another heated kiss. "Let's get this show on the road before our two monkeys start rattling around in their cages."

Hours later, once the sun finally rose on twelve inches of freshly fallen snow, they bundled the girls for their trek out onto the twenty acres of forest on which the house sat.

"You do know this is crazy, right?" The sight of him took her breath away. The way cold turned his cheeks ruddy and his winter coat accentuated his size. Even when she'd been little, he'd made her feel safe—like anything was possible.

"This coming from the guy who took all the desks from the school to spell out your class year on the football field?"

"Child's play." He took one step outside of the circle drive the local plowing service had cleared and stood in snow up to his thighs. "Got any ideas on how to carry the chain saw and two babies through this?"

"You're the SEAL."

"Really? Is that how this is going to be?" The way the corners of his eyes crinkled when he smiled made her want him all over again.

"You started it. Just be glad I can't hold Vanessa and make a snowball at the same time, or you'd be pummeled."

"Like this?" Before she could even form a plan for making a one-armed snowball, he'd already succeeded, lobbing it straight at her head.

"Beast!" The shocking cold of snow against every inch of her face had her laughing, but seeking revenge. A chase ensued. "I hate you!"

"No, you don't," he teased, always an infuriating few steps ahead.

When he finally slowed enough for her to nail his bare neck with a handful of lightly packed snow, he growled upon impact, landing her and Vanessa in a playful tackle against mounded snow.

Breathing heavy and smiling, she said, "You're horrible, attacking poor defenseless girls like that."

"Aw, I'm not so bad." The sizzling heat of his slow, sexy grin did crazy, happy things to her chest. Sheer anticipation of wanting his kiss made it impossible to breathe. Consulting Vivian, he asked, "You think I'm fun, don't you?"

The infant gave him a toothless grin.

"See? All the ladies love me." He leaned in close enough for his warm breath to tickle Hattie's upper lip.

Yes, Mason, you would be so easy to love.

In an attempt to steer the conversation away from her heart, she asked, "How is any of this helping me get a bigger Christmas tree?"

He laughed, then kissed her. "As seems to be a trend when I'm around you, something's getting bigger."

"You're horrible!" And so ridiculously sexy she could happily occupy this spot for hours.

"Admit it, you can't get enough of me...." He kissed her again and again, and as much as she wanted to deny him, she lacked the strength. Like a chip or cookie, when it came to his kisses she had to have one more.

"Okay, yes, I'm hopelessly addicted to you, so will you now get my tree?"

"Have you always been this demanding?"

She raised her chin and smiled. "Yes. So kiss me one last time and then get moving. Since the snow's deeper than we thought, the girls and I will stay here."

"Deal."

Only after Hattie and the girls waved Mason on his way, she found herself craving still more...

MASON COULDN'T HAVE said why, but his mission to find Hattie her quintessential Christmas tree had taken on an absurd sense of urgency. Above all else, he wanted to see her smile—better yet, be the one responsible for producing that smile.

He trudged at least a half mile through thigh-deep snow

before discovering a twelve-footer that even Hattie would be hard-pressed to deny was impressive. Not too wide and perfectly symmetrical, it was a true beauty—just like the woman he'd be bringing it home for.

While priming the finicky chain saw, it occurred to Mason that over the past few weeks—especially since sleeping in a real bed next to Hattie—Melissa and Alec's house had started feeling more like a home. But what did that mean? Was it the actual house he felt comfortable with, or the occupants? All it took was remembering that morning's kisses and the twins' adorably goofy grins to tell him without a doubt, the ladies of the house had placed a spell over him.

Weeks earlier, he'd found himself living for the navy. It spooked him how suddenly new commitments had taken precedence.

But was he honestly committed to Hattie and the twins? Or had he succumbed to the privileges of playing house with benefits?

Frustrated with this train of thought, he used a collapsible shovel he'd stashed in a backpack to dig out around the tree's base—no easy feat as beneath the snow, it'd been broader than he'd anticipated.

No worries, though. He'd told Hattie he'd bring her a tree and by God, that was what he'd do.

His next course of action was to start the small chain saw he'd also hauled along. He yanked repeatedly at the saw's pull start, only nothing happened. Even as a kid he'd had a hatred for two-cycle engines. Apparently, they hated him back.

He tugged and tugged, primed and primed, until finally giving up and opting for an old scout hatchet he'd brought for backup.

With the sky darkening and the temperature dropping,

he figured he'd better put his back into it or he'd be there all night.

When he'd been a full-time Alaskan, he'd been a fisherman—not a woodsman—so his ax man skills left a lot to be desired. He knew enough to make a V in the trunk, but best as he could remember, the placement of that V was critical as to which direction the tree would fall.

Hoping for the best, Mason made a judgment call when giving the larger-than-expected tree a final shove. Wood cracked, and with a mighty whoosh the tree was down.

Now he just had to drag it home...

TWO HOURS PASSED. When Mason still hadn't returned to the house, worry set in. The man was a navy SEAL. No doubt he could single-handedly take down a grizzly, then roast him for dinner, but Alaska was loaded with manly men and sadly, they died all the time.

Though Hattie's more rational side knew he was most likely fine, the part of her still shocked by the sudden loss of her sister and brother-in-law warned her not to take chances. After all of their horseplay, it'd been noon before he'd set off. This time of year, especially with cloud cover, they had barely two hours of daylight left—if that.

Pacing the kitchen, she dialed her parents' number, praying at least her father would recognize the potential urgency of the situation. "Dad, I'm sorry to bother you," she said once he picked up, "but I need your help. I'm afraid Mason may be in trouble."

"Be right there" was all he said before hanging up.

Snow was really coming down, along with the temperature, so Hattie popped the girls in their playpen, then took their monitor outside.

"Mason!" Falling snow combined with wind in the pines deadened the sound of her voice. "Mason, can you hear me?"

No response.

If something had happened to him all because she'd sent him out to look for a stupid Christmas tree, she'd never forgive herself.

Shivering with no coat, she dashed back inside.

Kneeling alongside the playpen, willing her pulse to slow, she said to the girls, "Right about now I'm wishing you guys were old enough to talk to. Better yet, that you were old enough to talk some sense into me about not needing everything to be perfect—especially not decorations."

When Melissa had been alive, she'd gladly assumed the role of family Martha Stewart, but that had never been Hattie's thing. Why now did she feel compelled to try to re-create things the way Melissa had done them? Could it be linked to her insecurities about Mason? How she still didn't completely believe he was as into her as she was him?

The doorbell rang, and Hattie rushed to answer.

Her dad was an avid backcountry snowshoer. Many times they'd gone together, and he carried her snowshoes with him.

"Thank you so much for coming." She crushed him in a hug.

"We'll find him. His tracks should be easy enough to follow."

"But I can't leave the babies."

"I'll watch them." Her mom's movements were sluggish, her expression grim, but she was really there, holding out her arms for a hug.

Hattie asked, "Are you sure you'll be okay?"

She nodded. "I'll be fine. We'll talk later, but for now, you two go on and bring Mason safely home."

Her dad was right in that, even with worsening weather, Mason's trail was clear. Seeing how deeply he'd sunk into the snow made her nauseous. Why had she insisted he do it?

The deeper into the forest they trekked, the harder snow fell and the darker the skies grew.

Hattie's chest tightened to the point she feared having some sort of attack. "Mason!"

"Maaason!" her father echoed. To her he asked, "How're you doing with your bum arm?"

"I'm fine. It's Mason I'm worried about."

"We'll find him. I told your mom that if we're not back in an hour, she should call for backup."

A few more steps later, Hattie was almost afraid to ask, "How'd you get Mom to come?"

"I didn't. She's got herself down to taking those tranquilizers only at night. She wanted to be here."

"Th-that's great," Hattie said. Her teeth started to chatter, only not from cold, but concern for Mason. Another new item on her list of issues was that if her mom was doing better, why hadn't she called? Was she still upset over the will?

"Mason!" her dad called.

"Lyle?" answered a voice from out of the dark. Then came an odd swishing sound.

"Mason! Thank God." When he came into view, tears fell fast and hard. As best she could in her awkward snowshoes, Hattie went to him, tossing her arms around his neck, kissing him full on his lips, not caring who saw. "I've been so scared something happened. What took you so long?"

After returning her kiss, he drew her attention to a hulking form behind him. "What do you think took so long? Your tree. In case you haven't noticed, it's a monster."

Lyle asked, "Why'd you pick one so big?"

Mason laughed. "Your daughter wanted one this size. I was afraid if I brought anything smaller, she wouldn't let me in the house. The only thing keeping me going was my fantasy of returning to a steaming spiked coffee."

Now quaking with gratitude for Mason being all right, Hattie shook her head. "You stupid, silly man. I would have promised you a lifetime supply of spiked coffee if you'd come home an hour ago."

"I'd have taken you up on that," he said with a sexy wink barely visible from the light of her dad's head lamp, "but I didn't dare come home without this tree."

"YOU'RE SAFE." Mason was shocked when Akna opened the front door for him, then made the sign of the cross on her chest.

"Sorry for giving you all a fright." He was too cold to put much thought into the implications of his ex-mother-in-law's appearance. For Hattie's sake, he hoped this meant a return to the closeness she and her mom had once shared. "This whole Christmas-tree thing has gotten out of hand."

When he'd voiced his complaint in Hattie's direction, she'd at least had the good graces to redden, but then he found genuine regret behind her half smile and was sorry for his continued teasing. "I never should've asked you."

"Now that the tree's down," Lyle said, "we might as well put it up. Your sister likes her tree in the front window, right, Hattie?"

Hugging the coat she'd only just removed, she nodded. "I'll get the little tree out of the stand."

Outside with Lyle, Mason tried and failed again to get the chain saw working so he could trim the trunk and bottom branches.

Lyle asked, "Mind if I take a turn?"

"Be my guest." Mason stepped aside.

Just his luck the stupid thing started right up, making him feel like a gangly twelve-year-old in front of the man whom he'd once held in high regard.

The chain saw's buzz and smoke polluted the calm night.

But after a few minutes' cutting and shaping, Lyle was done. "That should do it."

"Looks good." More than ready to get this chore finished, Mason grabbed the tree by the trunk's base to haul it inside.

"Hold up." Lyle blocked the porch stairs. "While I've got you alone, mind explaining that kiss?"

Chapter Sixteen

"Let me help." When her mother got up from the sofa, Hattie had a hard time even recognizing her. She'd lost a frightening amount of weight and dark shadows haunted her eyes.

"I've got it, Mom. You rest."

"I—I've done enough resting." Hugging herself, she stared at her reflection in the window's glass. "Despite my issues with Mason, I'm glad he wasn't hurt. Even the possibility of another accident was the wake-up call I needed. It's good being back with the girls."

Almost as if they sensed the dark mood, Vanessa and Vivian sat quietly in their walkers. Vanessa gummed a stuffed frog and Vivian stared daggers at a potted fern.

"Mom..." Their family had never been overly demonstrative, which made her mother's admission all the more meaningful, yet hard to hear. Hattie hadn't expected a grand statement, just for her mother to remember the family she still had who loved her so very much. "It's okay."

"I know, but let me get this out. I'll always believe what your sister did—signing her children over to you and a man who should've been out of all of our lives—was an awful betrayal. Then, instead of accepting her wishes like the honor they were, he just—just threw his parental rights away? H-he's awful. Worse."

When Akna started to weep, Hattie wrapped her arms around her mother's frail form. "What he did, it wasn't like that. Mason's a good man, Mom, but he has an important job to get back to. He's not ready to be a parent right now."

"Raising your sister's children isn't important?"

Hattie sighed. "That's not what I meant. It's complicated." If her mom knew exactly how complicated, she'd no doubt ground her.

"Sɪʀ?" Tʜᴇ ᴋɪss question had Mason clearing his throat. "I'm, ah, not sure what you mean."

"Then I'll be blunt." Lyle fit the chain saw back in its plastic case. "Hattie might be all grown up, but as far as I'm concerned, you've already hurt one of my daughters. If your plan is to create that kind of pain all over again, then—"

"Sir…" Mason clenched and unclenched his fists. "I mean no disrespect by this, but Melissa cheated on me. You're a man, so I assume you know what it means to support your family. If I'd been able to stay home every day with Mel, holding her hand every second after that miscarriage, don't you think I would've? Unfortunately, as the man of the house, I didn't have that luxury. To afford your daughter the kind of lifestyle she deserved, I had to work. Fishing was all I'd ever known."

A nerve twitched in Lyle's jaw. "I understand that, but make no mistake, if you're putting the moves on my Hattie, I will do everything within my power to stop you."

Seriously? "What don't you get about the fact that your daughter left me—to be with my best friend. She wasn't the one forced to join the navy, because everywhere I went in this stupid town, all my so-called friends stared at me with pity. Hattie gets me. She's a beautiful, loving woman fully capable of—"

Lyle's hard right to Mason's jaw rendered him momentarily speechless.

It took every shred of Mason's self-restraint not to meet the older man's punch with one of his own. But what would that prove? "Because you're no doubt still grieving, I'll give you a pass for that. What I won't do is accept blame for your eldest daughter making the conscious decision to break her marital vows. As for Hattie, I'm pretty sure she's old enough to make her own decisions."

His ex-father-in-law exhaled with a grunt of what Mason could only describe as disgust, then mounted the porch stairs. "We'll see about that."

"HE HIT YOU?" Hattie had just made the girls' dinner bottles and fixed them bowls of peaches when her father stormed into the house, telling her mother it was time for them to leave.

As suddenly as her parents had appeared, they were now gone.

"Yep." Mason fished in the freezer, eventually pulling out a bag of peas he held to his bruising jaw.

Instantly at his side, she asked, "What'd you do?"

His narrow-eyed stare told her she'd asked the wrong question.

"What is it with your family always assuming I'm the one in the wrong? Your old man wanted to know why I kissed you. He then declared you off-limits as far as I was concerned."

Covering her face with her hands, Hattie groaned. "You've got to be kidding."

"Wish I were."

"Now what?" Hattie held Vivian's spoon to her mouth.

"You're asking me?" He did the same for Vanessa.

"Clearly, both of my parents have lost their minds." Vivian winced, then grinned at her first taste of peaches.

"I don't get how they'd rather complain about you than be here with these two cuties."

"Good question." He used a damp washcloth to clean Vanessa's sticky cheeks.

"I'm sorry."

"For what? You didn't hit me."

"Yeah, but if it hadn't been for my stupid Christmas tree, none of this would've happened."

"Speaking of which, it's still out in the front yard. Once we get these two fed, wanna help me bring it in?"

She leaned in to kiss him. "There's nothing I'd rather do."

"Nothing?" He grinned, then winced, reaching for his bag of peas to hold against his jaw. "At the very least, after getting punched out by your dad, you owe me a rousing game of helpless patient/naughty nurse."

HATTIE FINISHED WITH the last of the blue Christmas lights she hung at the bar every year, then climbed down from the stepladder to admire her handiwork.

"Needs to go a good three inches to the right," said Rufus.

"Ignore him," Clementine said from the garnish station. "It looks good." She'd eaten about twenty cherries in the past thirty minutes, but in the holiday spirit of giving, Hattie pretended not to notice. "But I still don't understand how your dad punched out your boyfriend and the very next day you're back at work, decorating up a storm, acting as if nothing happened."

"I'd hardly call Mason my boyfriend."

"Then what would you call him?" She unloaded the silver metallic tree that occupied a place of honor at the base of the stairs.

"Does there have to be a label?"

"I don't suppose, but have you all talked about what happens when he leaves?"

"No." Hattie preferred not thinking about it.

The bar's door opened. Stepping inside on a gust of cold wind was Hattie's father.

Leaving Clementine to deal with the tree's many parts, Hattie met him before he selected a seat. "You hit him? Dad, that's not you." When her voice cracked, she swallowed hard. "You've always been one of the kindest, gentlest men I know. What's happening to not only you, but our family?"

"It's complicated." He removed his Conifer Cardinals ball cap. "All I know is Mason destroyed Melissa and he'll do the same to you. He's not cut out to be a family man—never has been, never will."

"Are you delusional?" When her raised voice drew stares from the customers seated at the bar, she tugged her father by his sleeve to a lonely row of booths. "You and Mom never wanted to accept the fact that your supposedly perfect daughter cheated on her husband, but she did. I'm sorry she'd had a miscarriage, but that never justified her sleeping around with Alec—her husband's best friend. Why can't you see that? Moreover, why can't you recognize Mason as the injured party in that whole mess? Melissa and Alec kept all their mutual friends. Mason didn't just lose his wife, but his entire world."

Her dad slowly exhaled. "Can you grab me a beer?"

"No. Not until you admit you were wrong to hit Mason and owe him an apology, but also that I deserve some happiness. If Mason makes me smile, then how can that be wrong?"

"Fine. You won't give me a beer, I'll take my business elsewhere."

"You're impossible," she called after her father when he slapped his hat back on and headed for the door.

"And you're delusional. Mark my words, that boy will bring you nothing but pain."

"He's not a boy, but a man," she whispered once her dad was gone. "And at the moment, I respect him more than you."

Rufus shook his head. "You shouldn't disrespect your father like that."

"Yeah? Well, thanks for the advice, but I'm damned sick and tired of him disrespecting *me*."

"REMIND ME WHY we're standing in line for the girls to see Santa for the second time this year?" The Saturday before Christmas, Mason pushed their stroller ahead by a measly foot down the North Pole Trail that was actually the longest stretch of Conifer's wharf that didn't have any businesses built off of it. Fresh pine garland had been hung from the railings and the choir from Eastside Church sang carols. Food stands sold funnel cake, cider and cocoa.

Even the weather was being cooperative, with plenty of sun and no wind.

He'd been to Conifer's annual Christmas parade and festival every year of his life until leaving for the navy. So why did it feel as if he'd landed on the moon without a space suit?

"Why wouldn't we bring them to see Santa? You saw him here when you were a kid, right?" She tucked Vivian's blanket more snugly around her shoulders.

"Sure. We all did, but I'm just saying the girls could get confused by the concept of multiple Santas, since they just met him at the tree lot."

"Whatever. Just stand there and look handsome."

Had they been alone, he'd have landed a light smack to her behind for being sassy. Unfortunately, they were surrounded by couples he and Melissa had graduated with. His skin crawled from the weight of their stares.

"What's wrong?" Hattie asked. "You're glowering as if someone stole your candy cane."

"I just hate how everyone's staring."

"Who?" She glanced around.

"I don't know. Just everyone."

"Since when did you become self-conscious? And for the record, I'm pretty sure Jingles the Elf Clown is drawing way more of a crowd than you."

They moved forward another couple feet. "Forget I said anything, okay? Let's just get this over with and head back to the house."

"Don't you want to go to the craft sale? For all they've done to help with the girls, I want to find something special for your dad and Fern."

"Please, Hattie, can we just—"

"Hey, Mason. Long time no see." Craig Lovett, the guy from Mason's senior class who'd had his birthday party at Alec and Melissa's that fateful last night, held out his hand for Mason to shake. "I'm in awe of you, man. You're an honest-to-God SEAL. You're living the dream."

His wife, Sue, who manned their stroller, tugged a lock of Craig's hair. "I thought *we* were *the dream?*"

Craig backpedaled by giving his wife a quick kiss. "Honey, you know what I mean. What guy wouldn't want to be a SEAL? I always planned to be one, but never found time. Is it true that during Hell Week you have to kill a shark with your bare hands?"

"Nah." Where did guys get this stuff? Craig had been such a jackass to him during the divorce that Mason was sorely tempted to yank his chain by claiming they had to kill not just *any* shark, but a great white. Instead, as he'd been trained, he took the high road. "No sharks, just plenty of running and heavy lifting."

"Oh." Craig's shoulders deflated. "Well, you did have

to stay underwater for twenty-four hours while breathing through a reed, right? I'd have nailed that."

Mason slowly dragged down his sunglasses. "Underwater breathing techniques are top secret, man. If I told you about them, I'd have to kill you."

"Sure. I get it. Whoa." He shook his head. "That's hardcore, but I could handle it. Maybe I should look into enlisting?"

Sue rolled her eyes before asking Hattie, "How are the twins? Losing both their parents had to be rough. Our oldest son, Frank, lost his hamster when he was two. I thought he'd need therapy to stop crying."

"Um, yeah." Mason couldn't be sure, but he'd have sworn Hattie glanced his way for help. If he'd read her right, she wanted to escape this couple as badly as he did. To Mason, she said, "I just remembered we were supposed to pick up those cookies I ordered at two and the bakery closes in ten minutes. We've got to go."

"Oh, gosh—" Sue scooted their youngest child's stroller aside when Hattie almost ran her down with the twins. "Well, it was nice seeing you."

"Mason," Craig called, "when you get a chance, stop by the store. I'd love hearing your battle stories."

"Will do," Mason said with a backhand wave.

Safely out of earshot, Hattie slowed to her more normal sedate pace. "Can you believe the nerve of that woman? Comparing Viv and Van's loss to losing a hamster? And did you really have to breathe through a reed for twenty-four hours?"

"What do you think?"

She laughed. "No, but considering you just chopped a giant tree, then dragged it back to the house and single-handedly crammed that sucker into a stand, at this point I'd pretty much believe anything about you."

"Why do you stick around here?"

She crossed the street that had been closed for the day to only foot traffic. "What do you mean?"

"Please don't take this the wrong way, but I don't remember high school being a particularly good time for you. Why do you hang around with people like that?"

"I don't. They were my sister's friends—used to be yours."

He winced. "Don't remind me. I've changed. They seem as self-involved as ever."

"I love Conifer. There's my family and the bar. Great friends like Clementine and all my regulars. There's low crime and lots of fun things to do. I can't imagine a better place to raise a family—especially now that I just happen to have one."

"I admire you." He opened the door to the rec hall, where the craft fair was being held. "Don't think I could do it."

"Did anyone ask you to?" Her snarky tone alerted him to the question's layers. What did she really want to know? Whether or not he was asking if she'd ever consider leaving Conifer? Or if he'd ever consider staying?

HATTIE MIGHT OUTWARDLY be humming along to "Silent Night" as she and Mason browsed the craft-fair items, but that didn't mean she was calm.

Before breaking her arm, she'd had a handle on the situation with Mason. She'd known exactly where she stood with him. They'd shared the blizzard party, and after that, had she not been stupid enough to trip down those stairs, he'd have been long gone. Since then, no matter how hard she'd tried convincing herself she wasn't attracted to him, and that she didn't even want him because he'd been Melissa's first, Hattie was beginning to fear her efforts futile.

Who was she kidding? Mason had always been a part

of her, but that didn't mean squat when it came to him making a meaningful commitment to her.

His charging to her rescue now was no different from when he'd carried her home after the sledding accident that had broken her ankle. He cared, but that was all. By his own admission, after what her sister had done to him, he was incapable of giving more.

Which was why she had to stop viewing him as the handsome man of her dreams and start seeing him for what he was—her sister's bitter ex. No more swooning over his ridiculous body and looks. It was time to be adult about the situation and stop acting like a love-sick preteen.

"Think Fern might like this?" With a goofy, game show–model flourish, he held up a house-shaped tissue-box cover. The tissue came out of the house's chimney. It was so well made, yet so kitschy, Hattie loved it and his over-the-top presentation.

"I bet she will." How did he do it? Just when she vowed to cure herself of her unhealthy Mason addiction, he went and did something adorable to drag her back in.

THIRTY MINUTES LATER, Hattie stood alongside Mason in Craig's sporting-goods store while he surveyed fishing poles.

"Dad's been bitching for years about losing his best rod steelhead fishing on the Situk River. About time he got back out there."

While Mason took forever selecting just the right one, Hattie remembered all the times she'd shopped here with Melissa and her mom for her dad. Father's Day and his birthday and Christmas, the three of them had been here, debating over whether to get fishing tackle or hunting gear. Back then, she never would have guessed how distant she and her family would now be.

Her parents would no doubt place all the blame for their

current state of affairs on Mason, but they'd be wrong. The man and woman she'd once believed infallible were human just like everyone else.

She wasn't sure whether to be happy or sad about that fact. On the one hand, it came as somewhat of a relief to know her parents were mortal. On the flip side, why had they chosen now to fall apart? Yes, Melissa had died, and because of that, part of their family was gone forever, but for her, for their grandchildren, they couldn't fall apart. More than ever, she needed them, but after her dad hit Mason, what would she even say?

Going to see them before her father apologized would make her feel traitorous.

"I think this one." Mason plucked a rod from the rack. "Dad will love it. What're you getting your dad?"

"A sack of coal. I'm still furious with him. Aren't you?"

While Hattie pushed the stroller, they headed toward the checkout. "At first, yeah, I was plenty pissed, but then I put myself in his shoes. He lost his daughter, and that loss doesn't make sense. One minute she was in his life, the next she was gone, so he's striking out. I just happened to be there."

They were next in line, which squelched the conversation—probably a good thing, as she'd need a moment to process Mason's charitable take on the situation. She waited until they were in the car to ask, "How can you be so forgiving toward my dad?"

Mason backed out of their parking space. "How should I act? Lyle used to be like my second father. I thought the world of him. His punch didn't hurt so much physically, as emotionally. I don't understand, though, how they still view the divorce as such a black-and-white issue, with me one hundred percent at fault."

"I've never gotten it, either." Out on the main roads, traffic was a nightmare. The pretty day this close to

Christmas was such a rarity that it seemed the whole town had come out to celebrate. "But I'm sure Melissa's bad-mouthing didn't help."

The moment Hattie mentioned her sister's bad sportsmanship regarding the divorce, guilt consumed her. Especially with Melissa gone, she shouldn't have been disloyal to the sister she'd loved.

But then, what did she owe Mason? In such a short time, he'd come to mean so much, which frightened her. From the start, what they'd shared was never supposed to be more than a temporary good time. A way to feel better when nothing in her life felt right.

At the next stoplight, Mason asked, "Melissa trash-talked me a lot to your folks?"

"I—I suppose." She tried looking down, but he placed his fingers beneath her chin, urging her to meet his gaze.

"What exactly did she say?"

"I don't want to do this. It doesn't feel right."

"Oh—but your sister making false claims about me to your parents was?"

"I didn't mean that."

They finally broke free of traffic, but for the next few miles, and then hours, Mason didn't speak a word.

Chapter Seventeen

That night, Mason stood in front of the twelve-foot tree he'd lugged from the forest to help Hattie decorate. They'd draped it in lights—the last available from both Shamrock's and the grocery store. They'd hung all of Melissa and Alec's ornaments—some Mason even remembered having been around back when they'd been married. So here it sat, this monument to the holiday, but what had it solved or proved?

Hattie's relationship with her parents was worse than ever. Melissa's perfect house had been maintained, but what did it matter if no one saw it but him and Hattie? The twins were supposed to be having a magical first Christmas, but as long as they had plenty of bottles, clean diapers and hugs, he got the impression they couldn't care less about the season's opulent trappings Hattie insisted they have.

So, in the end, after all of this work, what had he and Hattie accomplished? Part of him felt rather than celebrating the true meaning of Christmas, all they had done was construct an elaborate altar at which they were supposed to worship Melissa's memory. Only that wasn't what he'd signed up to do.

Come to think of it, what *was* he doing? It'd taken Hattie a couple days to get past the initial shock of her broken arm, but since then, her cast hadn't slowed her. So if she didn't need him, why hadn't he gone back to base? Why had he stayed in Conifer, playing house, when he could be making a genuine difference for his country?

"You ever speaking to me again?" Hattie had been downstairs, folding laundry. He'd offered to do it for her, but in typical Hattie fashion, she'd refused.

He shrugged.

Stepping up behind him, she slipped her hands around his waist, resting her head between his shoulder blades. "I am sorry. Before Melissa died, I one hundred percent took your side in the divorce. I still feel the same, but her dying tangled it all up in my mind. My sister never said anything *that* heinous about you—she just excelled at playing the poor, innocent victim. I guess the only way she could reconcile her actions into not being your garden-variety adultery was by claiming you were gone so often that she'd been forced to turn to Alec for support. Total B.S., but there you have it—the world according to Melissa."

Strangely unable to cope with even the few hours' separation their argument had caused, Mason placed his hands over Hattie's. "Thanks. As much as it hurts, now that I know the specifics of what your parents believe I did, that puts me somewhat on an even playing field. Trouble is, with your sister not here to back me up, we both know who they're most likely always going to believe."

"I am sorry...."

Turning to face her, he ran his hands along her upper arms. "Know what's funny?"

Her sad smile filled his heart to near bursting. "I honestly can't think of a single funny thing."

"Okay, so maybe *funny* isn't the right word. More *enlightening,* but the fact is that as long as I have you on my side, I don't care what your parents think."

She had no response.

"Wishing you felt the same?"

Nodding, she crushed him in a hug. "Everything's such a complicated mess. I don't know what to believe."

He kissed the top of her head. "How about we table the topic for now, turn off this obscene amount of lights and focus on what we do best...." Pressing his lips on hers filled him with the same excitement as when he stepped foot on American ground after having been gone on an extended mission. As much as it terrified him to admit it, all the way out here in tiny Conifer, Alaska, with his best childhood friend who'd somehow become more, when he hadn't even been looking, Mason had finally found home.

Only trouble was, how the hell was he going to keep it? More important, considering what an abysmal failure he'd been at family life before, was he 100 percent sure he wanted it?

TWO DAYS BEFORE CHRISTMAS, instead of going to her bar as Hattie told Mason she'd be doing, she stopped by her parents' home. Though Mason teased her about having adopted Melissa's quest for perfection, Hattie took it seriously. As the twins' mom, she had to be as diligent as possible with every aspect of parenting. While she'd never reach Melissa's degree of perfection, she would always try to do her best.

Approaching the front door, she felt her nerves take over.

Her mom usually went all-out with holiday decoration, but the same fall wreath that'd been on the door the day of Melissa's death was still there, droopy and faded and crusty with ice.

Hattie's relationship with her parents had degraded to the point she rang the doorbell instead of walking in.

"What a nice surprise." Of all people, Hattie hadn't

expected her mother to answer the door, but she was cautiously optimistic about seeing her mom out of bed. "Did you bring the twins?"

"No." In the entry hall, Hattie slipped her arms from her coat.

"I'm almost afraid to ask who's with them."

This again? "Mason. And he's great, Mom. They adore him."

She sighed. "Come on in. Can I get you anything? Tea?"

"No, thank you." The home Hattie had grown up in had always been cluttered, but clean. Now it just looked sad. Dishes and newspapers littered the counters. The dining room table was piled with photo albums. "Where's Dad?"

"Working late. Keeping busy seems to help him cope."

"What about you? Are you doing anything special for yourself?"

Akna sat on the sofa, then flipped through a pile of photos she'd taken from the side table. "I'm thinking of taking up scrapbooking. It'll be a big project, but you can help. I want to make a special book for each year of your sister's life. Maybe even two or three per year for those times when she was extra busy. I'm seriously debating leaving out her wedding pictures with Mason, though. This project is meant to celebrate her life, so it doesn't seem right to feature a time that caused her such pain."

Hattie had never wanted to bang her head against a wall more than she did now. "Um, please don't take this the wrong way, but why are you and Dad so fixated on blaming Mason for everything bad that ever happened to Mel?"

For a split second, her mother's wide-eyed, gaping expression caused a flicker of guilt. But then a myriad of beautiful memories Mason had shared with their family not just in the past, but recently, emboldened her to forge ahead.

"When I broke my ankle, do you remember who carried

me in from the woods? And whenever Mel procrastinated on school projects, who was always there for her to pick up the slack? Who helped with the yard work and gardening, never expecting to be paid in anything but your ham sandwiches or fish stew? Yes, Mel and Mason's divorce was ugly, but why can't you see he never wanted it? He loved her as much as we did—do. She was his life, and she essentially threw him away. How can you blame him when he was the injured party?"

Seeming flustered, Akna dropped her photos and stooped to gather them. "I thought it might be nice for us to share this scrapbooking project, but you're just upsetting me."

"Mom, I *need* you to be upset." Hattie helped clean the mess. "You have to snap out of your grief long enough to recognize Melissa's girls need their grandmother."

"If I believed that, she'd have left them with me, instead of you."

Heels of her hands pressed to her forehead, Hattie realized she might as well have been talking to the raggedy wreath on the front door. "Don't you get it? In leaving her kids to me, Melissa gave you and Dad a tremendous gift. She freed you from the day-to-day drudgery of constant feedings and baths and laundry so you could be their grandmother. She wanted them to grow up viewing you as a person to be loved and cherished and honored—just like Melissa and I did with your parents and Dad's. Why are you denying them that opportunity? What I especially don't understand is why you're blaming Mason for any of what happened."

What had started as her mother's silent tears now turned messy. "Why do I blame Mason? B-because if they'd never gotten divorced, your sister never would've married Alec, and she never would've been in his p-plane. Please, leave. J-just go…"

Hattie crossed the room to give her mother a hug, and then abided by her wishes. She'd done all she could to repair their relationship. The next move was solidly in her mother's court.

Pressing her hand to the front door, Hattie said, "You're welcome to share Christmas breakfast with us around nine. Fern and Jerry will be there. I've also invited Alec's mom and dad, though I doubt they'll come. It'd be a real shame for you to miss Viv and Van's first Christmas."

WHILE FERN BABYSAT the twins, Mason browsed Shamrock's with his dad, searching for just the right gifts for Hattie, the girls and Fern—the tissue house thingy they'd purchased at the holiday fair seemed more from Hattie than him. "What about a scarf and glove set?"

His dad laughed. "Son, I think you've moved a ways past that."

"How so?"

"Don't you think she's expecting a ring on her finger?"

Damn near choking on his own spit, Mason asked, "Where'd you get that idea?"

"You two are not only shacking up, but share a couple kids. I've seen you with all three of those girls and you look downright smitten. Why not marry Hattie? She's been trailing after you all doe-eyed practically from the day she could walk."

"Oh, come on…" They passed the jewelry department. "Marriage is a step I only intended to take once, and see where that landed me? Besides, you never married again after losing Mom, so why should I?"

Jerry picked up a box of chocolates, bouncing it between his hands. "The key word there is *lost.* What happened to you was different. Never said anything to you, but to me, your Melissa always struck me as a little too big for her britches. Everyone fawned all over her like her poo didn't stink, but by God, what she and Alec did to you did stink—to high heaven. None of that was your fault, so why have you spent so many years blaming yourself when sweet little Hattie's been here all this time, just waiting for you to realize she's the best thing the Beaumont family ever had to offer?"

Head spinning, Mason wasn't sure what to say other than, "Well, that's easy for you to say, but what about you and Fern? Anyone with eyes could see you two are more than just friends."

"Of course we are."

"Then you're finally admitting you feel a little something extra for her?"

"I should hope so, seeing how I married her ten years ago."

"You what?" Mason froze smack-dab in the center of the blender and toaster aisle.

"You heard me. We decided not to make a big deal out of it. I'm allergic to her dogs, and can't stand most of her shows, so she mostly stays up at her place." He winked. "Without fail, though, we never miss conjugal visits at my place every Saturday night."

"How come you never told me?"

Jerry reached for a pig-shaped cutting board. "Don't recall you ever asked."

"WHAT'RE YOU ALL DOING?" Hattie asked Mason upon returning home from her parents' to find him with the girls on their play mat.

"We're trying to say 'cow,' but all I'm hearing are a lot of *goo*s."

After tossing her coat on the back of the sofa, Hattie joined the cozy trio. "You do realize you're months ahead of schedule for their first words?"

"Most babies say their first official words around twelve

months, but clearly we're dealing with prodigies, so I'm anticipating words way sooner than that."

"Uh-huh…" She loved the way just being with him and the girls transformed the most mundane activities into pure magic. Tickling Vivian's tummy, she asked, "Okay, gorgeous, out with it. According to Drill Sergeant Mason, you should be speaking in full sentences by Valentine's Day."

Mason's complexion paled.

"You all right?"

He nodded. "It's inconceivable to me that by the time I see these two again, they could be walking and talking."

"I'm surprised that kind of stuff's even on your radar."

"Why?" He rolled onto his side, taking Vanessa along with him. She sat up, reclining against him. She looked so comfortable, so completely at peace, Hattie couldn't bear thinking of how ruined the girls would be when it came time for Mason to go. "I care a lot about these two."

"I know, but once you gave up your rights, I figured it'd be no big deal for you to walk away."

"Me, too.…" His normally easygoing smile struck her as hollow. Did he regret relinquishing custody of the girls? But even if he did, how would he raise them when his career dictated a large portion of his time was spent overseas?

She wanted to tell him about what had happened with her mom, but couldn't. As much as she needed to vent, Mason didn't deserve to be dragged into her mom's irrationally cruel coping methods. Hattie had done her best to remind her mother of happier times they'd all shared, but if she wasn't ready to listen, there was little more Hattie could say.

"Your dad and Fern are coming for Christmas, right?"

"Sure. Why wouldn't they? Oh—and before you answer, have I got news for you."

She sat up, perching Vivian on her lap. "Let's hear it."

"Prepare to have your mind blown—my dad and Fern are married."

"What?"

"Dad and I were out shopping this afternoon when he admitted they tied the knot ten years ago."

"That's the craziest thing I've ever heard."

"I thought so, too."

"Why aren't they living together?" He rattled off a long list of reasons that actually sounded level-headed. "Okay, but why the secret? Someone should've at least thrown them a reception."

He smoothed Vanessa's hair. "They didn't want anyone butting into their business. Sound familiar?"

"Maybe a smidge." Laughing, she held her thumb and forefinger barely apart. "But I'm sure my dad will stop by soon to apologize."

"I'm not holding my breath."

CHRISTMAS MORNING, Hattie was first to wake. Usually the girls slept until seven, which gave her a little time to gather her thoughts and drink her first cup of coffee before slipping into mommy mode.

Moving slow as to not wake Mason, she inched from the bed, only to get a fright when he snagged her around her waist. "Where do you think you're going?"

Hands over her mouth, she laughed. "You scared the you-know-what out of me."

"Sorry. My intention was to scare the pants off of you."

"Get your mind out of the gutter." Her halfhearted slug landed on his delicious biceps, which in turn made her appreciate his idea all the more.

"Why? It's much more fun in the gutter."

After he'd thoroughly kissed her, she had to agree.

By the time they shared a shower guaranteed to land

them on Santa's naughty list, the girls were up, demanding their breakfast.

Mason offered what had now become their usual routine. "Divide and conquer?"

"Deal."

After feeding the girls, Mason made a fire in the living room hearth.

Hattie turned on the tree lights and set out three platters of cookies she'd made the night before. Since Clementine's mother had gone on a holiday cruise, she would be over for lunch with her boys. Fern and Jerry were stopping by for breakfast and lunch. She didn't dare hope her parents would make an appearance for even one meal, let alone two.

Back upstairs, Hattie fussed with the girls' red-and-green dresses and put Velcro-latch bows in their hair. She added red tights and black patent shoes. For their first Christmas, she hoped Melissa was smiling down upon her adorable brood.

Downstairs again, she asked Mason, "Mind watching the monkeys for a few minutes? I need to get ready."

He gave her a funny look. "What do you mean? You look great."

She set the twins on his lap. "I'm a hot mess. The pictures we take today will be with the girls the rest of their lives. I don't want them ashamed of Aunt Hattie."

Once he'd placed the twins safely in the sofa corner, he tugged her to his lap. "You are amazing. Whether you're wearing sweats and my T-shirt or a ball gown, in my eyes, there's never been a more beautiful woman."

"Don't..." She glanced down at her ragged nails.

"What?" He kissed her just as the sun peeked over Mount Kneely. His warm lips, the scent of the coffee they'd just shared on his breath, raised goose bumps on her forearms and set happy tingles to flight in her belly. How did he do it? Make her feel like the most special woman on earth with a simple kiss? How had her sister ever found him lacking? Skimming his fingertips over her riotous hair, he stared at her with an intensity she found difficult to meet. "Sun's making your skin and hair glow. You're so beautiful."

"Stop..." she whispered when he nuzzled her neck.

Heart racing, she wished she knew whether or not he honestly meant his kind words—or were they just lines he used on all his girls back in Virginia? How was she ever supposed to know?

Chapter Eighteen

"Too bad for me that this time," he said with a final kiss to her nose, "I have to stop because if I don't, we're never going to open presents."

By the time Hattie finished dressing in her favorite plum turtleneck, black slacks and heels, then straightening her hair and applying makeup, she felt armored to resist Mason's most ardent advances.

She was most vulnerable to him when relaxed. When she wasn't thinking rationally, but emotionally. When she stopped focusing on what was best for her and her nieces and succumbed to Mason's heady charm.

At the base of the stairs, she paused a moment to freeze the idyllic image in her head. Mason had turned carols on the stereo and knelt in front of the girls, who shared the sofa.

"Peekaboooo!" he teased over and over to their delighted shrieks. In a perfect world, she'd give anything for him to stay, but perfection didn't exist. Something, whether it was too much salt in her pumpkin pie or her father punching the man of her dreams, would always be bound to go wrong. From here on out, she'd enter any situation expecting the worst, and then, if even the smallest thing went right, she'd be grateful instead of disappointed.

The bottom stair creaked, alerting Mason to her presence. When he wolf-whistled, she blushed. "Damn. You cleaned up nice. Do I need to change?" He wore pajama pants and no shirt. As far as she was concerned, he looked his sexy best.

"You're fine until company comes." *Fine* was an understatement!

"Cool. Now, can we open presents?"

She laughed. "Sure. But you're playing Santa."

HOURS LATER, the living room filled with smiling faces, Mason gazed across a sea of wrapping paper to see Hattie cradling Vivian. She tickled the girl's belly, eliciting a giggly response. In that moment, a fundamental part of him changed. Ever since Melissa had left him, Mason believed himself not only incapable of commitment, but he'd loathed the thought of it. Now? He couldn't fathom being without not only Hattie, but the twins he'd somehow grown to love every bit as if they were his own little girls. It no longer mattered they'd been created from Melissa and Alec's bond. If anything, he loved them all the more because of it, because if Melissa had never left him, Mason might never have realized the truth that had been right there all along—Hattie was the girl for him.

Always had been.

Always would be.

As if they were connected by an invisible string, she looked up. Her sweet, simple blown kiss proved his undoing. The act that finally made him understand the profound piece of advice his friend Calder had shared.

You know when you know.

"MOM! DOUGIE CHEATED!" Clementine's oldest son's booming voice made Hattie wince.

"Did not," three-year-old Dougie proclaimed. They played his new Candy Land game Santa had brought.

Clementine topped her famous candied yams with mini-marshmallows. "Sorry they're so hyper. I warned you that if you craved a nice, peaceful holiday, we were the wrong crew to invite."

Hattie waved off her concern. "They're adorable. And the last thing I want is quiet. It'll only remind me of my parents, who I fear are holed up in their creepy-dark house, dining on TV dinners."

"Thought you'd decided not to worry about them?" Fern noted, checking on the ham she'd brought to their party.

Mason and his dad watched football with the babies on the downstairs TV.

"Easier said than done. I'm frustrated with them, but also worried. What's it going to take for them to come back to the real world?"

"Time." Fern slipped her arm around Hattie's shoulders. "This is probably the last thing you want to hear, but a year or two from now, they'll probably be back to their usual selves, doting on the twins and meddling in your business."

"Oh—they've already got that covered." Clementine tossed the empty marshmallow bag in the recycling bin. "Hattie, did you tell Fern about your dad hitting Mason when he saw him kiss you?"

Hattie shot her friend a dirty look. "I thought we weren't talking about that?"

Fern waved off her concern. "I knew hours after it happened. In the time he's been back, Mason and his dad have grown real close."

Hattie shut her eyes, wishing for so many things she couldn't fit them all into a single prayer. Had her parents not been grief-stricken to the point of insanity—better yet, had Melissa never died—how might things be different? What if she and Mason had had their reunion by chance, and then romance had blossomed? Would her folks have then embraced their relationship? Would Hattie trust he was attracted to only her, and not the ghost of her sister he may still see in Hattie's eyes or smile?

"Whew…" Mason closed the door on the last of their guests. "I was beginning to fear they'd never leave."

"Me, too." At ten, the twins had long since been bathed and tucked in by Fern and Jerry, who seemed to enjoy their new role as adoptive grandparents so much that they'd hardly argued at all. As much as she'd enjoyed being around her friends, she'd still sorely missed her family.

In the kitchen, she and Mason worked in tandem to unload the dishwasher.

Nearly finished, she asked, "Am I a bad person for not having taken Van and Viv to see my parents? Was I too harsh, expecting them to come here?"

He snorted. "You're asking me? To my way of thinking your parents and Alec's have a lot of lost time to make up for with their granddaughters, and no one to blame for it but themselves."

Abandoning their task, she hugged him. "In case I haven't told you lately, thank you—for sticking around after I broke my arm, for not returning my dad's punch. Thanks for everything. I'll be so sorry to see you go."

He tensed. "About that… What would you say if I didn't?"

Hands pressed to his chest, she didn't dare hope that was what he meant. His heart beat so hard, she felt its comforting rhythm. "Are you thinking of asking for another extension on your leave?"

"Not exactly." When he dropped to one knee, then took her left hand, her pulse took off on a perilous course. With his free hand, he reached into his back pocket, pulling out a simple, yet lovely diamond solitaire ring. "I found this when I was out shopping with my dad. I want you to marry me, Hat Trick. I'm tired of playing house. Let's do it for real."

Was this a dream? "M-Mason...I don't know what to say."

"I should think it's fairly obvious."

"Yes, but—"

"Then you will? Marry me?"

Yes! her heart screamed.

"I'm sorry, but no," her head forced her to say. How long had she dreamed of a moment like this, yet without all the baggage? With 100 percent trust this was wholly what he wanted—*she* was wholly what he wanted.

"I'm sorry, what?" Brow furrowed, he shook his head. "Did you just turn me down?"

"What did you expect? There's this whole mess with my parents to sort out and the fact that you live about a gazillion miles from here. Not to mention the not-so-little concern that maybe the whole town's right, and I am stepping right into my sister's life. It's all a little too convenient, don't you think?"

His gaze narrowed. "Did you really turn down my proposal because you're on the outs with your parents or afraid of what the town thinks?"

Chin raised, she didn't back down from his angry stare. "Can you blame me for having doubts? Everything between us happened so fast...."

He tossed his hands in the air. "Gee, Hattie, I guess when I asked you to marry me, not because of some sense of duty, but because I thought I loved you, I kind of expected *your* opinion—not your mom's or dad's or Sophie's or that old curmudgeon's who never leaves your bar."

Throat painfully knotted from the effort of holding back tears, she had to ask, "Do you? Love me?"

"A few minutes ago, I might've said yes. Now?" He shook his head. "Hell if I know."

MASON GAVE EACH girl a goodbye hug and kiss, whispering his love, but only when he stormed down to the garage, then careened out of the driveway behind the wheel of Alec's Hummer did he breathe.

What had just happened? Had he honestly taken the step his dad and Calder had advised, only to be summarily shot down?

He'd done everything for Hattie and her sister's girls. He'd been prepared to give up everything—including the career he credited with saving his life after Melissa's betrayal damn near killed him. He'd done all of that and for what?

Five minutes later, he reached his dad's only to find Fern's truck in the drive.

Swell.

Figured the one time he really needed to talk with his father, Jerry had more important matters on his mind. And here it wasn't even Saturday. Regardless, he rapped on the door until his old man answered.

"What're you doing?" his dad asked. "Everything all right with Hattie and the girls?"

Mason sighed. There wasn't a short version to the story, and since he was mortified about having his proposal shot down, he told a necessary white lie. "I, ah, got called in. It's short notice, but it comes with the territory."

"Hate seeing you go," Jerry said before pulling him into a tight hug. "But I sure am proud of you, son."

His dad would never know how much Mason needed that affirmation—that he was on track in at least one portion of his life.

After saying goodbye to Fern, and getting a hug from her, too, Mason drove to the airport. His dad wanted him to stay with him until his flight, but Mason politely declined. He needed to be alone. Have time to think. At this time of night the airport terminal would be closed, but on his phone, he went ahead and made a reservation on-line to fly out first thing in the morning. He'd sleep in the car. His dad knew everyone, and promised Mason that if he left the vehicle's keys with airport security, he'd get it back to Hattie.

Most everything he owned was at the house, but screw it. Belongings were replaceable. Only thing he couldn't buy was a new heart.

HATTIE WOKE TO find her eyes swollen and red and an empty pillow alongside her instead of Mason resting his hand on her belly. The loss was crushing. The fact that she'd brought this pain on herself? Certifiable.

But what else could she have done?

Rolling over, she gripped the blanket, drawing it up to her chin. Where was he now? Maybe once he calmed from the initial shock of her frank rejection, he'd under-stand it was for the best.

But was it? Fear hanging heavy at the base of her stom-ach told a different story. What if turning him away for what she perceived to be all the right reasons turned out to be her life's single biggest mistake?

Over the baby monitor came the sound of Vivian's cries.

Before Hattie could pull on her robe and poke her cold toes into slippers, Vanessa had chimed in. Had it really only been yesterday Mason had helped her with the morn-ing routine? She now wished she hadn't taken a moment of his presence for granted.

He meant everything to her, but to be with him meant destroying her family, which was already so badly broken.

"YOU'RE A SIGHT for sore eyes."

"Thanks." Mason closed the door behind him and en-tered the apartment he shared with Cooper. Since their friends Calder and Heath had married, they were the last remaining bachelors on their SEAL team. Thanks to Hattie, Mason suspected he was done when it came to anything more than sharing a drink with the fairer sex. Ha! Fairer sex, his ass. A more appropriate title would be that women were the shortsighted, incapable-of-trust sex.

"Have a good holiday?" Cooper asked, pausing "Call of Duty" on his Xbox.

"Swell."

"Me, too." Cooper had never been the overly talkative type, and it looked as if he hadn't changed since Mason had been gone. "Well, it's been a long day. Think I'll grab a quick shower, then turn in."

"Sounds good, man. See you in the a.m."

"WELL, IF YOU ASK ME, I say good riddance." Hattie's mom fanned a pile of scrapbooking paper while her father added another log to their hearth's fire.

Hattie couldn't wrap her head around her parents' one-eighty. Mason had been out of her life for a week, and the second they'd heard through the Conifer gossip hotline that he'd left town for good, they'd run right over to Melissa's extending not only the mother of all olive branches, but multiple offers to help with her nieces.

Just as Hattie feared, the girls were on the verge of being inconsolable with Mason gone. Perpetually irritable and weepy, they seemed like different babies from the ones they'd been only a short time ago.

Her dad jiggled Vanessa on his knee. "Me and my fist would like to claim credit for sending him on his way, but he's always been a smart kid. He no doubt finally got the clue he wasn't wanted around here."

"Would you two knock it off," Hattie snapped. When Vivian cried in her carrier, Hattie lifted her, pacing while trying to soothe the cranky infant. "This is Mason we're talking about. He's a longtime family friend who's helped me more times than I can count—and both of you. Look how his leaving has affected your granddaughters. When he was here, except for the first couple weeks after losing Melissa and Alec, they never acted like this."

Her mother slapped her craft papers to the coffee table. "So, you're saying your sister's memory was only worth two weeks?"

"I didn't mean that at all," Hattie said above Vivian's increased wails. "I just think that where Mason is concerned, you two are being disrespectful. Mason's a good guy—a great guy. I'm sorry he left." *All the more so, because a huge reason why I turned him away was out of respect for you.*

"SNOWMAN, MY THREE-YEAR-OLD girl runs faster than you! Get the lead out!"

"Yessir, Master Chief." In the week Mason had been back on the job, he'd sorely missed his peaceful days playing Mr. Mom. Soon enough, his body would be back in top-notch form, but he feared getting his head back in the right place may take longer.

When the team stopped running for a water break, Calder approached him. "You look like crap."

"Thanks, man. Love you, too."

"Thought you were going to marry the girl?"

"What gave you that dumbass idea?" Mason splashed half the contents of his water bottle over his head.

Calder checked to make sure they were alone, then said in a low tone, "I told you the secret. Remember? How *you'll know when you know.*"

After finishing off the water, Mason said, "Obviously, I didn't know."

EVEN TWO WEEKS after their latest argument, Hattie refused to leave her nieces with her parents, so she had them with her while cleaning out her old apartment. Trevor, a long-time bartender and friend, had stepped up so much when she'd broken her arm and after Mason had left that she'd promoted him to night manager. Along with the title, he'd be moving upstairs. At least he would as soon as all of her old junk was gone.

Hard to believe she'd once been such a pack rat.

Mason ran a tight ship. Living with him had taught her the benefits of streamlining her lifestyle.

She missed him with a gnawing, nagging pain that rarely went away. While she still couldn't be sure he hadn't proposed out of nostalgia for her sister or just plain old pity over not wanting her to be a single mom, she constantly second-guessed her decision.

If she'd said yes, would he be here with her now?

But would that have even been fair, considering how much he loved his job?

Vivian grew bored with her play mat and wasn't afraid to show it with a good old-fashioned tantrum. By the time Vanessa chimed in, Clementine charged up the stairs to check on the commotion.

She lifted a wide-eyed, sniffling Vivian for a hug and said, "Too many more screams like that, and you'll give Auntie Clem a heart attack."

"Sorry." Hattie calmed Vanessa. "I'm almost done. Just need to go through this box of purses."

"No worries." To Vivian, she said, "You're coming downstairs with me. It's about time you learned to appreciate cherries."

"Thanks," Hattie called after her friend.

Reaching far back into a cedar cabinet, she grabbed the last of the purses she was donating to charity. It was the black dress purse she'd carried the day she and Mason saw Benton for the reading of her sister's will.

She clutched the purse to her chest, willing herself not to cry.

"Van, we should've fought for him, huh? Told your nosy grandparents we don't care what they think."

THREE WEEKS LATER, while the girls "ran" wild in their walkers, Hattie was scooping ashes from the fireplace when her cell rang.

Even though Mason had his own assigned ring tone, she couldn't help wishing it'd somehow be him.

After wiping her hands on a rag, she grabbed her phone, only to swallow her usual disappointment upon seeing the caller wasn't Mason, but Benton—Melissa's lawyer.

"Hattie?"

"Yes… Hi. Are you making preparations to head out to your mine for the season?" She sat on the hearth, where she could keep an eye on the rowdy, shrieking twins.

"Not exactly. Do you have any free time today to stop by?"

"I—I suppose. Is everything okay?" Her stomach tightened. Had Alec's parents decided to contest the will?

"Oh, sure. Just stumbled across something I thought you might like to have."

AFTER A QUICK SHOWER, Hattie dropped the girls with her mom, then drove straight toward Benton's. Judging by the stacks of paperwork and folders lining his reception area, he'd been cleaning his office. Or maybe the better term would be *rearranging,* as it didn't appear he'd disposed of much—more like he'd moved it around.

"Benton?" Hattie called into the gloom, stepping gingerly around a few files that'd fallen.

"Back here!" he shouted from his office.

She found him under his desk, picking up paper clips. "Need help?"

"Nope. Just about got them all." He raised up, only to conk his head on the underside of the desk. He winced, rubbing the offended spot. "Guess I had that coming."

She sat on one of the folding chairs. "No one deserves that kind of pain. Hitting your head's the worst."

"Hold your judgment until after you see this." He held out a sealed envelope.

"What is it?"

"A letter—from Melissa. I guess the day you were all in here for the reading of her will, it must've fallen. I'm deeply sorry. I never even knew she'd stashed it in the packet."

Hattie held the letter in her trembling hands, and shock didn't begin to cover her myriad of emotions. Elation for the privilege of one, last message from her sister. Anger for Benton having been so careless as to have lost it. And honestly, a little trepidation as to what her sister had found so important to convey that she'd needed to share from beyond her grave.

"I'll leave you in private." He stumbled from the room, closing the door behind him.

For a few minutes, Hattie sat perfectly still.

Then she tore open the envelope, but struggled removing the contents as her hands refused to stop trembling. When she'd finally unfolded two pieces of the embossed stationery Melissa had ordered after her wedding, she read the dear words through tears.

Sweet Hattie—

If you're reading this, my premonitions have come true and Alec and I have gone to a better place. You may find it strange—me leaving my two angels to you and Mason—but to my way of thinking it was the most natural, honorable act I could've done.

I have to admit I was never the kind of woman

Mason deserved. I was never good like you. You were always off helping someone while I pursued the perfect tan. In death, I guess I finally found the strength to admit I could be a little shallow—or, okay, maybe a lot!

Laughing along with her sister's spirit, Hattie brushed tears that refused to stop falling.

Before I seem too down on myself, let me reassure you that while I lacked in some areas, overall, I was the bomb. But, dear sister, so are you, which is why I want my girls raised by the kindest, sweetest, most gentle person I know. *You.*

Now, here's where Mason comes in. One of my greatest regrets was hurting him. I blamed him for being gone on long fishing trips as the cause of our breakup, but in all honesty, I couldn't stand being alone. That was never a life I wanted. Alec was always hosting parties and had his big, gorgeous house. I always wanted to be a real-life princess and Alec gave me that chance. In the end, I betrayed Mason and hurt him deeply.

You and Mason shared a connection I never had with him, even while we were married. Your friendship at times felt stronger than our supposed love. Looking back, I think I viewed him as a conquest, a trophy to be won. He's a good man who deserves good love—your love.

Hattie, please don't do anything stupid like let Mom and Dad dictate how you live your life. They mean well, but what I want for you and my children is to *live* well. As I'm writing this, I know I'm not long for this world. My dreams of dying scare me, but not as much as the thought of my girls growing up all alone. Who knows, maybe these crazy dreams are the result of too much wine and I'll live to be a hundred, but if not, with you as Vivian and Vanessa's mom, I know they'll be well cared for and loved. And if Mason sticks around, and you two finally realize how great you'd be together, then maybe I'll go to the spirit world in good favor.

Please raise my girls as much as possible in the old ways of cherishing children. It makes me happy to believe our family's spirits live on in them.

Finally, even if you don't find true love with Mason, please don't ever stop searching. You've always been the smarter of us two, but in this case, please don't overanalyze when it comes to love, but go where your heart guides you. When the time comes, you'll know what to do.

I adore you, dear sister. Please don't ever be sad when thinking of me. I pray you and my girls smile when saying my name, as I will do the same for all of you.

—M

Barely able to read the last part through tears, Hattie reached to Benton's desk for a tissue. How ironic was it that if she'd read this letter months ago, absorbing her sister's advice to follow her heart, she would have recognized what she now realized she'd instinctively known all along—Mason was, had always been, the right man for her.

Figuring it would do little good to beat herself up about letting him go, she instead chose a more proactive route to self-help by jumping headfirst after her dreams.

"LATELY, IT'S BEEN you asking me this," Mason said to Heath in between training dives, "but are you all right?

You were out of it down there. It's not like you to space on your decompression time."

"I'm good." He bit into a power bar. "Aw, who am I trying to kid? Nothing could be further from the truth."

Mason leaned in closer. "What's wrong?"

"You know how Patricia and I have been trying for a baby? Turns out she hasn't been able to conceive because of a tumor."

Mason's stomach sank. Patricia was one of the nicest gals he'd ever known. "It's benign, though, right? She's gonna be okay?"

"Hope so. Don't know what I'd do without her."

Mason knew the feeling. Most days, being without Hattie and the girls felt akin to breathing with one lung.

Only out here on open water was he able to find some semblance of peace. Otherwise, he couldn't help wondering what she and the girls were doing. How many new things had the twins learned?

"Didn't mean to drag you down," Heath said. "I need to stay positive. I'm taking the rest of the week off to be with her during her tests."

"I'll be thinking of you both. Hopefully, she'll be fine."

"From your lips to God's ears…"

The rest of the day they were too busy for chitchat, but during what little downtime Mason did have, he couldn't help but think what a raw deal Heath and Patricia were getting. Here were two people who loved each other but, by a cruel twist of fate, may not have much more time together.

Conversely, he and Hattie might've had all the time in the world, but she'd thrown it away.

HATTIE GLANCED AT the address she'd typed into her phone's map feature, double-checking it against the real thing in front of her.

Tipsea's. This was the place.

"You ready for this, ladies?" Vivian and Vanessa ignored her in favor of grabbing for a butterfly that had made the mistake of entering the twins' air space. "Some help you two are."

She forced a deep breath of muggy, brine-laced air.

So far, she liked Virginia. The warmth of not only the temperature, but the people.

Summoning her every ounce of courage, Hattie yanked open the bar's door, intent on meeting Maggie.

"Let me get that for you," a naval-uniformed passerby offered when she struggled to fit the girls' stroller inside.

"Thanks. Guess this place wasn't designed to be kid friendly, huh?"

He laughed. "Not exactly, but have fun."

"Thanks." It took her eyes a while to adjust to the gloom. Whereas her bar had tons of windows overlooking the bay, Tipsea's provided a dim-lit hideaway for its patrons. Neon beer signs glowed from every wall and six pool tables were half-occupied in a gaming area. This early in the afternoon, the dance floor was empty, as were most of the tables and booths. Four men ringed the bar: two sat nursing their draft beers; the others played video games. The scent of beer and what would no doubt be a great cheeseburger flavored the air.

A slight woman with snow-white hair rounded the bar, holding out her arms for a hug. "You have to be Hattie."

Hattie laughed. "Did my posse give me away?"

"Just a smidge. Come on. Let's get y'all to the office. Hank!" she called to the bartender. "I'm headed to the back. Holler if you need me."

"Will do," he said with a wave and curious glance in Hattie's direction.

Hattie was pleasantly surprised to find Maggie's office to be a bright, homey retreat from what she'd seen so far.

"Thank you for agreeing to meet with me," she said once Maggie sat on a comfortable floral sofa.

Hattie had taken the matching armchair.

"My pleasure. I have to say, your offer took me off guard, but after thinking on it a bit, partial retirement does hold a certain appeal."

"I'm glad. If everything works out, this will hopefully launch an exciting new chapter for us both."

"I REALLY DON'T feel up to this," Mason complained to Cooper on their way to Tipsea's. It might be St. Patrick's Day, but all the green beer in the world wouldn't bring back his smile.

"Knock it off. You haven't left the apartment for anything other than work in weeks. A night out with the guys will do you good."

Wishing he'd driven himself so he'd have an escape vehicle, Mason shook his head, mumbling, "This is B.S. I'm too old to be kidnapped."

"Whatever. Just shut up and quit complaining. I promise, you'll have a great time."

The second Mason hit Tipsea's rowdy crowd, he attempted turning right back around to hail a cab, but Cooper grabbed hold of his arm. "Seriously, man. You need to head for the bar."

"Not thirsty."

"Hells bells..." Cooper tugged him past a dancing leprechaun and a blonde in a green bikini.

What did it say about Mason that he wasn't interested? He should've been over Hattie by now, but more than ever, he feared that day may never come. Cooper said, "Loosen up and at least try having a good time. Look—" he pointed toward the bar, where a smoking-hot brunette wore blinking, green antennae "—the bartender's giving away green shots."

Mason took another long look at the woman, a serious look, and then she met his stare and the shock of finding Hattie standing behind his favorite bar damn near had him swallowing his tongue.

"Is it really her?" he asked Cooper, even though his friend and Hattie had never even met.

"If you mean your girl, Hattie, according to Maggie it is. She threatened me bodily harm if I didn't bring you down here tonight." He waved to a few guys on another SEAL team. "Now that I'm done babysitting, have fun."

She said something to one of the other three bartenders on duty, then approached him. Her brown eyes shone with emotion. He wanted to say something smartassed that would show he didn't care she'd come to him, but how could he do that when he did care—more than anything.

In the middle of the crowded bar, he wrapped his arms around her, breathing her in. "I didn't know I was capable of missing a person like I've missed you."

"I feel the same," she said. "I'm sorry. I wanted to accept your proposal, but the whole time we were together, it felt like such a dream, I guess I never believed it could actually be true."

He kissed her and his world once again made sense. She tasted of strawberries and mint and that special something that always reminded him of her. "I never would've asked if I hadn't planned on spending the rest of my life with you and the girls. Speaking of which, where are they?"

"With friends of yours. Calder and Pandora. Maggie introduced me to them. She says Pandora works for the best child-care agency in town."

After a light shake of his head, he asked, "How is it you know all of my friends? How long have you been in town?"

"Only a week, but it felt like a lifetime without seeing you. Maggie and I are now partners. Clem and her mom are looking into buying my bar, and I rented out Melissa and Alec's house. I wanted to get settled here first—just in case you took wooing."

"What's that mean?"

She pressed her lips to his, teasing him with her wicked tongue. "You know, if you'd still been mad at me, I would've needed a job and house to retreat to. In your terms—a base of operations, because no matter what your response was to seeing me, from now until forever, you're mine."

"I like the sound of that." After more kissing and being jostled by the crowd, frustration got the better of him and Mason found himself wanting Hattie all for himself. "Mind getting out of here?"

"Thought you'd never ask."

With Hattie's fingers interwoven with his, Mason led her out of the bar and into their new life, speechless and choked up over the realization that for once in his life, a woman he loved ran to him instead of away.

He never thought he'd believe it, but maybe Melissa's Inuit dreams had some substance to them after all.

Resting her head on his shoulder, Hattie softly sighed. "I love you. Pretty sure I've always loved you."

"I love you, Hat Trick—only I was too dumb to realize it until it was almost too late." From the front pocket of his jeans, he withdrew the ring he'd carried with him every day since leaving. "Before we go a step further—marry me?"

She feigned taking a moment to think about it.

"Not funny," he said with a growl and kiss. "Answer, or I may rescind the offer."

"Yes. Of course." Arms around him, fingers raking his hair, her lips confirmed her words.

"That's better." He slipped on her ring, kissed her finger, then asked, "Where are we going?"

"I thought you knew? My rental car's back at the bar."

Tilting his head back, he groaned. "I wish you'd have said something a block earlier. We could've already been back at my apartment doing naughty things." He paused to whisper some of the specifics he'd been dreaming of for weeks.

Even the shadowy streetlights couldn't hide her blush. "That's awfully presumptuous, sailor. You really gonna talk to your future wife like that?"

He winked. "Every night—mornings, too, if the girls aren't up too early."

"Oh—well, in that case, we should probably get moving. We have a lot of lost time to make up for."

"You read my mind. How's the leg room in the backseat of your car?"

She laughed. "For what you have in mind, we're gonna need a model upgrade."

"Bummer. Guess if I've waited this long, though, a few more minutes won't kill me."

"Speak for yourself. Come on." Hattie ducked into the lobby of a boutique hotel, booked a room, then reacquainted herself with every inch of Mason's delicious body. Gone were all of her feelings of awkwardness and mistrust, replaced by a confidence she viewed as the greatest gift he'd ever given.

Sure, her ring was pretty, but most gorgeous of all was the way Mason made her feel inside and out. He'd changed everything about her for the better, and if it took the next sixty or so years, she'd spend every day of the rest of her life thanking him.

Epilogue

Hattie hadn't believed she'd find an even larger group of friends outside of Conifer, but she couldn't have been more wrong.

Dancing barefoot on the beach in celebration of her and Mason's June wedding were not only her new favorites like Calder and Pandora, Maggie, Heath and Patricia and Cooper, but even her old crowd who had flown in for the happy occasion. Of course, Fern and Jerry, along with Clementine, Joey and Dougie, as well as Clementine's mom. The most surprising guests of all were Hattie's parents.

At first, they'd stayed on the fringe of the celebration, but the longer the night went on, the more they joined in.

"Mind if I steal you and the groom for a sec?" Her dad took her hand, then shockingly reached for Mason's. With tears in his eyes, Lyle said, "I owe you both an apology. L-losing Melissa was the toughest thing I've ever been through. Mason, I hope one day you can forgive me for allowing my grief to drown my common sense. Hitting you was deplorable—especially when I now see how much joy you bring my sweet, beautiful Hattie." He paused a moment to collect himself. "Anyway, I don't mean to go on all night, but I also want to thank you both. Hattie, even when we didn't deserve it, you kept reminding your mom and I about how much we still had left to live for. Mason, no matter what, you've always been the true definition of a gentleman. I couldn't dream of anyone I'd rather have watching over my daughter."

"The honor's all mine, sir."

Both men embraced.

And then Akna joined in on the hugs.

But then, just in case the night grew too maudlin, Jerry and Fern were on hand, providing them all with their usual antics.

"You can't put that in there," Fern said when her husband slipped his bowl of ice cream into the chocolate fountain.

"I don't see why not. How else am I s'posed to get chocolate syrup on my scoop of vanilla?"

"You're impossible," Fern declared. "I can't take you anywhere."

"Like you're such a prize?" He appraised her full-skirted, purple-striped dress, yellow pumps and Shirley Temple curls. "What am I saying? Woman, you're the hottest thing west of the Mississippi—or I guess tonight that'd be east. Come on over here and give your Big Daddy a kiss."

Hiding her laugh against her new husband's chest, Hattie could scarcely contain her happiness. Even the girls seemed to be having a great time, flirting up a storm with Calder and Pandora's son.

"Back when we were in grade school," she said, "could you ever imagine our lives would turn out like this?"

"Honestly, at the time, I was more driven by schemes of how to nab the cookies from your lunch bag." He caressed her belly. "But now that I not only have you, *and* all of your future lunch treats, I am pretty psyched to see what our future holds."

Heart pounding from having kept her tiny secret for

three months, she asked, "What if I told you your hand is currently resting on our future?"

After taking a moment to process her words, his smile lit the night. "For real? You're pregnant?"

She nodded. "Is that okay?"

"Okay?" He lifted her only to swing her around and around. "It's perfection."

Funny he should choose that word, because she'd spent so much time working toward making everything in her life perfect. However, the one thing she'd learned from all of her attempts was that it wasn't possible. Only with Mason by her side, turned out perfection had been within reach all along. All it had taken was following her sister's sage advice to "go where your heart guides you."

In Hattie's case, that meant walking straight into her handsome SEAL's loving arms.

* * * * *

JINGLE BELL BABIES

KATHRYN SPRINGER

Kathryn Springer is a lifelong Wisconsin resident. Growing up in a 'newspaper' family, she spent long hours as a child plunking out stories on her mother's typewriter and hasn't stopped writing since! She loves to write romance because it allows her to combine her faith with her love of a happy ending.

Prologue

July 11, 1:15 p.m.

"One of the funnel clouds that touched down in the area yesterday and struck the small town of High Plains was determined to be a level F3. Already the Red Cross, local law enforcement agents and volunteers have banded together to begin cleanup—"

Jesse Logan stabbed his finger against the power button of the radio. He didn't need to hear a reporter condense the past twenty-four hours into a neat sound bite, or try to describe the damage a second funnel cloud had caused when it slashed across the prairie, directly toward the Circle L.

Jesse had seen the devastation firsthand; he was standing in the middle of it.

The kitchen lay in shambles around him. The twister had spared the outbuildings but clipped the side of the ranch house, taking out a section of the wall, while leaving his mother's antique china cabinet in the corner of the room intact. Glass from the shattered window littered the floor, strewn among soggy tufts of insulation and chunks of sodden wallboard.

Jesse picked up a piece of wood and was about to pitch it into the growing pile of debris when he realized it was one of the legs from the kitchen table.

His fingers tightened around it, ignoring the splinters that bit into his skin.

Yesterday morning he'd sat at the table, before going out to do his chores.

And yesterday afternoon...

A fresh wave of pain crashed over Jesse, making him wonder if he wasn't still caught in the throes of a nightmare. Except his eyes weren't closed.

The crunch of tires against gravel momentarily broke through his turbulent thoughts. For a split second hope stirred inside his chest as he sent up a silent prayer that the car coming up the driveway would be a familiar one.

It was.

The hammer slipped out of Jesse's hand and grazed a crease in the hardwood floor as the High Plains squad car stopped in front of the house. Colt Ridgeway's tall frame unfolded from the passenger side.

As the police chief approached, the stoic set of his jaw and the regret darkening his eyes told Jesse everything.

No. No. No.

"This is going to be hard for you to hear, Jesse." His friend's quiet words barely penetrated the rushing sound in Jesse's head. "Late this morning...found Marie's vehicle...tree fell on the driver's side..."

Like a child, Jesse wanted to press his hands against his ears and shut out the truth.

Where are You, God? Are You even listening? How much more do You think one man can take?

The silent cry burst out of a place deep inside him.

Hadn't he gone through enough?

"Marie must have been trying to outrun the tornado," Colt continued softly. "I'm so sorry for your loss, Jesse. Sorry for you...and your girls."

Jesse couldn't answer. Couldn't tell Colt the truth. Not

yet. That his wife hadn't been trying to outrun the tornado—she'd been running away. From him.

When the driving rain had forced him to abandon his chores the day before, he found Marie's note on the kitchen table. Next to it, the simple gold wedding band and diamond engagement ring he gave her the night he proposed. An heirloom that had been in the Logan family for generations.

He'd had to read through his wife's letter twice before the meaning sank in but the words had remained branded in his memory.

> *Jesse,*
> *I have nothing left to give. If I stay on the ranch, I'll never become the person I was meant to be. You were the one who wanted a family, so I'm leaving the babies with you. I'm going back to Kansas City and I'll contact you when I'm settled.*
> *Marie*

The storm bending the trees outside hadn't compared to the one raging inside of him.

Frantic, Jesse had immediately called the nurse's station in the Manhattan hospital, where their premature triplets had been in the NICU for the past two months. The nurse had verified that Marie hadn't shown up that afternoon to sit with the girls.

He braved the weather to drive to the hospital anyway, hoping that his wife had had a change of heart and gone there instead of the airport.

She hadn't.

Jesse stayed with his daughters the rest of the evening, waiting for a phone call. It wasn't until one of the nurses on duty had asked him if his ranch was located near High Plains that he learned about the tornadoes.

Unable to get through to his hired hands or his sister, Maya, Jesse spent a sleepless night in the family lounge and most of the morning waiting for the state police to remove the barricades from the roads.

When he was finally able to return to the ranch, Jesse had gone from room to room, calling Marie's name. Praying that news of the storm would have fanned an ember of concern in her heart and brought her home. If not for him, then for Madison, Brooke and Sasha.

At the thought of his precious girls, Jesse was struck by an overwhelming desire to hold them again.

"I have to get back to the hospital." He pushed past Colt.

"Jesse, wait. Don't be stubborn." Colt put a restraining hand on his arm. "You're in no shape to go anywhere. Let me call someone for you."

He immediately thought of his younger brother, Clay, but he shook the image away. Colt was right. He wasn't thinking clearly.

His sister, Maya, should have been the one who came to mind first. Not Clay. Clay had shirked his responsibility to the ranch and the family years ago.

If his brother hadn't even bothered to call when Maya had told him Jesse's triplets were struggling for their lives in the NICU, what made him think Clay would be here for him now?

In that respect, Marie and Clay had been alike. Both of them ran away when things got hard. Jesse knew it was up to him to pick up the pieces. Alone. Again.

He swallowed hard against the lump lodged in his throat. "I'll call Maya," he managed to rasp.

"Jesse…" Colt frowned.

Don't say it, Jesse thought. His self-control was hanging by a thread. He couldn't think about his own grief though, he had to think about the three babies he'd left sleeping peacefully in their cribs only a few hours ago. He had to keep it together. For his daughters.

As if Colt could read his mind, he nodded slowly. "I understand. And don't worry about the...arrangements right now, Jess. Take as much time as you need."

THE AUTOMATIC DOORS parted as Jesse reached the front of the building. He'd spent so much time at the hospital over the past eight weeks that many of the staff knew him by name. Two volunteer auxiliary workers stopped talking and nodded solemnly when he passed the information desk.

He'd only taken a few steps down the corridor when a man stepped out of the cafeteria and intercepted him.

"Jesse."

Jesse froze at the sound of the familiar voice, although he barely recognized his father-in-law. The deep lines in Philip Banner's face and the haunted look in his eyes told Jesse he already knew about Marie's death.

Instinctively, Jesse extended his hand to grasp his father-in-law's, but the man stepped away, rebuffing the overture.

Jesse flinched. Philip had never bothered to hide his disapproval. As one of the state's leading prosecutors, Marie's father had had high hopes his only child would marry well. A cattle rancher from Kansas didn't fit his model of the ideal son-in-law. Philip and Sharon had kept in close touch with their daughter after the wedding, but barely acknowledged Jesse's existence.

Jesse had hoped his in-laws would soften when they found out they were going to be grandparents, but if anything, the news had made them more resentful. Instead of anticipating the girls' arrival, Sharon seemed to blame Jesse for Marie's difficult pregnancy.

"Have you seen the girls yet?" It occurred to Jesse that

Philip and Sharon may have come to the hospital for the same reason he had. To hold the triplets and try to find some comfort in knowing that a part of Marie lived on in her daughters.

Philip ignored the question. "Sharon and I need your permission to take Marie..." His voice cracked and he looked away, as if it were difficult to look Jesse in the eye.

Jesse stared at the man, unable to comprehend what he was asking. And then the truth hit him. They hadn't shown up out of concern for Jesse. Or his baby girls. His in-laws had been close by because they'd been part of Marie's exit plan. They'd probably made arrangements to meet her at the airport—to lend their support in case Jesse followed— before escorting her back to Kansas City.

"You want to take her—" Jesse couldn't say the word *body* "—back to Kansas City?"

"We have a family plot in the cemetery." Philip's expression changed and now bitterness scored the words. "Marie never belonged here with you. You know that. Last week she called and asked us if she could come home. It's where she wanted to be. It's where she should be now."

Home.

Jesse had a flashback of the day the obstetrician told them the ultrasound revealed they were expecting triplets.

Jesse's initial shock had quickly changed to delight. He'd always wanted a large family. When it came right down to it, what difference did it make whether there were years or minutes between the births of their children?

And if he were honest with himself, he'd hoped that starting a family would ease the tension growing between them.

During their courtship, Marie claimed she couldn't wait to have children, but after the wedding she'd avoided the topic. Jesse hadn't minded it being just the two of them for a while, but Marie's reaction when she'd found out she was pregnant had disturbed him. Overwhelmed, she'd started to cry and begged him to take her home.

He'd thought she meant the ranch.

Now, seeing the anger and grief on his father-in-law's face, Jesse was forced to admit the truth behind Philip's claim: Marie had never considered the ranch her home.

Jesse had lost his wife long before the tornado struck.

The words stuck in his throat but he pushed them out. "I'll talk to the director at the funeral home. The two of you can work out the arrangements."

Philip nodded curtly, pivoted and walked away without a backward glance. No *thank-you*. No mention of his granddaughters.

The little energy Jesse had left drained away. On emotional autopilot, he took the elevator to the NICU. When he reached the nursery, he heard someone singing softly to the girls.

But it wasn't his sister.

Sitting beside the crib where his daughters slept was Lori Martin, the young, auburn-haired nurse he'd met once or twice. Jesse hadn't gotten to know her as well as he had the other nurses, because her shift ended before he arrived to sit with the girls every evening.

The soft smile on Lori's face and the expression in her eyes made Jesse's chest tighten.

It wasn't right.

Marie should have been the one singing to them. Loving them. And yet she'd left them...all of them.

Jesse's fists clenched at his sides.

Marie was gone, but he had three reasons to live: his daughters. And Jesse decided to make sure no one would hurt them again.

Chapter One

December

"You could have given Maya some hope."

Jesse stiffened at the sound of Clay's quiet voice behind him.

The memory of their sister's stricken expression had seared Jesse's conscience. He knew he'd been out of line, but the last thing he needed was his younger brother beating him up about it.

He'd been doing a pretty good job of that all by himself.

"Maya's been worried sick since Tommy ran away," Clay pointed out. "All she needed was to hear you say you'd find her son and bring him home."

"I did say that."

"'I'll bring him home *either way,* Maya.'" Clay's voice deepened—an exaggerated imitation of Jesse's low baritone—as he recited the words Jesse had spoken just before leaving the house. "In my opinion, you could have left two little words out of that promise."

"I don't remember asking for your opinion." Jesse tightened the cinch on Saber's saddle before leading the gelding from the stall. "Is it fair to give Maya false hope?"

"Now, are you asking my opinion?"

Jesse scowled. Since Clay's unexpected return to High

Plains a month ago, his brother claimed to have changed. Jesse didn't believe it for a second. Not when Clay still managed to get to him like a burr under a saddle blanket.

"Maya needed encouragement. Would it have been so hard to give her some instead of being...Mr. Gloom and Doom?"

Jesse felt the sting of the insult. "*You're* telling me what Maya needs?"

"I know I messed up by leaving." Clay met his gaze. "But that's all in the past now."

"How convenient."

Clay's jaw tightened, the only outward sign that Jesse's words had found their mark. "If I remember correctly, you were always the glass half-full guy in the family."

That was before his glass got tipped over—and stepped on.

"I can't tell Maya that Tommy's all right if I don't know it's true." Jesse wanted to believe they'd find Tommy safe and sound. The whole family—Jesse included—had embraced the precocious little boy. Even before Maya had married Gregory Garrison, and they'd started formal adoption proceedings, Tommy had become part of the family. As far as Jesse was concerned, signing the adoption papers was merely a formality. He'd been "Uncle Jesse" for months.

But he had to deal with facts, whether anyone else wanted to or not. And the facts—that Tommy was only six years old and had been missing for three days—didn't exactly tip the balance in their favor.

When they'd discovered Tommy had run away, volunteer search parties formed immediately, to comb the area. Colt Ridgeway even arranged for a search-and-rescue dog to aid in the effort. But the ranch's vast acreage—ordinarily a source of pride for Jesse—had worked against them.

After Tommy disappeared, Maya had taken a quick

inventory and found that he'd taken some food, his coat and a backpack. The discovery had eased their minds— for the first twenty-four hours. But as resourceful as the little guy had proven to be, a coat wasn't enough to ward off the December wind penetrating the sheepskin lining of Jesse's jacket. And food eventually ran out....

Jesse decided to change the subject before he said something else he might regret. "Be sure to tell Nicki that I appreciate her willingness to watch the triplets again today, while I look for Tommy."

"She knows." There was a glint in Clay's eyes. "And don't you mean while *we* look for Tommy?"

Jesse stepped out of the barn and stopped short at the sight of Sundance, an ornery pinto mare, saddled up and ready to go. Her pinned ears let him know she wasn't very happy about the situation.

He hesitated, tempted to change his plan in order to watch Sundance send his brother into orbit. Maybe another time. "You remember the lay of the land. It would make sense for you to take another group out."

"It might," Clay agreed. "But I'm going with you."

"I'll make better time by myself."

A shadow crossed Clay's face, but then he shrugged. "Even the Lone Ranger had Tonto."

"And Edgar Bergen had Charlie McCarthy," Jesse muttered.

"Do I need to remind you that I'm a grown man and 'you're not the boss of me' anymore?"

Hearing the familiar quip made Jesse's lips twitch. Clay had hurled those words at him frequently while growing up. There was a reason he'd wanted to break away from the rest of the search parties and go it alone. But for some reason, Jesse found himself giving in.

The gleam of laughter in his brother's eyes brought back memories of a time when they'd actually been at ease in each other's company. Before Clay dove into teenage rebellion and turned his back on everything Jesse believed in.

They'd come to an uneasy truce at Thanksgiving, when Clay asked if he could move back to the ranch. Jesse guessed the request had something to do with the lovesick look in his brother's eye whenever his new fiancée, Nicki Appleton, came into view, but some things were hard to let go of. Clay had walked away from his birthright once before. What was to say he wouldn't do it again?

As they passed the house, Jesse saw Maya step out onto the wide front porch. Regret sawed against his conscience again. Not because he'd spoken the truth but because it had hurt his sister.

"Give her some hope," Clay had said.

How could Jesse explain that he and hope had parted company six months ago? If the road to hope led to disappointment, what was the point?

By the time they reached the gate, Maya was waiting for them.

Jesse had to force himself to look his sister in the eye. When he did, the light he saw shining there was a far cry from the worry that had darkened those eyes earlier.

"Michael just called." Maya no longer referred to the minister of High Plains Community Church—her new husband's cousin—by his formal title. "He and Heather Waters are organizing a candlelight prayer vigil for Tommy this evening. He said the people who can't physically join in the search felt led to join together and pray. I know you and Clay are going to find him today, Jesse. I can *feel* it. God is going to show you the way."

Jesse tried to hide his frustration. Maya's faith had always been her North Star, pointing toward the truth. Not too long ago, his sister's unwavering conviction would have challenged him. Strengthened him. But now the only thing her words stirred inside of Jesse were the ashes of what remained of his dreams.

"Keep believing, Maya." Clay came up alongside her. He leaned over the saddle and pulled her into his arms, ruffling her hair as if she were Tommy's age. "God knows exactly where Tommy is. And you're right. We're going to find him. By nine o'clock tonight you'll be tucking him into bed."

Jesse wanted to put a muzzle on his brother. How could Clay get Maya's hopes up like that? Was he the only person in Kansas who was willing to face things the way they were, instead of the way he wanted them to be?

Maya aimed a grateful look at Clay and her smile came out in full force. For the first time in three days.

Jesse clicked his tongue and Saber agreeably stepped forward. The minute they passed through the gate, he nudged the gelding into a canter.

Unfortunately, Clay caught up to him before Jesse's temper had time to cool. "Was that really necessary?"

Clay didn't pretend to misunderstand him. "Yes."

"You shouldn't let her hope for the best."

"And you shouldn't let her imagine the worst," Clay retorted.

Hadn't they already had this conversation?

Jesse wondered if they'd ever see eye to eye on anything.

He tamped down his anger, bit his tongue and forced himself to focus on the reason he'd teamed up with Clay in the first place.

Tommy.

After the boy disappeared, the county sheriff had organized the search, dividing up Jesse's property on a map and assigning each group of volunteers a certain section. Given Tommy's age and size, they'd started close to the ranch house and gradually expanded the search to include the hills and grazing land.

The teams had met back at the ranch after a fruitless search earlier that morning, and when the sheriff instructed everyone to recheck the areas they'd already searched, a shiver of unease had skated through Jesse.

Staring down at the map, he had had an overwhelming urge to scrap the grid and go with his gut. And his gut told him not to waste time covering the same ground again.

He just hadn't expected his brother to tag along.

They rode in silence until Jesse turned his horse down a worn cow path.

"Where are we going?"

"The river," Jesse replied curtly.

To his surprise, his prodigal brother followed without a peep. Accustomed to Clay chafing every time Jesse took the lead, he found he couldn't let that slide. "No argument? No 'do you really think a kid Tommy's age could have made it that far on his own'?"

"You did."

Jesse twisted around in the saddle to stare at his brother.

"It's a long shot," Clay continued. "I mean, you went to the cave on horseback and Tommy is on foot."

Jesse's mouth dropped open. "Cave?"

"Oh, don't look so surprised. It wasn't much of a secret. I followed you there all the time."

"You followed me." Jesse couldn't believe it. He'd been certain the secret hiding place he'd discovered had actually *been* a secret.

The ranch had been his playground as a child, and he'd explored every inch of it. And not always with his parents' permission or his siblings' knowledge, either. At least, he *thought* it had been without his siblings' knowledge.

"Of course I did." Clay's shoulder lifted in a casual

shrug. "But I knew you wanted to be alone, so I let you think you were."

Wanted to be alone...

Bits and pieces of a conversation he'd had with Tommy suddenly trickled through Jesse's memory like the beginning of a rock slide. And then it all came crashing back.

Thanksgiving Day, Tommy had complained that Layla, Maya's three-year-old daughter, was always following him. In the name of male bonding, Jesse had sympathized and told Tommy that his irritation was perfectly normal. He confided that as a boy he also had times when he needed to get away from his younger sister and brother.

"Did you go to your room and lock the door?" Tommy had asked.

Jesse had laughed at the question. He and Clay had always shared a bedroom, so there'd been no privacy there.

That's when he mentioned his favorite "thinking spot" had been a secret cave, its location marked by a strange U-shaped tree whose roots formed the ceiling of the hideaway.

Jesse's mouth suddenly felt as dry as dust. What he'd failed to mention to Tommy was that the last time he'd checked the cave—about five years ago—it had collapsed.

"Jesse? What's wrong?"

Instead of answering, Jesse urged Saber down the hill.

"I REALLY APPRECIATE YOU helping out at the last minute, Lori."

"I'm glad you called." Lori Martin flashed a quick smile in Nicki Appleton's direction as she peeled off her coat and hung it on a colorful, rainbow-shaped wall peg. "I worked today and missed the e-mail about the prayer vigil."

"Reverend Garrison pulled it together pretty quickly, but when I offered to oversee the nursery tonight, I had no idea there'd be such a large turnout." Nicki smiled and blew a wisp of curly blond hair out of her eyes. "I definitely have my hands full in here. I'll give you a choice, though, since you came to my rescue tonight. Do you want to give the triplets their bottles or play demolition derby with the boys over there in the corner?"

The triplets.

Instinctively Lori moved toward the three infant seats arranged in a semicircle on the floor where Nicki sat. Sure enough, there were the Logan girls, a trio of adorable little blossoms dressed in various shades of pink.

She hadn't seen them since October, when she'd volunteered to take a turn in the nursery during the morning worship service. She'd been thrilled at how much the girls had changed—but a little taken aback that the strong connection she'd felt for them hadn't.

As a nurse who provided specialized care for premature infants, Lori walked a fine line between providing the best care possible while not letting herself get too emotionally attached. But from the moment she'd witnessed those tiny girls in the incubator, she'd fallen in love.

Maybe it was because Marie Logan, the babies' mother, had spent more time sipping coffee and flipping through magazines in the family lounge than she had sitting next to her daughters' cribs.

Lori tried to be understanding. It was never easy for a new mother to be released from the hospital and have to leave her children behind. But right from the beginning, Marie seemed to be consumed with her own needs rather than the needs of her daughters. She treated the nursing staff as if they were her personal servants, and her constant criticism frequently brought the aides to tears.

At the end of one particularly stressful morning, Lori took Marie aside and asked if she could pray with her. Marie's bitter response chilled her.

"The reason I'm here is because God is punishing me

for my mistakes. It's not like He's going to listen to anything I have to say."

Before Lori had a chance to convince Marie that wasn't true, the woman had fled from the room. Several days later, Marie's body was recovered in the wreckage from the tornado.

Rumors flew around the pediatric ward that Marie had left her husband and the babies shortly before the tornado struck High Plains. Lori didn't want to believe it, but the day Jesse Logan had arrived to take the triplets home, she'd seen the truth etched in the deep lines fanning out from his eyes.

Midnight-blue eyes that were a perfect match to the ones staring solemnly up at her.

"I'll feed the triplets." Lori reached for Sasha and was rewarded with a beautiful heart-melting baby grin.

Only three and a half pounds at birth, Sasha had been the smallest of the trio. She'd also fought the hardest to survive.

By the time Sasha left the hospital—a full week after her two sisters—she'd stolen the hearts of the entire nursing staff.

"Are you sure?" Nicki raised a teasing brow. "They remind me of a nest of baby birds who all want their dinner at the same time."

"I help, too." A bright-eyed, pajama-clad toddler drifted over and hugged Nicki's arm.

"That's the truth." Nicki gave her foster daughter an affectionate squeeze. "Kasey has been a big help with the babies over the past few days."

Lori grinned as Sasha latched on to the bottle with both hands, as if she hadn't eaten for days. "When did you start taking care of the Logans?"

"It's not permanent. I've been helping out with the girls while Clay and Jesse look for Tommy Jacobs." Nicki's expression clouded. "That's why they organized the prayer vigil tonight. He's been missing for three days and…it's taking a toll on the family."

Lori imagined that was an understatement. She'd heard about Tommy through the prayer chain at High Plains Community and wasn't surprised to learn that Maya's older brothers had taken an active role in looking for their nephew. Or that the entire congregation had reached out to the family.

"I don't mind helping Jesse out when he needs a sitter now and then, but between Kasey and my job at the preschool, I have my hands full," Nicki continued. "I'm not sure who is going to take over and be Nanny Number Six."

Lori's attention, which had been irresistibly drawn to Sasha's tiny fingers, snapped back to Nicki.

Number six?

"Are you saying that Jesse Logan has gone through five nannies?"

"In five months." Nicki nodded. "That has to be some kind of record."

Lori silently agreed. And she couldn't believe the five nannies had all been at fault. Anyone taking on the enormous responsibility of caring for triplets—and premature ones at that—would accept the job with a clear understanding of the challenges they would face.

What had happened?

A sudden image of the handsome but stern-faced rancher flashed in Lori's mind. She couldn't imagine Jesse being an easy man to work for.

"The last nanny Jesse fired had only been at the ranch for forty-eight hours," Nicki continued. "She put in an application at the preschool where I teach, but was embarrassed to tell the director why Jesse had let her go. Apparently, he had a problem with the bedtime songs she sang to the triplets."

"You're kidding."

"I wish I were." Nicki sighed. "Anyway, the word is out, and no one has responded to the classified ad Jesse put in the newspaper for the last two weeks. Clay and I are praying that the right woman comes along. Soon."

A memory stirred in Lori's mind but she immediately pushed it aside. It bounced back.

Not a good sign.

The day after the tornado, she'd been called in early to cover another nurse's shift. Everyone was shaken by the news of the devastation, and with tears in her eyes, one of the nurses whispered to Lori that she'd heard Marie Logan had died.

Lori knew the triplets had no comprehension that their lives had been irrevocably changed, but she'd gone to them immediately. And while she sat next to the crib and sang to the girls, she'd felt someone's presence in the room.

Jesse stood in the doorway, watching her.

She'd wanted to comfort him—to tell him she was praying for him—but the hard look in his eyes warned her that he wouldn't welcome any sympathy.

As Lori slipped out of the room, she'd asked God to let her know if there was a way she could help the Logan family.

Had He waited five months to give her an answer?

Chapter Two

Discouragement gnawed at Jesse as he paused to survey the barren landscape. The frontline winds that had spawned the funnel cloud in July had left their mark on this end of the property, too.

"Jess—wait a second."

Jesse glanced back and saw Clay dismount and reach for something in the brush.

Jesse's heart kicked against his chest. Ever since the tornado, he'd been searching for the heirloom engagement ring Marie had left on the kitchen table that day. He'd found the soggy remains of the note and her wedding band in the rubble, but there'd been no sign of the diamond.

Several times a week for the past five months, Maya faithfully checked the community Lost and Found to see if anyone had turned it in. Reverend Garrison had even made a special announcement during one of the community meetings to let everyone know how much the ring meant to the Logan family. One weekend, he'd even brought his teenage niece, Avery, and a small volunteer crew from the youth group out to the ranch to comb a section of the property for missing items.

"I can't believe how far a twister can carry little things like this," Clay remarked, examining something in his palm.

"What is it?" If Clay had found the ring, he'd have told

Jesse right away. Silently, Jesse berated himself for giving hope a temporary foothold.

Hadn't he learned that particular lesson already?

"A key chain…with a whistle on it."

Jesse was at his brother's side in two strides. "Let me see that."

Clay's eyebrow shot up. "It's yours?"

Jesse stared at the piece of plastic cradled in his brother's palm. "It's Tommy's."

"The tornado dropped it this far from town?"

The tornado. Or Tommy.

On a hunch, Jesse raised the whistle to his lips and blew.

Clay winced. "Making sure it still works?"

"Shh." For a moment, Jesse thought he'd imagined the faint cry woven into the wind. But Clay's sharp inhale told Jesse he'd heard it, too.

"Uncle J-Jesse?" The roots of an overturned tree moved and a familiar freckled face poked out.

When Tommy saw the two men standing there, he scrambled out of his hiding spot and barreled toward them.

Jesse swung the boy up into his arms and Tommy burst into tears.

As CLAY RADIOED the good news to the deputy in charge of the search, Jesse settled Tommy in the saddle in front of him and buttoned him into his coat. The boy's ragged sigh shook his thin frame and went straight through Jesse.

He still couldn't believe that Tommy had managed to stumble upon the collapsed cave.

When the tornado had chewed its way across the property, it upended the tree that had once marked the cave's location, but created an opening large enough for a six-year-old boy to squeeze into. Sheltering him not only from the elements but from any predators lurking in the area.

Clay had murmured something about answered prayer. Jesse hadn't argued the point. Maybe God had stopped listening to him, but at least He had heard Maya. At the moment, Jesse could be grateful for that.

"Are you sure Mom…Maya…and G-Greg aren't mad at me?" The words were muffled but Jesse could hear the undercurrent of worry in Tommy's voice.

Jesse frowned. Tommy had been calling Maya and his brother-in-law "Mom and Dad" for the past few months.

"I'm sure. They've been worried about you…." His throat tightened. They'd *all* been worried about him. "And they're going to be happy to know that you're okay."

"Even if I did sumpthin' bad?"

"What do you mean?"

"I made Layla cry. Not on purpose," Tommy added quickly. "But I don't think they believed me. And then I heard Maya tell you there's a problem with the 'doption. I know what that means. There's a problem with *me*."

Jesse sucked in a breath. No one could figure out why Tommy had run away from home, but now it all made sense. He'd overheard part of a conversation Jesse had had with Maya.

"Believe me, Tommy, that's not what she meant. Everyone loves you—you're part of the family."

"For real?" Tommy's chin tilted toward Jesse and the dirt-smudged face brightened.

"For real. The problem with the adoption isn't you, champ. The problem is that it isn't going as fast as Maya and Greg would like it to," Jesse explained. "Trust me. They can't *wait* for you to be their little boy."

Tommy snuggled against him. "We better get back so she isn't worried anymore. I'm glad you came, Uncle Jesse. I was getting kinda cold. And I ran out of—" he battled a yawn "—peanut butter."

"THEY FOUND HIM." Nicki picked up Kasey and twirled her around in the middle of the room, much to the toddler's delight. "Clay just called my cell phone. Tommy is fine. Tired and hungry, but fine. Maya and Greg are meeting Jesse at home."

Lori closed her eyes and offered a silent prayer of thanks.

"I'm going to sneak into the service and tell Reverend Garrison so he can announce the good news." Nicki spun one more wobbly pirouette as she glided toward the doorway with Kasey in her arms. "Thanks for staying to help, Lori. I'm sure you had other plans for the evening. Plans that *didn't* include total chaos!"

Lori smiled but didn't confess that total chaos was a welcome change from her silent apartment, a bowl of pretzels and the latest cozy mystery she'd picked up at the grocery store checkout.

While Nicki entertained Kasey and the other children throughout the evening, Lori devoted her attention to the triplets.

Brooke and Madison had taken their bottles and had eventually fallen asleep, but Sasha was clearly a night owl. The baby remained wide-awake, content to cuddle in Lori's lap as they put several miles on the rocking chair.

Lori, who held and cared for babies all day, couldn't ignore the deep connection she felt with the triplets. Several times during the course of the evening, Nicki had commented on how comfortable they seemed to be with her.

It seemed unlikely they would remember her....

Lori glanced down and met Sasha's solemn gaze.

If she didn't know better, she'd think that Sasha was reminding her of the promise she made to God that day.

It wasn't exactly a promise. More like an...offer.

A suggestion, really.

"I love my job at the hospital," Lori murmured out loud. "They need me."

Sasha, who'd been cheerful most of the evening, suddenly let loose a heart-wrenching whimper.

The timing of which had to be an absolute coincidence, Lori decided.

"Oh, no, you don't. That's not fair." She lifted Sasha higher in her arms, nuzzling the rose-kissed cheek. Encouraged by the baby's soft chortle of laughter, Lori closed her eyes and planted a trail of noisy kisses up the baby's pudgy arm.

Sasha's tiny feet began to pedal rapidly inside the flannel blanket.

"Oh, really? I can find little toes, too, so you better—"

A door to the nursery snapped shut and Lori's eyes flew open.

And there stood Jesse Logan.

His sharp, blue-eyed gaze flickered over the infant seats near Lori's feet where Brooke and Madison slept, before moving to Sasha, who recognized her daddy and gurgled happily, waving her arms to get his attention.

Lori gave Sasha points for bravery.

How—for even a split second—could she have entertained the notion that God wanted *her* to be Nanny Number Six?

Jesse didn't look like a man who needed anyone's help.

Although there was no getting around the fact that the man was extremely handsome, the set of his jaw didn't look as though it allowed much movement—and certainly not on something as frivolous as a smile. The silky fringe of dark hair beneath his Stetson didn't soften features that looked as if they'd been sculpted by the elements.

"Mr. Logan." Lori rose to her feet, gently trying to disengage her shirt from Sasha's grip.

There was a spark of recognition in his eyes.

A thought suddenly occurred to Lori, and she lifted her free hand to her hair for a quick, exploratory search. At one point during the evening, Kasey had clipped a pink elephant barrette on the end of Lori's braid.

Yup. Still there.

Lori suddenly wished she hadn't run home to exchange her scrubs for faded jeans and a sweatshirt. At the hospital, there'd been a professional boundary in place. Jesse Logan—patients' father; Lori Martin—nurse.

But now? Now she was simply a Good Samaritan. A Good Samaritan whose hair was in a tangle from being tugged on by—count them—*six* little hands all evening. And then Kasey had added her own special touch.

"Where is Nicki?" Jesse's loose-limbed stride carried him across the room in less than two seconds.

Now he stood close enough for Lori to pick up the subtle, earthy scent of wind and leather that clung to his coat.

Lori wasn't petite by any standards, but she had to tip her chin up to look at him. His height was a little intimidating. And so was his expression.

Instinctively, she tightened her hold on Sasha.

"Nicki is talking to Reverend Garrison. My name is on the sub list for the church nursery, so she asked if I was free to help her watch the children this evening." Lori wasn't a babbler by nature, but there was something unnerving about being with a man who didn't waste words. Not to mention a man who didn't seem to like to *use* them, either. "I don't know if you remember, but we met—"

"I remember you."

Okay, then.

Lori tried again. "The girls have really grown." She couldn't prevent a chuckle. "But they haven't changed all that much, have they?"

Jesse's finger flicked the brim of his cowboy hat, pushing it up. The movement chased the shadows away, revealing the full impact of cobalt-blue eyes set in a face stained a deep golden brown from the sun.

"What do you mean?" Those eyes narrowed and Lori realized he'd taken her comment as a criticism. "Their pediatrician says they're developing on schedule."

"I meant their personalities," Lori explained, wondering if she'd just witnessed the same look the five nannies had seen moments before they'd been fired.

No wonder he was having a difficult time filling the position!

"Brooke still lets you know that she wants something *yesterday.*" She smiled down at the baby, who continued to move restlessly even in sleep. "And you know Madison is going to be the peacemaker of the group. When Brooke started crying tonight, Madison offered her own thumb to calm her down. And Sasha's quiet, but she takes in everything around her—"

"You can tell them apart?"

Lori blinked at the terse interruption. "Can't you?"

"Of course I can." Clearly offended, Jesse swept off his hat and tunneled his hand through his hair. "Maddie is bald, Brooke has a birthmark on her left shoulder blade and Sasha is the smallest."

Lori stared at him in amazement. He'd zeroed in on some of the triplets' physical characteristics.

Didn't the man realize his daughters had three very distinct *personalities? Temperaments?*

Needs?

It suddenly became important for Lori to make Jesse understand.

"It's not just what they *look* like on the outside. Madison loves to be cuddled but Brooke doesn't have the patience for it. My guess is that she'll be the first one to crawl. Sasha is attracted to color and motion...."

Lori's voice broke off as Jesse dropped to one knee in front of Madison's infant seat.

Conversation over.

She'd lost him. It suddenly occurred to Lori that Jesse Logan was probably the type of man whose entire life revolved around his ranch. A man who believed that providing food and a roof over their heads made him a good father to his daughters.

The second-shift nurses had all raved about Jesse's devotion to his children because he'd shown up at the NICU every night. That didn't prove anything to Lori. Sitting beside their cribs could have simply been one more thing for Jesse Logan to check off his to-do list. A duty instead of an act of love.

They'll need more, Lori wanted to protest. *So much more.*

Jesse's indifference raked over debris from her past and scraped up old memories. Memories that Lori thought had long been put to rest.

"What do you want from me, Roxanne? I said I'd own up to my responsibility and I did...but that doesn't mean I have to pretend to be happy about it...."

Lori swallowed hard and tried to shut out her father's voice, shaken that the words sounded as clear as if he'd spoken them the day before, instead of fifteen years ago.

The room began to shrink and Lori felt an overwhelming urge to escape.

"I'll find Nicki." With Sasha still in her arms, Lori headed toward the door.

She wasn't surprised when Jesse didn't respond.

Emotions churned inside of her. How could she leave the triplets, when they needed someone who would lavish attention and love on them?

When they needed *her.*

She made her decision. Pausing in the doorway, she turned and looked over her shoulder...

Just in time to see Jesse cup his hands over his mouth and blow on his fingers. Warming them.

Lori's breath caught in her throat.

And that's when she saw it. The subtle sway of his body before he managed to balance his weight on the heels of his boots. The slight dip of his shoulders beneath the heavy coat.

Exhaustion.

The bone-deep kind that sucked away a person's energy—chiseled holes in their perspective. The kind that stole a person's ability to think.

And talk.

Lori's feet felt rooted to the floor and her heart began to pound. "Mr. Logan?"

Jesse's head snapped up and once again his face looked as if it had been carved out of stone.

Lori hoped she wouldn't live to regret her next words. "Are you still looking for a nanny?"

Jesse tried not to let his frustration show.

Of course Lori Martin had heard he was looking for a new nanny. The entire population of High Plains probably knew he was looking for a new nanny.

He'd fired two or three—okay, so maybe it had been five—although he wasn't sure if he could count the last one. Just when he'd opened his mouth to say the words *you're fired,* she'd beaten him to the punch and informed him that she quit. But did that mean he deserved to be treated like a pariah? The last time he'd gone to the newspaper to put in an ad for another caregiver, the woman behind the reception desk had actually laughed. *Laughed.*

Was it his fault that none of the nannies he'd hired had been able to do the job properly?

His sweet-tempered sister's popularity had opened the door to a few favors. But so far, nothing permanent.

He'd been grateful to Nicki for agreeing to watch the triplets over the past few days while they searched for Tommy, but she had her hands full with Kasey, the active toddler she'd recently been granted permission to adopt.

Clay had offered to shoulder more responsibility in the mornings so Jesse could drive the girls to a day care in High Plains, but that was his last resort. And he had to make that decision in about six hours.

Pride stopped him from letting anyone see how desperate he was. Especially the young, brown-eyed nurse who'd managed to coax a belly laugh out of somber little Sasha.

He could still hear the lilt of Lori's laughter, mingled with his daughter's, as he'd stood outside the door of the church nursery. It had rolled over him with the warmth of a spring breeze. And the sight of her raining kisses on Sasha's chubby arm affected Jesse more than he cared to admit.

"That's right." The words sounded curt, even to his own ears, but it was the best he could do.

Small talk was simply beyond his capability at the moment.

Three days of searching for Tommy, in addition to keeping up with his regular chores and getting up with the triplets during the night, had begun to take its toll. His limbs felt as if they'd been replaced with wet concrete.

Lori Martin lingered in the doorway and Jesse wished she'd go away. And not because his gaze strayed to the soft tendrils of sunset-red hair that had escaped from her braid. Or because Sasha looked perfectly content to remain in the woman's arms.

Nope. Because he was practically dead on his feet and didn't need any witnesses to the fact. Someone who would report back to Nicki. Who'd report to Clay. Who'd report to Maya....

He had an idea. As much as Lori Martin obviously loved children, he knew exactly what would make her beat a hasty retreat.

"I didn't realize you were interested in the position. When can you start?" Jesse injected just enough sarcasm to scare her off. And let her know exactly what he thought about people gossiping about him.

Lori Martin met his gaze. And smiled sweetly.

"Right now."

Chapter Three

You're hired.

Those two simple words echoed in Lori's mind as she reached the end of the long dirt road, and the car's headlights illuminated a turn-of-the-century two-story house with a stone foundation.

Jesse's house.

Maybe she should leave the engine running.

Lori hadn't expected Jesse to turn cartwheels at her impulsive offer the night before, but his cool response had her questioning her decision. And her sanity.

I can do all things through Him who strengthens me.

The verse in Philippians she'd read during her devotional time that morning filtered through her panic and calmed what some people would have called "the butterflies" in her stomach. To Lori, it felt more like a herd of mustangs had taken up residence there.

She took a deep breath and turned off the ignition.

The front door opened and Jesse stepped onto the porch, his lean, broad-shouldered frame backlit by the soft glow from the window.

He'd been waiting for her.

Lori got out of the car, tempted to leave her suitcase in the trunk. Just in case.

I can do all things through Christ, Lori reminded herself. *All things.*

She'd made a promise to the girls—and to God—and she intended to keep it.

Scraping up her courage, Lori popped the trunk and wrestled her suitcase out. She took a step back and smacked into something warm and solid.

"I can take this." Jesse's fingers closed over the handle and brushed against hers as he took control of the suitcase.

The chilly morning air was making her shiver. Had to be that....

"Thank you." The mustangs had multiplied, but Lori forced a smile.

"Is this all you have?" She sensed a scowl in the darkness.

"I packed what I needed to get me through the next few days." If she lasted that long. "My rental came furnished, but I plan to pick up the rest my things later in the week."

Jesse acknowledged her words with a curt nod as he retraced his steps back to the house.

Did the man know how to smile?

All things...

The verse dissolved like sugar in water as Lori followed Jesse inside and caught her first glimpse of her new home.

"You can go on in." Jesse's gruff prompt encouraged her to take another step forward.

A *reluctant* step forward.

It was obvious that two bachelor ranchers and three babies equaled chaos.

Jesse coughed as he ushered her into the living room. "The place is a little...neglected. I had a housekeeper. Up until last week."

So. He'd fired her, too.

Which explained why the room looked as if the tornado had gone through his house the day before, instead of five months ago.

Bright plastic toys were scattered like confetti from one end of the room to the other. Laundry—men's faded chambray work shirts mixed in with tiny, colorful sleepers—lay draped over the three infant swings lined up in front of the window.

And what was that smell?

Lori took a few more steps forward and something crunched beneath her foot. Glancing down, she saw the remains of a pretzel ground into the carpet.

"The housekeeper did most of the cooking, too." Jesse discreetly swiped up a sock and crossed his arms to hide it from view.

Not that they'd had much time to talk about her specific duties yet, but it would have been nice if Jesse had mentioned she would be in charge, not only of the triplets, but of the entire household.

"I started asking around to find someone else, but…" His voice trailed off and Lori filled in the blanks.

Your former nannies spread the word about you.

The former nannies he'd apparently fired without a qualm.

But Madison, Brooke and Sasha needed her, so Lori was determined not to start off the day—let alone the first fifteen minutes—on the wrong foot.

"Don't worry about it. I don't mind cooking," she said cheerfully. "I make the best eggplant Parmesan you've ever tasted."

"Eggplant…" Jesse frowned. "I don't think I've ever tried that."

"Oh, I'm sure you'd remember if you had. It's delicious. In fact, it's considered a staple in a vegetarian diet." But probably missing from the menu of a certain cattle rancher.

"Vege—" Jesse choked on the rest of the word. "You're a…vegetarian?"

Lori waited a beat, hoping he'd realize he was being teased. It would prove a sense of humor lurked somewhere below that serious demeanor. "No."

Jesse frowned.

Apparently not. "I was kidding."

"Kidding?" Jesse repeated the word suspiciously.

"Making a joke…." *Never mind.*

"Right." Jesse continued to stare at her, and Lori wondered if, in spite of her best intentions, she was going to break her predecessor's forty-eight-hour record. Abruptly, Jesse turned away. "I'll show you to your room. The girls are still asleep, but I guess that's not a surprise, considering how late they went to bed last night."

Lori envied them. She'd stared at the ceiling for hours, asking God if she'd made the right decision.

It wasn't as if she were a risk-taker by nature. And considering Jesse Logan's track record with the triplets' former nannies, one might argue that taking the job definitely put her in that category.

After she'd helped Jesse bundle the girls into their snowsuits the night before, Lori told him that she'd be there by six-thirty the next morning. She didn't know much about ranching but assumed Jesse's day started at sunup. The mixture of relief and gratitude in his eyes told her that she'd guessed correctly.

Fortunately, Lori had the day off from her job at the hospital, which would give her time to contact the personnel department at the hospital and talk to Janet, her supervisor.

Another factor that had proven God was at work in the situation. In fact, the longer Lori had thought and prayed about it, the more she realized that seemingly small and insignificant details now looked like signposts, directing her down a different path than the one she'd been on.

She wouldn't have known Jesse was looking for a nanny if Nicki hadn't called and asked for her help in the church nursery the night before. And just last week, Lori's landlady mentioned her niece had moved back to High Plains and needed a place to stay. She asked if Lori wanted to renew her lease, which was due the second week in December. Lori had told her that she planned to stay—but the lease agreement remained on her desk, still unsigned. Lori couldn't help but think that her landlady would be happy to offer the unit to a family member.

Even if Lori believed in coincidences—which she didn't—it would have been impossible to ignore the verse she'd read during her devotional time—the one she'd memorized while packing her suitcase. The one she silently repeated as she wove through a maze of baby jumpers and followed Jesse to the second floor.

A spacious landing opened up at the top of the stairs, and Jesse turned down the hallway to the left.

"You can have the room that adjoins the nursery." His husky voice dropped to a whisper as he nudged the door open.

Lori braced herself, ready to pretend to be enthusiastic. Only, this time she didn't have to pretend.

The color scheme was a serene combination of subdued ivory, sage-green and a vibrant shade of blue that reminded Lori of Jesse's eyes....

The sky, she quickly corrected the errant thought. It reminded her of the *sky.*

She ventured farther into the room, aware that Jesse had put her suitcase down and moved aside to allow her to explore.

A queen-size antique four-poster bed, covered by a double wedding-ring quilt, dominated the room. Hand-hooked wool rugs had been strategically placed in front of the matching nightstands and the window. All places where bare feet might linger.

A sepia-toned photo of a man and woman held a prominent place on the wall above the headboard. Instead of staring somberly at the camera, typical for photographs taken during that era, the young couple was smiling at each other.

"My ancestors, Will and Emmeline Logan." Jesse stood beside her and Lori's heart did that crazy skip-hop thing again. "Will and Zeb Garrison founded High Plains in 1858, and Will married Emmeline a few years after that."

Lori forced herself to concentrate on the photo instead of the appealing, masculine scent of the man standing beside her.

More than a hundred years separated the two men, and yet the family resemblance was uncanny. Will Logan had the same bone structure—angular jaw and deep-set eyes— but his smile held a hint of mischief. "Was it your great-grandfather who started the Circle L?"

Jesse nodded. "He built the house for Emmeline. The ranch has been run by one of their descendants ever since."

Lori felt a stab of envy. What would it feel like to be part of such a strong family line? To share a legacy that had bonded its members together for more than a hundred years?

Her own family had splintered and fallen apart the summer after Lori had graduated from high school.

"It's beautiful," she murmured. "You must feel very blessed."

"Not everyone would agree with your opinion." Jesse pivoted sharply on his heel. "I'll show you the rest of the house and then I have to get to work. Clay is probably already in the barn waiting for me."

Lori found herself staring at his retreating back.

Not everyone would agree...

Agree with what? That his home was beautiful—or that he'd been blessed?

THE HEADACHE that had anchored its claws in the back of Jesse's skull during the night finally worked its way around to his temples.

He hadn't expected Lori Martin's innocent questions to bring back an avalanche of memories...and regrets.

Marie had never described the house as beautiful. The first time she visited she labeled it "quaint," and Jesse, who'd taken it as a compliment, remembered thanking her. But several months after the wedding, she'd complained the rooms were too small and she felt cramped without adequate storage space. Without discussing it with him first, she'd talked to her father. Philip not only had an architect draw up a new blueprint, but then generously offered to pay the expenses so they could build something more suited to their style.

What Marie didn't understand was that the ranch *was* Jesse's style.

And he thought it had been hers.

Memories lapped against the walls Jesse had shored up around his heart.

The truth was, both of them had assumed a lot about each other.

They'd met at a rodeo, when Marie had come to town on what she described as a "girls' getaway" weekend. She sat down next to Jesse on the makeshift bleachers, her eyes sparkling with mischief as she told him that her friends had dared her to kiss a cowboy.

Unable to resist her charming smile, Jesse planted his favorite Stetson on Marie's head and kissed her on the cheek instead, surprised at his own boldness.

They had dinner that evening. And the next.

Marie extended her weekend stay to an entire week. When she finally left, she took Jesse's heart with her. After more than ten years of pouring his heart and soul into making the ranch a success, he'd been ready for someone to share it with.

Jesse had always been the levelheaded one when it came to life and relationships, but in spite of Maya's reservations, he proposed to Marie on Valentine's Day and they married less than six months later.

Unfortunately, it hadn't taken long for Jesse to realize that Marie had a romanticized, Hollywood view about life on a ranch. Emergencies ignited like brush fires, and as the owner of the Circle L, it was Jesse's responsibility to put them out. Night or day. Marie started to resent the hours he spent apart from her. She resisted Maya's attempts to befriend her, and refused to become part of the tight-knit community, but still complained that she was bored.

Bitterness scoured the lining of Jesse's stomach. He'd opened his heart and taken a risk. And in the end he'd lost.

He didn't blame Marie, he blamed himself. He'd written a fairy tale of his own—one in which he and his wife would work side by side during the day and sit together on the porch swing in the evening, waiting for the first star to appear in the sky. They'd laugh together. Raise a family together. The way his parents had.

But the reality? More arguments than laughter. And too many nights when Jesse had sat on the porch swing alone while Marie sat inside watching television or talking on the phone.

He didn't feel *blessed*.

"Mr. Logan? Jesse?" Lori Martin stood beside him, concern reflected in the depths of her amber eyes. "Is something wrong?"

Jesse's lips twisted.

Maybe she was worried that she'd agreed to work for

someone who was losing his mind. Not that Jesse blamed her. A few times over the past few months, he'd wondered about that himself.

He frowned as his gaze dropped to the constellation of pale cinnamon freckles dotting the bridge of Lori's nose.

Funny, he hadn't noticed them until now.

With a jolt, Jesse realized he hadn't noticed how young she was, either. Probably in her mid-twenties. Her smile seemed to appear without warning or reason, and the lively sparkle in her eyes was evidence of a life that hadn't been touched by disappointment.

Lucky her.

Lori's response to his bluff the night before, when he offered and she accepted the nanny position, had left him stunned. It wasn't until Jesse watched her car glide up the driveway that he let himself believe she'd really accepted the position. And even then, he half expected to see her do a U-turn and hightail it back to town.

He'd stopped asking God for help a long time ago, but if Jesse didn't know better, he'd be tempted to think He was still looking out for him anyway.

Lori felt her face grow warm and she shifted uncomfortably under Jesse's intense perusal. Had her mascara smeared? Did she have a smudge of grape jelly on her nose?

An unhappy squawk on the other side of the door saved her from having to ask.

She and Jesse instinctively turned toward the sound.

"Brooke." They said the name at exactly the same moment.

Lori grinned at the expression on Jesse's face and she shrugged. "She's always the first one awake and ready to eat in the morning."

A shadow darkened Jesse's eyes. "I keep forgetting that you…know them."

Know them. Love them. Had even held them in her arms before Jesse....

Lori decided those thoughts were best kept to herself as she stepped into the nursery to say good morning to the girls.

She blinked, giving her eyes a moment to adjust to the shock.

Someone had painted the room...pink. But not a delicate, seashell-pink. A bright, vibrant, sensory-overload shade of Post-it Note pink.

But aside from the color of the walls and the identical white cribs lined up against the wall, it didn't look like a nursery.

No pictures on the walls. No mobiles over the cribs. The windows lacked curtains and, other than the beds, there wasn't a stick of furniture. Not even a rocking chair.

Lori's gaze moved to an enormous cardboard box positioned under the window. She decided it didn't count.

A sudden noisy chorus rose from the direction of the three cribs, and Lori no longer had time to dwell on the décor. Or lack thereof.

"When one wakes up, they all wake up." Jesse shook his head. "I stopped setting my alarm a few months ago— it seemed a little unnecessary."

Lori went to Sasha first, even though the baby wasn't exercising her lungs the way Brooke was. She'd captured her toes and was studying them with the same serious, intense expression Lori had seen on Jesse's face. She reached into the crib and Sasha's dimpled hand closed around her finger.

"Good morning, sweetheart. How did you sleep?" She glanced at Jesse. "Do you have a changing table somewhere?"

"It's in the box," Jesse muttered.

The box under the window.

Madison rolled over to watch the show, her thumb tucked firmly in her mouth. Lori blew her a noisy kiss. "Patience, sweet pea. I'll get to you in a minute."

Out of the corner of her eye, Lori saw Jesse's scowl.

It occurred to her that, if he'd fired someone for the songs she'd sung to the girls, maybe kisses were against the rules, too.

Not on *her* shift.

She'd spent hours caring for babies, and she knew that the more stimulation they received—the more people who touched and spoke to them—the more they thrived.

"If you have work to do, I can take it from here." And she'd be much less nervous if Jesse wasn't watching her.

Jesse hesitated.

"Really. We'll be fine." With Sasha in her arms, Lori breezed over to the changing table...*box*...and with one hand, flicked open a blanket before laying the baby down. She kept one hand on Sasha's tummy while reaching for a clean diaper from the stack on the floor.

Jesse hadn't taken the hint, and Lori felt the weight of his gaze as she deftly changed Sasha's diaper. It wasn't until *all* the babies had on fresh diapers that he finally retreated.

Lori sighed with relief.

"I must have made it through round one," she whispered to Madison.

The baby grinned.

"I know, I know." Lori winked at her. "I won't get cocky. Now, let's go down to the kitchen and find some breakfast."

And get ready for round two.

Chapter Four

"So, what do you think? Is this one going to work out?"

Clay's innocent expression didn't fool Jesse for a second.

He knew he should have followed his gut instincts. But no, in spite of his better judgment, he'd gone down to the barn and put himself in the crosshairs of Clay's wicked sense of humor.

As far as Jesse was concerned, the topic of the nannies that had come and gone over the past few months wasn't open for discussion. But if there was an invisible line drawn in the sand, his brother had to cross it.

"Time will tell." Jesse chose the safest response.

Clay rolled his eyes.

"She's very...calm," Jesse offered.

Really calm.

Lori hadn't seemed a bit rattled by the prebreakfast commotion. Jesse was always a little overwhelmed in the morning, when all three girls woke up within minutes of each other, bawling like newborn calves for their breakfast.

In his mind's eye, he saw Lori's lips purse as she blew a kiss to Madison. He shook the image away, but another one—of Lori tickling the bottom of Sasha's tiny foot while Brooke wailed for her share of the attention—took its place.

"Patient," he added.

"That should work in your favor."

"I meant patient with the girls."

"Right. Sorry." Clay grinned. "And she didn't run screaming back to High Plains when she saw the living room. That's a good sign."

Jesse had thought so, too.

Not that he hadn't tried to keep up with the housework. And the laundry. And the cooking.

Even with two hired hands pulling ten-hour days and Clay coming onboard to help, Jesse had a difficult time staying on top of things at the ranch. It took every ounce of his energy to take care of the triplets in the evening and find a few free hours to work on the books. When he'd let the last nanny go two days before Tommy turned up missing, the house had taken a downward spiral.

Who was he kidding? Downward spiral? It had already hit bottom. Crashed and burned.

"I'm having dinner with Nicki so I won't be around this evening." Clay reached out and clipped Jesse lightly on the shoulder with his fist. "Lori sounds too good to be true. Don't mess this up."

"Me?"

"I've got two words for you: *five nannies*."

"I wasn't the problem." Jesse glared at his brother. "They weren't what I…expected."

The teasing sparkle in Clay's eyes faded. "Jess…" He paused, as if trying to find the right words. "You can't expect the girls' nanny to be like their…mother. It's not the same. It's not going to *look* the same."

His brother didn't realize the truckload of irony in that statement, Jesse thought. Marie hadn't wanted to be a mother. He'd watched her emotionally distance herself from the girls—the same way she had with him.

He had prayed. Back then. He prayed she would eventually come around. He prayed she would see the girls for the miraculous gift they were—but those hopes had been crushed when he found the note and her wedding rings that day.

A wave of bitterness swept through him. Belief in answered prayer. Hope. At one time, Jesse had had a surplus of both. But that was before he'd realized they left a lingering aftertaste of disappointment.

"I know this has been hard for you, Jess, but I'm here to help." Clay met his gaze. "Not just with the ranch but with…everything."

"Yeah, but for how long?" Jesse retorted.

As soon as he saw the shadow skim through his brother's eyes, Jesse silently berated himself.

"For as long as you want me to, whether you believe it or not." Clay's quiet promise weighted the air between them.

He sauntered out of the barn and Jesse closed his eyes.

What had happened to him?

Over the past six months, Jesse had been waiting for a sign that the well of bitterness inside of him was beginning to dry up. But instead, he felt as if it were constantly being replenished by an unknown source.

Maya told him that he had to let God work in his heart but Jesse wondered if he was beyond repair. Sometimes he thought the only thing that kept his heart beating was his daughters' sunny smiles.

SHE COULD *do* this.

Lori surveyed the living room and took a moment to regroup.

Triplets fed and dressed: check.

Laundry started: check.

Supper in the Crock-Pot: check.

Kitchen—

Lori winced. That room definitely fell under the promise: *I can do all things through Christ who gives me strength.* She planned to tackle that particular project while the girls took their morning nap.

After giving the triplets their bottles, Lori spread out a hand-pieced quilt on the floor of the living room and put all three babies in the center. While they worked their way to the edges, she deposited the toys into a large wicker hamper and sorted through the clothing draped over the swings.

Apparently, the men in the household had discovered a handy place to hang up their laundry after it came out of the dryer, saving the work of having to fold it and put it away.

Lori shook the wrinkles out of a faded denim work shirt and the subtle scent of sage and soap drifted into the air.

Jesse's.

She separated it from the stack of stylish, Western-style shirts that she had a hunch belonged to Clay Logan.

Lori didn't know Jesse's brother well, but he was engaged to her good friend and former neighbor, Nicki Appleton. She'd also seen him help rebuild the Old Town Hall, which had been leveled by the previous summer's tornado. He'd jumped into a battered old Chevy and took off down the road shortly after she'd arrived. And there'd been no sign of her new employer all morning.

She had no clue what the household routine involved, but the less contact she and Jesse had, the easier it might be to keep her job.

Unless…

"Uh-oh. Is there a nanny cam hidden somewhere, girls?" Lori anchored her hands on her hips and scanned the room, her gaze zeroing in on the only thing decorating the mantel above the stone fireplace—an unassuming silk fern.

"A tempting thought, but no."

The husky, masculine drawl sent a shiver chasing up Lori's spine, followed by a head-to-toe blush that probably turned her skin the same shade of red as her hair.

Lori whirled around. Jesse must have entered the house through an entrance other than the front door and snuck up on her.

"You're…here." *One point for your keen observation skills, Lori,* she chided herself.

Jesse shrugged off his duster and draped it over the back of the sofa. All three girls recognized their father's voice and immediately began to vie for his attention.

"It's ten o'clock," Jesse said.

Lori wondered if there was something significant about that particular time. Was she supposed to have lunch ready? The coffee on?

Or maybe Jesse performed daily inspections of his children and the nanny, like Captain Von Trapp in the movie *The Sound of Music.*

Now you're being paranoid.

"Ten o'clock," she repeated cautiously.

"I come in every day at ten."

"You're…finished for the morning?"

Jesse looked at her in disbelief. "Hardly."

So she'd been right. It *was* an inspection.

Lori took a deep breath. "I fed and dressed the girls. Supper is already in the Crock-Pot, but you didn't mention anything about lunch. You are a little low on groceries." She deliberately downplayed the sorry state of the refrigerator's contents. "So I will need to run to the grocery store within the next day or two. If there's something you'd like me to do right now—"

"You can go," Jesse interrupted.

Go?

Go as in *leave?* Return to her job at the hospital?

Lori looked down at the triplets and panic rushed through her.

She couldn't leave. The girls needed her. She wasn't sure what she'd done—or hadn't done—but somehow she'd broken the record for the shortest employment history with Jesse Logan.

"But what if I don't want to…leave?" There. She said it.

Jesse's eyebrow shot up. "I appreciate your dedication, Miss Martin, but I know how tiring taking care of the triplets can be. Put your feet up. Read a book. Take a walk. I don't care what you do, but the next half hour belongs to you."

Lori stared at him in disbelief. "You're giving me a *break?*"

Jesse sighed. "I'm trying, but you don't seem to be co-operating."

"But what about the girls?"

He gave her a wry look. "I think I can keep an eye on the girls."

Lori hesitated, still confused by his unexpected offer. "I have half an hour? To do anything I want to?"

"You are down to twenty-seven minutes now, but yes, that's generally the definition of a break."

Lori ignored the edge in his voice. "All right, then. I'll see you in twenty-seven minutes."

"Miss Martin?"

Lori sucked in a breath. Now what?

"You have…something…on your shirt."

Lori glanced down. So she did. A crusty river mean-dering down her shirt from collar to hem. Compliments of Brooke, who'd discovered a unique way of letting the person feeding her know when she was finished with her bottle.

"Thanks. I think."

"And your…foot."

Lori glanced down but couldn't identify what was spattered across the toe of her tennis shoe.

"Hazards of the job." Lori, who had experienced worse, couldn't help but smile. "And please, call me Lori."

Jesse didn't smile back.

It didn't matter, Lori decided, as she practically skipped across the living room.

She still had a job. And half an hour—well, twenty-seven minutes—would give her just the right amount of time to tackle one of the projects on her list.

JESSE'S PULSE SETTLED back into its normal rhythm.

It was one thing to have Lori smile at his daughters, another to have her smile at *him*. And even with the remnants of Brooke's breakfast on the front of her shirt, she looked way too fetching.

Jesse pulled his unruly thoughts back in line.

Knowing how demanding the morning routine could be, he expected Lori would welcome a few minutes of alone time. But that wasn't the reason why, barring any unforeseen emergency on the ranch, Jesse had started the tradition of the ten o'clock break. It was important to give the nanny a break, but he also had his own, more selfish, reasons.

In order to get through the rest of the day, he needed to spend some time with his three favorite girls.

Jesse flopped down next to the quilt and carefully settled Sasha in the crook of his arm. His smallest daughter had gained weight over the past few months, but to Jesse, she still felt as fragile as spun glass.

When he brought Sasha home from the hospital, he'd been terrified to hold her—certain he'd either drop her or, worse yet, accidentally break her in half.

At the urging of the hospital social worker, he and Marie had taken a special class offered to the parents of pree-

mies. The staggering amount of information hadn't put
Jesse's mind at ease, but he'd waded through it anyway—
never dreaming that in a few short weeks he'd be raising
the triplets alone.

Jesse knew everything there was to know about ranching, but when it came to being a father, he felt completely
out of his element.

As the months went by and the girls showed no signs of
additional health complications, Jesse had relaxed a little.
But, nanny or not, he still checked on them at least once
during the night, and in the morning before he went out
to start his chores.

Draping Maddie between his knees, Jesse watched
Brooke wiggle away from him, intent on reaching one of
the colorful toys scattered on the quilt.

His gaze swept the room again and he couldn't believe
how much Miss Martin...*Lori*...had accomplished in just
a few hours.

The room even *smelled* better. Like cinnamon and ap-
ples.

When he'd heard the sound of Lori's voice coming from
the living room, he assumed she was on the telephone. But
as he got closer, he realized she was talking to the girls.
Hands planted on her slim hips, she'd been staring suspiciously at a fake fern and asking about a nanny cam.

The idea did have merit.

Modern technology like that would have come in handy
when he'd discovered Nanny Number Three sound asleep
on the couch while his hungry daughters wailed upstairs
in their cribs.

Clay implied that he'd been too critical of the women
he'd hired, but Jesse didn't know how he could be anything else. He worked long days, so the girls' caregiver
would have an enormous influence on them. She had to
be someone he could trust.

Someone like…Lori.

That he felt that way when he barely knew the woman surprised him. But there was something about her that instantly set her apart from the other nannies he'd hired. And fired.

Being an RN certainly qualified her to handle any medical emergencies that arose. She hadn't seemed upset by the fact that his daughters had decorated her clothing with their breakfast. And judging from the tantalizing smell filtering in from the kitchen, she knew how to make more than eggplant Parmesan.

And her smile…

He refused to think about her smile.

"We've got half an hour, ladies." Jesse turned his attention back his offspring. Much safer. "What would you like to do?"

In response to his question, Maddie began to gnaw on his knee and Sasha's tiny fingers closed around one of the buttons on the front of his shirt.

"Playtime. Got it."

For the next twenty minutes, Jesse let his world shrink to the size of the quilt spread out on the floor.

He cuddled Maddie, put together a chain of oversize plastic beads for Sasha and read a colorful cardboard copy of *Goodnight Moon* out loud. Three times.

Brooke had created a sport out of shedding her socks, so Jesse had to stop occasionally and wrestle them back on.

"It's footie pajamas for you tomorrow, Miss Logan," Jesse grumbled good-naturedly as he set Brooke in his lap once again and retrieved the tiny sock she'd discarded on her quest to reach the stuffed octopus Maya had bought as a coming-home present for the girls.

Brooke decided to protest the loss of her freedom and started to whimper. Like a chain reaction, Madison joined in, and then Sasha.

"You, too, sunshine?" Jesse reached for Sasha, whose forehead crumpled as she burrowed against his chest.

"If the three of you don't cheer up, You Know Who has to step in." Jesse eased Sasha out of his arms and laid her on the quilt next to her sisters.

The chorus picked up intensity.

"All right. You asked for it." Picking up the pink blanket an elderly member of High Plains Community Church had made for the girls, Jesse draped it over his head. "Don't say I didn't warn you. Here comes...*Flannel Man.*"

He roared the words—the girls always seemed to appreciate the drama—and made a growling noise deep in his throat. Shaking his head, he set the tassels on the blanket in motion.

Madison and Sasha stopped crying immediately, but Brooke, always his toughest critic, remained the last holdout.

Jesse dropped down on all fours. "Brooke Emmeline Logan—do you dare to challenge Flannel Man?"

Brooke's excited response not only drowned out the rest of the sentence but threatened to shatter the glass in the windows.

Jesse groaned and rolled onto his side. "I surrender. I surrender. Flannel Man has been vanquished."

Brooke's victory shriek rattled the china in the cabinet.

Three happy babies. Mission accomplished.

He peeked out from under the tassels of the blanket, just to make sure, and saw a pair of tennis shoes. A pair of tennis shoes with a glob of *something* spattered across the toes.

Lori.

Chapter Five

The living room was directly below the nursery, and Lori had just finished straightening up when she heard the girls begin to fuss.

She glanced at the clock. Ten-thirty on the dot. Nap time.

The commotion downstairs escalated, and the sound of a low but distinctively masculine growl—followed by a piercing shriek—turned Lori's knees to liquid.

Was Jesse...*scolding*...the girls? For simply doing something that all babies did?

Automatically, her feet carried her out the door and down the stairs. As Lori rounded the corner and rushed into the room she saw Jesse.

At least she was pretty sure it was Jesse.

Someone lay stretched out on the carpet next to the babies. Twitching. With a pink blanket over his head.

"Flannel Man is vanquished!" Jesse's dramatic groan drew another decibel-loaded shriek from Brooke.

Flannel Man?

Lori clapped a hand over her mouth as she took in the fascinating scene and ventured closer. Only Jesse's shadowed jaw was visible below a fringe of tassels.

Suddenly the tassels shook, his body stiffened and Jesse jackknifed into a sitting position.

"What is it?" He yanked the blanket off in one swift motion. Eyes as blue as star sapphires locked with hers, daring her to comment.

"It's been a half hour, so I thought I should…um, put the girls down for their nap now." Lori struggled to keep her expression neutral.

When they'd met the night before, she'd judged him to be an indifferent father, similar to the man who had raised her. And now she'd caught him *playing* with them. A silly, imaginative type of play which hinted that a sense of fun lurked below Jesse's serious exterior.

He rolled fluidly to his feet, anchoring his hands on his hips. The silky dark hair went every which way, and Lori fought a crazy, inexplicable urge to reach out and smooth the tousled strands back in place.

She shoved her hands into the front pockets of her jeans. *What. Are. You. Thinking?*

"A half hour?" Jesse shot a disbelieving look at the grandfather clock in the corner of the room and Lori could have performed a cartwheel when it backed up her claim and began to chime.

He crossed his arms. "Okay. Go ahead."

Lori recognized a test when she saw one. And a person with two arms and three babies to transport upstairs and put to bed definitely qualified.

Lori was tempted to ask if she could please deal with Flannel Man instead. He seemed a *teensy* bit more approachable.

Under Jesse's watchful eye, she put Madison in the portable playpen and bent down to scoop up Sasha and Brooke, settling one on each hip.

They immediately struck up an unhappy duet.

"I think they want Flannel Man to perform an encore." Lori chuckled.

Jesse didn't.

Okaay. No encores.

"I'll be right back for Maddie." Heart pounding in her ears, Lori took the girls upstairs and settled them into their cribs.

Without knowing the girls' naptime routine, Lori had to improvise. She found a floppy stuffed horse under Brooke's comforter and tucked it in the corner of the bumper pad where the baby could see it.

"Do you have a friend, too, Sasha? Where is she hiding?" Lori spotted the baby's pacifier, but there was no sign of a favorite toy.

"It's a white cat. On the floor under the crib."

Jesse stood several feet behind her, Madison sprawled in his arms, looking completely content.

Lori didn't know the household rules yet, but was tempted to create one of her own—Jesse had to leave his cowboy boots on when he came inside. At least the jingle of his spurs would warn her of his approach.

She reached out to take Maddie from him and settled the baby on her back in the crib. Even before Lori finished tucking the crocheted blanket around her, Maddie's eyes drifted closed.

"Thank you for bringing her upstairs." Lori kept her voice low so she wouldn't disturb the girls.

Jesse didn't answer and Lori followed the direction of his gaze to the window. Or rather, to what used to be in the cardboard box *underneath* the window.

"You used your break to put the changing table together?"

Lori caught her breath as Jesse stalked across the room. Probably to inspect her work.

"The directions weren't that complicated. And it came with one of those little black toolie things." Lori decided not to mention the plastic bag of "spare" parts left over from the project.

Jesse cleared his throat and looked away. "Are you referring to an Allen wrench?"

Had he almost...smiled?

When Jesse's gaze cut back to her and Lori saw his shuttered expression, she decided she must have imagined it.

"I guess so." Belatedly, it occurred to her that maybe she'd overstepped her boundaries. Or insulted him. After all, the changing table had sat unassembled for months, and she'd put it together in less than an hour. "I hope you don't mind, but you said I could use the time to do whatever I wanted."

For a few seconds the only sound in the room was the soft, rhythmic sound of the girls' breathing.

"I meant to get to it." Jesse sounded distracted as his hand traced the decorative edge of the wooden rail. "The tornado took out half the kitchen when it came through. I had to deal with that first."

His fingers closed around the rounded corner post and Lori noticed a thin band of white bisecting the sunwashed skin at the base of his ring finger.

The place where his wedding band had been.

Her heart clenched. Jesse had had so much to bear over the past few months. Marie Logan's death—the single fatality from the tornado—had hit the close-knit community hard, but Nicki had hinted that Jesse repeatedly rebuffed offers from people to help.

"It takes time to rebuild," Lori offered quietly. "To put things back together."

Jesse's teeth flashed but it couldn't be classified as a smile. "Some things are never the same."

"The same, no," Lori agreed without thinking. "But God has the power to make something new."

"I'm sure you speak from experience." Jesse's cynical tone implied just the opposite.

Lori bit her lip. She *did* speak from experience, but sensed Jesse would argue that her loss couldn't compare to his.

Maybe it didn't look the same, but she understood what it was like to move forward into an unknown future and trust that God would be there every step of the way.

The girls need a father who loves You, Lord. A father who believes that You can be trusted no matter what happens in their lives....

"I won't be able to come in for lunch today, but we can discuss the specifics of your job after supper," Jesse said abruptly. "I have to get back to work now."

Lori watched him stride from the room and a piece of her heart went with him.

It was becoming clear that the trials Jesse experienced had eroded the foundation of his faith. In his anger, he'd chosen to walk away from the only one who could heal the wounds of the past. He doubted that God loved him.

Lori briefly closed her eyes.

She understood that, too.

JESSE SLIPPED INTO THE HOUSE through the back door and took a detour to the laundry room.

So much for good intentions.

He'd promised Lori they would sit down together and go over the list of her responsibilities, but an emergency came up. He'd spent half the night in the barn, delivering a premature calf. Most of the fall calves had been born already, but a rancher could always count on having a few mamas who didn't do things by the book.

By the time Jesse discovered the cow in distress, the hired hands had already left for the day and Clay was on his way to High Plains to spend the evening with Nicki. Leaving Jesse to play midwife alone.

After several hours spent alternating between cheerleader and drill sergeant, he'd helped the exhausted mother bring a tiny but perfectly formed calf into the world.

Shrugging off his coat, he caught a glimpse of his reflection in the mirror above the laundry sink. Silently, he tallied up the damage. Hair damp with sweat, smudges of dirt on his face and bloodshot eyes. He didn't exactly smell like a red rose, either.

"I hate to say it, but that calf looked better than you do," Jesse told his reflection.

Fumbling with the buttons on his denim shirt, he stripped down to his T-shirt and tossed the offensive piece of clothing into the washing machine before Lori discovered it.

When he'd shown up for his morning play date with the girls, he noticed the clothes hanging on the baby swings had been folded and separated into three piles.

Another duty Lori had taken on that she shouldn't have.

Jesse didn't expect her to take care of everyone's laundry. He and Clay were big boys and could fend for themselves when it came to things like that. Something he would have brought up for discussion if they'd had the opportunity to talk.

Unfortunately, he hadn't been back to the house since Lori caught him—no, caught *Flannel Man*—surrendering to three seven-month-old babies.

The memory of being caught with a pink blanket on his head made Jesse wince.

So maybe it wasn't a game stamped with the official seal of parental approval, but he'd found out that whenever Flannel Man made an appearance, his daughters' tears miraculously dried up.

That was good enough for him.

But the sound of Lori's laughter when she'd teased him about the girls wanting an encore had lingered in Jesse's memory all day, like the melody of a song he couldn't get out of his head.

He turned on the faucet and cupped his hands under the stream of hot water, letting it wash away the blood stains and thaw out the joints in fingers stiff from the cold.

No matter how patient Lori seemed to be, Jesse doubted he was at the top of her list of favorite people now. After all, he'd hired her on the spot, without taking time to outline her duties, and then proceeded to abandon her—and his children—for the next ten hours.

And he'd skipped dinner.

If she thinks she's going to be responsible for everything around here, she'll be the first nanny you won't have to fire. She'll walk out the door all on her own.

Jesse dried his hands off on a towel and a familiar tightness constricted his chest as he made his way down the hall to the kitchen, hoping to scrounge up some leftovers.

The contractor he hired after the tornado had done a meticulous job reconstructing the kitchen, but Jesse still couldn't enter the room without reliving that day and the events that followed.

Since then, he avoided it as much as possible, choosing to eat meals in his office or on his way out the door. The room, once his favorite place to linger, now only served as a visible reminder of the things he'd lost.

His mother, Sara Logan, had always referred to the kitchen as "the heart of the home." Looking back, Jesse knew there had to have been some truth in that, because even though the old-fashioned parlor had been converted into a spacious, formal dining room before Maya was born, the entire family congregated in the kitchen instead.

It was there that Sara had created a welcoming oasis guaranteed to appeal to a weary husband, two growing boys and one horse-crazy daughter. They'd turn up there at various times throughout the day, lured in by the aroma of home-baked bread or a plate stacked high with crispy, paper-thin sugar cookies. The birds in the apple tree outside the window provided soothing background music. And more often than not, their mother would be sitting at the table when they came inside. Ready to talk…and listen.

When Jesse lay in bed at night, he could hear the soft murmur of his parents' conversation as the kitchen table became the connecting point between their days.

Every memory Jesse had of his mother was linked to the kitchen. Sara Logan's *heart of the home* had been a reflection of *her* heart. But in less time than it took to bridle a horse, the tornado had reduced it to a pile of stone and timber.

"An act of God."

Wasn't that what people called a tornado? Lori had sounded so convinced that God was in the business of rebuilding, but hadn't He been responsible for the storm's devastation in the first place? Jesus had calmed the winds once before—why had He turned his back on High Plains that day?

Why did He turn His back on me?

Jesse's footsteps slowed. Maybe he should skip the leftovers and spend an hour or two going over the budget instead. He remembered he'd left a jar of peanuts on the desk. If Clay hadn't gotten to them first.

"Jesse?"

Lori emerged from the kitchen and Jesse's thoughts scattered in a dozen different directions.

Dressed in loose-fitting gray sweatpants and a yellow T-shirt, she'd taken the braid out of her russet hair and it skimmed her shoulders like a glossy curtain.

How Lori managed to look as fresh and perky as she had when he'd seen her earlier that day was a complete mystery. In contrast, Jesse knew he looked as if he'd been forced through his grandmother's antique wringer washer. Backward.

"I thought you'd be asleep by now." Jesse couldn't help it that the words came out low and gritty, sifted through the gravel that suddenly filled his throat.

"You didn't come in for supper."

Jesse searched Lori's eyes, looking for signs of resentment as he braced himself for what would happen next. Lori would plead temporary insanity for giving up an eight-hour workday for a job with an absentee employer who required her presence 24/7. And expected her to cook, too.

And then didn't bother to show up for supper.

"I had to help a nervous mama deliver a calf." It was the truth, but as far as excuses went, Jesse figured Lori wouldn't accept it as a legitimate one.

Cows dropped calves all the time without assistance, but when that first-time mama had bellowed and rolled confused, mournful eyes in his direction, Jesse didn't have the heart to abandon her.

"I can understand that." Lori quickly corrected the statement with a soft laugh. "Oh, not the calf part. The nervous mama part."

The sound of her laughter blew holes in Jesse's defenses. Which explained why a few seconds later he found himself standing in the kitchen. A different kitchen than the one he'd been in that morning.

Lori hadn't simply straightened up the kitchen; she'd transformed it.

Jesse instantly recognized the lace tablecloth draped over the scarred surface of the oak table as one that his mother had used for company. Jesse's father had dabbled in woodworking and surprised her with the table as a gift for their tenth wedding anniversary.

The tornado had snapped off two of the legs, but Jesse

couldn't bring himself to add it to the pile of debris. Instead, he'd hammered it back together and returned it to its rightful place in the center of the room.

His gaze lingered for a moment on the candle that served as a centerpiece before moving to Lori, who stood at the counter dishing up something from the Crock-Pot.

"My favorite thing about one-pot cooking is that the food doesn't dry out, even if you can't get to it right away."

To Jesse's astonishment, Lori handed the plate to him. The tantalizing aroma of roast beef, red potatoes and baby carrots made him forget all about the bowl of peanuts on his desk.

He stood rooted to the floor until he felt the touch of Lori's hand under his elbow, guiding him to the table. She clucked her tongue.

"Sit down before you fall down, cowboy."

Chapter Six

Lori wasn't sure what shocked her more, her boldness or the fact that Jesse obeyed.

Needing a few moments to compose herself, she left him sitting at the table and made a beeline for the coffee-pot. Her hands trembled as she topped off one cup and poured a fresh one for Jesse.

She'd bathed the triplets and put them down for the night. Cleaned up the kitchen. Stashed a breakfast casse-role in the refrigerator for the next morning.

Everything had been under control—except, she ac-knowledged ruefully, her emotions.

"Are you sure you want to do this, Lori? Jesse Logan reminds me of a dog with its leg caught in a trap—so fo-cused on his own pain that he snaps at the people trying to help him."

Lori winced as the conversation she'd had with her for-mer supervisor at the hospital scrolled through her mem-ory. Janet Novak didn't believe in sugarcoating the truth, but Lori had always appreciated the fact that her boss was brave enough to speak it.

They'd talked on the phone shortly after the triplets had fallen asleep for the night. Janet was reluctant to accept her resignation, and asked Lori to consider using two weeks of her accumulated vacation time to determine whether she really wanted to give up her position at the hospital to be a full-time nanny.

Janet had also expressed reservations about the stability of the position and how Marie's death seemed to have changed Jesse. But instead of stirring up more doubts over the decision, her supervisor's caution only strengthened Lori's resolve.

After witnessing the way Jesse had playfully entertained his daughters that morning, Lori wanted to believe that below the painful experiences—the ones that had hardened like layers of sediment over Jesse's heart—was a man who could find hope again.

Until that happened, she would be there to love and care for the babies. And to pray.

But none of those things, she knew, explained why she waited up for Jesse to come in.

While restoring order to the kitchen, Lori tried to convince herself that she'd stayed up because she needed a clear definition of what was expected of her. More information about the triplets' schedule, pertinent details regarding directives from their pediatrician, special instructions.

But all it took to decimate her confidence was the sound of his footsteps in the hall.

And coming face-to-face with him?

More mustangs.

Beads of water clung to the tips of his tousled, dark hair, and glistened on the shadowed jaw, evidence he'd taken off the top layer of grime in the laundry room. In faded jeans and a plain white T-shirt that molded to the contours of his muscular torso, Jesse could have stepped off the cover of *Today's Cowboy*.

"Cream or sugar?" Lori waited until she was fairly certain her voice wouldn't come out in a squeak.

"No." Jesse paused. "Thank you."

The husky rumble of appreciation in his voice restored some of Lori's courage. She pulled out the chair opposite him and sat down. "You're welcome."

Their eyes met across the table and held for a moment until Jesse looked away.

The silence should have been uncomfortable, but for some reason, it wasn't. Maybe because Jesse tucked into his dinner with a masculine enthusiasm that made Lori glad she'd followed her instincts and put the roast in the Crock-Pot that morning.

"So…?" Jesse cleared his throat. "How did it go today?"

"Great."

"Great?"

"You sound surprised. What haven't you told me?" Lori grinned.

"Just about everything," Jesse muttered.

Lori figured that was as close to an apology as she was going to get. It would do for now.

"I understand emergencies," she said quietly. "They're a fact of life in the NICU. Let's consider today a practice run and start over tomorrow."

Jesse's chair suddenly scraped against the floor and his knee bumped the table, causing the flame of the candle to dance. "Thank you for keeping supper hot for me. It's been a long day, so maybe we should hold off on our meeting until tomorrow morning."

Jesse deposited his dishes in the sink and was on his way out the door before she had time to protest.

Lori had the strangest feeling he was running away.

But from what?

"MADE IT THROUGH the night, did you?" Jesse knelt down in the straw, mindful that Mama Cow had taken a protective stance over her calf. "Hey, I'm the one who helped you bring her into this world. Remember?"

Curious, the calf took a few wobbly steps closer, stretched out its neck and lipped Jesse's sleeve.

"Sorry." Jesse chuckled. "Breakfast is served over there." He tried to gently disengage the calf's mouth, but the touch of his hand spooked the tiny animal. It kicked up its heels and bolted.

Similar, he thought ruefully, to the way he'd responded the night before. He'd expected Lori to be angry that he hadn't kept their appointment. He hadn't expected...understanding.

Or a plate of hot food.

Sit down before you fall down, cowboy.

Lori's gentle humor had made it sound as if they shared a common purpose. That they were teammates rather than opponents.

But Jesse had grown accustomed to being alone.

He'd also grown accustomed to the bone-deep numbness that had settled into his soul and formed a seal around his heart after Marie's death.

Once Jesse had suffered a mild case of frostbite. When the feeling began to return to his fingers, the pain had been excruciating.

He'd relived the experience the night before.

For the first time since the tornado, he hadn't broken out into a cold sweat when he entered the kitchen—or been bombarded with painful memories. Instead, he'd felt enveloped in its warmth...and in the warmth of Lori's presence.

Let's consider today a practice run and start over tomorrow.

The trouble was, Jesse didn't know if he *wanted* to start over. And he didn't want to look too closely at the reason why.

If that made him a coward, Jesse could live with that.

He skipped breakfast, sent Clay out to feed the cattle

and started the morning chores, but at five minutes to ten, cowardice was no longer an option.

The phone started ringing when he walked into the house, so Jesse took a detour into his office to answer it. "Logan."

"This is Toby at Anderson Furniture Gallery—"

"You must have the wrong number."

The man must have sensed he was a split second away from talking to dead air. "Wait a moment! Is Lori Martin there?"

Of course she was, but Jesse had no idea where. Come to think of it, the house was unusually quiet. "I can take a message."

"Wonderful." Toby's relief was palpable. "Please tell her there is a fifty-dollar charge for deliveries outside the city limits."

"Delivery charge for what?" Belatedly, it occurred to Jesse that it really wasn't any of his business.

"Ms. Martin called yesterday to inquire about purchasing a rocking chair."

Jesse frowned. "I'll pass that on and have her call you back."

"Thank you, sir, and have a great—"

The phone clattered back in its charger.

A rocking chair?

As Jesse stepped out of his office, a bansheelike cry above his head pierced the silence.

Brooke.

He took the stairs two at a time and turned left when he reached the landing.

"Don't cry, sweetie."

Jesse's footsteps slowed.

Once Brooke started the waterworks, trying to stop them was like trying to prevent a river from overflowing its banks. His eldest daughter's penchant for drilling holes in peoples' eardrums was the reason why he'd let Nanny Number Four go.

He'd come in earlier than usual one morning to make a phone call and heard Brooke raising the roof. Knowing she'd been fussy during the night, Jesse immediately went to investigate and make sure everything was all right. Halfway to the nursery, he heard the nanny respond with a harsh imitation of Brooke's wail followed by several seconds of scolding.

By the time he reached the top of the stairs, Sasha and Madison had joined in.

Two hours later, Nanny Number Four moved out.

"Brooke…honey. It's all right."

Brooke's wail reached a crescendo, and Jesse peeked into the room, not sure what he'd see.

The sight in front of him wrenched out a smile before he could prevent it. Lori sat in front of Brooke's infant seat, waving her arms, the upper half of her body shrouded by a blanket.

"Look, sweetie. Here's…*Flannel Man.*"

Since the blanket didn't muffle the feminine, musical sound of Lori's voice, Jesse knew there would be no fooling the small audience watching her. Especially Brooke.

"Identity theft is a crime, you know."

At the sound of Jesse's voice, Lori wanted to scuttle into the closet and hide. If the man had fired a nanny for singing the "wrong" songs to the triplets at bedtime, her job was definitely on the line for impersonating a superhero.

She lifted the corners of the blanket and peeked out.

And saw Jesse…smiling.

Lori blinked several times to be sure. Just in case the blanket covering her head had somehow temporarily cut off the flow of oxygen to her brain and affected her vision.

No. Still smiling. An irresistible smile that softened the stern jaw and deepened the blue of his eyes to the color of a summer evening sky.

Her heart somersaulted in her chest as Jesse sauntered into the room. Lori would have stood up but had a hunch that her knees wouldn't support her. They felt a little… spongy.

But who could blame them?

After Jesse's abrupt departure during their conversation the night before, Lori had gone to bed wondering if she was on shaky ground. When she'd made her way to the kitchen to mix up the girls' bottles that morning, she discovered a note taped to the refrigerator. Evidence that Jesse had decided to save himself the time and trouble of an actual face-to-face meeting and condense her duties onto a three-by-five card instead.

"Giving Lori a hard time this morning, princess?" He knelt down in front of Brooke, whose tears evaporated like water on a hot skillet at the sight of her daddy.

"I was doing fine until you blew my cover," Lori muttered, rising to her feet with as much dignity as she could muster.

"It wouldn't have worked anyway." Jesse's words stopped her dead in her tracks as she made her way to the door. "You were missing Flannel Man's secret power source."

Lori turned around.

Was Jesse teasing her? It was difficult to tell, given the fact that his heart-stopping smile had come and gone as quickly as a shooting star.

She moistened her lips. "Secret power source? And what would that be?"

Jesse shrugged. "A secret."

Lori shook her head.

Of course it was.

"SOMETHING SMELLS DELICIOUS. Any chance I can try a sample?"

Lori chuckled at Clay Logan's hopeful expression as she took a pan out of the oven. "It's nothing fancy—just peanut butter brownies. The roast chicken is for supper tonight."

"Dessert?" Clay clapped his hand over his heart and pretended to stagger into the kitchen. "Roast chicken? Let me tell you something, Miss Lori. After two weeks of living on hamburgers and beans, that sounds pretty fancy to me."

Lori couldn't help but be warmed by the praise. Somewhere along the line, Clay had learned the importance of positive feedback.

Unlike Jesse. When it came to the eldest Logan brother, Lori was beginning to think that *not* being fired meant she was doing a good job.

"I found a box of recipes in the cupboard, and I hoped this one was a favorite." Lori nodded toward the decorative tin on the countertop, the one she'd accidentally stumbled upon during a quick inventory of the kitchen the day before.

The majority of the recipes were handwritten on traditional recipe cards, but several had been jotted down on scraps of paper.

"That looks like Mom's." Clay's smile faded slightly. "But I'm surprised Maya didn't take it when she moved into town after…"

His voice trailed off and the flash of pain in his eyes revealed an old hurt, leaving Lori at a loss for what to say.

"Maybe Maya didn't know the box was there," she suggested cautiously. "It was buried pretty deep in the back of the cabinet."

She hadn't lived in High Plains long enough to know all the details of his family history, but the night she'd volunteered in the nursery, Nicki had mentioned the Logans' parents had died together in a car accident years ago.

Oddly enough, although Clay was the one standing in front of her, Lori felt a rush of compassion for Jesse. He lost both parents and his wife…and for several days after the triplets' birth there'd been a question whether or not Sasha would survive.

No wonder the man's heart had gone into lockdown.

Unaware of her turbulent thoughts, Clay picked up the tin and his thumb grazed a trail over the top of the cards. A faint smile lifted the corners of his lips.

"When I was about six or seven, I remember Mom asking Grandma Logan to write down her recipe for Christmas fudge. Gram insisted she didn't have one, so Mom followed her around the kitchen with a pen and pencil, taking notes while she made it. Dad and Grandpa rounded us kids up and herded us into the den to watch television." He gave a low laugh. "If I remember right, Dad's exact words were 'children should see a fireworks display at the Fourth of July celebration, not Christmas.'"

The thread of affection in Clay's tone made it clear the adults had seen the humor in the situation.

"You must have a lot of good memories growing up here." Lori smiled wistfully. Over the past few years she'd come to accept that her own memories of "Christmas past" were best left there—in the past.

Clay's smile widened. "I remember the year we got a toboggan for Christmas. Mom and Dad had two rules. Rule one: no fighting over it. Rule two: Jesse got to sit in front and steer the thing because he was the oldest."

"But you wanted to."

"Good guess." Mischief danced in Clay's eyes. "I waited until everyone was busy and took my chance. Except things didn't go quite the way I expected. My foot got caught in the rope and the sled flipped over. By the time I got to the bottom of the hill I had a sprained wrist and a bloody nose—"

"And you sneaked up the hill to try it again the next day."

Lori felt the sudden drop in temperature, as if someone had opened a window. She didn't understand the tension that suddenly crackled in the air but she recognized its source.

Jesse.

Chapter Seven

The stare down between the two men lasted so long that Lori wondered if she was supposed to declare a winner. Instead, she aimed a bright smile in Clay's direction.

"Points for perseverance," Lori said, keeping her voice light. "What happened then?"

Clay dragged his gaze away from Jesse and shrugged. "My big brother stopped me."

Jesse's expression darkened. "That time."

The tick of the clock on the wall sounded as loud as a shotgun blast in the split second of silence that followed the words.

"That time," Clay agreed softly.

What on earth is going on? Lori thought. She deliberately stepped between them to draw Jesse's fire. "Is everything okay upstairs? I was just about to check on you and the girls."

"I put them down for their nap already. They seemed a little out of sorts this morning."

Mmm. Kind of like someone else she knew.

Jesse's gaze cut back to his brother. "Did you need something?" He managed to turn the simple question into a challenge.

"The vet called to let you know the shipment of antibiotics you ordered is in." Clay's tone remained even, but his hands clenched at his sides. "I can go into town and pick it up this afternoon."

Lori recognized an olive branch when she saw one. But what did Clay have to apologize for?

"Fine," Jesse finally said.

No "thank you, Clay." No softening of that granite jaw. No flicker of warmth in his eyes.

Lori wanted to smack her hand against her head. Or his.

Discouragement battled her earlier optimism. When Jesse interrupted Clay's story, Lori had assumed the tension between the two brothers was the result of a recent difference of opinion or misunderstanding.

But now something told her that its roots went deeper into the past.

Lori knew from experience the influence a child's environment could have on his or her life. How it colored their perspective. Influenced the way they viewed others…and themselves.

He's so focused on his pain he snaps at the people who are trying to help him.

But did that include his own brother?

Clay set the recipe tin back on the counter and gave her a polite nod. "Lori. You're doing a great job, but be sure to let us know if you need anything."

"I will." It was nice to know someone was on her side.

Jesse's scowl deepened. He didn't budge when Clay reached the door, and, for a split second, Lori was sure the two men were going to collide. At the last second, however, Jesse shifted his stance and Clay brushed past him.

"Excuse me." Lori decided it would be wise to follow Clay's lead. Before she grabbed a chair from the kitchen table and put Jesse in a time-out for rude behavior.

Instead of moving to the side the way he had for Clay, Jesse stepped in her path, effectively blocking her escape.

Lori's nose twitched and she suppressed a smile, finding it difficult to be intimidated by a man who smelled like baby powder. Not that intimidation was Jesse's intent, but the man did have a talent for imitating a thundercloud.

"You had a phone call. Someone named Toby from the furniture store."

The rocking chair she'd inquired about. And Jesse had taken the call. It was too late to wonder if maybe—just maybe—she should have discussed the addition of a new piece of furniture with him prior to calling Anderson Furniture Gallery.

"I'll call him back later." She tried to inch around him, but Jesse's gaze pinned her in place.

"Why do you need another rocking chair? We already have one."

He had to be kidding.

Was it possible he really didn't have a clue why she wanted a rocking chair in the nursery?

Lori searched his expression and saw...confusion.

Okay, maybe it was possible.

"Yes, you do," she agreed. "But it's in the living room."

Jesse didn't respond, obviously waiting for the rest of the explanation.

Burying a sigh, Lori obliged. "If one of the triplets wakes up in the middle of the night, I don't want to stumble all the way downstairs to rock her back to sleep."

Not to mention that said rocking chair was an enormous tweed rocker-recliner that looked as if it could easily swallow a hundred-and-fifteen-pound nanny whole. Or that she'd learned the hard way the night before that trying to slip out of the room to calm one baby somehow tripped an internal "triplet radar" that woke up the other two. Instead of comforting one baby, she'd had three to settle back down.

Jesse didn't look convinced.

"Is that what you usually do?" Lori made another valiant attempt to bridge the communication gap. "Bring them downstairs one at a time to rock them back to sleep?"

"No." Jesse tunneled his fingers through his hair and frowned. "They like to be boggled, not rocked."

"Boggled?"

A red stain worked its way up his neck and spread across his handsome features. "You know, a cross between a bounce and a…joggle."

Lori bit down on her lip to prevent a bubble of laughter from escaping. "Oh. Right. *A boggle.*"

"It works." Jesse crossed his arms.

Noting the defensive gleam in his eyes, Lori realized it probably wasn't the best time to point out that Sasha had been content to sit in her lap and rock for hours the night she'd helped Nicki in the church nursery.

But Jesse was the boss, and she was determined to break the nanny curse.

"I'm sure it does." Lori tamped down her disappointment. "And I'm sorry. I should have asked you about a rocking chair first. It won't be a problem to cancel the order."

"Is it fancy?"

Now it was Lori's turn to be confused. "Fancy?"

Jesse arched a brow. "The rocking chair?"

"Oh, no, not at all." Lori felt her freckles start to glow. "I saw it in the window display last week. It's maple, but it does have a pretty seat cushion." A horrifying thought occurred to her. Did Jesse think she was going to present him with the bill? "I don't expect *you* to pay for it, of course, because I'm the one who wanted—"

"There's a rocking chair up in the attic that belonged to my grandmother." Jesse cut through her rambling. "I can't guarantee what kind of condition it's in anymore, though."

"I'm sure it'll be fine." Lori tried not to let her excitement show. She had explored her new surroundings enough to be thoroughly charmed by the bits and pieces of Jesse's family history that added up to create a cheery warmth in his home. "Do you mind if I take a look?"

Jesse hesitated and then jerked his head toward the stairs. "Come on."

Now it was Lori's turn to balk. "I know you're busy. Just point me in the right direction and I'll find it."

"Indiana Jones would have a hard time finding it," he said dryly. "And I think I can spare a few minutes."

Jesse waited at the top of the landing while Lori took a quick peek at the triplets to make sure they were still asleep.

"We're good to go," she whispered, backing quietly out of the nursery.

Jesse gave a curt nod. "This way."

"This way" proved to be down the opposite hall and into a small bedroom.

It took Lori a split second to realize it belonged to Jesse. With a pang of guilt, she realized he'd given up the larger bedroom so she could be closer to the triplets.

"The staircase leading to the attic is in the closet." Jesse opened the doors and disappeared inside. "I haven't been up there since...for a few years...so I have to move some boxes out of the way."

Lori took advantage of his absence to study the room.

The simple, masculine décor reflected the man she was beginning to know, from the neat stack of books on the nightstand to the shoes lined up against the wall.

Just as she suspected, everything served a purpose and was displayed in its rightful place...except for the collection of picture frames shaped like flowers sprouting from the top of his dresser.

The splash of primary colors against the dark woodwork was so unexpected that Lori paused to take a closer look.

Judging from the girls' smiling, dimpled cheeks, she guessed the photos had been taken within the past month. Fascinated, Lori's gaze drifted to a daisy-shaped frame. Each "petal" held a miniature photo of the girls, but in the center was a picture of Jesse sitting in a leather chair, all three babies fanned out on his lap. He wasn't smiling—naturally—but the photographer had captured the mixture of love and pride on his face as he looked down at his daughters.

One of the frames on the dresser had fallen over, and automatically, Lori reached out to stand it back up.

Her heart missed a beat as she found herself staring at a close-up of Jesse and Marie. It must have been taken on their wedding day, although the ornate altar and soaring stained-glass windows didn't look familiar.

But then again, neither did the couple in the photo.

Marie, dressed like a fairy-tale princess in an elaborate satin, beaded gown, smiled at the camera while Jesse stared down at his bride with an adoring expression. His rugged features looked carefree rather than wary, the blue eyes warm and unguarded.

What happened between them? Why did Marie leave?

The questions tumbled over one another in Lori's mind.

Her brief interactions with Jesse's former wife at the hospital had been disturbing—a hint into the heart and mind of a woman desperately unhappy with her life.

Lori couldn't understand why. Most of her dreams had revolved around having a family. A loving husband. Children. A welcoming home. All the things Marie Logan had chosen to walk away from.

A loud thump followed by a muffled groan jerked Lori back to reality.

"Someday I hope I get the chance to ask Will Logan what he was thinking when he designed the house." Jesse poked his head out of the closet a split second after Lori set the frame down. "I guess we're set."

Lori peeked into the closet just in time to see Jesse swipe away a skein of filmy cobwebs in the doorway above his head. She shuddered. Maybe the tweed rocker-recliner in the living room wasn't so bad....

"Watch your head." Jesse started up the steps, his broad shoulders barely clearing the narrow stairwell.

And the rest of me, Lori silently added, as one of the wooden planks bowed beneath her weight.

Jesse paused suddenly and twisted around to look at her. "Be careful when you get to the top. The last step is a bit of a challenge."

Lori looked past him and squinted into the shadows. "I don't see a...last step."

"That's why it's a challenge." Jesse's elusive smile flashed in the gloom.

Lori swallowed hard. Jesse's smile should be accompanied by a warning from the surgeon general. Twice in one day was about all her heart could take.

"You can do it. Take my hand." Jesse must have thought it was fear that kept her frozen in place, when his smile was to blame.

Lori took a deep breath as Jesse's fingers closed around hers. She felt the gentle scrape of calluses against her palm...and the little pulses of electricity that danced up her arm.

Jesse's breath hissed between his teeth.

Shaken, she wondered if he'd felt it, too.

As soon as Lori's feet connected with the floor, Jesse let go of her hand and stalked away. Lori willed her knees to keep her upright.

She couldn't be attracted to Jesse. God had brought her to the ranch for the triplets. To make sure they grew up knowing they were loved.

Jesse does love his daughters.

The thought swept in and Lori silently acknowledged the truth in it. The man could be as tough and unyielding as a piece of cold leather, but in the presence of those babies, Lori caught a glimpse of another side of him. A softer side.

But she hadn't thought of it as a *dangerous* side. At least not where she was concerned.

Until now.

JESSE COULDN'T look at Lori.

Not that *not* looking at her made a bit of difference. Especially when the light floral scent she favored had followed him to the opposite corner of the attic. And every nerve ending in his body still tingled from the simple touch of her hand.

Jesse stifled a groan.

He didn't *want* to feel anything. Been there, done that— and had the open wounds to prove it. Even the people closest to him had lacked staying power—and there had to be a reason.

Who was he kidding? *He* was the reason.

"It looks like a flea market up here!"

Jesse heard Lori's muffled voice, but all he could see was the top of her head as she worked her way through the maze of discarded furniture and boxes. He dragged his gaze away from the gold threads the overhead light illuminated in her hair. He took a quick inventory of his surroundings and discovered that Lori was right.

Marie preferred a more contemporary style, so she had

started to replace the contents of the house with more modern furnishings. Jesse had encouraged her, hoping she would feel more at home, but he hadn't realized until now how many things had been banished to the attic.

"I think I found it!" There was no mistaking the lilt of excitement in Lori's voice. "Come and look."

In order for Jesse to "look," he had to be closer to her. Which meant he had to stop hiding in the corner with the spiders.

Working his way over to Lori, he found her on her knees. Eyes shining as she used the hem of her shirt to brush away the dust coating the seat of a rocking chair.

He shook his head. "Wrong one."

"What do you mean?"

"I forgot about this one, but I'm pretty sure it came in on the wagon train with Emmeline. The family founders passed on the pack-rat gene, I'm afraid. We never get rid of anything."

"You shouldn't." Lori looked dismayed at the suggestion. "Oh, it's not the things themselves that are so important, but the stories they tell. They're connected to your family history, and as the girls get older, you'll be able to share the stories behind them." Her voice softened. "They won't have to struggle to figure out who they are and where they fit. They'll know."

If only it were that simple, Jesse thought. He wasn't even sure where *he* fit anymore.

He stared down at the chair, not wanting Lori to see how her words had affected him. She made it sound like a positive thing—sharing the Logan family history with his daughters.

What stories will you tell them? A mocking voice infiltrated his thoughts. *How about the night you and Clay argued and he left the ranch for good?*

He hadn't meant to eavesdrop on Clay and Lori's conversation in the kitchen, but when Jesse heard his brother putting a humorous spin on the toboggan incident, anger had welled up inside of him.

His perspective of that day differed a bit from his brother's.

Clay's little adventure with the sled and the subsequent trip to the emergency room had resulted in their parents' disappointment—with *him*. His mother and father never came right out and said it, but as the older, responsible one in the family, Jesse had been forced to shoulder the unwelcome burden of keeping his younger sibling out of trouble. Trouble that had only multiplied as Clay's spirited antics eventually spiraled into full-blown rebellion—and ultimately led to the tragedy that had cracked the foundation of their family.

Were those the stories he was supposed to pass on?

"Jesse?"

His skin jumped at the tentative touch of Lori's hand on his arm. But what stunned him even more was the compassion in her eyes—as if she could read his troubled thoughts. As if she *understood*.

But how could she? Lori hadn't experienced the devastating losses he had. She appeared to have a strong faith, but Jesse doubted it had been tested to the point where she felt as if she'd stumbled into a place beyond God's hearing. Beyond His reach.

A few weeks after the tornado struck High Plains, Jesse overheard a customer at the feed store admit that every time the sky clouded over he couldn't help but stare at the horizon. Waiting for the next funnel cloud to appear.

Jesse could relate. Only, he wasn't waiting for the next storm to arrive—he was waiting for the next person he cared about to leave.

Lori swallowed hard.

She'd touched Jesse. *On purpose.* Knowing he wasn't a man who sought out help or comfort.

Offering encouragement had been part of her job in the NICU but this felt different. This was…*Jesse.* Lori wanted to do something—say something—to coax him away from the ledge of dark memories that had drawn him in. To remind him that he wasn't alone.

Amazingly enough, it worked. The bleak look in Jesse's eyes faded, replaced by a wariness that told Lori his defenses were back up and running. Now that she had his attention, she wasn't sure what to do with it!

"This rocking chair will be fine, don't you think?" She casually withdrew her hand from Jesse's arm—ignoring the current rocketing down to her toes—and set the chair in motion.

"It doesn't look very sturdy."

Lori's training kicked in, and while he watched, she gave the chair a brief but thorough examination. "One of the spindles is a little loose, but I should be able to glue it."

"Right." Jesse's expression was skeptical. "And you'd somehow manage to fit that in between taking care of the triplets, making home-cooked meals and restoring the house to its original state of disrepair."

Lori caught her lower lip between her teeth and peeked up at him from underneath her lashes. Guilty as charged. "You noticed that, huh?"

"I noticed."

He noticed, but it was difficult to tell from his expression whether or not he approved.

"According to the three-by-five card taped to the refrigerator, I do have some free time in the evenings," Lori reminded him. "And I have a ten o'clock break every morning…*and* Sundays off."

Jesse's eyes narrowed. "That's *your* time. To relax and regroup."

"Great." She gave him a sunny smile, dusted her palms against her jeans and reached for the rocking chair. "Because I find all those things you just mentioned *very* relaxing."

Chapter Eight

"What are you doing?"

Lori's foot slipped off the rung of the ladder. If the sound of Jesse's voice hadn't been enough to send her into cardiac arrest, the steadying touch of his hand against her leg a split second later packed enough power to finish her off.

Her breath stuck in her throat.

"I'm hanging up this...garland." The garland that had slipped out of her hand and drifted to the floor before she could finish threading it through the brass chandelier.

"That's funny. It looked to me like you were trying to break your neck," Jesse growled up at her.

The ladder *was* a bit rickety, but Lori wanted to argue she'd been doing just fine until he'd blown in like an early winter storm.

Early being the key word.

She'd hoped to have the house completely transformed by the time he returned. To surprise him.

Well, mission accomplished, Lori thought, as she delicately shifted her weight to regain her balance. Jesse did look surprised. Just not *pleasantly* surprised.

Something she should have gotten used to by now.

A week of living in Jesse's house had driven Lori to cross-stitch her "I can do all things through Him who strengthens me" verse from Philippians 4:13 on a book-mark she tucked in her bible. But as an extra reminder, she'd written it on a three-by-five card and taped it to the refrigerator—next to the one Jesse had put up outlining her duties!

The man was turning out to be a study in contradictions. Just when she thought she had Jesse figured out, he did something completely unexpected. Like offering a helping hand. Or smiling.

No matter how tired or preoccupied Jesse looked when he came into the house at ten o'clock every morning, when Lori showed up a half hour later, he seemed...rejuvenated. As if he needed the time with his daughters as much if not more than they did.

He would disappear into his office every evening after supper but reappear in time to help her bathe the triplets and get them ready for bed—something Lori hadn't expected when he'd hired her as a live-in nanny.

Ever since the day they'd gone up in the attic to find the rocking chair, she and Jesse, out of necessity, formed a tentative alliance. But every time their paths crossed, the interaction reminded Lori of the couples on those popular television dance competitions, who had to learn the steps of a new dance together. Sometimes the result was awkward. Sometimes humorous. And sometimes it was downright painful.

Considering the expression on Jesse's face, Lori had a feeling this was going to be one of the downright painful encounters. Because, once again, it looked as if she'd stepped on his toes.

"Could you please hand me that piece of garland?" Lori decided to bluff her way through. A misstep was only a misstep if a person couldn't recover quickly enough to make it look like part of the routine.

Jesse reached down and picked up the length of artificial balsam, studying it with the same suspicion he might a chunk of meteor he found smoking in the pasture. "Where did this come from?"

"I saw a box of Christmas decorations in the attic when we were looking for the rocking chair. Umm, where are the girls, by the way?"

Her pathetic attempt to distract him failed.

"Maya asked if she could keep them a few more hours. She's going to bring them back later this evening." His gaze broke away from her and zeroed in like a laser pointer on each new addition to the décor. The ceramic ginger-bread village, with its miniature figurines that now pop-ulated the mantel. A hand-carved nativity scene on the coffee table. The old spinning wheel Lori had wrestled down the stairs and, in a burst of creativity, embellished with a spray of artificial holly berries.

She'd also started a fire in the fireplace, more to pro-vide a welcoming atmosphere than to chase the chill out of the room.

Finally, Jesse's inventory was complete, and he looked up at her. "It's Sunday."

"Yes, it is." Lori knew that. She and Clay had driven into town together to meet Nicki and Kasey at High Plains Community for the morning worship service. Maya and Greg had been there, too, with Layla and Tommy in tow. Maya had mentioned that Jesse accepted her invitation to spend the afternoon with them, but Lori hadn't realized the triplets would be enjoying an extended visit with their aunt.

"Your day off," he added.

She knew that, too. It was on the three-by-five card. "Am I putting up the decorations too soon?"

"Too soon?" Jesse repeated the words. "No, what I meant to say was that it wasn't necessary."

"But…it's the triplets' first Christmas."

A shadow skimmed across Jesse's face before he

averted his gaze. "They won't remember it. I didn't expect you to go to all this trouble."

Maybe the babies were too young to appreciate—or remember—their first Christmas, but that didn't stop Lori from wanting to make it special.

Her brave foray back to the attic reminded her a little of Christmas morning, yielding an incredible bounty of treasures buried inside those dusty boxes.

Along with the traditional glass balls, she'd discovered a box containing fragile handmade ornaments—three small handprints preserved in plaster of Paris. Each one had a name written on the back—Jesse, Clay and Maya. Underneath those, carefully protected by a layer of crisp paper snowflakes, was a team of clothespin reindeer, complete with pom-pom noses and toothpick antlers.

Not sure what to display, she'd made three trips up and down the stairs and brought everything down. And once she started unpacking boxes, it had been difficult to stop.

"It's no trouble," she said softly, tempted to add that she was looking forward to the days counting down to Christmas.

For the past few years, with nowhere to spend the holiday, she volunteered to take extra shifts. It gave her a sense of satisfaction to know that, in a small way, giving her time that way meant someone else would be able to spend Christmas with their loved ones.

But this Christmas would be different. It would be the kind of Christmas she'd always dreamed of. She'd already found several recipes she wanted to try—including the one for Grandma Logan's Christmas fudge—and she decided to wrap white lights and garland around the staircase banister.

"Still, I—"

"Special delivery!" A cheerful bellow drowned out

Jesse, as Clay poked his head inside the door and grinned at Lori. "Seven feet tall. And as big as a round bale of hay."

"You brought a tree." In her excitement, Lori practically slid down the ladder....

And landed smack dab in the warm circle of Jesse's arms.

The top of Lori's head bumped against Jesse's chin. His arms automatically went around her slender frame as he put out one foot to keep his balance.

Too bad that only worked on the *outside*. Because Lori's unique fragrance—the one that reminded him of wildflowers—was already creating havoc on the inside.

"Sorry," Lori gasped, eyes wide as she twisted in his arms and stared up at him. "Are you all right?"

Not even close, Jesse thought as he silently willed his hands to let go of her.

Over the past week, he'd tried to maintain a safe distance between them, but he was beginning to suspect there was some kind of conspiracy to thwart that plan.

For one thing, all three of his precious daughters had taken to expressing their displeasure—rather loudly—whenever Lori left the room. Not even Flannel Man could cheer them up. Jesse knew he should have been relieved the girls had bonded with their new nanny so quickly... if he also hadn't noticed they seemed to be the most content when he and Lori were *both* in the room with them.

And out of sheer necessity, he and Lori were together. A lot.

The triplets' presence at dinner kept everyone's attention focused on them, and after the meal Jesse could escape to his office or the barn. But later in the evening he and Lori joined forces to carry out what she had cheerfully dubbed the "three Bs." *Baths, bottles and blankies.* Jesse would have described it as the hour and a half of absolute pandemonium that preceded the triplets being tucked into their cribs for the night.

That Lori was able to have a sense of humor about a challenging triathlon involving wriggling *wet* babies— followed by wriggling *hungry* babies—had made it even more difficult to maintain the safe distance that Jesse thought he needed to be, well…safe.

The kitchen Jesse had spent the past five months avoiding once again welcomed him when he stopped in for a break or to have lunch. But it wasn't just hot coffee and the promise of Lori's cooking that caused him to linger. He was becoming uncomfortably aware that lately he found himself looking forward to seeing Lori during the day.

No matter where Jesse went, he could hear the sound of her warm laughter flowing through the house, eroding his determination to keep their relationship strictly employer and employee.

It was one of the reasons he'd accepted Maya's invitation to spend the afternoon with her family and let Lori enjoy her day off—he wanted to make sure the boundaries were firmly in place. For his sake more than hers. But he hadn't expected Lori to use her afternoon off to transform his home into a Christmas wonderland.

"I can't believe you brought us a tree." Lori practically skipped across the room toward Clay. "I wasn't sure when I'd have a chance to drive into High Plains and get one."

"You can thank my fiancée. She mentioned the two of you had a long conversation about the perfect tree after church this morning. When we took Kasey to pick one out after church, Nicki saw this one and thought of you." Clay swept off his hat. "I would have been home sooner, but Greg, Reverend Garrison and I decided to volunteer at the Old Town Hall for a few hours."

Jesse waited for his brother to comment on the fact that he'd declined an invitation to join the work crew, but Clay just looked around the room and grinned. "Wow. You've been busy today, too. It looks great in here."

"Really?" Lori's smile bloomed and Jesse felt another hard pinch to his conscience. Instead of complimenting her efforts, he'd told her that she shouldn't have bothered. "I hope the decorations don't make the room look too crowded."

The corners of Clay's lips kicked up. "Nope—it reminds me of the way the house looked when we were kids. Mom pulled out all the stops at Christmas. Dad always teased her by saying she was trying to compete with the North Pole."

This was the second time Jesse had heard his brother fondly reminisce about their childhood and he couldn't believe how selective his brother's memory was. Had Clay conveniently forgotten all the Christmases he'd been a no-show after their parents had died, ignoring Maya's tearful pleas for him to come home?

"Well, where do you want the tree?" Clay sauntered into the room and propped his hands on his hips. "Are you planning to decorate it tonight?"

"I can't find the stand. It wasn't in the attic with the rest of the things."

"Jesse probably knows where it is."

Both Clay and Lori turned toward him, and Jesse tried unsuccessfully to steel himself against the avalanche of memories that Clay's little side trip down memory lane had triggered.

Growing up, Christmas had always been a big deal, but their parents had never let the busy pace and gift-giving get buried under the real reason they were celebrating. Neil and Sara Logan's faith had been an integral part of all the preparations, from the extra baking their mother dropped off to elderly members of the congregation to curling up on the sofa together on Christmas Eve and listening to their father read the story of Jesus's birth from the book of Luke.

After living alone for so long, Jesse had looked forward to sharing the holiday with Marie, hoping that, as a couple, they could resurrect some of the family traditions he'd put aside while concentrating on the ranch.

But the first Christmas they'd spent together as husband and wife had been Jesse's wake-up call to the differences in their family backgrounds.

He had agreed to spend the holiday with Marie's parents because he knew how much she missed them. But in the Banner mansion, the house was decorated by a professional, who changed the "theme" every year. Marie's family didn't even trim the tree together, one of Jesse's favorite traditions. He could have dealt with that if it hadn't been for his new wife's complete indifference toward anything related to the true meaning of the day. She'd paid more attention to what her friends were wearing at the Christmas Eve service than the sermon.

They ended up arguing most of the drive back to High Plains, and Marie refused to speak to him for two days.

Merry Christmas.

Jesse averted his gaze. "No, Jesse doesn't know where the Christmas tree stand is."

At his abrupt response, Clay's eyebrows disappeared under the brim of his Stetson. Jesse didn't care. He wasn't ready to think about Christmas. Or pretend to look forward to Christmas. Not this year.

But apparently he was in the minority.

The whole town had pitched in over the past few months to rebuild the Old Town Hall. The mayor and Reverend Garrison hoped to have the project finished in time to commemorate Founders' Day with a special potluck and dance on Christmas Eve followed by a community celebration Christmas Day.

Jesse couldn't scrape up the desire to attend either one, and had turned down an invitation to speak at the gathering. Even though Mayor Lawson had reminded him that as a direct descendent of Will Logan, the man who had driven a stake in the ground near the High Plains River on Christmas day in 1858, people would expect him to attend.

Just the way Clay and Lori expected that he knew where to locate a tree stand on a moment's notice.

He cast an impatient look at his brother. "I don't know where it is because I haven't put up a tree for years. That's why I told Lori she shouldn't have gone to all this trouble. I usually spend Christmas at Maya's and I assume Lori will be going home."

The color drained out of Lori's face and Jesse took a step forward, concerned at the sudden change in her expression.

The oven timer in the kitchen pierced the sudden silence.

"Lori? Is something wrong?" Clay asked.

"No." She ducked her head and moved toward the door, refusing to meet their eyes. "I…need to check on something in the oven. Please excuse me."

She slipped out of the room and Clay aimed a scowl at Jesse. "What was that about?"

"I have no idea. You were standing here, too." Disturbed, Jesse listened to the sound of Lori's footsteps in the hall.

Clay's eyes flashed. "It's obvious you won the part of Scrooge this year, but I don't see why it should bother you that Lori wants to decorate the house or put up a tree."

"It isn't about that. It's about her taking time for herself," Jesse shot back, still shaken by the expression on Lori's face. "I know how demanding the triplets can be. Correct me if I'm wrong, but Lori deserves a day off."

"Since you're giving me permission, I will correct you."

Clay met his gaze without flinching. "Because I thought having a day off meant doing what you want to."

"It does." Jesse frowned. Hadn't he just *said* that?

"So..." Clay drew out the word in a way that made Jesse's back teeth grind together. "Did it occur to you that maybe Lori was doing exactly what she wanted to do on her day off?"

"Extra work? Work she didn't need to do?" Jesse raked a hand through his hair. "You see how hard Lori pushes herself around here. If she doesn't slow down a little she's going to burn out and—"

Quit.

Jesse's mouth dried up, preventing the word from tumbling out. And hard on its heels rode another thought. He didn't *want* her to quit.

The speculative gleam that appeared in his brother's eyes made Jesse wonder if Clay hadn't filled in the blank.

"Listen, I don't claim to understand women—"

"That's a relief," Jesse muttered under his breath.

Clay ignored the comment. "All I'm saying is that what you consider extra work might not be work at all, from Lori's perspective. Think about it this way—we love the ranch even though the long hours and the constant demands would suck the life out of most people. To us, though, it gives back more than it takes. If I had to guess, I'd say that's the way Lori feels about taking care of you and the girls. You hired her to run the house but she's turning it back into a home."

That thought didn't terrify Jesse as much as the longing that unfurled inside a dormant chamber of his heart. He'd made the mistake of reaching for that dream once. Before he knew what it felt like to lose everything.

"I didn't hire her to do that. I don't *need* her to do that." If he said the words out loud, maybe it would make them true. His head knew it, but for some reason his heart stubbornly—and unexpectedly—refused to agree.

Clay blew out a sigh. "Maybe it's what *Lori* needs. Did you think about that? Nicki mentioned she was totally devoted to her job at the hospital—a job she gave up at a moment's notice to come here. Did you ever stop to ask yourself—or her—*why?*"

Without waiting for an answer, his brother stalked out of the room.

Chapter Nine

The sudden silence brought quiet but not peace.

Maybe it's what Lori needs.

Clay's words repeated in Jesse's head as he slumped down on the sofa and closed his eyes. Big mistake. His memory took advantage of the momentary lapse in his defenses to replay part of the conversation that had taken place in the attic.

The day he'd asked—with a touch of sarcasm that now made him wince—how she planned to find time to fix the rocking chair in between taking care of the triplets, cooking and bringing the house back to life. Lori had smiled and claimed she enjoyed doing all those things. That she found them relaxing.

But he hadn't listened. Hadn't wanted to believe it.

The image of her stricken face popped back in his mind and the next breath Jesse took actually *hurt*.

What had he said?

He lurched to his feet and got tangled in the handle of a canvas bag beside the sofa. Shaking it free, he accidentally released a ball of yarn. By the time Jesse chased it down, it had rolled under the coffee table and was about to disappear under the recliner.

"Gotcha." Jesse snagged it and started to wind up the loose strand. It led him back to a pair of knitting needles stuck in what looked to be a Christmas stocking still under construction. Jesse was no expert, but even he could see the level of skill it had taken to add a name above the prancing horse with a garland of holly around its neck.

Brooke.

On a hunch, he rummaged through the contents of the bag. Inside he found another one depicting a sweet-faced angel and bearing Sasha's name. There was also an enormous ball of sparkly white-and-gold yarn he guessed would soon take shape and become a stocking for Maddie.

Jesse felt the truth slap him upside the head.

He'd assumed the nanny he hired would carry out the list of duties posted on the refrigerator and take advantage of the free time in her schedule to live her own life. He hadn't expected one who not only gave a hundred percent of her time and energy to his daughters but also freely opened her heart to them.

Loved them.

The fog of pain Jesse had been living under lifted briefly, and he wondered why a woman as sweet and giving as Lori didn't have children of her own. Why didn't she have a husband who loved her to distraction? Who started and ended the day with her in his arms?

Jesse ruthlessly squelched the memory of the way Lori had fit perfectly in his arms.

Further proof that he needed to keep his distance.

If Jesse were honest with himself, he knew his negative, knee-jerk response when he'd found Lori decorating the house for Christmas hadn't sprung so much from bittersweet memories of his parents as it had from fear. Fear that he was getting used to things he shouldn't. Dangerous things. The sound of Lori humming softly to his daughters as she got them ready for bed. Having someone to share a smile with over the triplets' antics. A light glowing in the kitchen window that drew him in like a weary traveler when he walked back to the house after finishing the evening chores.

A woman like Lori deserved a man whose heart hadn't been shredded with shrapnel from his past. A man who believed in love, not someone who knew all too well how fleeting that particular emotion could be.

HOME FOR CHRISTMAS.

Lori's vision blurred as she took the steaming pan of corn bread out of the oven and sank against the counter.

It wasn't as if she could blame Jesse for assuming she had a home to go back to.

She'd found that most people didn't ask about her extended family. The few times her coworkers, when discussing their own holiday plans, had asked her when she was going home, Lori would simply explain that her parents had divorced years ago and now lived on opposite sides of the country. Leaving her in the middle.

To Lori, it seemed as if she'd been caught in the middle most of her life. Caught between two unhappy people who seemed to agree on only one thing—that once the "duty" of raising her ended, they would be free to live their own lives.

And they had.

She received the obligatory Christmas card from her mother every year and a phone call on her birthday, but the letters she'd sent to her father had been returned with no forwarding address.

The lack of warmth in the house where she'd grown up had fostered her childish dreams of a day when things would be different. She would create her own home—a place where everyone who stepped through the door would feel welcomed. Special. *Loved.*

But this isn't your home, she chided herself. *It's Jesse's.*

And if he doesn't want you to spend Christmas here, then you have to find somewhere else to go.

If she talked to Reverend Garrison, Lori was sure he could connect her with an organization that needed volunteers to serve meals to shut-ins or the homeless on Christmas Day. There were hurting people everywhere who needed an encouraging word or someone to spend time with them. She could be that person. She'd done it for years.

So why didn't acknowledging that lift the weight pressing down on her heart?

Because this year you want things to be different. You want to be with the triplets on Christmas.

The truth filtered into her thoughts and just as Lori accepted it, another one followed close behind.

And you want to be with Jesse.

Lori pushed away from the counter, wrapping her arms around her middle as she took a distracted lap around the kitchen table and tried to push away the errant thought.

The light-headed, fizzy feeling that came over her whenever Jesse walked into the room simply meant that he was a handsome guy and she happened to be blessed with twenty-twenty vision.

Keeping a professional distance from a man who held everyone at arm's length should have been easy. If it weren't for the fact that over the past few days, when Jesse lowered his guard, she'd caught fascinating glimpses of a man who had the capacity to care deeply.

His more playful side came out when he interacted with the triplets, and his commitment to family was evident in the daily phone conversations he had with Maya. And although tension obviously existed between him and Clay, the thinly veiled regret she saw in Jesse's eyes whenever Clay was in the room told Lori he had a desire to make things right with his brother.

Jesse might act as if past experiences had stripped his heart bare, but Lori knew all it needed was some tending. There was still life there.

If only Jesse would recognize how much God loved him and wanted to fill the empty places that each loss had gouged out of his soul, he would have a great capacity to love.

And he would be easy to…love.

The thought that maybe, just maybe, she was already halfway there terrified her.

When Lori allowed herself to daydream about her future husband, she had always pictured a man who laughed easily and was never stingy with his affection. The opposite of her father. And even though she couldn't compare the two men, she knew that Jesse didn't trust easily.

It was the reason he'd fired five nannies before hiring her out of sheer desperation. The reason he rebuffed Clay's offers to take on more responsibility for the ranch.

The reason why getting close to him would be risky. And Lori was no risk taker. At least she hadn't been, until the day she set down her suitcase in Jesse Logan's driveway.

Her growing feelings for her employer were a complication she'd have to pray about. But at the moment, all she wanted to do was escape the cloud that had settled over her when he told Clay that she would want to spend Christmas at "home."

The irony? She'd been pretending that's where she was.

Lori blinked back the tears that stung the backs of her eyes. Jesse's reaction when he'd discovered her decorating the house couldn't have made it any clearer. He expected her to stick to the duties outlined on the index card.

As if Lori's feet had an agenda of their own, they carried her out of the kitchen and down the hall. She grabbed her jacket off the hook near the back door and slipped outside.

As busy as the triplets kept her during the day, Lori hadn't taken time to explore the ranch. Jesse had once suggested she use her free time to take a walk, so she decided to take him up on it.

As she came around the corner of the house, Jesse's dogs, Max and Jazz, bounded up to greet her. She'd seen the pair of Australian shepherds chasing each other around the barn on occasion, but hadn't had an opportunity to introduce herself properly.

"Are you going to give me a tour?" Lori reached down to ruffle one set of silky, speckled ears and then the other as the animals vied for her attention.

One of the dogs barked an affirmation and Lori chuckled, feeling her mood lift slightly. "Okay, then. Lead the way."

Maybe some fresh air would give her a fresh perspective. And while she prayed that Jesse would open his heart to God's love, maybe He would give her some wisdom so she would know what to do about her own.

SHE WAS GONE.

Jesse looked in the kitchen and saw a pan of golden-brown corn bread cooling on the countertop and a kettle of chili simmering on the back burner, but there was no sign of Lori.

He bounded up the stairs but found the nursery empty, too. When he finally scraped up the courage to rap on her bedroom door, there was no response.

Where *was* she?

Panic scoured the lining of his stomach and Jesse hesitated in the hallway, unsure of where to look next. Or if he *should* look.

Clay had disappeared, too, so he couldn't ask him if

knew where Lori might have gone. Not that Jesse would have risked getting another lecture from his younger brother. He wasn't used to Clay standing his ground and sharing his opinion about something.

Jesse walked to the nearest window and looked outside to see if Lori's car was still parked next to the barn. His relief at seeing the bright blue compact didn't completely dispel his growing concern over her disappearance.

He retraced his steps, forced to face the fact that Clay's insight into the reason behind Lori's actions may have been right.

He wasn't used to that, either.

In the past, Clay had operated under the "when the going gets tough, the tough take off" motto. The little brother Jesse had grown up with had been impulsive. Slow to think things through and quick to act.

That was part of the problem. Jesse was having a hard time relating to Clay because he was no longer a boy. Growing up, the Circle L had formed the foundation of their relationship. When Clay stormed away and turned his back on the ranch that night, they'd lost their common ground.

"You're still brothers."

Something Maya had reminded him that afternoon. Jesse had never understood her unwavering belief that God would eventually help Clay find his way home and their family would be together again.

Now that they were, the rules had changed. *They'd* changed.

With tears in her eyes, his sister had pleaded with Jesse to start over with Clay. Jesse wasn't sure he could. In order to start over, didn't a person have to let go of the past? Or maybe, in his case, the past had to let go of *him*. Sometimes Jesse felt as if there were shackles around his feet, preventing him from moving freely. From moving forward.

Maya would say that's where God came in, but Jesse's faith had been so weakened, he no longer trusted it to hold him up, or to fill the empty pocket in his soul when someone else he cared about walked out of his life.

Right. That's why it's so much easier to push them away first.

Jesse blamed the sudden tightening in his chest on the unnatural quiet filling the house. He took the stairs two at a time and glanced into the living room. The logs in the fireplace had burned down to a glowing nest of coals, and even though the decorations gave the room a festive look, something was missing.

Or someone.

Someone to whom he owed an apology for whatever it was that he'd done that had snuffed the sparkle out of a pair of wide brown eyes.

If he could *find* the someone.

Jesse opened the front door and found his view obstructed by the monstrous evergreen that took up half the porch.

What had his lunatic brother been thinking? They'd be lucky if the thing would fit through the doorway.

Turning sideways, Jesse pushed through it, wincing as needles jabbed through the faded denim fabric of the shirt he wore. He accepted the pain as penance. In the two weeks since Lori had moved to the ranch, Jesse never had known her to be moody or withdrawn. She didn't even seem to need time away from the demands of taking care of three babies—and two bachelor ranchers.

Which made her unexpected disappearance even more troubling.

His gaze searched the outlying pastures in vain for a glimpse of copper, knowing Lori's hair would stand out against the hills like a cardinal on a snow-covered branch.

Maybe he should check the barn. Clay usually fed the

horses around this time, and Lori could have ended up there. A tiny knot of envy uncurled in his chest at the thought of the easy, uncomplicated friendship Lori had struck up with his brother. As much time as she and Jesse spent caring for the triplets, Lori didn't seem as comfortable with him.

Why is that, do you suppose? Jesse silently countered in disgust. *Clay came home bearing gifts while you almost caused her to fall off the ladder.*

And speaking of gifts…

The glare Jesse leveled at the offending object should have caused it to spontaneously combust. Maya told him she would have the triplets home by seven, so now the sequoia—*spruce*—in the doorway was not only an obstruction but a safety hazard.

"Thanks, little brother," Jesse muttered under his breath. "You left me no choice."

MAX AND JAZZ veered toward the barn, more than ready to rest after a long romp in the hills, while Lori continued up the driveway. While she'd set off to clear her head, she hadn't realized daylight had retreated, bowing to the shadows that crept in and filled the spaces between the buildings.

She quickened her pace, wondering if Maya had returned with the triplets. She hadn't planned to be gone so long.

Someone had left the porch light on, and as Lori got closer to the house, she noticed the Christmas tree was gone. No doubt Clay had already muscled it through the door. If Jesse hadn't put it through a wood chipper first.

Lori sighed. The fresh air had given her a fresh perspective. And the still, small voice inside told her that she owed Jesse an apology. She'd gotten so caught up in turning the house into a replica of the one in her dreams that she hadn't stopped to take his feelings into consideration.

When it came to Jesse, Lori was learning to look below the surface to the emotions simmering there. He may have sounded all calm and logical when he pointed out there was no reason for her to waste her time and energy on Christmas preparations, but the pain that honed an edge on the words revealed the truth.

She couldn't believe she hadn't thought of it before.

Five months ago, Jesse would have been looking forward to celebrating Christmas with his wife and their new babies, not being a widower and single father at the age of thirty-four. No wonder he'd looked as if she'd set fire to the living room instead of simply adding some decorations.

Show him that You haven't abandoned him, Lord. Remind him that the gift You gave at Christmas—Your Son— proves You love him...and help me put my own feelings aside and know that wherever I spend Christmas, You'll be with me.

Lori followed a trail of pine needles into the house and down the hall and paused in the living room doorway. Peeking into the room, she couldn't hold back a smile of delight.

The tree stood right where she'd imagined it. In the corner of the room, next to a whimsical, keyhole-shaped window fashioned from delicate pieces of stained glass.

The branches moved and Lori realized there was someone wedged between the tree and the wall.

"Clay, I didn't see you back there." Lori rushed over. "Thank you for putting the tree up! Did you need some..." *Help.*

The rest of the words died in her throat. Because it wasn't Jesse's brother who fought his way out from behind the branches.

Chapter Ten

Lori flushed under the weight of Jesse's gaze as it swept from her wind-kissed cheeks down to her feet, stopping to linger—with disapproval—on the cute pair of suede shoes he must not have considered official, regulation ranch wear.

"You found the tree stand." Lori made a desperate grab at one of the thoughts bouncing around in her head and managed to blurt out a complete sentence.

Instead of answering, Jesse stepped forward and Lori sucked in a breath as he reached out and caught her hands, folding them between his. The warmth of his skin melted a path down to her half-frozen toes.

"No gloves? No shoes?"

Lori glanced down at her feet. "I'm wearing shoes."

"Those aren't shoes." Jesse stalked toward the fireplace, shedding pine needles on the carpet as he tugged her along behind him. "Sit here for a few minutes and thaw out."

He didn't have to tell her twice. Lori sank onto the stone hearth, which felt better than her electric blanket, and closed her eyes blissfully.

When she opened them again, Jesse was still looking at her, the blue eyes unfathomable.

Lori swallowed hard. "Thank you for putting up the tree."

"It was blocking the door."

Of course it was. Lori forced a smile and rose to her feet. "I should put the ornaments on before Maya gets back with the triplets."

"You have—" Jesse glanced at the grandfather clock "—about twelve minutes and thirty seconds."

That would give her enough time to string the lights....

Except that someone already had.

She turned to stare at Jesse. "You put the lights on."

One of the broad shoulders lifted in a casual *so what if I did?* shrug.

"Were they...umm, blocking the door, too?" Lori ventured.

Jesse's bark of laughter surprised them both.

It also surprised Maya, who stood in the doorway, her eyes wide with disbelief. Disbelief that slowly changed to a speculative gleam, as her gaze shifted from her eldest brother to the new nanny.

Oh. No.

Lori had seen that expression before. Whenever one of her coworkers pulled her aside to tell her they had a cousin/brother/neighbor/friend who wanted to meet her.

"Unca Jesse." Layla's excited chirp momentarily distracted the adults, as she dashed into the room followed by a slender teenage girl with a self-conscious smile. "This is my new cousin Av'ry. She watches me and Tommy sometimes, but she likes your babies, too."

"So do I." Jesse smiled at Avery.

Lori let out a relieved breath as the little girl launched herself at Jesse, who scooped her up in his arms. His niece giggled before planting a smacking kiss on Jesse's stubbly jaw. She drew back and shook a pudgy finger at him. "You're scratchy. Daddy's face doesn't feel like that."

Jesse arched a brow. "That's because your daddy talks to people all day and your uncle Jesse talks to horses."

Layla giggled again and Lori couldn't help but notice that Maya's eyes had misted over. She guessed the woman's emotional response came from hearing Layla call Greg Garrison "Daddy."

In a small town, everyone knew everyone else's business, so Lori had heard that Jesse's sister and Greg had recently exchanged wedding vows after a whirlwind courtship. The couple had started their marriage with a ready-made family in Maya's three-year-old daughter, Layla, but they were also in the process of adopting Tommy.

"Tommy talks to Charlie, too," Layla informed him.

At this, Jesse glanced at Maya. "You found Charlie?"

Maya's expression clouded. "Not yet. A few weeks ago someone called, claiming they saw a dog that matched Charlie's description down by the river, but Greg drove down there and didn't see any sign of him."

"Tommy says he'll be home for Christmas," Layla said. "He prays every night for Charlie. I heared him."

Jesse cleared his throat and gave his niece a playful tap on the nose. "Where are my babies, by the way? You promised to bring them back."

"In the car with Daddy. He said let him know when the toast is clear."

"Mmm." Jesse pretended to consider that bit of news. "Are you sure he didn't say *coast?*"

"Nope," Layla said decisively, as she struggled to get down. "I'll get Tommy." The moment her feet touched the floor, she was off and running.

"Tommy is outside playing with Max and Jazz," Maya said softly. "He's been adjusting well to living with us but he really misses Charlie. Greg and I have talked about getting him a new puppy for Christmas, but maybe it's too soon. Tommy still believes Charlie is going to come back."

Before it occurred to Lori that it wasn't her place to offer advice, she shook her head. "You should wait."

Jesse tossed her an impatient look. "Maybe it is a good idea. Charlie isn't coming back."

"You don't know that." Lori didn't want to argue with him—could be grounds for being fired, after all—but she did think it might be too soon to replace Tommy's pet.

Jesse's lips tightened. "The dog has been missing since the tornado hit. I think it's better if you didn't let Tommy keep wishing for the impossible."

"But we don't know it's impossible," Maya said, her smooth forehead furrowing. "I think that's where Tommy's hope comes from. Every Sunday he asks me to read the praise corner in the church bulletin. After the tornado, Michael asked people to share stories of God's faithfulness, and each week, there isn't an empty spot on the page. This morning, a woman wrote that a family album with all her children's baby pictures was returned to her. Completely intact."

"It's nice to know that some people are finding the things they lost."

Sympathy flashed in Maya's eyes. "Jesse, you know we haven't given up hope about finding the ring."

"I have," Jesse said flatly.

Avery, Lori noticed, was listening to their exchange with wide-eyed interest.

A sudden commotion in the hall shut down the conversation and Clay wandered in, holding a bundled-to-the-chin and very wide-awake Sasha. "I hate to break up the party, but Greg and I could use some help with the baby brigade. And Maya, you should think about trading in that van for a coach bus."

Maya's lips curved into an affectionate smile as she looked at her niece. "We thought for sure the triplets would fall asleep on the way home, but they must have been afraid they were going to miss something."

Tommy appeared in the doorway, and the sadness in his eyes lifted a little as he caught sight of the tree.

"Are you going to decorate your tree tonight, Uncle Jesse? We made popcorn strings for the one we put up." His expression was earnest as he looked at his uncle. "The babies are too little to put the ornaments on, but we can help."

"We help," Layla echoed solemnly.

Lori couldn't look at Jesse. She was the one who'd inadvertently gotten him backed into a corner, so it was her responsibility to rescue him. Even though a tree-trimming party had always been high on the list of those childish dreams of hers that had been causing so much trouble lately.

She caught her lower lip between her teeth. There had to be a gentle way to turn down the children's heart-melting offer to help...if she could think of one.

"Lori?" Jesse's husky voice stirred up those mustangs again. She dared a look in his direction, and felt her heart buck at the sight of his rueful smile. "Do we have any... popcorn?"

Hope took wing inside of her. "I think we do."

"Great." He looked as if he actually meant it, but Lori knew better. The last thing he wanted to do was be reminded of his loss; but Tommy and Layla's feelings meant more than his own. It was one of the things she was beginning to love about him.

Like about him. One of the things she was beginning to *like* about him.

"Do you mind making some?"

"Yes. I mean *no*." Lori stumbled over the words as Jesse's smile widened into the captivating, take-no-prisoners smile that never failed to steal her next breath. "No, I don't mind. Not at all."

Tommy and Layla turned to their mother, who knew

what was coming and held up both hands in surrender. "I suppose we can stay another hour to help Uncle Jesse and Lori, but that's it. Do you mind staying a little bit longer, Avery?"

"Great. I'll unwrap Sasha while Lori and Jesse collect the rest of their chicks." Clay toted his niece over to the sofa.

Lori ducked her head and made for the door before anyone noticed her freckles start to glow.

Their chicks?

Clay probably hadn't realized what he'd said. Or if he had, it was only a reference to the fact that she and Jesse cared for the babies together. It was a business relationship.

She knew that when Jesse hired her. But lately, all her good intentions had turned into wishes. She wanted more.

"DID YOU MAKE this one?"

Jesse glanced at the cardboard candy cane dangling from Lori's fingers. "I plead the fifth."

"So, yes." Lori grinned. "Most people stick with red and white. I think it's very…creative."

"I think I wanted to use every color of glitter my Sunday school teacher put out on the table."

"Glitter?" Layla, who'd found a cache of tiny wooden carousel horses in the box of ornaments, perked up at the word.

Jesse cringed, imagining what would happen to a tube of glitter in the hands of a budding three-year-old Michelangelo.

"It's on the candy cane ornament your uncle made when he was little, sweetheart." A smile lurked in Lori's eyes as she held it up for Layla to see. "We were just admiring it."

Jesse couldn't help but notice the smile had been there all evening. It hadn't faded during the hundredth time she'd wound up the girls' infant swings, when Tommy accidentally dumped a bowl of popcorn over or when Layla draped gobs of tinsel on the spinning wheel when no one was looking.

Whatever had been bothering Lori, she must have left it outside in the hills, because she was obviously in her element.

Knowing that didn't let Jesse off the hook. He'd told Clay he didn't want Lori to suffer from burnout, but she seemed most content when surrounded by noise and activity. Which only reminded Jesse that he'd been out of line before.

"Pretty." Layla judged the candy cane "good" and went back to playing with the horses.

Lori leaned forward to hang it on the tree, but Jesse reached out and snagged her wrist.

"You aren't going to actually put that where people can see it?"

"Of course I am."

"No one is watching." Jesse lowered his voice. "Candy canes have been known to mysteriously disappear, you know. Never to be seen again."

Lori drew back, feigning alarm. "You wouldn't dare. This is part of your past."

"So?"

"So that means it belongs."

The woman was a walking Hallmark card. "It's proof that my mother never threw anything away."

Lori snorted. *Snorted.* "Trust me. In about four years, you'll have to build a separate storage unit to put every finger painting and Popsicle stick picture frame your daughters make in preschool."

Jesse opened his mouth to argue, and then snapped it shut as he tried to visualize tossing out anything of his daughters.

"Exactly." Lori laughed and every pulse point in Jesse's body leaped in response.

Self-preservation had him inching away from her. A challenge, considering that Layla and Tommy flanked them like bookends. Layla sat next to him, singing softly to her new friends, and Tommy stood beside Lori, trying to find out how many ornaments a single branch would hold.

Where were his sister and her husband, for crying out loud? Didn't they know Jesse had his own noisy brood to keep an eye on? Clay had joined in the festivities for a while, but then pulled a disappearing act, probably to make his nightly phone call to Nicki.

Jesse twisted around just in time to see Greg holding a sprig of mistletoe above Maya's head. His sister blushed like a junior high kid at her first dance.

He was thrilled his little sister had fallen in love with a guy who actually deserved her, but couldn't prevent the wave of regret that crashed over him. Two years ago, when he met Marie, he thought he'd found what those daytime talk shows liked to refer to as a "soul mate." Now he suspected the term was nothing more than an advertising gimmick to sell more roses on Valentine's Day.

Did Lori like roses?

The thought breezed in uninvited and Jesse frowned. If she did, he didn't think she'd favor the perfect, elegant ones from a floral shop. No, given the enthusiasm Lori expressed for all the old stuff around the place, she'd probably prefer the wild, unkempt clusters of heirloom-pink roses that climbed the stone foundation of the house in late summer.

Alarms went off left and right at the sudden security breach inside his head.

"Mommy and Daddy are gonna kiss," Layla announced without looking up.

Avery, who sat on the sofa paging through a dog-eared copy of *The Gift of the Magi*, rolled her eyes.

"They do that." Tommy heaved a long-suffering sigh.

"'Cause they love each other," Layla said knowingly.

Tommy wrinkled his nose. "It's still gross—isn't it, Uncle Jesse?"

Jesse didn't want to think about kissing. Or *talk* about kissing. Especially not with Lori sitting so close. He glanced at her, careful not to let his gaze drift to the soft pink lips always on the verge of a smile. Her slender body was rigid, eyes staring straight ahead, and her lips—yup, in spite of his noble intentions he'd looked anyway—were pressed together in a somber line.

It was obvious the topic was awkward for her, too.

Suddenly Lori's shoulders began to shake and she started to laugh.

And Jesse, in spite of himself, couldn't help but join in.

Maya's and Greg's heads snapped around, and Maya's blush deepened when she realized everyone's attention had shifted from the tree to her and her new husband.

Greg cleared his throat. "I think it's time the Garrisons went home," he announced. "Lori and Jesse have to put the babies to bed, and tomorrow is a school day for you two."

Tommy sighed again.

"I like school," Layla said primly.

"You would." Tommy crossed his arms and scowled.

Layla burst into tears.

"Whoa. Time-out, guys." Greg put his hands together like a referee. "We're all getting tired."

Without being scolded, prompted or cued, Tommy suddenly wrapped his arms around Layla and gave her a fierce hug. "Sorry."

Layla sniffed. "I forgive you."

Tommy fished inside his pocket and pulled out a mashed Tootsie Roll. "You can have this."

Squealing with delight, Layla pounced on the misshapen piece of candy and started to unwrap it. With a relieved smile, Maya herded the two children toward the door.

"We could all take a page from their book, couldn't we?" Greg murmured.

Jesse couldn't have agreed more. It was too bad all family conflicts didn't get resolved with an apology and a Tootsie Roll.

"I'll start the three *B*s," Lori murmured, as she rose to her feet. "You can see your sister and her family out."

Jesse noticed the candy cane still clutched in her hand. "You're going to hang that on the tree the minute my back is turned, aren't you?"

Lori flashed her thousand-watt smile. "Absolutely."

Chapter Eleven

"It's good to hear you laugh again." Maya whispered the words in Jesse's ear as she went up on her tiptoes to hug him goodbye.

"I laugh," Jesse muttered.

"Not often enough." The affection in Maya's eyes matched her tone. "She's amazing, Jess. A real answer to a prayer—I don't know how you managed without her."

Jesse didn't bother to pretend he didn't know who she was referring to. Sometimes it seemed as if Maya knew him better than he knew himself. "The girls seem to like her."

"The girls?" Maya repeated the words with a raised eyebrow.

"Yes. The girls." Jesse's eyes narrowed, daring his sister to continue down the path she was not so subtly hinting at.

He knew her, too.

"The house looks the way I remember it when we were growing up. All of Mom's old decorations." Maya smiled wistfully. "I'm glad she kept everything—and that you decided to put it up this year."

"It's not as if I had a choice."

Maya tilted her head. "She's good for you."

Here we go again, Jesse thought. "She's good for the *girls*."

Maya didn't appear as if she'd heard him. "Tonight...I wished Mom and Dad were here. They would have loved watching Tommy and Layla have fun. And they would have spoiled the triplets rotten."

"Don't go there, Maya."

"Why not?" Her chin lifted. "I miss them, Jesse. Every day. Even though I can't see them anymore, I can still hear their voices. If we want to honor their memory, we have to remember what was important to them."

"The ranch." Jesse scraped an impatient hand through his hair. "Why do you think I'm still here?"

"Not the ranch." Maya's frustrated look judged him as dense as smoke from a brush fire. "Family."

She was referring to him and Clay again. He sighed. "You're pushing."

"Someone has to." Maya huffed the words, but Jesse could tell by the way her shoulders relaxed that she had decided it was time to back off. Until a teasing sparkle danced in her eyes. She peeked at him from under her lashes. "You are so stubborn, I'm surprised that Lori puts up with you."

He rolled his eyes. "And you are so transparent."

"Thank you." Maya beamed. "I take that as a compliment." She gave him another hug that threatened to cut off the flow of oxygen to his brain. "Thank you for putting up with us tonight."

"Thank Lori." Jesse nudged his sister toward the door, but Maya had to get the last word in.

"I did. Now make sure you do, too."

Jesse didn't bother to mention that not only did he owe Lori a thank-you, he owed her an apology, too.

JESSE MET LORI at the bottom of the stairs.

"They're already asleep?"

"I'll have to give them their baths in the morning. I

think watching their cousins decorate the tree completely wore them out."

Jesse wasn't surprised. It had worn *him* out. "Layla is just as precocious as her mother at that age. I remember Clay complaining to Mom once that Maya made his ears tired."

What made him think of that?

Jesse rocked back on his heels, unsettled by the thought. On the other hand, why should it come as a shock that an evening submersed in what his sister had warmly referred to as "making memories" had stirred up a few of his own?

For a little while, like a spectator swept into the middle of a holiday parade, Jesse had gotten caught up in the festive mood. He and Clay had even shared a knowing look at Tommy's excitement when Maya told him he could put the final touch on the Christmas tree—the gold star at the top.

Jesse wondered if witnessing a replay of that once-sacred Logan tradition had opened up a floodgate of memories for Clay, too.

Growing up, that particular honor had always fallen to Jesse. The year Clay turned seven, he questioned why Jesse always got to put the star on top of the tree. Jesse had seen the deep disappointment on his brother's face and asked their parents if they could each put up a star.

"'Cause there is room for two," he'd told them.

Every Christmas after that, finding a tree that had room at the top for two stars had become a challenge that involved the whole family.

Unfortunately, Jesse's brain hadn't stopped with that memory. It hit fast-forward and took him to another place. The conversation that had taken place the night of his brother's senior prom. After he'd bailed Clay out of jail.

"Face it, Jesse. There isn't room on the ranch for both of us. You and I both know that Dad was grooming you to take over the Circle L. You don't need me."

"Don't be an idiot. This is your home. But if you're going to keep making decisions that ruin your life, at least go somewhere else so that Maya and I don't have to watch it happen."

Jesse hurled the words at his brother in anger, verbal fallout from the aftershocks of that late-night call from the police department. When he'd first heard the dispatcher's voice, he assumed the worst. He thought Clay was dead.

He hadn't expected his brother to leave the Circle L the next day. For good.

They'd always had a difficult time communicating, but the words they exchanged in the barn that night had become embedded in their relationship like a splinter. All these years, it festered below the surface, never quite healing. And Jesse didn't know how to remove it.

"I think Brooke is going to give Layla a run for her money in the precocious department."

Jesse's attention snapped back to Lori, as her soft voice filtered through the dark shadows cast by the memory of that night.

"You are probably right," Jesse muttered. And multiplied times three, the thought of being so outnumbered was more than a little terrifying to a rookie dad.

"Don't look so worried. You'll do fine."

Jesse wasn't so sure. And the fact that Lori had accurately read his mind was somehow equally as terrifying.

In the short silence that filled the air, Lori skirted around him. But instead of going up the stairs, she headed in the direction of what used to be Jesse's normal, everyday living room, before its radical transformation into a life-size Christmas card.

"Just to warn you, that tree will tip over if you put another ornament on it." He found himself following her.

"I promise, no more decorating." With one finger, Lori

drew an invisible X over her heart. "I thought I should do damage control before I collapse, too."

Jesse's eyes narrowed. She didn't *look* as if she were about to collapse. Strands of copper hair had escaped the elastic band of her neat ponytail, but the amber eyes hadn't lost their glow. He was relieved it had returned—even if he had to put up with the adverse side effects from the warmth of her smile. Rapid pulse. Shallow breathing. Light-headedness.

Lori went straight to the sofa and lifted one of the cushions, revealing a layer of popcorn as thick as insulation.

How had she known it was there?

Shaking his head, Jesse gathered up the rope of silver garland his niece had draped around her shoulders like a feather boa.

"It could have been worse, I suppose," Jesse said. "Layla and Tommy could have insisted we break out the glitter and make more ornaments."

"Mmm." Lori knelt down, taking a sudden but keen interest in a string of lights drooping off the end of a branch.

"You volunteered to make ornaments with them, didn't you?"

The telltale flush of pink stealing into the porcelain cheeks answered his question.

"Next Sunday after church. On my day off," she added swiftly, as if anticipating his response.

Now he had guilt. And it tripped a switch on his memory. Once again, he saw Lori's stricken expression when he'd said...

What had he said?

Jesse still couldn't shake the nagging feeling there'd been more to her reaction than hurt feelings over his bungling attempt to spare her extra work.

"They'll like that." Jesse began to pick strands of tinsel off the spinning wheel, and they promptly attached themselves to his flannel shirt as if it were a magnetic field. "Isn't this stuff banned in the United States?"

"No, but it's definitely something the babies could get tangled in because it doesn't like to stay put," Lori said. "I didn't say anything because I didn't want to hurt Layla's feelings."

Because, Jesse's conscience cuffed him upside the head, *there are people who are sensitive about that sort of thing.*

"She'll notice it's gone the next time she visits," he pointed out.

"It won't be gone. It will be displayed in this special, star-shaped Christmas tinsel box."

The clear plastic container she presented for his inspection looked vaguely familiar.

"I think that was intended to hold half a pound of jelly beans." Green apple and cinnamon, if Jesse remembered right.

"Now it's going to hold tinsel." Lori held it out and Jesse dutifully transferred the clingy strands from his shirt into the container. "It will be safe from the triplets, but it'll have a place of honor when Layla visits."

"Where do you come up with this stuff?" Jesse wondered out loud, amazed by her creativity when it came to children. "Does it come naturally, or were your mom and dad famous parenting experts or something?"

Apparently, he was rustier at the whole teasing thing than he'd thought, because Lori's warm smile didn't surface. Instead, her eyes darkened with something that looked like...pain.

Something Jesse was shocked to see there, but recognized as easily as he recognized his own reflection in the mirror.

"No." Lori felt the container slide between her damp palms as she carried it to the mantel.

Jesse trailed behind her, collecting empty boxes and

nesting them together along the way. "No to the first part, or no to the second?"

Lori had hoped a simple, straightforward answer would have been enough to satisfy Jesse's curiosity. She strove to keep her voice light. "No to both."

It wasn't as if she could tell him that there was nothing particularly unique or even instinctive about the way she related to children. Most of her ideas stemmed from wishes. The things she'd needed—wanted—*her* parents to do.

"Are you from a large family?"

The container wobbled. Lori didn't trust her hands to steady it, so she pushed them into the front pockets of her jeans. "I'm an only child."

An only child who didn't want to have this conversation.

She spotted a box of Christmas lights and made a break for it. Finding a vacant space on the floor—right next to the Christmas tree Jesse hadn't wanted—she drew out a knot of lights, hoping he'd be more than ready to retreat to his office where there wasn't a red velvet bow or ornament in sight.

He didn't.

Instead, he dropped into the chair beside her and picked up one end of the lights she'd started untangling. Connecting them by a single, dark green wire.

"Do your folks live around here?"

"No."

Jesse eased from the chair onto the floor beside her and she stiffened at his nearness. He reached into the box, tugging another set of lights free.

A long minute of silence stretched between them and Lori realized he was waiting for her to elaborate.

"Mother lives in New York." She held her breath, hoping he wouldn't ask the obvious: *What about your dad?*

"Do you usually spend Christmas with her? On the East Coast?"

Lori's fingers twisted together in her lap. "I picked up extra shifts at the hospital. People want to be with their families, and since I was single, I was the logical person to work over the holiday."

Jesse easily read between the lines. Lori had worked longer hours to help out her coworkers. But why hadn't she wanted to be with *her* family? Seeing how much she loved fussing over Christmas, wouldn't she want to go home?

The jolt that went through Jesse made him wonder if God hadn't just reached in and reconnected some faulty wiring in his brain. Before he could linger on the fact he'd just acknowledged God still might have a bead on Jesse Logan, the conversation they'd had earlier that afternoon rushed back in.

"I usually spend Christmas with Maya and I figured Lori would be going home."

Silently, Jesse lined up the casual statement against the wounded look in Lori's eyes that afternoon and came up with a match. Lori hadn't reacted to his implied criticism that she'd overstepped her bounds by decorating the house—she'd been hurt by his casual assumption that she had a place to spend Christmas.

Jesse felt the sting, as the truth sank into his thick skull. He'd assumed Lori was the way she was—all sunshine and smiles—because she'd been raised in a nurturing, loving family, protected from life's storms.

When he hired her, he hadn't thought that she'd given up her own home to move into his. She no longer had a living room to trim with colored lights, nor little bows nor a Christmas tree. Nor people to share those things.

His family had fractured after the death of their parents, but when Jesse thought about it, there were a lot of good memories to draw from. Loving parents. Laughter. Something he'd taken for granted.

Jesse drew in a slow breath, feeling his way through unfamiliar territory like a cowboy air-dropped into the middle of downtown Chicago. Now that he knew what he'd said, he wasn't sure how to make it better.

Five minutes later, he still wasn't sure. But he had to come up with something, because the lights were almost knot-free, and something in Lori's posture warned him that she was poised for flight.

"I was thinking about the dedication they're planning on Christmas Eve for the Old Town Hall," Jesse said casually. "My baby sister ordered me to go, but she's on the restoration committee. Between her responsibilities and her own family, she'll be pretty swamped. If you could stay with us over Christmas and help me with the girls, I'd pay you overtime."

Lori's next breath stalled in her chest, as hope bloomed there like an answer to a prayer she didn't even remember praying. But God must have seen it, tucked away in a corner of her heart.

"I could do that." Lori said. "But I won't accept any extra pay. It would be my gift."

Jesse was silent for so long that Lori wondered if he'd heard her. She decided God had given her an opportunity to follow the urging of that still, small voice she'd heard on her walk.

"Jesse? I'm… I owe you an apology." The words came out in a rush, keeping pace with the tempo of her racing pulse. "I didn't stop to think about how you might feel about Christmas this year. Without Marie. All the changes in your family. I should have talked to you first, instead of getting carried away with the decorations. It's your house."

She needed to keep reminding herself of that. Because it was starting to be so easy…too easy…to think of it as home.

Jesse's earlier silence had been disquieting enough, but this one stretched out so long Lori was tempted to grab her knitting bag and finish Sasha's Christmas stocking while she waited for his response.

"These are outdoor lights, you know."

Okay. Not the response she'd been expecting. But curiosity got the best of her. "How can you tell?"

"They're all clear bulbs. Mom used to wrap the porch rail outside with white lights."

Without closing her eyes, Lori could imagine how beautiful that would look.

"I could probably find some time to put them up. If you want me to."

Lori momentarily forgot it was safer to avoid looking directly into Jesse's blue eyes. But she wasn't sure she heard him right.

The regret she saw there squeezed the air from her lungs. But what did he have to feel sorry about?

"Really?" The word came out in a pitiful croak. "Thank you."

"And just for the record, you don't owe me an apology." Jesse's voice was low as he stared at the tree. "I owe you one. I didn't think about taking pictures of the girls with the Christmas tree in the background. Or how Layla and Tommy would enjoy the decorations when they came to visit. Sometimes I can't see…" He struggled to find the right words and finally gave up with a shrug. "Just do whatever you want to when it comes to Christmas preparations, and I promise to stay out of your way."

Lori knew what he'd been trying to say. Sometimes he couldn't see beyond his own pain.

Warmth spread through her, as Lori wondered if he

even realized the significance of the moment. He wasn't fooling her. He'd picked up on her reluctance to talk about her family and guessed something wasn't right.

Jesse *had* seen beyond his own pain...when he'd caught a glimpse of *hers*.

Chapter Twelve

Jesse shifted his weight under the pickup truck, trying to dislodge the irritating object burrowing into his right shoulder blade.

By trial and error over the years, he'd taught himself how to fix the equipment that inevitably broke down. Clay had always been the one with a knack for coaxing engines back to life, but he wasn't available. For the past week, his brother divided his time between putting in a full day at the ranch and then driving into High Plains to act as foreman for the crew trying to get the Old Town Hall ready in time for the Christmas Eve celebration. The project was going on practically round the clock.

It crossed Jesse's mind that Clay was trying to earn the town's forgiveness for all the teenage pranks he'd pulled back in the day.

"You have to forgive him, Jesse. It's eating you alive."

Maya's words came back to him and the wrench slipped between Jesse's grease-stained fingers and clattered to the floor, missing his ear by an inch.

His sister was becoming more confrontational about the tension between him and Clay, and Jesse was getting tired of being her favorite target. When they'd talked on the phone the night before, she had the nerve to tell him that Clay was more than willing to make amends, but Jesse was the one who seemed reluctant to put the past aside.

All Jesse knew was that it *was* getting harder to hold the past up as a shield, protecting his defenses. Not when he no longer wanted to be Clay's boss. He wanted to be his brother. He wanted the easy camaraderie that he saw between Maya's husband, Greg, and his cousin, Reverend Garrison. He wanted to ease the burden of keeping track of the ranch's financial records onto Clay's shoulders, so he could spend more time with the girls in the evening.

And more time with Lori?

The unexpected voice in Jesse's head sent a chain reaction through his body that caused it to jerk. His shoulder bumped against the tire, which loosened a scab of rust above his head that rained down bits and pieces of metal like a broken piñata.

Great.

Lori was nowhere around and she was still a health hazard.

It was the reason he'd skipped supper and wandered through the outbuildings until he found an emergency that needed attention. Because he found it easier to deal with a fickle engine than fickle emotions.

Jesse wanted to spend time with her. And *wanting* to spend time with her had forced him to spend more time in the barn—so he *couldn't* spend more time with her.

No wonder the past few days had been pure torture.

If he timed things right, he could slip into the house at ten o'clock, when Lori was in her room for the night.

His fingers patted the dusty concrete floor to find the missing tool. The next thing he knew, someone's fingers brushed against his, soft as a whisper, and put the wrench in his hand.

Jesse didn't even have to turn his head an eighth of an inch to know who his mystery helper was. The subtle scent of wildflowers cut through the pungent smell of motor oil and grease, like the first spring breeze after a long winter.

His gaze slid over and collided with Lori's. She was on her knees next to the truck, peering at him with curious brown eyes. Her cheeks were pink from the cold, but her smile warmed him more than the space heater humming in the corner.

"Clay said you had an emergency before he left for town. I thought maybe it was one of the cows again."

Jesse had found the wrench—with a little help—but now he struggled to find his voice. "No cows this time. Just a broken driveshaft."

"I didn't know how long you'd be out here, so I brought you a cup of coffee and a sandwich."

Sure enough, Jesse caught a whiff of java. His nose twitched like Saber's when he tried to lure the horse into the round pen with a bucket of grain.

"Are the girls asleep?" He knew they were, or Lori would have never ventured outside.

"I have the baby monitor in my pocket." Lori's hand patted a bulge in her coat pocket. "The triplets all seemed a little tired today. Maybe they're having a growth spurt or starting to teethe. Anyway, I gave them their baths and put them to bed a little earlier tonight."

Jesse tried to ignore the guilt that the innocent comment stirred inside of him. He usually helped with the "three *B*s" every night, but he *had* warned Lori when he'd hired her that unexpected emergencies would come up. And even though the old pickup, rusting in the garage since the previous April, didn't quite constitute an emergency, it had provided an excuse for him to avoid having supper with Lori. Alone.

"You can leave it on the bench. I'll get to it in a minute." *As soon as you go back up to the house,* he thought.

"Thank you," he added, because his mama had raised a gentleman.

Your daddy didn't raise a coward, either. But here you are, hiding under a truck.

Lori didn't budge. Jesse knew, if he moved his head a fraction of an inch to the right, he would see the delicate curve of her jaw.

He clenched his teeth and tried to focus on the task at hand, but his traitorous gaze drifted on its own accord to the glossy braid draped over Lori's shoulder, gleaming like polished mahogany against the green wool coat she wore.

Jesse heard a noise that sounded like the cap of a thermos being unscrewed, followed by the splash of liquid into a cup.

Don't look. Don't look. If you ignore her, she'll go away.

"Sasha sat up without any help from the bumper cushion this afternoon," Lori said, a hint of satisfaction creeping into her voice. "Her muscle tone is improving more every day."

Jesse blinked. Had she known he was concerned about that? Had he left the book on child development on the coffee table?

"I wish I'd seen it."

"You can," Lori said cheerfully. "I took a picture of her with my cell phone."

Jesse closed his eyes and groaned.

"Are you all right?"

"I'm fine. There's a…a rock or something digging into my shoulder." Immediately after he said the words, he realized his mistake. Lori was a nurse. Lori was a natural caregiver. Lori was already positioning her body to wriggle under the truck to help him….

"I think I will have that sandwich." Jesse shot out from underneath the pickup like a bronco released from a chute, then rolled to his feet. In the time it took to draw his next breath, Lori's efficient hands were brushing dirt off the back of his shirt.

He shied away. "It's fine. Thanks."

"Look." Lori flipped open her phone and, sure enough, there was a grainy image of his youngest, listing a little to the right but sitting up without assistance.

Jesse felt his throat tighten. The picture was another small affirmation that Sasha was going to be okay.

The day before, he and Lori had taken the girls to their appointment with Dr. Cole, and the pediatrician marveled at how far the triplets had come since their last checkup. She made a comment about all the TLC they must be receiving and gave Lori an approving look.

Right before they left, Dr. Cole pulled Jesse aside.

"Do you want my professional opinion, Jesse?" she murmured, while shuffling through the paperwork. "Don't let this one go."

That was the trouble, Jesse thought. The growing realization that he didn't *want* to let Lori go.

At the moment, however, his contrary nature wished she would. Unfortunately, she didn't seem to be in any hurry to leave him alone to enjoy his own, miserable company.

"This shed reminds me of the attic." Lori slid the phone into her coat pocket, retrieved the cup of coffee from the bench and handed it to him.

"I know. My family layered stuff in here like sediment." Jesse propped a hip against the hood of the truck. "Some of it dates back to the original homestead. Including the cobwebs."

Lori smiled and Jesse realized that had been his intent. To make her smile.

You are heading for trouble, buddy.

Jesse wanted to dive under the truck again. He hadn't been prepared for his heart and his head to wage a war over his growing feelings for Lori. He'd even come up with a list of reasons why he needed to keep a lid on them.

He was too old for her. Weighted down by too much baggage. What he had to offer wouldn't be enough, and eventually she'd find their relationship lacking. She'd find *him* lacking. And like Marie, she'd leave.

He wasn't convinced there was a whole lot of his heart left to offer someone. Especially someone like Lori.

"What is this? A metal detector?" Lori paused to inspect the high-tech gadget leaning up against the wall. "It looks new. Is it yours?"

"Yes," he admitted reluctantly.

"Do you look for things that belonged to your family when they settled the ranch?"

It would be easy to let her think that but for some reason, the truth popped out of Jesse's mouth. "I've been looking for Emmeline's diamond engagement ring. I'm sure you heard about it."

Lori tilted her head and frowned. "No. Should I have?"

"When Marie... The ring was on the kitchen table with her wedding band." No point in mentioning the note. "After the twister hit, I couldn't find it anywhere. People were finding things scattered all over the county, which was the reason Greg started the Lost and Found. Maya mentioned that Reverend Garrison made a special announcement about the ring one Sunday. He gave everyone a description and told people a little bit about its history."

"I worked a lot of weekends, so I must have missed it," Lori murmured. "That's what you and Maya were talking about the other night?"

Jesse shrugged. "She checks the Lost and Found every week. Hoping."

"But no one has found it yet."

Jesse didn't miss Lori's gentle emphasis on the *yet*. He wished he shared her and Maya's optimism. "At one point, it looked as if someone had turned it in, but the diamond was fake."

"I don't understand. Someone deliberately turned in a ring that looked like the one you'd lost?"

Jesse shifted uncomfortably. Even his cynical self had a hard time believing someone could be that coldhearted. But what was he supposed to think, when the evidence pointed in that direction?

"I'm not sure it was deliberate," he said slowly. "But the rings were similar in style. It's probably gone for good. What are the chances of finding a ring lost out there in the prairie grass?"

Knowing the chances were slim hadn't stopped him from looking, though. When it came right down to it, Jesse felt responsible for that ring, and not only because it happened to be a family heirloom. Until he found it, it was another reminder that he'd lost something else he'd been responsible for. Something entrusted to his care.

Like Clay. And Marie.

"The diamond meant a lot to your family?" Lori ventured.

"It was passed down to the oldest son for generations. But if it's found, it would eventually go to Brooke."

Lori read between the lines. Jesse didn't think there would be any Logan sons. He didn't plan to marry again nor have any more children.

She wanted to wrap her arms around his lean waist... and shake the stuffing out of him.

Ever since the evening Jesse had inquired about her family, she sensed a subtle change in him. He'd been crankier than usual. He snapped at Clay. He could barely look her in the eye.

He'd also wrapped the porch rail in tiny white lights, hung a wreath on the lamppost and started to hum Christmas carols to the girls at bedtime.

Lori praised God for it all.

Jesse might not realize what was happening, but she didn't have to be a nurse to recognize the symptoms. Jesse was caught in a battle...with himself. And, if she wasn't mistaken, with God.

She prayed daily that God would not only break through the walls around his heart, but that He would give her wisdom to know how to protect hers.

Jesse wasn't the only one struggling. Lori had her own battle to fight.

No matter how often she reminded herself that Jesse was her employer, her heart didn't seem inclined to agree. It wasn't simply a matter of chemistry, either, although watching Jesse emerge from under the pickup—his dark hair tousled and a smudge of grease on his angular jaw— had given her heart a better workout than a half hour of aerobic exercise.

She thought she'd come to terms with her single status, content to trust God's timing when it came to finding love. The babies in the NICU had filled her arms and her heart.

Lori hadn't felt a void in her life. Until now.

She'd always taken for granted that the man God brought into her life would return her feelings. Not someone like Jesse, who had a deep capacity for love, but no longer trusted it.

His shuttered expression told her that he already regretted telling her about the missing heirloom.

Too late. Lori mentally squared her shoulders. Everyone else might back off when Jesse leveled that cool stare in their direction, but she was made of sterner stuff. Not to mention the fact that she had a very effective weapon to wield against the temptation to turn tail and run back up to the house.

I can do all things through Him who strengthens me.

In this case, the *all things* was reaching out to Jesse. Whether he wanted her to or not.

"I could help you look for the ring in the early mornings, before the triplets wake up," she offered.

There was a moment of absolute silence, and Jesse said, very carefully, it seemed to Lori, "I appreciate it, but there's no point now. The local weatherman predicted that the snowfall over the next few days is going to be significant." He tossed back the last of his coffee and pitched the empty sandwich bag into a bucket against the wall. "Thanks for bringing supper."

Lori recognized a hint when she heard one, but she was reluctant to leave Jesse alone, even if it was what he thought he wanted.

"You're welcome."

Jesse's eyes narrowed. "You look half-frozen."

"I'm fine." She forced a smile as her numb toes curled in denial.

"Your cheeks are red."

Lori put the blame on Jesse, not the temperature. She blushed whenever those stunning blue eyes turned in her direction. Why couldn't she have been a brunette instead of a redhead with pale skin that acted like a barometer for her emotions?

She resisted the urge to press her mittens against her face. "Are you coming back up to the house now?"

"Not yet." Jesse knelt down and rummaged around in the toolbox beside the truck. "Not for a long time. Could be hours yet. You know how tricky driveshafts are."

Lori didn't, but she wasn't ready to give up. Call her crazy, but she enjoyed Jesse's company—when he wasn't trying so hard to be disagreeable. The more time they spent together, the more she realized his gruffness was an effective way of keeping people at arm's length.

Lori might have been put off, too, if it hadn't been for

the triplets. Jesse's love for his daughters peeled back the layers of his heart and revealed his true character.

The trip to the pediatrician the day before would have tested anyone's patience, but Jesse had responded to every unexpected situation—including a leaky diaper—with a gentle confidence that increased her respect for him even more.

Made her want to be with him even more.

Aware of Jesse watching her, Lori pretended to be interested in the collection of rusty horseshoes hanging on the wall. A movement in the shadows caught her attention, and she peered into the darkness, startled at the sight of a pair of gleaming yellow eyes peering back at her. Her pulse evened out when she realized it wasn't an oversize rat but a harmless calico cat curled up on an old couch.

She reached out a hand and rubbed her knuckles under the cat's chin. "I've never seen him before."

"He keeps to himself most of the time."

Something in common with his owner, Lori thought wryly.

"What's his name?"

Jesse hesitated a fraction of a second. "Cat."

Lori chuckled. "That's the best you could do?"

"It's as good as any." Jesse shrugged. "Cats don't answer to a name, anyway. They answer when they feel like it."

She smiled when the animal's eyes drifted closed. "Well, he must be pretty spoiled to have his own velvet couch to sleep on."

"Velvet couch? I don't think anyone stored furniture out here." Jesse stalked over to investigate and dismissed her claim with a shake of his head. "This isn't a couch. It's an old cutter."

"Cutter?"

"A sleigh." He rearranged the clutter until the sleigh was completely visible. "See the runners?"

Entranced by the sight of the old-fashioned sleigh, Lori crowded closer. "You didn't know it was here?"

Jesse rubbed his jaw. "I forgot about it, to tell you the truth."

Lori clucked her tongue. "I can't believe that."

"Believe it." Jesse kicked one of the runners with the toe of his boot. "This isn't exactly a practical vehicle to have on a ranch—especially in the Flint Hills."

"It might not be practical, but it's beautiful." Lori's fingers smoothed the dusty velvet cover. "Did you ever use it?"

"Me? No." He looked disturbed by the question.

"Why not?"

"It's kind of a...*froufrou* thing, isn't it?"

"Froufrou?" Lori repeated. "Oh, I get it. There's no saddle, and you wouldn't be able to win the race against the dogs when you come back to the barn for lunch."

Jesse stared at her and Lori winced. Maybe she shouldn't have mentioned that. It sounded as if she spied on him. And she didn't. It's just that he looked good on a horse. Really good.

The corner of Jesse's lips twitched and Lori swallowed hard. No way. He couldn't have known what she was thinking.

She forced her stubborn vocal chords to do their job. "Someone must have thought it was fun, or it wouldn't be here."

"I can't imagine hitching up one of the horses to this contraption."

"You may have to someday. When the girls are a few years older, you might want to take each of them for a ride around the yard. Make it an annual tradition at Christmas."

"Wait a second." Jesse's eyes narrowed suspiciously.

"This sounds like the 'making memories' stuff that my sister is always preaching about."

"It doesn't matter what you call it," Lori said patiently. "It boils down to *time*. And attention. Girls need to know they're special. Every time one of them tries to get your attention, she's asking you if she's important. If she's worth noticing. It will be easier to understand and accept God's love if they have a father who shows it first."

She hadn't meant to sound so passionate, but instead of becoming angry or defensive, Jesse regarded her thoughtfully. "Did yours?"

Lori's breath hitched in her throat. "I…" She moistened her chapped lips. "I… You have work to do, and I should probably check on the girls."

"Lori—" Jesse's voice reached her at the door, but she pretended not to hear.

It occurred to Lori as she hurried up the driveway that she was guilty of the very thing that frustrated her about Jesse.

She'd run away.

Chapter Thirteen

It took every ounce of Jesse's self-control not to follow Lori up to the house.

You wanted your own company, he reminded himself disgustedly.

Why would Lori want to spend time with him anyway?

He was rusty at small talk and his heart had disconnected from his brain a long time ago, giving him a distinct disadvantage when it came to understanding certain things. Like why a hundred-year-old sleigh could be an effective tool for connecting with the women in his life.

He tossed the wrench back in the toolbox and closed his eyes to block out the memory of Lori's expression when he'd asked her about her father.

It didn't work.

Once again, he'd caught a flash of sorrow in her eyes and it made him curious. No, it made him want to comfort her.

Another feeling he wasn't prepared for.

"It's none of my business," he told Cat. "That's one of the reasons we're out here in the cold garage and she's up at the house."

Not to mention it was safer that way. *He* was safer that way.

Cat obviously disagreed, because he yawned and

jumped down from the sleigh before disappearing into the shadows. Leaving Jesse to carry out his self-imposed exile alone.

For the next hour, Jesse fixed the driveshaft, swept up the floor and straightened the horseshoes on the wall. At ten o'clock, he closed the garage and headed up the driveway, relieved to see the house was dark except for the light Lori always left on in the kitchen.

The smell of gingerbread greeted him at the door.

Lori had been baking up a storm over the past few days, much to Clay's delight. She'd copied their grandmother's fudge recipe, frosted enough sugar cookies to feed an army and always kept water simmering on the stove for hot chocolate when he and Clay came inside.

When Jesse gave Lori the green light to continue her Christmas preparations, she proceeded to turn the entire house into a wonderland for the senses.

Jesse's lips curved. If he were honest with himself, he'd had more fun watching *her* than he had watching the house's gradual transformation over the past few days.

He shed his coat and boots in the laundry room and paused outside the kitchen door, positive she'd gone upstairs for the night. Maybe it wouldn't hurt to see what she'd made....

"Gingerbread with whipped cream."

Jesse whirled around and found Lori behind him. For some inexplicable reason, the room always seemed brighter when she was in it.

"I thought you'd be upstairs." *Or I'd still be in the garage.*

"Sasha woke up for a few minutes." Lori smiled. "Are you hungry?"

"No." Jesse hoped his stomach wouldn't growl and make a liar out of him. "I have some work to do on the computer."

For a split second, disappointment clouded her eyes. "I understand."

No, you don't, Jesse wanted to say. But he wasn't about to try to explain that every minute he spent in her company made him want to spend another...and another.

Jesse thought his heart had shut down after Marie's death, but whenever Lori was near, he felt as if it were slowly coming back to life.

He couldn't explain that, either. Not when he didn't understand it himself.

LORI SAT UP IN BED, wide-awake. It felt as if she'd been asleep for hours but a glance at the clock told her it was just after midnight.

The faint whimper from the nursery wasn't an unusual sound to hear during the night, but this one, followed by a rasping cough, had Lori reaching for her robe.

Guided by the glow from the night-light, she padded quietly over to Sasha's crib. Even before Lori saw the baby crowded into a corner, she sensed something was wrong.

As she bent over the rail, Sasha let out another low, pitiful cry and rubbed her face fitfully back and forth on the mattress.

"Hey, peanut," Lori whispered, using one of Jesse's favorite pet names for his youngest daughter. "What's the matter?"

Sasha reacted to the sound of her voice with a mournful whimper. Lori picked up the baby and her heart dropped as she felt the heat radiating through Sasha's terry cloth sleeper.

A hundred-degree temperature—maybe higher, she guessed.

Lori carried Sasha to the changing table and pulled open one of the drawers, glad she'd taken the time to stock it with basics, like a brand-new thermometer.

As she took the baby's temperature, Brooke woke up and sneezed several times in a row, which jump-started a confused, unhappy cry.

"I'll be there in a minute," Lori promised, in a soothing voice. "Now, let's see what we've got here." She bit her lip as the digital readout appeared on the tiny screen. "One hundred and one. Oh, sweetheart. I'm sorry."

Sasha tried to work up a smile, but another cough twisted her body. Lori picked her up, cuddling her close as she went to check on Brooke.

One look at the baby's fever-bright eyes and rosy cheeks and she knew Brooke was running a temperature at least as high as her sister's.

Panic scrambled for a foothold and Lori took a deep breath, knowing her nurse's training would only go so far. Her faith would carry her further.

She closed her eyes.

Lord, please protect the girls. You know how small and vulnerable they are. And help me have the energy and strength to care for them—

"Lori? Is everything all right?" Jesse's husky voice coming from the doorway interrupted her prayer.

She hated to tell him the truth. "Sasha and Brooke aren't feeling well."

The light flipped on and Lori saw Jesse bearing down on her, clad in a pair of black sweatpants and tugging a loose-fitting T-shirt over his head. Judging from his tousled hair and blurry eyes, he must have been sound asleep, until Sasha's cries woke him up, too.

Sasha kicked her legs weakly and made a valiant attempt to smile at her daddy—something that wrenched Lori's heart.

"What can I do?" Jesse looked wide-awake now.

"You can hold Sasha for a few minutes while I take

a look at Brooke." Lori gently transferred the baby into Jesse's arms and saw the flare of panic in his eyes.

"She's burning up."

"She has a hundred and one temp." Lori deliberately kept her voice even to keep Jesse calm.

It didn't work.

"You already took it? Is that high? Is she teething? Does she have a cold? An ear infection?"

"I'm not sure yet." Lori picked up Brooke and walked back to the changing table. The baby's soft, miserable sniffle was somehow worse than the loud protests they'd grown accustomed to hearing from the eldest triplet. "Brooke feels a little warm, so we'll check her temp, too."

"They have the same thing?"

"It looks that way." Lori kept one eye on the rise and fall of Brooke's chest as she changed the baby's diaper. Other than the congestion in their noses, both the girls' breathing sounded fairly normal. But after Jesse left, she planned to listen to their lungs with the stethoscope tucked away in her dresser.

"Maddie?" Jesse's gaze shifted to the only occupied crib in the room.

"She seems to be fine. Sound asleep through all the commotion."

"She takes after Clay." Jesse's growl sounded more affectionate than gruff for a change. "You could have lit a stick of dynamite by his head when we were kids and he would have slept through it."

Lori held up the thermometer and Jesse pressed closer, waiting for the verdict.

"One hundred and one."

"Is that high?"

"It's elevated, but not dangerously so for a child. I'll give her and Sasha a dose of medicine to bring down the fever and make them feel more comfortable."

"And then what?"

"You go back to bed and I'll take it from here."

Jesse's eyes narrowed. "You've got to be kidding."

"I'm a nurse." Lori struggled to keep her voice light so he wouldn't worry. "It's not the first time I've stayed awake all night with a fussy baby in my arms."

"But this time you've got *two* babies and *one* set of arms," Jesse pointed out. "I'm staying. I wouldn't be able to sleep anyway. Not knowing…"

His voice trailed off and the lost look in those indigo eyes made Lori want to comfort *him*. It was frightening enough for a parent when a normally healthy baby contracted a cold, but much harder to deal with when the baby's health had been fragile from birth.

Lori pushed aside her own concerns about the girls for the moment and tried to think of a way to ease his mind. She flashed a mischievous smile. "I won't turn down the help. Do you want the rocking chair or would you rather *boggle?*"

Jesse stiffened and Lori hoped he would understand that she wasn't making light of the situation but trying to ease the tension.

His lips curved into a smile. "You and Sasha take the rocking chair. Brooke and I will boggle."

"Deal."

The next few hours passed by in a blur. Both Brooke and Sasha dozed off for short periods of time and then woke up with distressed cries, as another coughing jag or sneeze disrupted their sleep.

Brooke's fever went down significantly as the night wore on, but Sasha's stubbornly inched toward one hundred and two. Every time the baby looked up at her with confusion in those wide blue eyes, it tore at Lori's heart.

She checked temperatures every hour and tried to coax both Brooke and Sasha to drink some fluids. Jesse had more success at getting Brooke to take a bottle than Lori did with Sasha, so they traded babies several times.

In spite of the worry banked in Jesse's eyes, he was a huge help. She didn't know how she would have managed without him.

Fatigue dragged at Lori's limbs and tugged at her eyelids as she rocked Sasha.

"What else can we do?" Jesse paused as he and Brooke took another lap around the room, his expression dark with worry and helplessness at his inability to ease his daughters' suffering.

"Their ears don't look infected, so if it's a virus, as I suspect, it has to run its course. I'll call Dr. Cole in the morning, but there isn't a lot we can do but try to keep them comfortable."

"It doesn't seem like enough."

A pitiful chirp came from Maddie's crib and they exchanged grim looks. Jesse was at his daughter's side in a moment and his ragged exhale warned Lori the night was about to get longer.

"Should we recruit Clay?" Lori offered the tentative suggestion, not sure how Jesse would react to the idea of asking his brother for help.

"He isn't here. He called a little bit after ten and said he planned to spend the night at Maya's. They're so close to finishing the Old Town Hall that he wanted to work as long as possible. I guess it's just the two of us."

The two of us. Maybe she was getting punchy from lack of sleep, but Lori liked the sound of that.

"I'll take her temperature." She put Sasha down in her crib and gave the baby's toes an affectionate tweak. "Don't worry, I won't forget about you."

As it turned out, Maddie seemed to have the mildest symptoms of the three, but now that she was awake, she didn't want to miss out on any of the attention.

Jesse ended up holding both babies while Lori retrieved Sasha from the crib and continued to rock her. A few minutes later, she heard Jesse's footsteps pause close by.

"Lori? Are you asleep?"

Lori's eyes snapped open. "Of course not!"

"Your eyes were closed."

"I was praying." She was too tired not to tell the truth.

Chapter Fourteen

He should have known.

Over the past few hours, his own desire to pray for his daughters had been overwhelming, but as soon as the words formed in Jesse's heart, his head questioned whether it would do any good.

He remembered the times when he'd been sick, and his mother would sit on the side of the bed, fluffing pillows and doling out cough syrup. Like Lori, her whispered prayers for comfort and healing had been a natural part of her nursing regime.

After his parents' death and Clay's departure, Jesse hadn't found much comfort or healing in prayer.

Maybe because you stopped talking to God?

Jesse couldn't deny the truth.

The night of the tree trimming party, Maya had told him their parents would have wanted them to remember the things they had valued the most. Faith. Family. Things Jesse had somehow forgotten when he focused his attention on keeping the Circle L as successful as it had been when his father was alive.

Lori's honesty struck a chord in Jesse, and he found himself responding the same way. She seemed to have a way of bypassing his defenses and getting right through to his heart.

"I used to believe that God listens. Now I'm not so sure." What Jesse hadn't realized until now was how much he wanted to believe it. "I'm not sure about anything anymore."

Lori didn't appear to be shocked by the disclosure. "He does listen. Because He loves us."

"I wish I could be sure about that, too." There. He said it. Jesse waited for the disapproval, or worse, disappointment, he knew he'd see in Lori's eyes for voicing those kinds of thoughts out loud.

"You can be."

"Really." Jesse would have raised an eyebrow but his face was too tired to do anything more than twitch. She sounded so certain. Maybe because nothing had ever happened that caused her to doubt it, he reminded himself cynically.

"You believe in Him, don't you?"

The simple question broadsided Jesse and his chin jerked in affirmation before he thought it through. "Yes."

Lori didn't look shocked by that, either. Although Jesse knew she would have seen precious few signs of his faith over the past few weeks.

His lips twisted. Who was he kidding? More like the past few years.

Lori's eyes met his and Jesse expected to see sympathy. What he saw instead was acceptance. And then determination.

"When I was a freshman in college, Lynnette, one of the girls on my floor, led me to Christ," she said. "Lynn invited me home to spend Christmas with her family, and she could tell I was still struggling with something that happened in my…past." Lori looked down at Sasha, who lay quietly in her arms, as if reluctant to disturb the outpour of memories.

"I was questioning God. Wondering why He'd allowed

it to happen. She said it was normal to have questions, but there was one I *never* had to ask. Does God love me? She said He answered that question at the manger, when He sent His son to earth. I realized that if I believe God loves me, I can trust Him to walk with me—or carry me—through the difficult things that happen."

For the past five months Jesse had received—and most of the time simply endured—dozens of well-meaning platitudes. Somehow, Lori's simple reminder of God's love began to erode the mortar of grief in the walls around his heart.

"Would you like to hear the verse she encouraged me to memorize?" Lori asked.

Jesse almost smiled. "Do I have a choice?"

A hint of a sparkle shimmered in her eyes. "Not unless you want to take the babies' temperatures next time."

Jesse winced. "Tell me the verse."

"It's from the book of Lamentations. *'Yet this I call to mind and therefore I have hope. Because of the Lord's great love we are not consumed, for His compassions never fail. They are new every morning,'*" she recited softly.

Unfortunately, Jesse knew what it felt like to be consumed.

What he didn't know was how to struggle free from the past.

"Calling it to mind," Lori said softly, as if she'd read his thoughts. Again. "It means *choosing* to remember that God loves us. No matter what happens. And we cling to that and go on from there, trusting that His great love means we are never without hope. He'll never leave us."

The note of sincerity in Lori's voice made it sound as if she spoke from experience and wasn't repeating something she'd read on the back of the church bulletin.

"What?" Lori shifted under the intensity of his gaze.

"That's why you love Christmas, isn't it?"

"Love Christmas?" Lori looked bewildered at the sudden turn in the conversation.

"I thought you just liked to fuss over the decorations and the making memories stuff," Jesse mused. "But it's because of what your friend, Lynnette, said, isn't it? About the proof of God's love being settled at the manger."

"Weren't we talking about you?" Lori's cheeks turned an appealing shade of pink as she averted her eyes.

Jesse was a little stunned to discover that he wanted her to trust him. Her abrupt departure the night before told him his question about her father had touched a nerve. She generously gave to others but seemed to draw back when it came to allowing others to reach out to *her*. He wanted to know her. Scary stuff for a man who'd decided that he wasn't going to let anyone get close. But he hadn't anticipated he would want to get closer to *her*.

Brooke let out an unhappy squawk, granting Jesse a brief reprieve from another unexpected revelation. He took her for another lap around the room to give his brain a chance to catch up with his heart. He'd never opened up about his faith—or lack thereof—after Marie died. Not even to Maya or Reverend Garrison.

"Jesse?" Lori called to him softly, as he finished lap number three. "Look who finally fell asleep."

"Sasha." Relief surged through Jesse as he looked down and saw that his daughter's eyes were closed, the fringe of dark lashes fanned out on pudgy, tear-stained cheeks.

"And Brooke." Lori's weary smile bloomed as her gaze lingered on the baby in his arms.

Jesse had been so lost in thought, he hadn't realized Brooke had fallen asleep. He laid his cheek against hers and the satiny skin felt cooler to the touch.

Thank You, Lord.

For once, Jesse didn't suppress his natural inclination to talk to God. For the first time in a long time, it felt…right.

"I'm going to put Sasha back in her crib now and see if she'll sleep for a while. Before it's time…" Lori stifled a yawn. "To get up."

Jesse noticed the pale streaks of silver lightening the horizon and grimaced. "I think it *is* time to get up."

"Then I'll hook up an IV to the coffeepot."

He choked back a laugh, a little amazed at how quickly—and easily—it had surfaced.

Lori gave him a stern look and put a finger to her lips, careful not to wake up Sasha as she carried her across the room.

Jesse followed suit and put Brooke down, too. He and Lori turned away from the cribs at the same time and ended up face-to-face.

She was beautiful. Even with lavender shadows under her eyes and unkempt wisps of hair framing her weary features.

Without thinking, Jesse reached out and lifted a loose strand of copper hair, tucking it behind her ear. It felt like satin between his fingers, just like he knew it would.

Lori's eyes widened as Jesse's fingertips traced a whisper-light path down the side of her neck.

"Thank you," he murmured. "For…everything."

Lori nodded, and the fact that she didn't move away made it that much harder not to take her in his arms. The only thing that stopped him was knowing that if he did, he wouldn't want to let her go.

"Hey, what's going on?" Clay's cheerful baritone boomed from the doorway. "Did my nieces decide to get up extra early to help with the chores this morning?"

His brother's timing, Jesse thought grimly, could have been a little better. And yet again, maybe he'd appeared in the nick of time.

LORI WATCHED JESSE nudge his brother into the hallway, and she forced her sluggish feet to follow, still a little dazed by the expression she'd seen in Jesse's eyes.

He'd wanted to kiss her.

Confusion churned in her stomach. Lori had assumed her feelings for Jesse were one-sided. Given her limited experience when it came to relationships, she didn't know if he was aware of—let alone felt—the tiny electrical charges that pulsed between them if they accidentally touched while giving the triplets their baths or traded babies during the bedtime routine.

Only, this time Jesse's touch hadn't been accidental.

She'd seen the conflict in his eyes when he looked down at her. Or maybe she'd seen her own emotions reflected there.

"The girls were up most of the night with high fevers," Jesse explained to Clay in a terse whisper, as he pulled the door closed behind them. "They just fell asleep a few minutes ago."

Clay's smile faded, replaced by concern as he looked at Lori. "Are they feeling better now?"

"Their temps seem to be going down," she replied.

"There must be something going around. Nicki mentioned that Kasey seemed lethargic yesterday. She even left work early to put her down for a nap in her own bed."

"Mmm. A nap."

Jesse's sharp look told Lori that she'd said the words out loud.

"Why don't you go back to bed for a few hours," he suggested. "I can hold down the fort until they wake up."

Clay slanted a skeptical look at his brother. "You look dead on your feet, too. Maybe *I* should be the one who holds down the fort. Since I wasn't here to rock a baby to sleep, the least I can do is make breakfast."

"Sounds good to me."

Clay looked shocked at his brother's easy acceptance of the offer.

Lori's heart lightened. Over the past few days, Clay had given Jesse's bad mood a wide berth, and Lori hoped the change she was witnessing in Jesse now was continued proof of God's faithfulness.

Jesse was His child and He wasn't going to let him go.

Once again, she was amazed at how the Lord brought good things out of difficult situations. Walking the floor with the triplets all night had opened up the door to a conversation she and Jesse might never have had under ordinary circumstances. It also had given her another glimpse into Jesse's heart. She no longer saw a man who'd rejected his faith, she saw a man struggling to rebuild his life on the foundation of that faith, but not sure how to go about it. What he didn't seem to realize was that rebuilding took time and patience. And forgiveness.

"I'll get started. Scrambled eggs and sausage? Pancakes? Fried potatoes?"

"Yes," Lori said instantly. "And coffee."

Clay chuckled but Jesse didn't join in. In fact, now he seemed to be avoiding her eyes. She was relieved when he accompanied his brother to the kitchen, sharing the details of the long night they'd had with the triplets on the way down the stairs.

She hoped there was one detail he *wouldn't* share.

Nothing happened, Lori reminded herself, ignoring the pulse that still jumped in the hollow at the base of her throat. The very spot his hand had lingered at after he'd tucked her hair behind her ear.

Jesse had simply…thanked her.

But for what? For helping with the babies? For encouraging him to go back to the core of his faith? For reminding him that God loved him?

The questions spun confusing circles in her brain, as

Jingle Bell Babies

Lori retreated to her room for a quick shower. The warm water revived her enough that she was able to ignore the comfortable bed as she pulled on a pair of jeans and a sweater.

Guided to the kitchen by the sizzle of bacon frying, Lori found Jesse already sitting at the kitchen table, his lean fingers linked around a mug of freshly brewed coffee.

Clay smiled and pointed the spatula at an empty chair across the table from Jesse. "Sit. Recover."

"He took over," Jesse murmured.

"Only because you're tired. I figured it was only fair that I take a turn at being the boss." Clay winked at her as he set a cup of coffee in front of her. "You should have called Maya's and let me know about the triplets. I would have come home right away."

Jesse was silent for a moment. "I didn't think…"

"I would," Clay finished the sentence. "Sometimes all you have to do is ask, Jess. That's what family is for."

Lori tensed, waiting for a terse comeback, but Jesse shot his brother a rueful look. "It's beginning to…sink in."

"What's beginning to sink in?" Maya breezed into the kitchen with Greg close behind. "That you aren't a superhero?"

Lori's lips twitched and Jesse leveled a *don't say one word about the guy in the pink tasseled blanket* look.

"It's too early in the morning for company," he complained, sinking a little lower in the chair. "Especially when a guy's been up all night."

"Company?" Maya rolled her eyes. "We're not company. We're here to take a shift." Her lively gaze swung from her brother to Lori. "You were right, Clay. They do look terrible."

Jesse scowled at Clay as the reason for Maya and Greg's

impromptu visit became clear. "I thought you outgrew tattling."

Clay loaded a stack of buttermilk pancakes onto a platter and brought it to the table. "It's only tattling when you're under the age of ten. After that, it falls under the category of sharing information."

Maya pulled out a chair and sat down next to Lori. Jesse's sister had the radiant look of someone who'd actually gotten a good night's sleep.

"Don't you two have jobs?" Jesse asked as she reached for his cup of coffee.

"I have a very understanding boss." Maya gave her husband a saucy wink.

"A boss who can take the day off when there's a family emergency," Greg added.

"Don't worry about a thing," Maya said blithely. "Grab a long nap, both of you, or you'll never make it through the day, let alone another night, if they're up again." After taking a sip of Jesse's coffee, she plucked the fork out of Jesse's hand and stabbed one of the sausages on his plate. "I'll clean up in here."

"I'll bet you will." Jesse accepted another fork from Clay.

Lori's head started to swim. Whether it was from sleep deprivation or an attempt to follow the conversation, she wasn't sure.

"I don't think I'll be able to fall asleep," she offered tentatively. "I can always catch a quick nap later this afternoon, when the triplets do."

Maya folded her arms. "Good. That means you'll get two naps today. One this morning while I'm here, and one this afternoon."

"You might as well give up," Jesse said. "There's no talking to her when she gets stubborn."

"It's a Logan trait." Maya looked pleased rather than offended by the description.

"You get no arguments from me," her husband chimed in.

Lori still wasn't sure. "You'll wake me up if their fevers spike again?" she asked. It wasn't as if she didn't trust Maya with the triplets—the babies loved their aunt—but she wanted to be certain they hadn't developed any new symptoms.

"Of course I will. Clay and Greg can start the barn chores and I'll take care of my nieces."

"Greg? Barn chores?" Jesse looked doubtfully at his brother-in-law, dressed in wrinkle-free khaki pants and a crisp, button-down shirt.

"The pointy end of the pitchfork goes in the hay," Greg said.

"Good enough." Clay handed the spatula to his sister and clapped his brother-in-law on the shoulder. "Let's go."

"It looks like we're outnumbered." Jesse turned toward Lori, his elusive smile surfacing once again. "The p.m. shift is temporarily off-duty."

The room shrank and Maya and Clay's good-natured banter faded to a low hum in the background as their eyes met across the table.

Lori stood up so quickly the chair almost upended, and she excused herself to escape to the safety of the hallway.

Jesse had made it sound as if the two of them were a team. For a moment, she felt as if she were part of the family, instead of the woman Jesse had hired to take care of the triplets during the day.

But Lori realized she was no longer content simply to be part of a "team." What she wanted more than anything was to be part of a family. But not just *any* family.

Jesse's family.

JESSE'S FEET FELT LEADEN as he stumbled back up the stairs. He decided to check on the triplets one more time, and then take Maya up on her offer to take a nap.

After he patiently gave his sister a brief recap of the triplets' sleepless night, Maya had once again taken advantage of the opportunity to remind him how blessed he was to have a nurse caring for the girls.

Not that Jesse needed to be reminded. Lori had done more than comfort the babies throughout the long night. She'd sensed how worried he was and tried to calm his fears, too.

What am I supposed to do, Lord?

This time Jesse didn't even question why it was becoming easier to turn toward God for direction, instead of away from Him.

If he were honest with himself—something that was also occurring more and more frequently—he knew Lori was partially responsible for that, too.

She hadn't backed down when he'd expressed his frustration and his doubts, but gently challenged him to look beyond his pain and return to the source of his faith. Her laughter had a way of chasing away the shadows that crowded in....

And he'd almost kissed her.

Jesse stifled a groan. Could he blame that momentary lapse of judgment on sleep deprivation? Or the fallout from being worried about the girls?

Or was it because Jesse was unable to muster up the strength to resist his feelings for Lori?

Before she moved in, he'd convinced himself that he was through with love. It had proven to be too unpredictable. Too risky.

He'd rushed into a relationship with Marie before they'd really gotten to know each other.

Jingle Bell Babies

Jesse paused on the stairs, gripping the banister like a lifeline.

He'd tried. He'd really tried. But in the end, he'd failed to make Marie happy. Wasn't that proof he wasn't cut from the same cloth as the other men in his family? The diamond ring—the one *he'd* lost—had become a symbol over the years. A testimony of the lasting love the Logan men had found. What did it say about him, that he could keep the Circle L going but not his own marriage?

Chapter Fifteen

The wind rattled the windows, and as Lori forced her eyelids open, she became aware of two things. It was snowing. And a glance at the clock on the nightstand told her that she'd slept almost four hours.

Rolling out of bed, she immediately made her way to the nursery. All three cribs were empty. No sign of Maya and the babies. Or Jesse.

Stumbling down the stairs, she made her way to the living room, where she discovered Maya and the triplets. Brooke sat in her infant swing, happily chewing on her stuffed octopus, while Sasha and Maddie kicked contentedly on a blanket near the Christmas tree.

"Good morning," Jesse's sister greeted Lori cheerfully as she padded into the room.

"It's afternoon." Lori hadn't meant to sound so accusing.

Maya didn't take offense. "Don't blame me. I was under strict orders to let you sleep."

"Strict orders?"

Maya grinned. "Straight from the top."

Jesse. Lori's stomach did a backflip. Would he think she was shirking her duties? She had hoped he would still be asleep, too. Then he wouldn't realize she'd slept away a good portion of the day.

"How are they feeling?" Lori's gaze bounced from baby to baby, searching for signs of illness.

Maya handed Sasha a ring of chunky plastic beads. "I took their temperatures half an hour ago. Brooke and Maddie's are normal again, but Sasha's is hovering around ninety-nine."

Ninety-nine was a marked improvement. Lori couldn't hide her relief as she knelt down next to the blanket and reached for the smallest triplet. "I planned to call Dr. Cole and let her know what's going on."

"Jesse already did. The nurse said there's a twenty-four-hour bug going around, and as long as the girls are taking in fluids and their temperatures stay down, she shouldn't need to see them." Maya smiled. "She must trust they're in good hands."

Warmed by the unexpected compliment, Lori cuddled Sasha and received another reward in the form of a wide, toothless smile. "That's my girl." She glanced at Maya. "How long has Jesse been awake?"

"He staggered downstairs about two hours ago." An emotion Lori couldn't identify skimmed across the other woman's face. "We're supposed to get a few inches of snow by this evening, so he was anxious to get outside. He said he had something to do that couldn't wait."

Remembering their conversation in the garage when she'd inquired about the metal detector, Lori instantly guessed what that something was.

"He's looking for the ring."

"I think so." Maya didn't look surprised that Lori had figured out the truth. "He blames himself that it's missing."

"That's silly." Frustration bubbled up inside her. It seemed as if Jesse blamed himself for a lot of things that were beyond his control. "It wasn't as if he had any way of preventing the tornado from touching down."

Maya was silent for a moment, and her troubled expression told Lori she was reliving the events of that day. "He found the rings and the note Marie left before the tornado came through but he left them on the table, hoping Marie would change her mind."

Lori's heart sank. That explained a lot. Why Jesse felt so responsible for the missing family heirloom. And why he'd struck the word *hope* from his vocabulary. He'd added his wife's abandonment to the list of dreams that hadn't come true. Prayers he thought hadn't been answered.

Didn't he recognize all the ones that had?

"That wasn't his fault, either."

"Of course not. But my big brother, for better or worse, feels personally responsible for everything that has to do with carrying on the Logan legacy. He doesn't realize he's not the only Logan around here." Maya shook her head. "As the oldest son, he feels the weight of everyone's expectations. Considering the Circle L has been around for about a hundred and fifty years, that adds up to a lot of expectations."

Lori couldn't argue with that. Rising to her feet, she carried Sasha over to the window. Snow continued to sift from the gunmetal-gray clouds overhead, dusting the prairie grass with a layer of white.

Not far from the house, she could see the lone figure of a man on horseback, the black duster he wore a stark silhouette against the hills.

"When Clay came back to High Plains last month, I prayed that he and Jesse would move forward...but Jesse is having a difficult time letting go of the past. He can't seem to forgive our brother."

"What happened?" As soon as Lori voiced the question out loud, she wondered if Maya would think she was overstepping her bounds.

"He didn't tell you?"

Lori shook her head, hiding her surprise at Maya's assumption that Jesse had confided in her.

"It started when Clay was a teenager." Maya's eyes darkened at the memory. "He rebelled. Claimed he didn't fit in here. He questioned everything we'd been taught and it just about broke Mom and Dad's heart. One night he and some friends got into trouble. Our parents went to pick him up… The accident happened on the way home. Clay had minor injuries but Mom and Dad…"

Maya's voice hitched and Lori waited until she was able to continue with the story.

"After they died, the tension between Jesse and Clay got even worse. Clay resented it when Jesse acted like a parent instead of an older brother. The night of Clay's senior prom, right before graduation, they had a huge falling out. Jesse never told me exactly what was said, but the next morning Clay was gone. He'd packed up his things and left before Jesse went out to start his chores. Clay finally called me and we kept in touch over the years, but I couldn't convince him to come home. I prayed a lot, knowing God had the power to reach him even when I couldn't."

Lori had been praying a similar prayer for Jesse for the past few weeks. The shift in his attitude when he'd confided his doubts about his faith had proven what she'd sensed all along. Like the prairie grass after a storm, Jesse had been beaten down, but the roots of his faith hadn't been completely destroyed. If he would only take a step forward, Lori knew God would meet him on the second.

Her own life was a testimony to that.

"When Clay came back to High Plains, I thought it would mean a fresh start for them, but he told me yesterday that he's getting discouraged. He still believes Jesse has never forgiven him for the death of our parents—or for leaving the Circle L."

"Maybe it's not Clay that Jesse hasn't forgiven," Lori said softly.

"What do you mean?"

"You were just talking about how he feels responsible for everything," Lori said. "Maybe the person Jesse hasn't been able to forgive is himself."

AN EXERCISE IN FUTILITY. That's what it was.

Jesse contemplated the acres of Logan land, stretching farther than the eye could see, against the chances of finding a tiny band of gold on the ground. Ground already covered with a dusting of snow.

What made him think he would find it now? He'd given up the search months ago, knowing it would be like looking for a needle in the proverbial haystack. Nothing had changed.

But I want it to.

Jesse rejected the thought. It didn't matter what he wanted. He had chosen to deal with reality. And the reality was that he still couldn't look his brother in the eye. Tomorrow was Christmas Eve and he hadn't bought gifts for anyone...and he'd fallen in love with his daughters' nanny.

How was that for reality?

Jesse closed his eyes and felt the snowflakes catch in his lashes. For a moment, he let his imagination loose. He imagined finding the ring and slipping it on Lori's finger.

A horn blasted several times and Jesse saw Maya and Greg's van rolling down the driveway.

Their departure meant Lori was awake.

He made Maya promise that she would let her sleep until she woke up on her own.

Because I'm still afraid to face her? And my feelings?

Maybe so. Or maybe, Jesse decided, he was just a glutton for punishment. So he spent another hour riding the fence line of the property where the tornado had touched down, searching for a glimmer of gold against the snow.

He finally called it quits as the sun went down. The snowflakes had changed into pellets of freezing rain that stung his face and greased the ground beneath the horse's hooves.

Jesse touched his heels against Saber's side and the horse turned agreeably toward the barn, anxious to get out of the weather, even if Jesse didn't seem to be.

HE MET HIS BROTHER on the way out of the building.

"How are the girls?" Clay asked.

"Much better."

"I picked up the mail while I was in town." Clay handed him a stack of envelopes, most of them the size and shape of Christmas cards. "I only stopped home to feed the stock. Mayor Lawson recruited Nicki and me to help with some last-minute details at the Old Town Hall."

There was a silent question in his brother's voice that Jesse ignored. Clay and Maya would have to be content with his presence at the festivities. He couldn't offer anything more.

"I'll see you later, then." He sifted through the mail as he walked up to the house, and a red stamp caught his eye. He paused under the lamppost to read it.

Lori's name was in the top left corner, but someone had written "Return To Sender" in large block letters over the name of the addressee.

Tom Martin.

He tucked the envelopes into the inside pocket of his coat before the snow dampened them. Stepping into the inviting warmth of the house, Jesse's numb fingers fumbled with the ice-encrusted zipper on his coat.

He heard Lori's gasp before he saw her standing in the

doorway. In a second she was at his side, conquering the stubborn zipper and peeling the coat off.

"I'm…"

Lori silenced him with a look and chucked his coat onto the dryer.

"Boots."

He complied immediately, sensing that if he didn't, Lori would assist him with the task. It took every ounce of his energy, but Jesse managed to scrape the frozen leather off his icy feet.

As he leaned forward, something crunched in his pocket. He'd forgotten the card.

"This is for you." He handed her the envelope he'd retrieved from his pocket. "You must have forgotten to change someone's address in your file."

Lori took it from his hand. "Thank…"

Jesse glanced at her sharply as her voice trailed off.

"Lori? What's the matter?"

She smiled wanly and tore her gaze away from the card. "I'm fine. Just a little tired. There's a fire going in the living room."

She straightened her shoulders and marched down the hall. Jesse limped along behind her.

When they reached the living room, Lori removed her knitting from the chair closest to the fire and propped her hands on her hips as Jesse gingerly lowered himself into it. Steam from a mug of coffee on the side table rose into the air, and he cast a brief but longing look at it.

"I poured it for you." Lori caught his glance.

"Is everything all right?" he asked. "You seem a little tense."

"Tense." Lori repeated the word. "Do you realize you rode off alone two hours ago? In an ice storm?"

The way Lori put it, it made him sound reckless. Irresponsible.

"You were looking for the ring, weren't you?"

And that, Jesse thought, made him sound just plain idiotic.

"I don't know why...." Except that he did. And it was her fault. Lori was beginning to make him believe that anything was possible.

"You don't understand," Jesse murmured. "The ring was entrusted to my care. Like the ranch." *Like Clay.* "You don't know what it's like to lose—" *someone* "—something that important."

"Yes, I do." The raw grief in Lori's eyes stunned him into silence. "I lost my...parents."

"I thought your mother lives in New York."

"She does." Lori's bleak smile didn't reach her eyes. "And the letter you gave to me is from my dad."

Tom Martin. Her father.

Jesse realized that he wanted her to trust him. In the past, he'd shied away from Maya's pleas to talk to her about what he was feeling, because he didn't think it would do any good. She couldn't fix it. But now he understood what his sister had really wanted. She wanted the opportunity to share his burden—something he wanted to do for Lori now.

"Will you tell me about it?"

After a split second of silence, Lori nodded.

"I told you that I'm an only child, but we were never what you would consider a close family. What I remember the most about our house was the silence. My parents didn't talk much—to each other or to me. Dad came home from work and closed himself off in the den while Mom got dinner ready. She would shoo me away whenever I tried to help. I just thought everyone's family was like ours. Until I overheard them arguing one day—about me."

A trickle of unease skated down Jesse's spine as Lori's voice ebbed away and then strengthened again.

"Mom was yelling at Dad—I'd never heard her yell before—telling him how sick she was of being blamed for ruining his life. She said things hadn't exactly turned out the way she'd planned, either." Lori paused long enough to draw a ragged breath.

"Dad said she had no right to ask him for anything, because he'd done his duty by marrying her when she got pregnant. With me. That's when it all made sense. They weren't too tired or too busy to spend time with me—they'd never *wanted* me. I was a constant reminder that they'd buckled under the pressure from their families to do the right thing. It was hard to accept the fact I was a mistake. But even though things weren't perfect, I told myself that at least we were together. Things could always change, right?" Lori shook her head. "They did. After I graduated from high school, my parents filed for a nice, polite divorce and then they…left. It was as if they'd been freed after eighteen years of bondage. I haven't heard from Dad since."

Anger welled up inside of Jesse. It was difficult to believe that the warm, loving woman he'd come to know had grown up in such a cheerless environment. Lori could have easily become bitter or mistrustful of people.

The way I did.

Jesse winced at the thought. But instead, the trials she'd endured had forged a heart of sensitivity and compassion.

"When I started college, I was a mess," Lori continued. "It was hard to accept that my parents were out there living their own lives, but had chosen to live them without me. If it hadn't been for God bringing Lynette into my life, I don't know where I would have ended up. I didn't think I was worth loving, but she told me that God loved me. If I hadn't reached out and grabbed on to that, I think the grief would have consumed me." The warm light returned to Lori's eyes and her expression softened. "You

see, I *do* understand, Jesse. There are different ways to…
lose people."

Jesse didn't answer. He couldn't.

Lori was right. Didn't it feel as if he had lost his brother
years ago? In some ways, the pain cut deeper than it had
after Jesse lost his parents. It may have been a different
kind of grief, but it was still grief.

It occurred to Jesse that Clay might be feeling the same
way. Weighted down with guilt. Believing all the things
Jesse had said one night out of anger.

He'd been afraid that his brother's reckless behavior
would lead to another headstone next to their parents, and
Jesse knew he couldn't stand by and watch it happen.

Clay thought Jesse continued to blame him for the death
of their parents, but that wasn't true. Jesse blamed himself.
For the death of their relationship.

Was it really possible to start over again? Rebuild?

Lori believed it was.

God can make something new. She'd told him that
shortly after they met.

Now Jesse had to make a decision.

Did he believe it, too?

Chapter Sixteen

Lori retreated to her bedroom, wishing she could rewind the last twenty minutes of her life.

Flopping down on the bed, she closed her eyes—but it didn't help.

What had she been thinking? Opening up to Jesse about the wounds of her past? She didn't want his sympathy— she wanted him to know what had helped her heal those wounds.

Her cell phone hummed on the nightstand and Lori fumbled to reach it. When she saw the name that appeared on the tiny screen, she flipped it open and managed to croak out a hello.

"Lori! I'm so glad you answered the phone." Janet's brisk voice came over the line. "Do you have a minute?"

Since she planned to hide in her room as long as possible, Lori could answer the question truthfully. "Sure."

"We haven't talked for a few weeks, so I thought I'd call and find out how things are going for you."

If only Janet would have called earlier! "Things are fine." *Just peachy.* "What about you?"

"Well…" The gusty sigh accompanying the word warned Lori that she'd given her former supervisor an ideal opening. "Yvonne gave her notice yesterday and Marlene is going on maternity leave next week. I'm definitely short-staffed, and the Fraser twins are due in a few days."

"I'm sorry." Lori meant it.

"Sorry enough to come back to us?"

Janet's laughter trailed the question, but Lori wasn't fooled. And even though she'd seen this coming, it hadn't prepared her for the viselike grip around her heart.

"Janet…"

"Don't answer me right now," her supervisor interrupted. "But please hear me out."

By the time Janet was finished making an offer that she hoped Lori wouldn't refuse, Lori was more confused than ever.

Was the timing of the phone call an answer to her prayer?

Lori hung up the phone and stared at the ceiling.

What do You want me to do, Lord?

"WHAT ARE YOU DOING out here?"

Jesse started at the sound of Clay's voice. Great. Just what he needed. A witness to his total emotional breakdown.

He tried to connect his jumbled thoughts but couldn't come up with a logical reason for being out in the barn at this time of night.

Other than the real one. That it had become his refuge over the years.

"What are *you* doing here?" Jesse turned the question on his brother. "I thought you drove into High Plains to work on the Old Town Hall."

"It's almost midnight. And it's done." There was an undercurrent of pride in Clay's weary voice as he sauntered over and flopped down on a bale of hay.

Forcing Jesse to state the obvious. "If you don't mind, I'd like to be alone."

"Alone." Clay's eyebrows rose. "Are you sure that's what you want, Jess?"

Jesse scowled. "You don't want to have this conversation. Remember what happened—"

"The night I followed you into the barn." Clay finished the sentence. "How could I forget?"

Silence settled between them, the air thick with memories.

"It's in the past."

"No it isn't." Clay met his gaze. "It's right here between us. And I'm not talking about the night of the senior prom. I'm talking about the night Mom and Dad died."

No way could he take two emotional hits in the same night. Not when he was still trying to recover from the last one.

Jesse took a step forward, escape on his mind, but Clay sprang to his feet and blocked his exit.

"Remember, Jess? You caught me sneaking out and you confronted me about the decisions I'd been making. You asked me if I was sure I wanted to—and I quote— 'go down that road,' because of where it might eventually lead. I went the wrong way. I admit that and I've been paying for it ever since." Clay's voice was hoarse. "I walked away from everything I believed in, and from the woman I loved. Now I'm going to ask you the same question you asked me that night. Are you sure this is the road you want to take? Because trust me, I've been there, and it's pretty dark."

Memories crashed over Jesse, momentarily stunning him into silence. He remembered the conversation as if it had taken place yesterday.

"And Jess." Clay's voice lowered to a whisper. "You have to realize that your girls…they may follow you. Is that what you want for them?"

Hot needles stabbed the back of Jesse's eyes.

Lori had been trying to tell him the same thing when she'd opened up and shared her past. She had been raised by parents emotionally crippled because they'd been unable to forgive and move forward.

She'd been brave enough to open that door and look back at her painful past because she wanted more for the triplets. She wanted more for *him*.

Clay exhaled in frustration. "Fine. Now I know how you felt when I didn't listen to you. I always thought you were the smart one, but if you can't see what's right in front of you, then you deserve to be alone and miserable."

Jesse knew what was in front of him. The future. And for the first time in a long time, he found himself looking forward to it.

"You dump all that on me and then you leave?" Now it was Jesse's turn to step in front of his brother as he pivoted toward the door.

"You wish," Clay retorted. "When is it going to sink through your thick hide that I'm not going anywhere?"

"Now." That simple admission gave Jesse the strength to continue down a new path. His throat worked. "I'm sorry. For the things I said. For the years we lost...."

He couldn't say any more. But Jesse found that he didn't need to, because Clay reached out and gripped his hand. And gave Jesse the courage to let go of the past.

"Merry Christmas, Jesse."

Jesse's face heated as he straightened and saw Colt Ridgeway standing several feet away. Of course the chief of police had caught him lurking near the perfume counter.

"It's Christmas Eve." Jesse inched away from a display of glass bottles.

"Close enough." Colt shrugged. "Doing some last-minute shopping?"

"Really last-minute," Jesse confessed. "The triplets were sick a few days ago and I lost track of time."

Colt regarded him shrewdly. "How are you doing these days?"

"Better." Jesse smiled. "Much better."

"I'm glad to hear that, Jesse." Colt pointed to a lavender bottle on a mirrored pedestal. "By the way, Lexi likes this one. Maybe Maya would, too."

"It's not for—" Jesse caught himself, but it was too late.

A slow grin spread across the officer's face. "See you tonight."

Jesse glanced at his watch and decided to pick up the pace a little. He didn't want to buy Lori perfume—he loved the unique scent of wildflowers that she favored.

He veered down the toy aisle and picked up a net bag full of colorful tub toys. The triplets were finally starting to enjoy bath time.

So was he. Kneeling next to Lori, shoulder to shoulder with an assembly line of shampoo, bubblegum-scented bath bubbles and lotion, any worries that dogged his heels during the day dissolved.

He loved the way Lori could turn the most mundane, ordinary tasks into something extraordinary.

She said she'd lost her parents, but as far as Jesse was concerned, Tom and Roxanne Martin had lost the most when they'd pushed Lori out of their lives.

"Can't wait to get Lori Martin back on the floor..."

The familiar name snagged Jesse's attention as two women wearing warm coats over their hospital scrubs passed him.

"Janet has been stressed out since she left. I heard she called Lori yesterday and offered her a big raise if she agreed to come back to the NICU."

"I couldn't believe it when she quit to take care of the Logan triplets."

"Lori did seem to lose some of her focus after they were born. She punched out late or skipped her lunch break to spend extra time with them. I wondered if she was getting too attached to them."

Both women parted as they reached Jesse, who stood frozen in the center of the aisle.

"Well, I hope she comes to her senses. In a few years, she could be running the entire floor. It wasn't exactly a strategic career move to trade a promotion in order to work as a nanny on a ranch in the middle of nowhere…" The woman's voice faded away as she and her coworker reached the end cap and turned the corner.

It hurt to take a breath.

Lori. Leaving. And she hadn't said a word.

Don't you get it, a mocking voice chided. *This is what you get for hoping. For starting to care again.*

Fists clenched at his sides, Jesse fought against the doubts that crashed over him.

Lord, help me. I refuse to go down this path again.

As soon as Jesse prayed, it felt as if a burden were lifted off his shoulders. His thoughts cleared as he allowed their conversation to cycle back through his mind.

It didn't sound as if Lori had agreed to return to her old job yet—only that her supervisor had asked her to come back.

It was up to him to convince her to stay. Jesse couldn't lose her now. He still hadn't told her that he and Clay reconciled. He hadn't told her how moved he'd been that she'd trusted him with the truth about her childhood.

He hadn't told her that he loved her.

Jesse closed his eyes.

Great timing, Logan. You finally come to your senses just when she's about to quit. She'll never believe you now, if you tell her that you love her.

Then he would just have to show her instead.

Galvanized into action, Jesse paid for his purchases and made his way to the parking lot. He turned the key in the ignition and felt his cell phone vibrate inside his coat pocket.

He ignored it, but less than ten seconds later it came to life again.

"Logan." He flipped open the phone and snapped out the word.

"Jesse? It's Reverend Garrison."

Jesse's heart slammed against his ribcage at the sound of the familiar voice. He knew that a call from the minister didn't necessarily mean bad news, but the conversation he'd overheard in the store had put him on edge.

"What can I do for you?"

"I was wondering if you could stop by the church for a few minutes. We need to...talk."

Jesse frowned. A minister who needed to talk. Something in the man's voice warned him that the conversation wasn't going to center around the weather.

What he wanted to do was get home to Lori. To tell her that he was in love with her. To beg her not to leave.

"It won't take long."

Five minutes would be too long. Especially when he'd been so resistant to the truth of his feelings for Lori. "I don't think I—"

"Please, Jesse."

Jesse sighed. Even though he'd resisted Reverend Garrison's attempts to draw him back into the fold after Marie died, the man had patiently waited in the wings, praying for him until Jesse came to his senses. The way a lot of other people had.

Which meant Jesse owed him a few minutes of his time.

"I'm on my way."

"Thanks. We'll be in my office."

We'll?

Jesse was about to ask who else would be there, but the minister hung up before he could question him.

Main Street was a flurry of activity. Most of the stores were closing early, so last-minute Christmas shoppers trudged through the snow, laden down with packages. Jesse noticed with amusement that most of them were men. He passed the Garrison building where Maya worked, and saw customers lined up outside of Elmira's Pie Diner, waiting for their orders.

The church parking lot was jam-packed with cars, but Jesse managed to maneuver his pickup into one of the few empty spaces.

He still couldn't believe the volunteers had finished rebuilding the Old Town Hall in time for the Christmas Eve celebration.

Mayor Lawson had invited him to speak at the Founders' Day potluck that evening, but Jesse had turned down the invitation. As far as he'd been concerned, he was the last person qualified to give a speech on "Moving Forward in Faith."

Now? Jesse smiled as he remembered his conversation with Clay. Now he just might have something to say.

Reverend Garrison stepped out of his office and waved to Jesse a split second after the front doors of the church closed behind him.

Jesse was used to seeing an easy smile on Michael's face, but today deep lines bracketed his mouth and his expression looked too serious for a simple social call.

Michael stepped to one side as Jesse warily approached. "I appreciate this, Jesse. Come in."

Jesse stepped into the office but stopped short as Heather Waters rose to her feet. He gave the attractive young woman a polite nod, a little mystified by her presence. Heather had returned to High Plains after a ten-year absence to assist the victims of the tornado, but because she was closer in age to his sister, Maya, he didn't remember much about her.

"Hello, Jesse." Heather's smile, like Reverend Garrison's, appeared forced.

The minister closed the door, effectively sealing them all inside the office. "You've met Avery. My niece."

For the first time, Jesse noticed the teenage girl huddled in one of the comfortable leather chairs, hugging her knees against her chest. Two brown pigtails didn't conceal her pale features as she stared intently at her lap.

"Of course. She helped Tommy and Layla decorate my Christmas tree one afternoon."

Avery mumbled something but didn't look up.

"Have a seat, Jesse." Reverend Garrison motioned to an empty chair.

Jesse hesitated. He didn't want a seat. Not when Lori could be packing her suitcase.

"Please."

Another *please.*

Jesse buried a sigh and sat down. "What's this about?" His impatience to get back to the Circle L—and to Lori—honed an edge on the words.

"Avery has something to tell you," Heather said softly.

The girl glanced at him and then quickly looked away, but not before Jesse saw a flare of panic in her eyes.

"Okay." Whatever was going on, Jesse didn't want to be responsible for making a kid like Avery shake in her boots. He stretched out his legs as if he had all the time in the world, and aimed a smile in her direction.

His plan backfired. Instead of putting her at ease, Avery slumped even lower in the chair and shot a distressed look at her uncle. Compassion filled Reverend Garrison's eyes, but he simply nodded.

"I wanted…" Avery choked on the words as she met

Jesse's gaze. "I wanted to tell you that I'm the one who put the fake ring in the Lost and Found a few months ago."

"You?" Jesse frowned.

Avery nodded miserably, tears springing to her eyes. "It looked kind of like the one everyone was searching for, but I didn't know for sure. I figured whoever lost it could buy a new one, and I wanted to keep the one I found. But then Uncle Mike said it was really old and it meant a lot to the person who lost it. That it was special. I never owned anything like that before but when I came to your house that night with Maya, I could tell that you were sad it was gone. I'm really sorry. I know I messed up."

Her voice trailed off and Reverend Garrison put a comforting hand on the girl's shoulder while Jesse tried to fit the pieces together.

Wait a second. Several of the words connected, and a cautious hope stirred in Jesse's chest.

"Are you saying…" His throat tightened. "That you *found* the diamond ring? The real one?"

Avery sniffed. And nodded. Before Jesse realized what was happening, she opened her hand. Cradled in her palm was the diamond ring that Will Logan had slipped on Emmeline's finger when he'd proposed.

Jesse stared at it in disbelief.

"Avery showed the ring to me this morning and I recognized it right away." Reverend Garrison's voice was apologetic. "We talked it over and decided you should be the one to determine the punishment."

"Punishment?" Jesse found his voice and grinned, startling the three people in the room. "Are you kidding? Avery deserves a reward."

He couldn't believe it had turned up after all this time. Today. This was no coincidence. This was an answer to prayer that took his breath away. A tangible symbol of God's continued faithfulness.

"Reward..." Reverend Garrison repeated the word cautiously. "I don't think you understand, Jesse. Avery found the diamond and *kept* it. She knows she should have come forward sooner—"

"I think Avery came forward at *exactly* the right time," Jesse interrupted. His hand shook as he took the ring from Avery. "I was going to replace it. Today, as a matter of fact."

Heather gasped and understanding dawned in Reverend Garrison's eyes.

"You..." Avery's eyes filled with tears. "You aren't going to call the police?"

"Everyone deserves a second chance." Jesse's hand shook as he slipped the ring into his shirt pocket. "Now if you'll excuse me, I'm going to ask for mine."

Chapter Seventeen

Lori placed Maddie's stocking on one of the weighted gold hooks on the mantel and stepped back to critique her effort.

All three stockings hung over the fireplace now—each one as unique as the precious baby she had made it for. As a last-minute change to the original design, Lori had trimmed the top of each stocking with a row of tiny jingle bells.

She had stayed up until her eyes began to cross, in order to finish the stockings in time for the gift opening that would take place at Maya and Greg's house on Christmas Day.

After the triplets were in their cribs for the night, she planned to finish wrapping the stocking stuffers she'd bought, while Jesse attended the potluck at the newly finished Old Town Hall.

For a moment, Lori let her imagination form a picture of the two of them attending the celebration together.

She shook the thought away. Why continue to torture herself?

Help me be content with what I have, Lord, and not want more.

After Janet's phone call, Lori had been awake most of the night, asking God to give her the wisdom to make the right decision. Given her conflicted emotions, the temptation to return to a stable job—one in which she didn't have to interact with Jesse on a daily basis—was overwhelming.

Her supervisor had practically begged her to return to the hospital, and Lori wondered if Janet's offer was divine intervention. Was God providing a way out?

But as the night wore on and she continued to pray about the matter, she had come to a conclusion.

She wouldn't leave. As long as Jesse needed her, she would stay at the Circle L. No matter the risk to her own heart, she was committed. She loved the triplets.

And she loved Jesse.

Lori had come to that conclusion during the wee hours of the morning, too.

She knew that part of Jesse's resistance, when it came to trusting people, stemmed from being abandoned. Lori refused to be one of the people he could add to his list of those who'd left. Like it or not, he was stuck with her.

The doorbell chimed and Lori paused to straighten the sofa cushions on her way to answer it. She wasn't expecting company, but since it was Christmas Eve, it was possible the postal service was making last-minute deliveries.

"Hello!" On the other side of the door stood a young woman in her early twenties.

"Can I help you?"

"I'm Melissa Olson." She gave Lori a wide smile. "And I'm here to help you."

Lori looked at her in confusion. "I don't understand."

"I'm here to babysit the triplets."

"I think there's been some kind of mistake." There had to be some kind of mistake! "Are you sure you have the right address?"

Melissa stomped her feet, depositing the snow that clung to her fashionable half boots onto the welcome mat in front of the door. "This is the Circle L, right?"

"Yes."

"Then I'm at the right address." She must have sensed Lori's indecision. "Mr. Logan called me," she added, as if that tidbit of information might be the key to getting past Lori and into the warm house.

Jesse had hired her? On Christmas Eve?

Lori bit her lip. Jesse had been gone since breakfast, and although he'd left a brief note explaining that he had some shopping to do, she couldn't help but wonder if the passionate retelling of her less-than-perfect childhood the night before had something to do with his disappearance.

It was entirely possible that she was looking at her replacement!

Melissa shivered. "Um, it's kind of cold out here...."

"I'm sorry. Please, come in," Lori said automatically.

The girl looked relieved as she entered the house, shedding her coat, scarf and mittens on the way in.

"Did ah, Mr. Logan...mention how long you would be watching the triplets?"

"No. He just said he'd pay me double. Poor college students like myself don't ask a lot of questions."

Well, Lori had a lot of questions. The most important one was why Jesse had hired a sitter for the babies, when she'd planned to stay with them that evening.

"But—"

"Don't worry about a thing," Melissa interrupted breezily. "I'm the oldest of six, and two of my brothers are twins. The babies are in good hands."

"I'm sure they are," Lori said weakly. "But I don't have plans to...go anywhere tonight."

"Really? Because Mr. Logan said you should be ready to leave at five-thirty."

"Ready to leave?" Lori squeaked.

"Yup. That's what he said. He'll be waiting out front." Melissa looked around the room. "Where are the babies? I can't wait to play with them."

"They should be waking up soon." Lori pulled the baby monitor out of her sweater pocket.

Melissa plucked it out of her hand. "Don't you want to change? You've only got fifteen minutes." A pair of wide green eyes looked pointedly at her long-sleeve T-shirt and comfortable jeans.

Lori grimaced. "I suppose I should."

She ran upstairs, opened up the closet and grabbed the green velvet dress she'd worn to the hospital Christmas party the year before. With its full skirt and sequined bodice, it was probably a little fancy for a church pot-luck, but she didn't exactly have a lot of time to choose an alternative.

A few minutes later, a soft tap on the door interrupted her thoughts. Melissa's lilting voice penetrated the wood. "It's five-thirty!"

"I'll be right down." Lori's hands shook as she twisted her hair into a casual knot at the base of her neck, secur-ing it with a pearl clip. She stepped into a pair of black ballet flats and flew down the stairs.

A quick peek into the living room told her that Me-lissa seemed to have everything under control. All three babies were awake and appeared to be fascinated by the new face in the room.

Lori went around and kissed each baby, resisting the urge to give the sitter detailed instructions. Melissa looked quite capable, and she had already coaxed a gurgle of laughter out of Sasha.

Grabbing her wool coat from the hall closet, Lori slipped out the door.

"Merry Christmas!"

Clay stood by the car, waiting for her. Lori managed a smile even as her heart sank.

Mr. Logan.

Of course. Clay was the one who'd arranged for a babysitter, most likely at Nicki's request. Clay's fiancée had expressed her disappointment that Lori wouldn't be joining them for the Christmas Eve festivities. Nicki and Clay had been hard at work on the Old Town Hall and had obviously put their heads together to come up with a plan to include her after all.

Clay opened the door on the passenger side and Lori slid inside the vehicle. She was tempted to ask where Jesse was but half-afraid of what Clay's answer would be.

How would he react when he found out that Clay and Nicki had hired another babysitter for his daughters?

On the way to High Plains, Clay entertained her with humorous stories about the work crew's latest bloopers while they scrambled to finish the last-minute details in time.

By the time they arrived at the gathering, the snow-covered churchyard was already filled with members of the congregation and visitors from the community.

A large section of the park—from the restored gazebo to the Old Town Hall—had been decorated for the occasion. Tea lights flickered inside the luminaries that lined the sidewalk leading up to the church, and evergreen swags were wound around the old-fashioned lampposts. Instrumental Christmas music played softly in the background, a perfect accompaniment to the laughter and conversation.

Clay, who'd been more than anxious to reach his fiancée's side, strode ahead of Lori while she paused to absorb the peaceful beauty of the surroundings. By the time she located him again, he stood at Nicki's side, Kasey perched on his broad shoulders.

The rest of Jesse's family clustered nearby, talking with Reverend Garrison and Heather, whose arm was linked with Avery's.

Lori smiled as she saw Tommy, a miniature replica of Greg in a navy suit and red bow tie, hunkered on the ground between his parents, surreptitiously building a tiny snowman.

But where was Jesse? And why didn't it seem to trouble his family that he wasn't there to share in the celebration?

Layla spotted Lori, and with a cry of delight broke away from the group.

"Lori! Lori!" The little girl ran up to her, the skirt of her wintergreen taffeta dress belling out above tiny, fur-trimmed boots. "I have a pretty dress, too. And sparkles on my mittens. See?"

"Your dress is very pretty," Lori agreed. "And I wish I had sparkles on my mittens."

Layla beamed.

"Were you surprised?" Maya joined them, stunning in a crimson wool suit and matching hat. She reeled Lori in for a brief hug and lowered her voice to a whisper. "I know it's hard for you to leave my nieces for a few hours, but you need a break occasionally, too!"

Lori was surprised and touched by Maya's warm greeting. How was it that in such a short time, she'd fallen in love with Jesse's entire family? Maybe it wouldn't hurt for one night—tonight—to pretend she really belonged with this precious group of people. It would be a Christmas gift to herself.

"It was nice of you to arrange for a sitter."

Maya's brown eyes danced with sudden mischief. "Oh, don't thank me."

Lori nodded in understanding. Nicki must have engineered the surprise, just as she'd suspected.

"Did Clay tell you that we have something else to celebrate tonight?" Maya glanced over her shoulder. "Greg and I signed Tommy's final adoption papers this morning."

Now Lori hugged her. "That's wonderful, Maya."

"Tommy said that now we are, and I quote, 'a forever family.' And then he wondered why we were crying!"

A forever family. Lori felt the familiar ache inside, even though she rejoiced with the couple over the good news. An image of Jesse and the triplets flashed in her mind.

Help me be content with the way things are, Lord.

"There's a larger turnout than we anticipated." Greg walked over and tucked Maya against his side. "Michael wants to gather around the tree out here, and sing some Christmas hymns before the service begins."

Lori summoned a smile as the minister approached. She'd prayed Jesse would have a change of heart and attend the service. She wasn't sure if she could enjoy the evening, knowing that he had, once again, distanced himself from the people who loved him.

Scraping up her courage, she decided to ask if anyone knew where he was. It wasn't like Jesse to abandon his chores and disappear for an entire day. "Maya, do you know—"

"Look, Mommy! There's a horse!" A childish voice suddenly broke through the quiet hum of conversation and the crowd's attention shifted to the street.

"It's a sleigh," someone murmured.

People craned their necks to get a better look. Kasey, still perched on Clay's shoulders, pointed a chubby finger and giggled.

"Maybe it's Santa," Layla said, wide-eyed.

Tommy's nose wrinkled. "That's not Santa. It's Uncle Jesse."

Lori's heart gave a little kick. It couldn't be. Jesse Logan and the musical jingle of bells did *not* go together.

Several people shifted, and she caught a glimpse of the sleigh as it came to a gliding stop next to the curb. A familiar figure dropped the reins and stood up, scanning the crowd.

Heads began to turn as curious faces looked to Reverend Michael for an explanation.

"Don't look at me." The young minister shrugged, but there was a knowing sparkle in his eyes. "This isn't part of the program."

"Lori?"

She froze when Jesse called out her name.

Clay grinned and gave her a friendly nudge. "I think that's you."

"But…" Panic choked off Lori's ability to finish the sentence.

"Go on." Maya gave her hand a reassuring squeeze. "I think my big brother has something to say to you."

"Finally," Clay muttered under his breath.

On their own accord, Lori's feet carried her forward. She felt people's smiles as they moved aside to let her pass.

Within moments she reached the sleigh.

And Jesse.

Chapter Eighteen

Jesse took a deep breath as Lori looked up at him, a confused expression on her lovely face.

God, I know You've been more than generous but I could use a little more help right about now.

Panicked, he tried to remember the speech he'd rehearsed on his way into town. If he said too much—or not enough—he could lose Lori forever. And now here they were, surrounded by dozens of curious faces who had pushed even closer to see what was going on.

Lori reached out to stroke Saber's nose. The gelding's appreciative snort came out in a plume of frost. "Is this part of the celebration? Horse-drawn carriage rides?"

Jesse blinked. Was it possible that Lori still didn't know what she meant to him? Why he was here?

How do I convince her, Lord?

With a flash of insight, he understood. In spite of Lori's strong faith, she still bore the scars of her childhood. The painful memory of parents who had never valued—or loved—her for the remarkable, beautiful person she was.

It was up to him to tell her.

Jesse knew what he had to do, even though his mouth went dry as dust at the thought. He had hoped everyone would be inside the Old Town Hall by the time he arrived. His original plan had been to wait for Lori to come out after the service so he could coax her into going for a sleigh ride with him. Once they were on their way, he would find a quiet, secluded place by the river to tell her how he felt about her.

Now he saw God's hand at work and he knew what would convince her that his feelings were real.

"I'm not giving sleigh rides," Jesse said. "I'm..." He was trying to propose, but he couldn't say that out loud or it would ruin the proposal. "I'm making a memory. For the girls. Like you suggested."

Great. He sounded as stilted and awkward as a kindergartner learning to read, but given the circumstances, short, choppy sentences were the best he could do. Especially when Lori was absolutely take-a-man's-breath-away beautiful. The sequins on her dress sparkled in the lamplight and the soft fabric traced the curves of her slender frame.

In spite of the chilly temperatures, Jesse broke out in a sweat.

Lori gave him a quizzical smile. "But the girls aren't here."

Jesse forgot about the crowd. He had Lori's attention and he wasn't going to lose it. He wasn't going to lose *her*.

He jumped down from the sleigh and went down on one knee in the snow. A murmur rippled through the people watching and Lori gasped when Jesse took her hand.

"This will be something the girls can tell their children someday. And their children's children."

Lori's hand fluttered in his but she didn't pull it away, which gave him the courage to go on. "I love you, Lori. You came into my life and you...you changed it. You changed me. Because of you, I found my faith again. We haven't known each other very long, but I know that I want to laugh with you and cry with you and grow old with you.

I wish I could tell you how much you mean to me, but I've never been good with words...."

And he ran out of them. Just like that. But maybe words weren't that important, Jesse decided. Because the expression on Lori's face told him everything he needed to know.

"Jesse Logan," Lori whispered his name. "You're better at finding the words than you think you are. It's one of the reasons I fell in love with you."

Jesse felt as if his heart was going to pound its way out of his chest. He pulled a small velvet box from his coat pocket.

Then he gave her a lopsided smile. "I was hoping you'd say that."

Lori's eyes widened. "What is that?"

"Part of the memory." He opened the cover and Emmeline's diamond winked up at them.

"You found the ring." Lori stared at the antique ring in awe. "What an incredible...gift."

Jesse had to disagree. He might have thought so before he'd met Lori, but now he realized that love was the true cornerstone of the Logan family legacy. Not the Circle L. Not the diamond ring.

That's what he had to convince Lori to believe.

"I found *you*, Lori. As far as I'm concerned, your love is the gift. Will you be my wife?"

She clapped her hand over her lips and nodded wordlessly.

Jesse slipped the ring on her finger. Out of the corner of his eye, he saw Maya and Nicki clinging to each other. Greg had perched Tommy on his shoulders for a better view while Layla bounced up and down and clapped her hands.

Jesse smiled and rose to his feet. "I think the entire community is going to be part of our memory."

Lori smiled back as he drew her into his arms. Her breath stirred his hair as she whispered in his ear.

"I wouldn't have it any other way."

Jesse closed his eyes. Neither would he. And he thought of another way to show her that he meant it.

He kissed her. In front of everyone.

Dazed, Lori opened her eyes when Jesse reluctantly released her. All around them, people were clapping and whistling.

Reverend Garrison stood a few feet away, a wide smile on his face.

"This wasn't exactly what I had in mind when I asked Jesse Logan if he would say a few words at the dedication of the Old Town Hall this evening."

Laughter rippled through the crowd and Lori felt the color flood into her cheeks. Jesse winked at her, his fingers tightening around hers. She couldn't help but glance down at the diamond on her finger, still caught in the afterglow of Jesse's proposal.

He *loved* her. He claimed that he wasn't good with words, and yet he'd proposed to her in front of his friends and family. In front of the entire town.

God, You are so good. Thank You for bringing us together.

Michael cleared his throat. "That said, in all honesty, I can't think of a better way to start this service—on the eve of our Savior's birth—than with an expression of love like the one Jesse just showed us," he said. "The ring he placed on Lori Martin's finger is the same ring that Will Logan gave to his intended bride—a pledge of his love and his commitment before God, to stay by her side no matter what the future held. The past few months have been difficult for our community, but we're here together, standing in the very same place the first settlers gathered years ago. Not only to celebrate the completion of the Old Town

Hall but to celebrate God's faithfulness. He has not—nor will He ever—abandon His people."

A chorus of *amens* burst out and tears banked behind Lori's eyes.

"People lost many things in the tornado, but the one thing we didn't lose was hope. Hope in God and faith in one another. It was those two things that moved Will Logan and Zeb Garrison to put a stake near the river on Christmas Day in 1858 and claim the empty sea of prairie grass around it. They named that place High Plains. According to local history, those men fell in love with two remarkable women—Emmeline Carter and Nora Mitchell." Michael paused and a smile teased the corners of his lips. "Although, from what I've read in the town archives, those relationships were not without challenges and trials. God was at work in their lives, too, and love prevailed." For a moment, Michael's gaze lingered on Heather Waters and a look of understanding passed between them.

Lori saw Clay and Nicki also exchange a tender glance. She knew they weren't the only couple who could relate to the truth of the minister's words. Many of the couples she saw had allowed God to work in their lives after the storm.

Her gaze moved from Jesse's brother and his fiancée to Nicki's close friend, Josie Cane, who stood in the protective circle of Silas Marstow's arms. Their daughters, Alyssa and Lily, stood beside them, hands clasped.

Not far away, Colt Ridgeway and Lexi Harmon had eyes only for each other.

"To dedicate the rebuilding of the Old Town Hall tonight, I would like to share a verse with you. My heartfelt prayer is that it will remind everyone of God's amazing love for us. I found this written inside the cover of the pulpit bible that Will Logan donated to High Plains Community Church after a tornado struck the town in 1860. The words are as true for us today as they were for the people that Will wanted to encourage back then."

"Yet this I call to mind and therefore I have hope. Because of the Lord's great love we are not consumed, for His compassions never fail. They are new every morning."

Lori felt the jolt that coursed through Jesse, as Michael quietly recited the same verse she had shared with him the night the girls had been sick. The one that had encouraged her to believe and trust God's love.

Michael bowed his head. "Please join me in a word of prayer."

Lori closed her eyes and the tears leaked out. She felt Jesse's fingertips gently brush them away.

"Lord God—" Michael stopped as a dog began to bark nearby. He would have continued, but Tommy's sudden shout echoed around the churchyard.

"It's Charlie!"

"Tommy, no." Greg choked out as the little boy broke away from the group. "It can't be him."

Tommy kept going. At the sound of the boy's voice, the dog turned and limped out of the shadows, tail wagging.

Everyone watched, awestruck, as Tommy dropped to his knees. Charlie barreled into his arms and the two wrestled together in the snow.

"It *is* Charlie." Maya clapped a hand over her mouth.

"Tommy *said* that Charlie would be home for Christmas." Layla looked at the adults around her, perplexed by their reaction. "Didn't you believe him?"

"The faith of a child," Reverend Garrison murmured.

"Home for Christmas," Jesse repeated softly. "What do you think?"

Lori tilted her head. "I like the sound of that."

"You're my home, Lori," he murmured. "You and the girls."

Her lips curved into a smile. "I like the sound of that even more."

Reverend Garrison shook his head, his expression bemused by the unexpected interruption. "We've witnessed God at work tonight in amazing ways. As we sit down to eat together, I encourage everyone to share some of the things that God has done in your lives over the past few months."

Jesse smiled down at Lori. "Should I go first?"

Lori rested her cheek against his shoulder, her heart full. "Maybe *I* should."

Jesse glanced at his brother and Clay gave them a knowing wink. "I think all of us will have something to say. It might take a while."

And it did. People gathered around the tables and the celebrations continued well into the evening, as dozens of stories were told of God's faithfulness. After the storm.

* * * * *

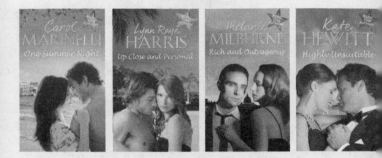